PRAISE FOR VIC

'A heartwarming novel … The st[...]
one, and this novel is a tantalisin[...]
— *The Weekly Times* on *The Last of the Bonegilla Girls*

'Victoria Purman has researched and written a delightful historical piece that will involve its readers from the first page to the last … written with empathy and understanding.'
— Starts At 60 on *The Last of the Bonegilla Girls*

'Victoria Purman has written a story about people exactly like my family, migrants to Australia … I came to this novel for the migrant story, but I stayed for the wonderful friendship Victoria Purman has painted between the four girls … The story is written in such a friendly, welcoming style that you can't help but be embraced by the Bonegilla girls and become one of them … don't be surprised if you find yourself crying at the end.'
— Sam Still Reading on *The Last of the Bonegilla Girls*

'A story told directly from the heart … *The Last of the Bonegilla Girls* is a wonderful ode to the bonds of female friendship and the composition of our country.'
— Mrs B's Book Reviews

'… a moving and heartwarming story [and] a poignant and compelling read, *The Last of the Bonegilla Girls* is … a beautiful story about female friendship and how it can transcend cultural and language barriers.'
— Better Reading

'… so rich with emotion, detail and customs that are almost unheard of these days, and thankfully so [because] the best way to get to know these characters is to read their story for yourself.'
— Beauty and Lace on *The Last of the Bonegilla Girls*

'*The Last Of The Bonegilla Girls* is a touching and compelling story of female friendship and celebration of what it means to call Australia home, no matter where the journey began … beautifully told … with an ending that will leave you dewy eyed and [with] a renewed sense of hope.'
— Bluewolf Reviews

Victoria Purman is a multi-published, award-nominated, Amazon Kindle–bestselling author. She has worked in and around the Adelaide media for nearly thirty years as an ABC television and radio journalist, a speechwriter to a premier, political adviser, editor, media adviser and private-sector communications consultant. She is a regular guest at writers' festivals, has been nominated for a number of readers choice awards and was a judge in the fiction category for the 2018 Adelaide Festival Awards for Literature. Her most recent novels are *The Three Miss Allens*, published in 2016, and *The Last of the Bonegilla Girls* (2018).

Also by Victoria Purman

The Boys of Summer:
Nobody But Him
Someone Like You
Our Kind of Love
Hold Onto Me

Only We Know

The Three Miss Allens
The Last of the Bonegilla Girls

The Land Girls

Victoria Purman

First Published 2019
Second Australian Paperback Edition 2020
ISBN 9781489281012

THE LAND GIRLS
© 2019 by Victoria Purman
Australian Copyright 2019
New Zealand Copyright 2019

Published by
HQ Fiction
An imprint of Harlequin Enterprises (Australia) Pty Limited (ABN 47 001 180 918), a subsidiary of HarperCollins Publishers Australia Pty Limited (ABN 36 009 913 517)
Level 13, 201 Elizabeth St
SYDNEY NSW 2000
AUSTRALIA

® and TM (apart from those relating to FSC®) are trademarks of Harlequin Enterprises (Australia) Pty Limited or its corporate affiliates. Trademarks indicated with ® are registered in Australia, New Zealand and in other countries.

A catalogue record for this book is available from the National Library of Australia
www.librariesaustralia.nla.gov.au

Printed and bound in Australia by McPherson's Printing Group

To the Mobbs family, who were all touched by war.
Though most have now passed on, thankfully they survived
the war to enjoy long and happy lives.
Roy Mobbs (RAAF) and his wife Olive; their daughter
Vilma; their sons Reginald (AIF) and his wife Davina;
Dudley (RAN) and his wife Marjorie; and all their children,
grandchildren and great-grandchildren.
A father and two sons served in World War Two in the
Middle East, New Guinea, the Pacific and in Darwin, while
on the other side of the world, my own family were made
refugees because of it.
I married one of Roy and Olive's grandsons and I feel so lucky
to be considered part of the Mobbs family.

Chapter One

Flora

December 1942

It was perhaps from a magpie chick, this soft thing nestled in Flora Atkins's palm.

Or a cockatoo, a sulphur-crested. It was weightless, lighter than a baby's breath. As white as if it had been soaked in lemon juice; a puff of summer cloud suspended in her hand.

When she exhaled, it danced and floated and she gently closed her fingers over it to keep it still.

Perhaps someone had ripped it from a young chook, gripping and tearing this new feather out of puckered, pink flesh, before slipping it into an envelope, their rage still white hot. Or perhaps they'd done it calmly, in a pre-meditated fashion, before dipping a nib into an inkwell on their writing desk so they could slowly and calmly inscribe the word *coward* on a card and slip it inside the envelope with the feather.

The card sat on the kitchen table, propped up next to the china sugar bowl. Flora's anger welled up inside her, stronger and harder, until she felt she might vomit.

'Don't they know?'

Her brother Jack sat, hunched over, his elbows on the table that was already set for dinner, his fingers in a tight knot. He hadn't even taken off his suit jacket, and his flat cap still sat low on his forehead.

If their mother was alive, she would have chatted Jack about wearing his hat indoors, but she wasn't there, hadn't been for fifteen years, and all her careful household rules had fallen by the wayside.

'Sit down, Flora.' Their father, John, turned off the stove under the boiling kettle. He filled the teapot and carried it to the table, setting it on the trivet. 'Cup of tea, love?'

She nodded. 'Yes please.'

The radiogram was loud in the living room—some jolly music she supposed—but with the buzzing in Flora's ears it was nothing but static. She pulled out a chair to sit down. She lowered the white feather next to her white gloves.

John filled Flora's cup. She had craved it the entire walk home from the tram stop at Camberwell Junction to their house on Waterloo Street, but now she didn't feel the slightest bit thirsty. Or hungry.

The three Atkinses stared at the feather, soft and beautiful and cruel.

'Where did it come from?' Flora finally asked.

'Pardon?' Jack asked, cocking his left ear in her direction.

'I was asking,' she said, slightly louder this time, 'did it come in the letterbox?' Her mind whirred. 'You don't think it was Mrs White, do you, or one of her daughters?' The Whites from number thirty-seven had lost a son the year before in North Africa, at the siege of Tobruk. Flora's heart sank at the idea. She and her father and Jack had mourned with the Whites at Tommy's memorial service. His young wife had held her new baby in her arms and wailed.

John frowned and shook his head. His grey hair flopped over his forehead and he pushed it back with a hand. He looked older than his fifty-five years. The deep wrinkles carved on his cheeks were crevasses. His brown eyes, the ones that she and Jack and their younger brother Frank had inherited from him, were flat and watery. He looked old, Flora realised. Worn out. A wife long dead, one son off fighting the Japanese, another unable to, and his eldest a thirty-year-old spinster.

'Your mother and Mrs White were friends. They went to school together. It couldn't be them, Flora.'

'Or ... or,' Flora stammered. 'What about the Craigies? Don't they still have cousins in London? Maybe something happened to them in the bombings and they—'

John held up a hand and Flora stopped. Her father's words were quiet, considered. 'I saw this during the last war. People on one side or the other about conscription. Should we force our boys to go and fight or not? I was too old and your mother and I had you kids by then. You two and Frank, of course.' Her father probably wasn't even aware he'd done it, but he'd blinked at the empty chair at the end of the table. 'Baby Frank. That's what we called him.' A smile curved his mouth. 'Even when he'd grown out of short pants.

'We knew about the white feathers then. My uncle got one. He was lame from falling off a horse and couldn't fight but that didn't matter. And everyone was all high and mighty about putting on a uniform, fighting for the king. But then there was Gallipoli and Pozières and Ypres. And after that, a lot of people thought none of our blokes should ever be forced to go off and die for someone else's war ever again.'

No one had forced Frank to go to war. He'd joined up back in July 1940 after the Battle of Britain had been all over the newspapers and the wireless. He'd come home one day, dirty from his work labouring on the dockyards, wearing a huge smile, which had only broadened when he told his family that he and his best mate Keith had enlisted.

'They've smashed the Luftwaffe, Dad,' he'd said, pacing the living room with a cigarette dangling from his lips, his flat cap waving in his other hand. 'The Hurricanes and the Spitfires did their job, all right. Now, they've got to send Hitler all the way back to Berlin.'

He'd kissed them all goodbye, marched to the Victoria Barracks and enlisted, and in short order had been sent to Trawool in central Victoria for training. He'd written them a letter at the beginning of October, after the whole battalion had marched the entire one hundred and forty-three miles on foot from Trawool to Bonegilla on the banks of Lake Hume, saying it was the best adventure he'd ever had.

He'd written to them from Palestine and Syria and was now training in Queensland after the journey home on *Laconia*, preparing to head north to the jungle. Their father had pinned a map to the back of the kitchen door and every time he heard news on the wireless about the whereabouts or activities of the 2/11th Field Regiment of the 8th Division, he marked the spot with an X and the date in pencil.

Frank's letters home were stored in a biscuit tin in the sideboard in the living room. He wasn't prolific, never had been one for school or books, but the pile had grown steadily during the past two years.

Jack rubbed a hand over his face and pushed his cup of tea into the middle of the table. 'The thing is, Dad, it's not someone else's war now. Not since the Japs bombed Darwin and made it into Sydney Harbour. They're coming after us, right here in the Pacific and in South-East Asia. Curtin had the right idea, bringing Frank and all our boys back from Europe to protect us here at home. We can't rely on the Poms to do it, can we? Not any more.' Jack listened to everything, read all the accounts in *The Age* and *The Herald*, and even stood for 'The Star-Spangled Banner' when it was played at the pictures right after 'God Save The King'.

He might not be able to fight, but he kept himself informed. The war was hard to avoid. Signs of it were everywhere. Posters were plastered in shop windows and in trams and buses, urging young men to join up. 'What are you doing to ensure victory for Australia, for Britain, for the Empire?' they beckoned. 'Are you satisfied that, come what may in the troubled months ahead, you will be proud of the part you played—be able to say—*I did my best*?'

There were advertisements in the newspaper, too, and even in the *Women's Weekly* as Flora browsed recipes or the latest short stories. There was almost nowhere to escape the calls to duty, the reminders not to gossip, the newsreels that asked Australians to do all they could to help smash the Japs or send tanks in to crush Mussolini or to knock out Hitler.

'What I don't understand,' Flora started, 'is how on earth someone could slip this in the letterbox, knowing Frank's off fighting. If they know you, how could they think—'

'Flora.' Jack hurriedly reached for his tea and the cup and saucer jumped and rattled. A wave of milky tea overflowed into the saucer. She looked across the table at him. His shoulders rose and fell. His lips were pulled together like the people in the posters—*loose lips sink ships*—and his eyes were hard and dark.

'Jack. I was just trying to—'

'You don't need to be suspicious of anyone in our street.' He removed his flat cap and held it tight in his fists. 'It wasn't the Whites or the Craigies or the Plummers or the Tilleys. Or anyone we know. During smoko today, a fine-looking young lady stepped in front of me on Swanston Street and handed that envelope to me.'

'On Swanston Street?' Flora asked, disbelieving.

Jack nodded, closing his eyes for a long moment. 'When I saw her coming my way, I thought she was handing me a pamphlet, you see, so I took it and thanked her. She gave me a little smile, and I let myself think just for a minute how lucky I was that a pretty girl had given me the time of day. And that smile on her face? She looked like she was spreading the word of God or some kindness. Imagine that. I thought she was being kind. I *thanked* her.'

A pain radiated up into Flora's throat, tightening it, and her heart seemed to crack inside her chest. 'Did she say anything at all to you?' she managed to say.

'Not a word,' Jack replied quietly. 'She strode off, looking right bloody proud of herself. I opened it right there in front of the newspaper stand near the corner of Bourke Street.'

Since she'd been fifteen years old, Flora had cooked for all the men in her family, washed their clothes, ironed their shirts, made sure her father ate dinner and got out of the house every now and then, counselled her brothers when their hearts were broken and their knees were scraped. Frank was always getting into some misadventure or other. But never Jack. Lovely, kind Jack. When he had been so sick with meningitis at fourteen, she'd sat by his hospital bed for a week. In many ways, she had felt more like a parent to her younger brothers than a sibling, and a motherly instinct rose in her gut now, churning, stinging, and made the pounding in her head stronger and louder.

'What a wretched young woman,' she said finally.

Her father sighed. His teaspoon clinked in his teacup. He'd learnt to cut down on his sugar since rationing had been introduced, but he'd never got out of the habit of stirring his tea while he thought.

'You've got that right, love. It must a sweet life, hey? To walk around Melbourne, all high and mighty, not knowing the facts about things,' John said wearily, his voice hoarse with a controlled anger. 'Jack's in a reserved occupation. All customs agents are exempt. And a whole lot of other blokes are too. Tram drivers. And watchmakers. Did they know that?'

Jack tapped his right ear three times. 'Dad, I couldn't go even if I wanted to.'

They stared at the feather. When Flora exhaled, her breath caught it and it floated and then settled again. She reached for it quickly, snatched it into her fist and stuffed it into the pocket of her skirt.

She forced a smile. If she smiled, she wouldn't cry. And she couldn't cry now. 'Let's not think about it any more.

People will always be ignorant and cruel and I'm not sure there's much we can do about it but keep to our own business. I've had a long day typing letters for Mr McInerney about shipping insurance and now I'm starving,' she lied. 'Shall I make us some supper?'

'There's three eggs from Mrs Jones on the sink.' John sat up straighter, his voice a little brighter. 'She dropped by today. She had a letter from her son and wanted to tell me all the news.'

'How's Robin going?' Jack asked, a note of false cheer in his tone too.

'He's keeping well, she says. Staying out of trouble.'

'That's good to hear,' Flora said. 'Nothing from Frank?'

'Not today, Flora,' John replied. 'Not today.'

While she knew the army had more important things to do than ensure letters home arrived in a timely fashion, they hadn't received a letter from Frank for a month. She tried not to think about what it might mean.

Flora went to the sink, pulled the blind and tugged the floral curtains closed against the approaching dark and the spying eyes of those enforcing blackout restrictions. Against those who presumed to make judgements about things they knew nothing about. Against those with white feathers. 'Why don't you both clean up? I'll get supper going.'

After vegetable soup and toast with boiled eggs for dinner, John moved into the living room to sit in his comfortable armchair and listen to 3UZ and the nightly discussions about the war. He liked the company there. On the mantelpiece above the coal grate there was a framed photograph of Frank wearing his khaki army uniform, its sleeves proudly bearing the insignia of his regiment. Next to it, her parents' wedding photo, taken in 1910 and a permanent fixture there every day since.

At the kitchen table, Flora sipped a cup of hot milk with Ovaltine, fighting her tiredness. She skimmed the headlines in the first few pages of *The Age*, trying not to take in too much detail about the war. Did knowing help at all with the worrying about what was happening overseas? And anyway, signs of it were everywhere she went in the city now. Melbourne had become the national headquarters of the Australian and American military, so the city—and the paper—could talk of nothing else. Shops advertised hamburgers and Coca-Cola to appeal to the thousands of Yanks at Camp Pell. Military cars and khaki lorries drove right through the centre of Melbourne and there seemed to be nowhere you could go without hearing an American accent. When the US troops had arrived in the months after Pearl Harbor, people in Melbourne were relieved. After the dark months of 1940, people knew that the English were too busy saving themselves to come to Australia's aid, and all eyes had turned to the United States with their troops and planes and tanks to help protect Australia from invasion.

But it wasn't just up to the Americans. Everyone was now being asked to do their bit to defend the country, and not just men. Women were being called on too, to release fit men from routine tasks to increase the frontline strength of Australia's fighting forces. Flora had seen the advertisements in the newspapers encouraging women that they could do a real job, 'A man's job!'

She had so far been able to look away from those entreaties without feeling the call herself. She was thirty years old, and the army and the air force and the navy wanted younger women, those with a sense of adventure, those possessed with courage and bravery. They didn't want women like Flora who'd spent the best part of the past fifteen years living a quiet life in Camberwell worrying over her father and brothers.

Flora turned the pages of the newspaper, quickly flicking past the death notices until she reached the Women's Section. She couldn't even escape the war there. There was a call for more women doctors for the RAAF, and an article offering handy sewing patterns for the remodelling of clothes. It was better to make do and mend than use rations to buy new garments, it advised.

A headline caught her eye: 'More Leaders for the Land Army'.

She lifted the paper so she could properly read the fine print. With paper in short supply, the print had become so small—and the brownouts made everything so dim—that she thought she might need glasses sooner rather than later. Land Army girls were going to orchards, flax mills and poultry farms. She remembered she'd seen a poster in the window of the post office on Burke Road. Her attention had been captured by the image of a young woman waving a pitchfork speared with wheat stalks, wearing a hat with a pin on the brim. She was smiling proudly in the sunshine with blue cloudless skies overhead.

'Do you need a hand cleaning up?'

She looked up to see Jack standing in the doorway.

'Well, I'm not going to look a gift horse in the mouth.' Flora folded the newspaper, put it on top of the icebox to save for the butchers on Saturday, and went to the sink. As it filled, she sprinkled soap flakes into the water and watched them bubble. Jack moved in next to her, on her right side so he could hear her with his left ear. One by one, she slowly washed each dish with a rag, her mind in a million places and none at all.

They worked in silence, voices from the radiogram in the next room a muffled background noise. Jack stacked the bowls and bread-and-butter plates in the cupboard next to the ice chest. He was amiable company, always had been. She glanced sideways at him as he wiped. He'd been taller than her since the year their mother had died, when he'd turned twelve and Frank ten. They not only shared the same brown eyes, but the same light brown hair of their mother. Flora liked having something of her mother's. She'd faded in Flora's memory after so many years, her voice now only a whisper in her memory. She'd lost the taste of her scones and her homemade lemon butter and the warmth of her embrace. They had been a close family, still were, yet she and Jack had grown even closer since Frank had gone to war. Their mother's premature death had already taught them that loved ones could be lost in the blink of an eye. They knew to hold on tight to each other.

Flora swirled the suds in the sink and searched for the knives and spoons. 'Did you read *The Phantom* today?'

'The ghost who walks? Man who cannot die?' Jack's voice took on a dramatic tone.

'Which evildoer is he vanquishing this month?'

Jack laughed and Flora let herself feel happy for a moment, the gloom over the day's events lifting just a little.

'You don't have to worry about me. I'm all right, Flor,' he said. 'Really.' He picked up a bread-and-butter plate and wiped it in a neat circular motion.

'Let me be angry for you, if you can't be angry for yourself.' He nudged her shoulder with his. 'Spoken like a true big sister. I can't say it doesn't cut me up, make me think of the sacrifices Frank is making that I can't, but what you said before? About people being ignorant and cruel but that we just have to keep to our own business? That's what I'm doing. This isn't the first time I've had looks from people, accusing me of skiving off.' He shook his head, as if it might wish the thoughts and the memories away. 'You see, Flor, my problem is and will always be that I look perfectly healthy on the outside. Tall. Strong. Bloody handsome, even.'

Flora laughed, felt a swell of pride in her chest. She'd watched him grow and flourish and thrive, despite his hearing loss and the teasing and taunting he'd received because of it. She lifted her shoulder and pressed her face into the fabric, pretending it was a bubble from the sink she was wiping away and not a tear. 'And don't forget, humble too.'

'No one can tell by looking at me that the hearing's half gone.'

'No, they can't. Which is all the more reason for them to mind their own business. What makes me angry is … people should know better, that's all, before they rush to judgement. Appearances can be deceiving.'

'So they should, and if we could change the world, perhaps that's where we'd start, hey? But let's talk about something else. How was your day at the office?'

'Oh, you know. The work never stops. Especially now.' The discussion about the feather was over, but that didn't mean she would forget it in a hurry. 'I went for a walk at lunchtime. The sun was shining for a minute or two so I thought I'd take advantage. I went up to Bourke Street to stretch my legs, stared at the Myer windows and wished they were full of pretty dresses like they were before the war, and then I hurried back to the office to eat my cheese sandwich at my desk. At afternoon smoko, I had to give one of the young girls a bit of a talking to. Norma. Pretty thing. She likes to talk. All the time.'

Jack raised a brow. 'Did you say pretty?'

'Yes, she's quite the dish. Blonde, almost white hair, and such a petite little thing. But sadly for you, Jack, she has a sweetheart. He's a butcher's apprentice, so he's exempt too. We hear about him all day long. Endlessly. Apparently he makes a rather delicious mutton sausage.' Flora rolled her eyes and Jack burst into laughter. She loved the sound of it, loved that she was able to make him laugh, that in the middle of a war there was still time for a joke.

Flora stared into the soap suds, popping the bubbles between her slick fingers. She had tried very hard not to envy Norma her youth and her beauty and her luck. Sometimes, Flora felt as if she were the last one left at a game of musical chairs, although when the music finally stopped, she was left standing all alone with no prize.

'I had to take young Norma aside and remind her about office etiquette. Mr McInerney prefers me to do the disciplining, you see. He thinks of the new girls like his granddaughters, he told me. Wants them all to adore him. What we both know is that if they're unhappy with the work, he'll lose them to something far more exciting that pays more, like the services or munitions factories.'

Jack shook his head in disgust. 'So he leaves you to do all his dirty work?'

'I'm rather forbidding, apparently.'

'You're telling me.'

Flora was, by a good ten years, the oldest woman in her office. One by one, each of the young girls had fallen in love, married and left, and it had become Flora's responsibility to train up every new girl and supervise them, with not a shilling extra in her pay packet. Even the young male clerks continued to earn more than she did.

'Flora?'

'Hmmm?'

Jack hung the damp tea towel on the hook on the back of the kitchen door. 'You're off in the clouds again, aren't you?'

'I'm tired, that's all.' She pulled the plug and the water gurgled down the drain. How self-indulgent it was to allow herself a moment to wallow over her life when Frank and thousands of other men and women were putting theirs at risk. Her problems seemed so inconsequential in comparison.

'Do you think he's all right?' Jack asked after a moment.

Flora forced a smile. 'You know Frank as well as I do. He's no doubt charming the pants off everyone he meets. God forbid he should ever meet a nurse.'

They leant back against the sink.

'He's going to come home, Flora. If anyone will, it'll be our Frank. The Japs wouldn't dare take a shot at him.'

'We shall not let ourselves think otherwise.' Flora hoped that the repetition of the sentiment might help it come true.

'So, what are you up to tonight, Flor? Going out to the pictures or something?'

'I have some war knitting to do. That'll keep me occupied until my eyes simply won't stay open any longer. Which will probably be,' Flora checked the clock on the wall, 'in about an hour, the way I feel.'

'C'mon, don't be such a bore. There's a dance on at the Trocadero. Why don't you put on a pretty frock and come with me? There are two bands on the line-up and there'll be dancing all night. I might even whirl you around the dance floor myself.'

Flora jabbed Jack with an elbow. 'No, thank you. You'll be too busy fighting off all the young ladies of Melbourne to be bothered dancing with me. Handsome men are in such short supply these days, Jack, which means your chances of finding partners are vastly improved.'

She knew immediately that she'd said the wrong thing. 'Oh, Jack, I didn't think—'

'It's all right, Flor. I know what you meant.'

Flora collected herself. 'I'm perfectly happy to stay right here with Dad, listening to the radio and knitting socks.'

'You and your socks.' Jack grinned. 'I reckon you've knitted enough for the entire AIF. You are allowed to have fun, you know.'

Flora found knitting to be a nice distraction from all that worried her. Without her mother to teach her, she'd struggled at first, having to unravel her first two attempts after making a right mess of the heel. But she was patient and committed and had found it easy going after that. Knitting had helped pass the time on nights too numerous to count. It had helped distract her from her loneliness, from thoughts of Frank. Her father quietly smoking. Songs on the wireless. Stitch after stitch. Row after row. Sock after sock. The routine quieted her mind. She tried to imagine the soldiers receiving her gift and how happy they'd be to have something clean and new. Socks were about warmth and comfort. She'd also tried muffs and balaclavas, but couldn't come at knitting the fingerless gloves in the instruction books. Trigger gloves, they were called.

'I don't feel like heading out. Anyway, I'm too old for fun.' Flora had never liked crowds particularly, didn't go to the football because of it, and Melbourne bustled now, every minute of the day and night, even with the blackouts. Sometimes she didn't recognise her own city.

'Forget about me,' Flora told her brother. 'Go and have a good time at your dance.'

'You sure?'

'I'm sure.' As if to reinforce the point, she stifled a yawn.

'Enjoy your night then. Knit one, purl one,' Jack said, leaving Flora standing by the sink with a damp tea towel over her shoulder.

'Jack,' she called out.

At the doorway, he turned.

'Empty the drip tray under the icebox before you go, won't you? It's almost full.'

'Will do,' Jack replied.

'And not down the sink. Pour it on the war cabbage in the front garden.'

'You are forbidding.' He winked.

Later that night, after Flora had admired the perfectly shaped khaki heel on her umpteenth pair of socks, she roused her sleepy father from his armchair and urged him to go to bed. She turned off the wireless, emptied his ashtray, took his teacup into the kitchen, checked the doors were locked and turned out the low lamp in the living room.

With a net pinned over her short hair, she tucked herself into bed with an old Agatha Christie novel, but the words swam and she couldn't concentrate on any of the twists and turns of the plot.

Their little house in Camberwell was quiet but her mind wasn't.

The image of the white feather burnt behind her closed eyes. When she'd gone to her bedroom to fetch her knitting earlier in the evening, she'd opened the top drawer of her dressing table and placed it inside her wooden jewellery box. It fluttered alongside her mother's string of pearls and matching pair of clip-on earrings that Flora loved so much but never wore any more, and a cameo brooch that had belonged to her grandmother, her mother's mother, from the Wimmera. Both women were long gone.

Flora remembered her anger, her pure, white-hot fury at the cruelty of the young woman who had handed the envelope to her brother.

Coward? Jack was anything but. That night, Flora could only swallow her anger, learn to live with it, and try not to let it make her rage.

Chapter Two

Betty

It took thirty-five steps. She'd counted them out a million times, at least.

Seventeen-year-old Betty Brower walked out her front door, down the cement path between the deep red rose bushes, turned left onto King Street, Rozelle, skipped twenty steps, and then turned left again through the Dohertys' wooden picket gate, six steps to the door, one step up to reach it, and pushed open the front door.

'Hooroo.' The darkly stained wooden door swung open with a squeak of its hinges and her voice echoed down the dim hallway.

A cup clattered in a saucer and a chair scraped on the kitchen linoleum. There was a mumble of voices and then, 'Don't you knock any more, Betty Boop?'

Betty smiled at the sound of Michael's laughing tone. She skipped into the house, past Mr and Mrs Dohertys' bedroom on the left-hand side (the door had been firmly closed forever and she'd never so much as peeked inside) and the boys' bedroom next on the right after that.

Only one son slept in the room now and she was familiar with every inch of it. The wall-to-wall Axminster carpet that Mrs Doherty had saved up for and installed back in 1938, much to the horror of her sons who'd rebelled against the floral design. Michael's collection of rocks on the window-sill, and the way the quartzite glittered in the early-morning sun. His Biggles books on the shelf that formed his bed-head. The leather rugby ball abandoned in one corner of his room. His scratchy grey woollen blanket with the white sheet turned over it at the pillow end, and the jar of three-penny bits on his dressing table that he was saving to buy a war bond. His brother Patrick's bed was pushed up against the opposite wall to Michael's, and was still as neatly made as the day he'd left for the war.

Just as Betty was two steps from the kitchen door, Michael leapt through the doorway.

Betty screamed in shock then glowered at him. 'Michael Doherty,' she exclaimed, slapping his arm. 'You scared me half to death.'

'Did not.' He'd grown so tall lately that he could rest an elbow on her head as if she were a hatstand, and he did it often just to tease her.

'Hello, Betty,' Michael's mother called from the kitchen. 'How was Woollies today?'

'Hi, Mrs Doherty,' she called out around Michael's broad shoulders. 'It was fine, thank you. Have I mentioned to you lately that your son is as mean as can be?' Everything about her best friend was bigger these days. Since he'd left school the year before and begun working at Cliff's greengrocer in Rozelle, he'd grown up and out. His shoulders were broader. His Adam's apple bobbed up and down now when he spoke. She'd poked it once when they were wrestling on the carpet in his room and he'd scared her senseless by making dramatic choking sounds and playing dead. For a few moments she'd honestly thought she'd killed him and was so scared that when he'd begun to laugh uproariously at her shock she'd paid him back by ignoring him for two whole days. The swipe of freckles that had always been splattered across his nose had almost faded into a tan. Almost. If she looked close, they were still there, the little pieces of the Michael Doherty she'd grown up with, the boy who'd been her best friend since she could remember.

'Me? Mean to you? Never.'

Betty pulled her lips together in a line and propped her hands on her hips. Michael tousled her hair.

She slapped his hand away again. 'Stop it. You know I have to keep it looking just so for work and if I have to pin it again, I'll make you pay. You can forget all about your surprise now.'

She patted her right hand on the small bulge in the side pocket of her skirt.

Michael's eyebrows lifted. 'Oh no, you wouldn't be that cruel. What's the surprise, Betty Boop?'

'If you think I'm going to tell you now, after you almost scared me half to death, you have another thing coming.'

He shifted his weight and brought one boot forwards, pressing on the toe of her black court shoes.

'Stop it!' she exclaimed. 'Now I'll have to polish my shoes again. You are being infuriating tonight.'

Michael pressed just the slightest bit harder on her foot. 'I'm going to pin you to the spot until you show me the surprise.'

She poked him in the chest. 'When you stop squashing my toes, I'll show you. Deal?'

'Deal.' They shook on it. Her hand in his. One, two, three shakes, as they always did. Michael slid his foot sideways off hers then got down on one knee. He pulled a folded white handkerchief out of his trouser pocket, flicked it out like Mandrake the Magician might when performing a trick, and pulled it taut between each hand. He lowered it and began polishing her shoe where his boot had left a dusty smudge.

Betty looked down, past the crisp whiteness of her shirt, skimming her gaze down the length of her woollen skirt to where it hit just below her knee, and down her stockinged leg to the turn of her ankle. She watched the wave of his chocolate-brown hair. Studied him as his hands tugged right to left and then left to right as his handkerchief soundlessly slid across the leather. And when he was done, he lifted his face to hers, sighed and smiled. There was a look in his eyes that she didn't recognise and it made her blush.

She slipped her fingers into her pocket and pulled out a Cherry Ripe bar. 'Your favourite.'

Michael got to his feet. His grin was wide. 'You really are an angel, Betty Boop,' he said softly.

She craned her neck to meet his gaze. 'Just a girl who knows where to find chocolate during the war, that's all.'

He slipped the bar in the top pocket of his shirt. 'Let's go.'

They'd always thought of the park at the end of King Street as their own. When they were children, they'd clambered over the gnarled roots of the Moreton Bay fig trees, playing marauding pirates with the other children from the neighbourhood. Once Betty had bowled him out playing cricket, knocking the stumps flying into the air, and she'd never let him forget it. He'd taught her to ride his bike by steadying her on the leather seat and then pushing her off with a shove and she'd wobbled and screamed and ridden thirty feet before falling off and skinning her elbow.

Now they were too old for such childish pursuits. Warmed by a Sydney December evening breeze, Betty and Michael lay on their backs on the grass, side by side, in the dark. It was a clear night and with the streetlights still dimmed for the blackouts, the full moon overhead shone like a sun. It was too dark now for the street cricket players who were home, fed and bathed, so the only sounds were the sporadic footsteps and conversation of their neighbours and the flap of bats' wings in the outstretched boughs of the Moreton Bay figs.

'I can't believe you found this.' Michael moaned as he chewed languorously, savouring every bite of his favourite chocolate. 'I don't even want to know how you got it but I'm damn well pleased you did.'

'A lady will never tell.' Betty unwrapped her second Columbine and popped it into her mouth, carefully folding the foil and slipping it into her pocket. She would have to remember to add it to the collection in the kitchen drawer when she got home, for donating to the war effort.

Chocolate and sweets had been in short supply since confectionary manufacturers had turned their efforts to supplying soldiers' rations, but Betty had made some unexpected connections through her friend from work, Jean. All the trouble and waiting had been worth it for this moment: the darkness and the silence and her best friend and chocolate melting in her mouth.

She liked surprising Michael. She liked everything about the Doherty family next door. When the family with two boys had moved in all those years ago, they'd welcomed her into their home with open arms. It was perfect: she had no siblings and they had no sisters. Mrs Doherty treated her like the daughter she never had. Betty's father saw the boys through the local school at which he was the head-master. He'd been her best chum for as long as she could remember.

'You are the best friend a fellow ever had, Betty Boop.'

She didn't need to see Michael's face to know that he was smiling. She knew his face as well as her own. She could see it even in the dark, the exact way it was just the slightest bit crooked, the right side of his mouth lifting a little more than the left. She knew that one of his ears stuck out more than the other, and she could pinpoint the exact place on his jaw that he bore a scar from the time he'd tumbled off his billy cart while barrelling down King Street with Patrick pushing him.

She nudged his leg with her knee. 'You're so predictable. You say that every time I bring you sweets.'

'How terrible of me, to remember what a wonderful friend you are only when you bring chocolate.'

'Terrible and very, very ungrateful,' she added with a laugh.

'You're wrong there, Betty. I am extremely grateful.' He shifted his long body, turning towards her, one elbow in the grass, resting his chin in his palm. 'Tell me. Did you get them from a blacketeer?' He lowered his voice, whispering dramatically and looking left and right to see they weren't being spied upon. 'Have you been meeting dodgy characters in laneways in The Rocks?'

'No, I have not.' She giggled.

'Wait. I've got it. You've turned your back on us Australian blokes and you've been flirting with an American, haven't you?'

'Me?' Betty responded with nervous laughter. The idea was ridiculous. She'd never gone near one, had bowed her head and walked on if she heard that accent. Truth be told, she was slightly scared of the Americans, of how glamorous they seemed, of their polite forthrightness, of the way they felt so comfortable roaming Sydney's streets in groups as if it had always been their city.

'Let me guess,' Michael started, flopping onto his back. 'A Yank walked into Woolworths, right up to your counter, leant over all the face powder and the bottles of potions and lotions you girls like to smear on your faces, and made a little small talk about how pretty you are, or some such rubbish.' Betty sat up, turned and looked down at Michael. His hands were splayed across his stomach, one knee was propped up and he stared into the night sky.

'Why, Michael Doherty. You sound as if you might be jealous.'

'I bet he impressed you with his *ma'am* this and *ma'am* that.' He breathed deep and sighed. 'Crikey. They're everywhere in Sydney, those bloody Yanks, splashing around all their money. You know they earn more than our troops, Betty? Almost twice as much as Patrick and my cousin Arthur and Peter and Dudley from school?'

Betty swallowed the last of her Columbine and stared ahead into the darkness. So many names. So many young men already gone to war. 'That doesn't seem fair.'

'That's how they can afford all these things to impress our local girls. They tip everywhere they go too. Show-offs.'

She didn't like keeping secrets from Michael and she didn't want him to think she'd been flirting with Americans. 'It's Jean,' she blurted. 'She got them. She knows Columbines are my favourite and I asked her if she could get a Cherry Ripe too, because it's yours. She's the one who got them from an American, not me.'

'Oh, right. Cheers to Jean then, I guess.'

Jean believed herself to be in love with Kevin, a sailor from South Carolina who was on one of the ships moored in Sydney Harbour. You couldn't look out at the water these days without seeing an American warship, anchored where sailing boats had bobbed before the war. Kevin had bought Jean silk stockings and cigarettes and taken her on dates to the Roosevelt nightclub in Kings Cross. Jean seemed to be having the time of her life.

Betty didn't want silk stockings or cigarettes or night-clubs or smooth-talking Americans. She'd never given her heart to anyone and the hope of such a thing happening seemed so unreachable now, as far away as the moon.

Betty breathed deep. The earthy smells of the grass and the Moreton Bay fig were so familiar. The war had changed so many things about Sydney. Shop windows were boarded up. There were no fancy Christmas displays in the windows. The streetlights were turned off and everyone had curtains drawn as soon as the sky darkened. Zig-zagged trenches had been dug in her father's school yard and in Hyde Park, and no one, for love or money, could buy red lipstick. She had to tell the same story over and over every day to hordes of disappointed and infuriated customers.

But this park, their park, the grass and the trees and the scent of it all, was the same. She hoped it would always be their little oasis in the upheaval the war had brought all around them. She never wanted this place to change, ever.

Michael turned to face her. 'It's my birthday next week.'

She huffed. 'You think I need reminding of when your birthday is, Michael Doherty? I've had your present wrapped for two months already. Hidden in a place that even you won't find it.' She drew up her knees, crossed her arms on them and dropped her forehead to hide in the small space there.

'I'm enlisting next week, on the fifteenth of December, the day I turn eighteen.'

Betty had pushed this day to the back of her mind, wishing that it would never come, that somehow she might be able to keep them both at seventeen forever. She had promised herself she would not cry. She would show the same strength that the whole Doherty family had shown when Patrick had joined the navy. They'd waved him off at Circular Quay with smiles and hoorahs and then returned home to silence and a strong cup of tea.

'And you'll be eighteen soon, too,' Michael said cheerily.

'February—' she started.

'Fourteenth,' he finished. 'How could I forget your birthday? You've been my Valentine every year since we were five years old.'

Betty wanted to be brave, truly she did. Not just for Michael but for Patrick and every other young Australian man fighting overseas. The last thing he would want to see was fear in her eyes. She lifted her head, looked over her shoulder at him and did her best to smile. 'You'll do us all proud, Michael Doherty.'

'I hope to.'

'I'm going to miss you terribly,' Betty said. 'What if it takes years to win the war? You'll be a man when you come back. I might not even recognise you.'

He smiled his crooked smile. 'Aren't I a man now?'

She looked him over. 'Not quite.'

'I'll be the same old me, I promise. Will you write to me, Betty Boop?'

'Of course I will. Every week.'

'I'll do the same. I promise. No matter where I am or what I'm doing.'

'Deal,' Betty said.

'Deal,' Michael repeated, and when he took her hand, they shook three times on the promise.

Chapter Three

Lily

Miss Lilian Thomas—known to her friends, family and many, many acquaintances as Lily but *never* Lil—lifted her delicate wrists and pressed down on the keys of the black Remington typewriter on a wooden desk at Miss Ward's Training College for Young Business Girls. Her eyes were fixed on the sheet of butcher's paper curled around the cylinder, and most particularly not at her fingers, because she was supposed to be learning touch typing, but with every strike of the keys her disappointment and frustration grew.

```
The qwixk brpwn fox jymped ocer the laxy doh.
```

'Will I ever learn this wretched thing?' Lily whispered. She reached for the platen knob, revolved it until the paper fed out of the machine and turned it over. Paper was too precious to waste—the war, you know—and if her teacher,

Miss Callen, had seen Lily giving in to her temptation to screw her mistake up into a crumpled ball, Lily would have been reprimanded in front of the entire class of fifty of Adelaide's finest young ladies. She took a deep breath, willed away her frustration, and began again, pressing the keys in the vain hope that she might accidentally spell the sentence correctly.

When her page was full of typed lines, when the clacking of the keys all around her had ceased too, she checked her tiny diamante watch. The hours seemed to stretch before her interminably.

It hadn't been her idea in the slightest to be thoroughly and systematically coached in shorthand, typewriting etc, which was the promise of the advertisement that had caught her mother's eye in *The Advertiser* back in October.

'You're simply aimless,' Mrs Thomas had told her over breakfast one morning in their elegant house in Buxton Street, North Adelaide. 'You've had nothing to fill your days since you finished school. And it won't do, Lilian.'

'I'm not aimless,' Lily had replied as she selected a polished silver butter knife and smoothed gleaming strawberry jam over her warm toast. The Thomas family's maid, Davina Hawkins, stood quietly at her side, pouring tea through a silver strainer into fine bone-china teacups decorated with cobalt blue and gold. She set the elegant matching teapot onto a trivet, poured a dash of milk into Lily's cup and then placed the beaded jug cover over the milk before slipping out of the breakfast room.

'You most certainly are. It's all dances and deb balls and recitals and frippery with you, Lilian. It's as if you don't even think about what's going on in the world.' Mrs Thomas stopped suddenly and sipped her tea with a sigh. Her mother seemed tired already and it was only eight o'clock in the morning. Lily looked down at her toast, embarrassed by the admonishment. When had she last had praise from her mother? Lily couldn't remember. How could her mother possibly be at all wise to what Lily was up to, with her own important work for the war effort? Mrs Thomas was barely ever at home, it seemed. She hosted Red Cross receptions to raise much-needed funds for the troops. Together with the ladies in her bridge club, she sat for hours knitting socks and vests and scarves for the soldiers, and her gardening club collected donations for packages to be sent overseas to the troops. They'd been particularly busy in the past few months, with Christmas fast approaching.

'No one serving king and country should miss out on a parcel from home.' Mrs Thomas tried hard to ensure her passions were shared.

There was a reason why her mother had thrown herself into war work with such particular dedication. Lily's older sister and only sibling, Susan, was Captain Dr Susan Thomas serving in the Australian Army Medical Corp in an Australian General Hospital in Egypt. She'd been dux of school in her final year, an outstanding medical student at the University of Adelaide and was simply the smartest woman Lily had ever met. Susan had been the apple of her parents' eyes, still was. Lily had arrived ten years after Susan was born, quite unexpectedly, and had upset the family's carefully planned dynamics. A change-of-life baby, that's what she'd been called, as if they might change their minds and send her back, and her arrival had further disappointed her father's scheme for a son to carry on the

Thomas tradition: to attend his school, become a member of the South Australian Cricket Association, and take up a job in the law firm he'd inherited from his own father.

They'd got Lily instead. A frivolous daughter who wasn't all that smart and who clearly couldn't even type. Her only saving grace was her looks. Her lithe figure, her bow lips, the slightly upturned nose and wide eyes captured people's attention, rather like Shirley Temple, although her blonde hair was dead straight and wouldn't remain curled no matter how many rags Davina tied in her hair at night.

In place of having their brilliant daughter with them in Adelaide, safe and sound, the Thomas family had to make do with a photograph of Susan in her uniform—a khaki tunic and skirt with large patch pockets, badges on each collar lapel and her army hat on a jaunty angle—which sat on the shelf above the fireplace in the front reception room. Every night, Lily crept in to say goodnight to that photograph and then prayed for Susan's safe return when the war was over.

Lily had put down her knife rather too quickly and it had struck her bread-and-butter plate with a clatter, which she'd regretted because it made her look petulant, and she wasn't.

'I do think about what's going on in the world, Mother. How could I not with all the soldiers everywhere I go in Adelaide? And we have the blackouts and rationing just like everywhere else. I'm not oblivious to—'

Her mother's brow furrowed as she interrupted her daughter. 'I know just the thing for your boredom.'

She'd acted swiftly, and that very day directly after breakfast she had visited Miss Ward on King William Street in the heart of Adelaide's commercial district, and secured for her youngest daughter a position in the best secretarial training college in the city.

And now, all these weeks later, Lily's fingers still stubbornly refused to strike the keys in the correct order to transfer the ink from the ribbon so the quick brown fox could jump over the lazy dog.

Miss Ward's guarantee was that every qualified student would secure a good appointment, which was a promise with a ring of truth to it since so many young men were away abroad and so many other young women had joined the forces or were working in munitions factories at Hendon.

Lily paused, checked the position of her fingers over the keys and pressed three quick strokes.

W a r

'How are you progressing, Miss Thomas?' Miss Callen was suddenly at her right shoulder. Lily leant forwards as if studying her terrifyingly bad typing up close might magically re-arrange the letters on the page. She lunged for the platen knob and w a r disappeared.

'I am trying, Miss Callen. Honestly I am.' She couldn't even convince herself that what she was saying was true. Her words sounded like lies.

Miss Callen's breathing became loud in Lily's ear. Lily stiffened at her teacher's proximity.

'How on earth are any of you going to achieve one hundred words per minute with such lackadaisical work habits?' She held a ruler in her hand and slapped it at the edge of Lily's desk, which made every young lady jump in her seat. 'Captains of industry are crying out for girls with secretarial skills. The quick brown fox jumped over the lazy dog. Again! And next week, shorthand!'

By seven o'clock, Lily had caught the tram home, through Victoria Square and up King William Street past Parliament House and the city baths on the Torrens, and then hopped off on O'Connell Street for the short walk home to Buxton Street. She'd completed half an hour of piano practice—wishing she could strike typewriter keys as fluently as she could black and ivory ones—and then began reworking an old gown of her mother's. She'd bought a pattern the week before from a haberdasher in Rundle Street and hoped she had the patience to create something that was, if not brand new, at least new to her.

She unpicked stitches and threaded her needle, humming along to the songs on the wireless in the corner of the room. And when the brass of Glenn Miller's 'In the Mood' filled the room, she leant back on her chair, her stomach fluttering. She and David Hogarth had danced to that song all year.

David. She liked every single thing about him. Handsome, intelligent and funny, he was from a family of graziers in the south-east. His three older sisters had married local property owners and his older brother, Bill, was serving in the RAAF. He'd come up to Adelaide as a boarder during high school and now had a flat, at Greenways Apartments at the top of King William Road, and a car, courtesy of his parents.

Lily had met David at a recital at Elder Hall the previous May and she'd been rather unashamedly instantly attracted to his dark blond hair and blue eyes that always seemed to have a sparkle in them. He played tennis on Saturday afternoons and practised two nights a week and it showed in his physique.

She was absolutely smitten with him.

They'd spent a lot of time together in the past six months. She was often on his arm at parties. He'd tried to turn her into a tennis player but, although she loved wearing her sister's old whites, she was hopelessly uncoordinated on the court. How on earth was she supposed to concentrate on the ball when he was on the other side of the net looking so dashing and being so patient with her lack of athleticism? They were regulars at West's Coffee Palace on Hindley Street when they felt like mixing it with the low crowd after a picture at the Metro. David was in his final year of law at the University of Adelaide but seemed to spend more time reading novels and poetry than legal texts. Perhaps if he'd been forced to attend Miss Ward's every day to learn typing he might be a little more grateful for the opportunities that had presented themselves to him. His father had gone to school with a man who was now on the bench and David had been almost guaranteed a clerkship, although Lily suspected he didn't fully appreciate either his intellect or his good fortune. They'd been on picnics to the Botanic Gardens and long drives up to Mount Lofty to admire the view over the city, and even talked until three in the morning once or twice.

But he'd never kissed her.

It had all been deliciously frustrating. Sometimes she believed she'd seen a look in his eye, detected that he might be moving in to press his lips to hers, or held her hand a little longer than he ought when he was helping her out of his car, but no. She remained unkissed, seemingly unloved. And entirely confused.

The music program on the radio ended and the familiar orchestral strains from the ABC announced it was time for the news. Lily hurriedly put down her sewing and rushed to turn it off. She was alone that evening and didn't have to listen to the war if she didn't want to. Davina was enjoying a night off seeing her family in Mile End, and Lily's parents were at a Red Cross fundraising dinner at the Town Hall. The house was quiet. She wandered into the hallway, ran a finger across the spotlessly clean side table in the hallway, her footsteps noiseless in the Persian rug, stopped to take in the scent of the red roses sitting in a crystal vase, and then swung open the double doors in the front reception room. This was where her parents entertained. There were more fresh flowers on the side table by the tapestry sofa, and the heavy brocade curtains were drawn. She went to the mantel and looked up at the photograph of her sister.

'Have you ever been in love?' she asked Susan.

Susan stared back at her from the photograph frame.

'I hope you have. I hope you've met another doctor in Egypt and he's swept you off your feet. Or perhaps you've fallen in love with a soldier, a working man, and as you've been treating his wounds he's fallen crushingly in love with you. What would mother and father say about that?'

Lily closed her eyes and saw David's smile and his blue eyes, felt the familiar thudding of her heart when she thought of him.

'It's complicated, isn't it, Susan … love? I've been asked out to dances and lots of other places by Tommy Skinner and he's a charming chap but he's not a patch on … you won't tell anyone, will you, Susan?'

Lily knew Susan would keep this secret.

'He's not a patch on David Hogarth. You'd like him, Susan, I just know it. He's incredibly clever but, I'll admit, not as clever as you. He's lovely. He dances like a dream and he loves poetry.'

Tears welled in Lily's eyes. 'Sometimes I think he might love me back, but then I'm not so sure. Sometimes I absolutely detest being eighteen.'

The next week, Lily went to the Metro with her new friend Clara from Miss Ward's for a seven-thirty screening of *Mrs Miniver* with Greer Garson and Walter Pidgeon; went to Wests to see Loretta Young's *The Men In Her Life*; attended sewing class in the evening; practised her piano until her fingers ached; and tried not at all to learn the shorthand for bill of lading. She had no idea what a bill of lading was and hoped she would never need to know. On Thursday she had coffee at the Gresham with Edwina Clarke and Serena Evans, old friends from school.

She hadn't heard from David all week.

On Friday evening, she was out with Tommy Skinner at Tux and accidentally drank a little too much sherry, which left her rather thick-headed for her stint with her mother on Saturday at the Red Cross trading table at the St Peters Town Hall. Her mother had been happy to work beside her daughter and Lily was pleased that the afternoon had passed remarkably quickly, so that she had time to go home and dress and fix her hair for the dance that night with Tommy at the Palais Royal on North Terrace. David hadn't asked her and saying yes to Tommy's invitation was a far better alternative than staying home on her own and pining.

It was a warm Adelaide December night. Lily really didn't need to be wearing her fur wrap over her pale pink chiffon shoestring-strapped gown but she looked rather glamorous in it, she thought, and had received approving looks from her parents as she'd presented herself at the top of the stairs when Tommy knocked on the front door. It had been nice to see them smile, and she'd made them laugh by pretending to trip on her way down. They'd shuffled her out the door looking quite proud of their daughter, and that filled her heart.

'Here we are then, Lily.' Tommy took her arm and guided her up the stairs to the curved brick entrance of the Palais and she felt rather like a Hollywood movie star arriving at a film premiere. Inside, art deco lights hung from the centre of the wide room, illuminating all the pretty girls and their dashing partners like a thousand stars twinkling in the sky.

'Lily! Lily!' someone called but the music and the chatter and laughter all around her was too loud for Lily to make out who it was. A young woman brushed past her and didn't stop to apologise, all her attention on the tall, uniformed American who was escorting her to the dance floor. Tommy led her to a table along the side of the dance floor, by the painted brick archways and the trailing ivy hanging above them. The table was scattered with velvet handbags, ashtrays half filled with lipstick-stained butts, empty bottles of lemonade and beer, and tall bottles disguised by brown paper bags.

'Have a seat, Lily.' Tommy pulled out a chair for her.

'Oh, no, I won't.' She slipped off her fur wrap and draped it over the back of the chair, and then put her clutch and gloves on the table. 'You promised me dancing, Tommy Skinner, and that's a foxtrot I hear.' She looked him over. He looked dashing in his black tuxedo, his white wing-tip collar and white bow tie. His hair was slicked back and, when he smiled at her so happily, in that moment she decided that if he tried to kiss her at the end of the night, she might well let him. He seemed to be the only man in Adelaide who wanted to try.

They danced a foxtrot, a tango, a waltz—twice—and a quickstep. Twirling around the dance floor in Tommy's confident arms, Lily let herself feel like the belle of the ball. They passed Bryan Gould dancing with Edwina Clarke, and Tony Allington and Serena Evans, and then twirled and laughed as they moved across the parquet floor, and as Lily took in the lights strung across the ceiling she tried to enjoy every step. She didn't want to think about going back to Miss Ward's on Monday and feeling like a complete and utter failure with a Remington. She didn't want to think about Susan and what she might be doing this very moment in a hospital in Egypt, and she couldn't think about David Hogarth either. He'd disappeared off the face of the earth, it seemed. She lifted her chin to look above the crowd and the sea of gowns and tuxedos, of slicked hair and set curls, of bow ties and pearls and glittering diamantes. How many of the Americans dancing at the Palais Royal tonight would be shipped off from this safe place to fight and die on islands they didn't yet know existed? How many Adelaide girls might fall in love with them before then, and have their hearts broken? What would happen to Susan and all the boys she knew who were abroad?

It was all Mrs Miniver's fault. She shouldn't have gone to see the Greer Garson film that week. In the closing moments, as the vicar sermonised to his congregation in the remains of their bombed church that this wasn't just a war of soldiers in uniform on the battlefield, but it was a war in the home and in the heart of everyone who loved freedom, Lily had cried, and when all around her people began singing along to 'Onward Christian Soldiers', she had wept. It had left her feeling tearful all week, when she'd always tried so much to be hopeful and cheerful.

'Gosh, there are so many Yanks here tonight,' Tommy said with a shout in her ear. They looked over to a huddle of uniforms by the bar.

'Yes,' Lily replied. 'They're everywhere, aren't they?'

'What's that they say about those fellows? Overpaid, over-sexed and over here?' Tommy rolled his eyes. 'All I know is they'd better keep their hands off our local girls. Don't you be tempted by one of those smooth talkers, Lily.'

'Pardon?'

She hadn't heard a word because she had seen David across the room. He was manoeuvring through the crowd of dancers towards her, and the thumping of her heart in her ears drowned out Tommy's voice and the music from the band and absolutely everything else.

'I said, don't you go losing your heart to a Yank,' Tommy shouted, leaning in close.

'No chance of that,' she replied dreamily.

One song ended and just as Tommy was about to launch Lily into a quickstep to one of Glenn Miller's new tunes, David was at Tommy's side.

'Skinner,' David said with a nod.

'Hogarth,' Tommy replied.

David turned his gaze to Lily. 'May I have this dance?'

Lily nodded politely. 'Why, yes, of course.'

Tommy bowed slightly and stepped back into the crowd. David reached for Lily's waist and pulled her in close. She rested one hand in his and put the other on his shoulder. Her fingers smoothed over the wool of his tuxedo and, too nervous to look directly at him, she stared at his black bow tie instead. He must have tied it hurriedly as one half was slightly bigger than the other and the knot was off centre.

'How are you, Lily?'

'I'm very well, thank you. And you?' She didn't want to sound cold but she was hurt about how he'd treated her.

'Fine.' He looked over her shoulder and his lips pulled together tightly.

'I didn't know you'd be here tonight,' she said.

'It was a last-minute decision, I have to admit.'

He was acting as if he'd rather be in the dentist's chair and she felt a flash of annoyance. 'You don't look to be in the mood for dancing.'

As if to prove her wrong, he pulled her ever so slightly closer and twirled her until she felt unsteady on her feet.

'David, it's hardly fair that you're cross that I came tonight with Tommy.'

He met her eyes and his brow wrinkled in confusion. 'What? No, I'm not. It's not that at all.'

Her heart sank. That had felt like her last hope, that he might be jealous and do something to claim her. What had he meant by toying with her all these months? The frustration and disappointment welled inside her. There were so few men left and the one she had fallen in love with didn't love her back. She tried not to cry but could feel she was on the verge of it—damn that Mrs Miniver all over again—and she tried to let go of him but when he realised what she was doing, he pulled her into his chest.

'Lil,' he said roughly and when she could bear to look at him his eyes were shining with tears. He leant down, his breath against her cheek. 'Bill was wounded in New Guinea. We found out on Tuesday.'

Lily's legs turned to rubber. She stumbled and it was only David's tight embrace that prevented her from falling to the floor. She pressed her cheek into the satin lapel of his tuxedo. 'Oh, no. Oh, David.'

They stopped twirling and stood, unmoving, in the middle of the dance floor.

Lily took her hand from his and gripped the lapels of his tuxedo, burying herself there in the safe warmth of him.

'I was hoping I'd see you here tonight. To tell you.' His chest rose and fell on a deep sigh and his lips pressed into the curl of hair at her ear as he told her, 'I'm joining the air force.'

Chapter Four

Betty

The door to the Woolworths staff cafeteria, in the building on the corner of Market and Pitt Street in the heart of Sydney, swung open and Miss Brougham strode in, blew a shrieking whistle and shouted, 'Evacuate!'

Betty almost choked on her cheese and pickle sandwich. Her friend Jean spluttered her tea. A hundred perfectly coiffured heads looked up towards the door, their mouths agape in that moment of silence and shock that precedes a panic.

'You heard me, girls,' Miss Brougham ordered. 'Grab your things and off we go. We're evacuating the whole store. Every single one of us.'

Someone screamed, high pitched and terrified, and then there were shushes all around.

'Are the Japs coming?' someone else shrieked.

'For goodness sake, girls.' Miss Brougham held the door behind her and with a wave of her hand beckoned them all to walk through it. 'It's a drill but if this is what we're to expect if they do make it into Sydney Harbour again, God help us all. Up, grab your things. Go, go go! It's a drill. The whole store, customers and all, are being evacuated.'

Betty pushed her chair back and reached for Jean's hand, and together they pushed their way through the crowd of girls to the door, to the flight of stairs at the end of the corridor, and down three levels out into the sunshine and crowds on Pitt Street.

'Bit of power's gone to her head, don't you think?' Jean rolled her eyes.

'That's unkind, Jean. If there really was a bomb, wouldn't you want everyone to get out safely?'

Jean tugged her hand. 'Crikey, Betty. I'm just having a bit of fun.'

Betty pulled her hand away and pushed ahead to the middle of the street. Of course the war was fun for Jean, full of handsome Americans and stockings and cigarettes and drinking in nightclubs and secret connections to find chocolate. And who knew what she was getting up to with the American soldier who was paying for it all.

The war hadn't seemed real for a long time, with the fighting so far away in Europe, in countries Betty had never heard of. But since the Japanese had taken Singapore, made it into Sydney Harbour and bombed Darwin and Pearl Harbor, things had been different in Sydney. Her parents woke every morning before six to listen to *Wake Up With Withers* on 2GB to keep up to date with the latest on the war. It all felt so close now, suffocating, as if everything she loved could be taken away at any minute.

And now Michael was going off to fight too.

Thousands of people, staff and customers, jostled around her in the street. Someone close lit a cigarette. A paper boy, sensing an opportunity, slicked through the crowd yelling, 'Newspapuh!' Someone tugged at the peak of his cap and he shook them off with a shrug. He adjusted the leather strap of his bag, which hugged his chest and bounced against his knee, and when an old man slipped him two pennies he handed over a *Sydney Morning Herald*. The customer tipped back his hat and took it upon himself to read out loud the latest details of the war to everyone around him.

'Allied forces have completely occupied the Gona area of the Japanese beachhead in New Guinea. It says here that Curtin announced it yesterday in the House of Representatives.'

'Where?' someone shouted.

'The House of Representatives,' he said. 'Canberra.'

'No, I mean did you say New Guinea?' A woman pushed closer, her large bosom brushing past Betty's shoulder. 'My husband's in New Guinea.'

A short young man and the round woman peered at the fine print on the front page. Betty could hardly hear herself think between the crush and the loud thudding in her ears. She looked up to the sky above Pitt Street and breathed deep, trying to block out all the nervous chatter around her and the pushing and shoving and the beeping car horns and shouts from the newspaper boy.

Was it safer to be out here on the street? Would she see the Japanese planes flying overhead as they followed the harbour past the Heads and right into the heart of Sydney?

Would she see the painted flag on the aircraft from all the way down there? Would she hear the throb and hum of their engines? And when a bomb was released from a Zero fighter, would she see it falling, getting bigger and bigger until everything turned black and her last thought in the world would be about who she would miss the most?

The next day, Betty tried her best all day to keep a brave face. Her customers would expect nothing less than a smile and a warm welcome from a Woolworths girl, and she was practised at both. What use was there in thinking about being bombed? The night before, she'd fallen into fitful sleep and had dreamt vividly all through the night about the London Blitz and the images she'd seen on newsreels of buildings collapsing and fire and smoke engulfing the city. When she got to work that morning, the air-raid drill was all anyone could talk about and she faced interrogations from every customer. She had quickly found her shopgirl smile and batted off their questions.

'Were you frightened?' asked a thin-lipped mother, clutching a white handkerchief and her little boy's hand. He had a finger firmly stuck up one nostril.

'Of course not,' Betty had replied as she'd handed over the woman's package. 'It was only a drill. A practice to keep all our customers safe.'

'That's not what I heard. My neighbour told me there really was a Japanese plane in the skies over Garden Island yesterday,' a matronly older woman pronounced with great authority as she purchased her deodorant cream. 'I'm only glad I was at my daughter's at Mosman instead of being here where we could all have been killed right where we stand.'

Her friend nodded in agreement. 'I heard that an elderly gentlemen had a heart attack right outside in Market Street. Is that true?'

Another customer, a young woman wearing a hat with a large spray of feathers on one side, swore that she'd seen Clark Gable himself directing evacuees from the building.

'Clark Gable? You mean, the movie star Clark Gable?' Betty's colleague Muriel sidled up to her to listen in to the conversation.

Betty was puzzled. 'I'm not sure he's even in the army.'

'He most certainly is,' the customer replied adamantly. 'He's a captain with a uniform and all. I read about it in *PhotoPlayer*.'

Betty did her best to reassure everyone but quickly came to realise that people believed what they wanted to believe, no matter what the truth was.

By lunchtime, she was tired of explaining and tired of her customers and their morbid curiosity. She found Jean at their regular table in the cafeteria and sat with her. Another day, another cheese and pickle sandwich and cup of tea. Another day closer to Michael's departure. 'I don't know about you, Jean, but if I hear one more question about—'

'The drill?' Jean interrupted. 'I don't know what people were saying to you down in Cosmetics but up in Haberdashery, I get the feeling people were actually a little bit disappointed that it was pretend.'

Betty chewed her sandwich. Mrs Doherty's pickle was vinegary and delicious and familiar and it made her think of Michael and his birthday all over again. She was tired after her night of wild dreams and her demanding customers, and she didn't want to think about the day before or what might come the next day and especially what was going to happen when Michael turned eighteen.

'Let's talk about something else. What are you reading?' Betty bumped Jean's shoulder and Jean moved her magazine between them so they could share.

'The *Women's Weekly* but it's such a bore. It's all war, war, war.' Jean flipped through the stories in the first few pages. 'Look at this. "Service with a smile! That's the spirit of those smart girls who are serving their country in the Australian Army, as members of the Australian Women's Army Service." The AWAS,' Jean muttered. 'Even the name is dreadful. Although I must admit, the uniforms do look smart.'

A smiling young woman wearing a hat with a gold badge at its brim stared at Betty from the page, but before she could read the small print Jean had flipped the magazine closed and over so its back cover faced up.

The full-colour advertisement caught her attention.

By Day, she's in the Land Army. By Night, she's the Darling of the Forces, thanks to Pond's Lips and Pond's Powder. The illustration was striking: a Land Army girl driving a tractor in a field, then being glamorously twirled around a dance floor by a Gary Cooper look-alike in a khaki army uniform and another man who looked almost exactly like Tyrone Power in a navy one, gold braiding in a loop at his sleeve, looking as if she couldn't decide whose invitation to accept first. Her white dress twirled and a beautiful rainbow-coloured wrap dangled from her elbow as she leant back to glance over her shoulder at Gary Cooper.

Betty read on.

Even if you are working harder than ever before for victory, there's no reason why your extra wartime duties should stop you from looking attractive. You can look lovelier than ever ... and without expensive beauty treatments. Pond's Powder and Pond's 'Lips' are inexpensive to buy, economical to use and definitely beauty-making. Pond's Powder clings for hours and hours ... it's made with the softest, finest texture. Pond's 'Lips' stay on and on and on—to the very last kiss.

Jean laughed. 'Look at that. "Six exquisite shades to choose from." That's a hoot. All any woman ever wants these days is red. Bright red. The Americans like that one best. I think it reminds them of that Betty Grable.' Jean winked. Betty was sure her face was flushing as red as the lipstick in the advertisement.

Her eyes drifted to the tractor and the plough. 'What do you think of this?'

'Pond's Powder?' Jean asked.

'No. The Land Army.'

Jean tried to keep her lips pulled tight as she giggled. 'I've seen the posters. Hasn't everyone? Girls milking cows. Girls ploughing fields, raking hay. Picking potatoes and all looking thrilled to be doing it. It looks awful. Give me Woolworths any day.'

'Don't you think it could be fun? Being out of Sydney, I mean. Working in the fresh air.' Away from air-raid drills and Japanese bombs.

'That's not my idea of fun.' Jean screwed up her face. 'All that dirt. And the smells.'

'It would be good to feel ... useful.'

'Seriously, Betty? The closest you've ever been to a cow is the milk in your tea.' Jean nodded at her friend's cup. 'I would never have picked you for the country type.'

Betty studied the magazine. Jean struck up a conversation with Daphne from Children's Wear who was sitting on her other side.

Betty's thoughts wandered. Was this to be her life? Her best friend gone off to fight and her days filled with waiting for news and selling face powder to Sydney's ladies? She'd never heard more complaints from customers than when supplies of lipstick had started to get tight. They could put up with tea and meat and sugar and butter rations, but it felt like the final straw to some when they couldn't find their favourite Coty's. Betty couldn't fight the feeling that it all seemed rather frivolous. What had changed in her? She'd been proud as punch when she'd left school at sixteen and won a job at Woolworths. Her parents hadn't been quite so proud. But the war had already begun. Sydney was different. She was different. Nothing was certain any more and a job was a job, after all. And she'd loved being a shopgirl.

But now women were joining up to the army and the air force in droves. She'd seen them proudly walking through Sydney's streets in their smart uniforms. She didn't know anyone who'd joined the Land Army but the articles in the newspaper said how important it was, helping to harvest food, not just for the fighting forces and those who were at home, but for sending over the sea to England, to people who were suffering so much because of the war.

Why had the idea so flirtatiously grabbed hold of her imagination? She'd never been to the country. She'd seen a pig once at the Royal Easter Show, a sow with enormous udders and ten perfect pink piglets nestling against her in fresh straw. Jean was right. She'd never even seen a cow up close, or a chicken, although the Gullisons four doors down had ten hens and a rooster that woke them all every morning with its boastful cock-a-doodle-dos.

Betty checked the time. She had five minutes until she was due back at her counter. She slurped the dregs of her tea, tucked Jean's magazine under her arm and went back to work.

'I'm home.' Betty turned the key in the front door of her house on King Street just after six-thirty that Friday night. She went first into her bedroom to toe off her court shoes. She slipped her relieved feet into her green felt slippers with the feather trim that moved like a wave when she took a step and padded into the kitchen. Not only had it been a long day, but it had been a long week and she still had work tomorrow before the week was over. Everyone worked six days a week now because of the war and even though she didn't do anything particularly useful for the war at Woolworths, lots of people had more money than they'd had for a long time and were determined to spend it.

Her father, Walter, sat at the kitchen table with the newspaper spread out before him, smoking a Capstan. Her mother, Alma, stood at the stove, wearing a floral apron, turning three lamb cutlets in a frying pan.

'I don't mean to sound ungrateful, Mum, but lamb again?' Betty asked with a frown.

'Yes, lamb again, Betty, although I think mutton might be the more accurate term for these chops. There's no beef to be found anywhere at the moment. Remember what the government keeps telling us? Buying lamb will help us win the war.'

'I suppose I could get used to it.' Betty smiled. 'Please at least promise me you've made mashed potatoes, Mum?' Betty went to her father, kissed him on the cheek and then crossed the kitchen to her mother, squeezing her arm.

'Of course. And we have tinned peas and some carrots from the garden. You sit down. I'm almost done here.'

Betty pulled up a chair. Salt and pepper cellars sat in the middle of the table along with a small crystal bowl of mint jelly. Betty knew it was Mrs Doherty's. Their neighbour cooked for everyone in the street: jams and pickles and spreads and sauces. Cakes and biscuits were her specialty, too. Betty's mother told her once that Mrs Doherty did it to distract herself.

'How was your day, Betty?' Walter asked.

'Fine,' she said. She jiggled a little in her chair and tried to still herself by holding her fingers together in her lap. 'After the excitement of yesterday and the drill, it seemed a little … ordinary, I must admit.'

Her stomach somersaulted. Nerves. Yes, that's what they were. Should she tell them after dinner? She hoped her courage hadn't deserted her on the long walk home.

She couldn't guess what they might say. After all, she was only seventeen. The lady in uniform at the Land Army office in Martin Place had stressed to Betty that any girl under twenty-one needed her parents' permission to sign up.

She felt once again their twinge of disappointment that she hadn't followed in their footsteps and become a teacher. Her father was proud of being a headmaster and her mother had recently been directed out of retirement to go back into the classroom, as so many young men were away and, war or not, children still needed to learn. Perhaps growing up around teachers had helped dissuade her from becoming one.

As she sat, twisting her fingers into knots, she wondered if her decision to join the Land Army proved they'd been right after all. If she'd been as happy as she'd claimed to be serving customers at Woolworths, she might not be entertaining the idea of throwing it all in to go to the country to pick potatoes. Or milk cows. Or drive tractors. The possibilities all seemed so thrillingly exciting.

The sizzling sounds from the stovetop ceased and a moment later Alma had placed plates before Walter and Betty. How many more times would she sit with her parents for dinner like this on a Friday night? How many more evenings would she spend the evening with them, listening to *Pepsodent Presents* on Sunday nights at eight?

Alma patted her daughter's shoulder. 'You all right, Betty? You've barely said a word.'

'As a matter of fact, there is something I need to talk to you about. Both of you.'

Walter regarded Betty over the top of his wire-rimmed glasses. 'What is it, Betty?'

She pushed her chair back. 'Wait here. I have something to show you.' She dashed to her bedroom, swept up her handbag and rushed back to the kitchen table. She opened the clasp and reached inside for the papers she'd been given at the Manpower Directorate: form A to enrol and an information booklet detailing everything else she needed to know. She laid them on the table.

'What's all this?' Alma asked.

'I've decided to …' Betty swallowed then took a fortifying deep breath. 'I'd like to sign up for the Women's Land Army.'

'I beg your pardon?'

'It's a vital war job. Lots of girls are enlisting.'

Her mother reached for the forms and stared at them. Her father stared at his daughter.

'I'm young and healthy. Well, in actual fact, a little too young. Dad, I'll need your permission and I hope you'll give it to me.'

Alma passed the papers to Walter. He scanned them and sat back in his chair. 'Betty, there's a list here of all the jobs that need doing. I don't know if you can do any of them.' He passed them back to Betty.

'Oh.' She hadn't studied the forms that closely. 'Let me see.' She scrambled to collect her thoughts as she read down the list. 'I've been looking after our vegetable garden this year, since Mr Curtin's austerity came in.'

Alma searched her daughter's face. 'That's not anything like real farm work. Like picking fruit or milking a cow. Or, what else does the form say? Driving a car or grooming and harnessing horses?'

'I'm sure I can do all of those things and more,' Betty replied, suddenly feeling nervous that her parents might not agree. Without her father's permission on the enrolment form she wouldn't be able to go.

'You don't need to do this, Betty. If you're bored with being a shopgirl there are lots of other things a young girl like you can do. You could still be a teacher. You have the smarts for it, you know that.' Walter took off his reading glasses and folded them. 'Or if teaching's not for you, I know the local bank manager. I'm sure he'd take you in as a teller. That's a good steady job until you get married.'

'Thank you, Dad, but I don't want to be a bank teller.' Betty glanced at her mother. 'Or a teacher. As a matter of fact, I don't really want to be a shopgirl any more either, if I'm being perfectly honest.' She frowned. 'I seem to spend half my day explaining why things are rationed and how coupons work. I don't feel like I'm doing anything for the war. Not like others are. I know I can help by getting out into the country and working for our farmers. There's a desperate labour shortage, you know, with all the boys off fighting.'

She watched her parents exchange glances.

She couldn't be sure but it seemed her father was trying not to smile. 'Yes, Betty. Crops still need harvesting and fruit still needs picking. Those of us in the cities need to eat and our troops abroad need food, too.'

Betty was sure her mouth had fallen wide open. 'You mean, you'll give your permission?'

'Are you absolutely sure this is what you want to do?' Alma asked.

Betty straightened her back and nodded in furious agreement with herself. 'Yes, I am. All you need to do is sign your permission on Form A and I'll be all set to go. I'll be earning thirty shillings a week, which is more than I'm on at Woolworths.'

'The work will be harder than serving at a counter,' Alma noted.

'I'm expecting it will be.'

Her father's gaze was direct and questioning. 'It says here you have to sign up for the duration of the war, or twelve months. Which one is it?'

Betty swallowed nervously. How could she explain to him how she was feeling? They didn't have a son. She was the only child and a girl. What was her family doing for the war effort? The Dohertys would soon have both sons away fighting. How could she look Mrs Doherty in the eye knowing she wasn't doing her bit, however small, when others were sacrificing so much?

'The whole time. I won't stop working until the end. It's not just a man's war, Dad. It can't be.'

Alma sniffed into her folded napkin.

Walter put his glasses back on, slowly, thinking for a long moment. 'All right. I'll sign my name where I need to. We're very proud of you, sweetheart, for wanting to do what you can.'

Betty's heart swelled. Being a shopgirl wasn't half as glamorous as being a Land Army girl was going to be. She could feel it. Wait until she told Jean. Wait until she told Michael.

'Thank you, Dad. Thank you, Mum. You won't be sorry, you'll see.' She hopped up from her chair and kissed them in turn before turning towards the door.

'Aren't you going to eat your dinner?' Alma called.

'I'm going next door. I have to tell Michael the big news.' She rounded the doorway into the hallway but stopped. She had a suspicion her parents' conversation would continue without her. She stilled, pressed her back to the hallway wall, cocked her head towards the kitchen. It felt wrong to spy but she couldn't help it.

'Did you have to rush to give your permission so quickly, Walter?' Alma whispered fiercely. 'We could have let her think about it a little more. I simply don't think she's ready for this. To be away from home for so long …'

'I know what you're thinking,' her father said.

'She's too young, Walter. Too light-hearted.'

'Naive, you mean?'

'Yes. She doesn't know the ways of the world, much less about horses or tractors or picking fruit. I'm scared for her, Walter.'

There was a long silence and Betty wondered if they'd guessed she was listening.

'We're lucky, you know, not having any sons. So many boys I've taught are off in Africa or Malaya or New Guinea. I think of those parents and what they're going through. What some of them have already been through.'

'You know the reason she's doing this.'

'What's that, Alma?'

'It's Michael. Can't you see?'

Betty leant in as close as she could to the edge of the doorway.

'It's his birthday next week. He's turning eighteen.'

'Oh, of course. You think she's …'

'Yes, of course she is and has been for the longest time.'

The clock on the mantelpiece above the stove ticked. Alma and Walter finished their dinner in silence. Betty tiptoed up the hallway runner and quietly closed the front door behind her.

'You've gone and done *what*?'

Betty and Michael stood under one of the Moreton Bay figs in the blackout darkness. The tip of Michael's cigarette danced like a firefly as he smoked.

Betty stood her ground. She didn't like his incredulous tone. 'You heard me. I'm joining the Land Army.'

'I did hear you, I just didn't believe you. What do you think you're doing with this ladies' army business?'

'What did you think? That I'd wait around here for you to come back or something?'

'No, I ...'

'Farmers are crying out for girls to go to the country and help, to do the work the men used to do.' Betty shook her head, feeling suddenly silly. Of course Michael knew that so many young men were away. 'I'm young and strong enough to do my bit. And those WRANS and AWAS and WAAAFs, they're not for me. I'm not that glamorous. I'm just a shopgirl from Rozelle but I can help out on the farms. I'm taking the forms back tomorrow. Dad's signed them. I'll be off to the country pretty soon, I expect.'

'The country?'

She huffed. 'Not you too. Why does no one think I can do farm work?'

'It's not that. It's just ... well, you sell ladies' cosmetics, Betty.' And when he laughed out loud, Betty felt silly and small.

'And it's boring me bloody senseless,' she shouted into the evening air.

'Are you absolutely sure?' In the glow of his cigarette, Michael's forehead creased in a question.

She nodded vigorously. 'Yes. Definitely. It's thirty shillings a week, plus a uniform and board. Better than what I'm earning selling ladies' cosmetics.'

'Well, who would have thought. Betty in the ladies' army.'

'The Women's Land Army. Get the name right, if you please.'

'So. I'll be off fighting the Japs and the Germans and you'll be milking cows.' Michael took a drag from his cigarette and blew the smoke over his shoulder.

This was belittling. She wouldn't take it. 'You really are infuriating, you know that, Michael Doherty?' She turned and walked away from her best friend. Within a moment, his hand was on her shoulder urging her to stop.

'Betty Boop, wait.'

She crossed her arms over her chest. Why was he the only one who was allowed to grow up? Just because he was a few months older than her. He urged her around to face him and bobbed down to meet her eyes.

'King Street won't be the same, will it, with both of us gone?'

'No,' she replied. 'It won't.'

'I'm going to miss you, Betty Boop. You know that.'

She knew if she were to open her mouth to speak she would burst into tears, so she nodded instead.

'Here.' Michael moved to her, his arms wide, and it felt like the most natural thing in the world to lean into him, to rest there, to feel his heart beating fast under her cheek. She held him tight and his strong arms squeezed her right back.

They held each other for a long while in the dark silent evening. Finally they loosened their hold on each other, but Michael's hand trailed down Betty's arm to her hand and they locked fingers. She held on tight.

'It'll be over soon. The tide's already turned in the war,' he said cheerily. 'That's what my dad says. I'll be home and back in King Street before you know it, Betty. And then I'll be buying you the chocolates, I promise.'

'You'd better.'

'When have I ever broken a promise to you?'

'Never,' she whispered into the night.

They walked home slowly, holding hands, bumping into each other clumsily as if they'd both just learnt how to walk. In the distance, a dog barked and the tinny sounds of a radio bled out into the street from someone's living room. When they reached Betty's house, they slowed. Things felt different between them somehow. Holding his hand made her feel nervous deep down in the pit of her stomach. In the moonlight, she noticed that his eyes, as brown as the chocolate on his favourite Cherry Ripe, seemed to be almost the exact same colour as his hair. How had she never realised that before?

Michael looked at his shoes and shuffled his foot along the footpath.

Betty smelled jasmine in the night air.

'Well,' he said.

'Well,' she replied.

'Betty ... I don't want to say goodbye. When I leave, I mean.'

'I beg your pardon?'

'I don't want you to come to Circular Quay with my parents to wave me off.'

'You don't?'

'I know we've got my birthday party next week and all, but can this be our goodbye? Right here? Right now? And then we won't have to speak about it again. We won't have to say the word.'

'All right,' she whispered.

'You'll write to me, won't you?'

Her voice caught in her throat. 'Of course. No doubt there'll be lots of adventures with cows and pigs that I'll be bursting to share.'

He stepped in closer. 'Betty.'

Her arms goosebumped.

'Don't get too lonely,' he whispered.

'Stay safe,' she implored.

'I promise.'

And when Michael leant down and pressed his lips to hers, they were kissing and his arms were around her waist and she grabbed his shoulders and he lifted her off her feet and suddenly she was flying.

Chapter Five

Flora

While her father and her brother sat in the kitchen listening to *Dad and Dave* and eating the last of the Christmas pudding, Flora Atkins was packing her suitcase.

She'd done something with all the rage she had felt about Jack's feather. She'd marched into the Manchester Unity Building on Swanston Street and lodged her application to join the Women's Land Army.

There was perhaps no one in her family more surprised than she was herself.

She'd provided all the paperwork she'd needed, including a medical certificate from the family doctor. Dr Carmichael had attested to her general health—if noting that she was a little on the thin side—and she'd been readily accepted. She'd ticked every box on the application form. Was she willing to cook? Tick. Ride? Tick. Drive? Tick. And on and on it went for the rest of the list: grooming and harnessing horses, milking, doing running repairs and poultry raising. Did she have any special experience in rural work? No. Did she have a particular preference for any type of rural work or any particular district she would be willing to go to? No, no and no. And did she have a companion desirous of being employed with her?

No.

She put two ticks next to the boxes marked *amateur gardening* and *poultry raising,* for extra emphasis. Since Prime Minister Curtin had urged all Australians to grow a Victory Garden to feed themselves, she'd attempted and successfully grown cabbage, potatoes and carrots. A small crop of tomatoes was coming along well too, although it would be up to her father and Jack now to tend to the fruit as it ripened over the summer months. She made a note to remind them that if they didn't watch carefully, the birds would eat them all. And as for poultry, she regularly sent leftover food scraps to Mrs Jones next door for her hens, for which they were repaid in fresh eggs, a good deal by any measure.

When she'd told her father and Jack what she'd done, they'd leapt up from their seats at the kitchen table, laughing and surprised. Her father had pumped her hand heartily and Jack had pulled her to him for an enormous hug.

'Your mother would be proud of you,' John had said, teary. 'She was from a farming family, you know. In the Wimmera.'

Flora knew that and also remembered that her mother's family had lost everything during the Depression.

'Well done, you,' Jack had said. 'Bloody marvellous, Flor. You can stick it to old man McInerney now, can't you?'

'Jack!' she'd gasped. 'I would do no such thing, even if I really wanted to.'

'He's got no idea what he's lost in you. Some farmer will be bloody lucky to have you on his farm. I know that much.'

Jack's faith in her was reassuring and she'd felt her cheeks flush with pride.

'Now, while I'm gone, you two had better pitch in and keep this house in order. Jack, you'll have to use the washing machine.' His eyes had widened slightly before he chuckled. She remembered how scared of it he'd been when he was a child, fearing his flingers would be pressed flat like the bed sheets if he got too close to the wringer above the boiler.

'And Dad,' Flora had continued, mentally ticking off all the tasks they would have to pick up now that she was leaving. 'Think you can manage supper and sweeping the floors every now and then?'

John had huffed good-naturedly. 'We'll be right, Flor. We'll survive on bread and dripping if we have to. Stop your fussing. You go and do what you've got to do. We'll be fine back here in Camberwell.' He'd wiped a tear from his eye. 'What do you think Frank would say about this caper, hey?' he'd asked.

'I know exactly what he'd say,' Jack had laughed. '"About bloody time you got out of the house and let those two blokes fend for themselves".'

That's exactly what he *would* say, and Flora could hear Frank's teasing voice in her head. She missed him so much.

'Think about it this way, Flor.' Her father had wiped his eyes. 'You could well be working on the farms that grow the spuds that make all those chipped potatoes for our lads abroad. You'll be helping to feed the troops. You'll be helping to feed our Frank.'

She'd held that thought close in the days since she'd signed up.

Mr McInerney had been near apoplectic when she'd given her notice. It was easy enough to get young girls to work for him, but replacing someone like Flora, with a decade of experience, who knew his business inside and out? 'What am I going to do with all the girls now, Miss Atkins, with you off gallivanting on some fool's errand? You think you can do a man's job in the country?' he'd spluttered. 'You don't have the strength for farm work, you know that. You've got office hands. You mark my words, Flora Atkins. You'll be back here quick as a flash, begging for your job back. And if you do, I would have to think very seriously about giving you your old position, given how quickly you decided to up and go off to that silly girls' army.'

Flora looked down at her bed, at her Land Army uniform, and pride swelled in her chest. There were gumboots, one pair of shoes, an overall dress, one pullover, a topcoat, one pair of gloves, a tie, two pairs of stockings and her hat, with a metal AWLA badge pinned to it, long socks, long work gloves and a black oilskin raincoat. She wasn't sure where she would be needing that in Australia in January, but never mind. Who knew how long she would be away for, and during which seasons. She folded her khaki shirts and the two pairs of bib-and-brace overalls, and tucked them in her suitcase. Her summer uniform, a short-sleeved shirt and skirt, hung on a hanger from her wardrobe door, ready to wear on her journey the next day to her first assignment. After that, she'd been instructed, it was to be worn strictly for official occasions such as receptions and church services and meeting local dignitaries.

Just in case, she'd packed a few extra things. Underwear, extra socks and a pair of men's elastic-sided boots, the kind her father wore to work at the council. She thought they'd be practical and not as difficult to walk in as the stiff and unwieldy gumboots. She made room for a notebook Jack had given her for Christmas, and the notepad, envelopes and stamps from her father.

'Promise you'll write every week,' he'd asked her as they'd sipped sherry by the Christmas tree. 'I'd love to know what you're up to. If you have time, that is, to write to your father. I know you'll be working hard. You put your work first. Always.'

Of course she would write. Her father would be lonely without her company and she vowed to keep her promise. The final items she put in her suitcase weren't practical but sentimental: a framed wedding photograph of her parents, and one of Frank in full uniform, colourised, his pink-cheeked grin staring back at the photographer like a wicked challenge.

She picked up the polished silver frame, admired her mother's beautiful lace wedding gown and the three-piece suit her father had worn. The sepia photograph was faded now, but her parents' faces still looked out, young and clear. They'd married young: her father was twenty-three and her mother just seventeen.

When Flora was seventeen, she'd imagined that by the age of thirty she would have been married for many years, looking after her husband and their children. She'd wanted three, two girls and a boy. But that had never come to pass. She'd never had a sweetheart and knew now that she never would. She'd been passed over and time had passed her by.

She had never been beautiful, had been too easily looked over when prettier girls turned heads. She was always a little too tall for men, at five foot eight in her bare feet. Her hair was brown, just brown, and she knew that she was plain. With her hair cut short now, in the wartime style promoted by actresses and celebrities, she was even more so. Their neighbour Mrs Tilley never failed to be forthright about how plain Flora was, and it seemed that with every passing year she was unmarried, Flora grew plainer still.

She'd spent her teenage years mourning her mother and looking after everyone else. Perhaps that had changed her in a way that young men had noticed. And by the time the sadness had started to lift she was twenty-five years old and well over any starry-eyed expectations about being swept off her feet. She'd made a life for a decade there in Waterloo Street in Camberwell, putting the three men first, and she might have continued to if Jack hadn't received the white feather and she hadn't seen the poster for the Land Army one more time on the tram.

Keep the farms going while the men are fighting.

While Frank is fighting. While Jack can't.

In an instant, she had found an outlet for her anger. If Jack couldn't serve, she would. She'd serve her country, work her fingers to the bone if she had to, if it meant Frank came home safe. In that moment, she made a promise to herself. One day the war would be over and her family would be together again. And she would serve until that day, until all four of them were once again sitting around their kitchen table in Camberwell, sharing a sweet cup of tea and the stories that made them a family.

There was a soft knock at her bedroom door.

'Flor?'

Flora tucked her parents' wedding photograph under her overalls. 'Come in, Dad.' The door slowly opened and John peeked around it as if he might be expecting someone else to be in the room.

'You right, love?' he asked.

'I'm almost packed.' Then she chuckled. 'Although I don't seem to have very much and my suitcase is already full to bursting. It must be the gumboots.' John glanced at the pile of folded khaki clothes.

'Boots,' he noted with a raised eyebrow. 'Like a real working man, hey?'

'They'll be practical. Although I haven't had the chance to wear them in before I go. I hope I don't rub blisters.'

'Thick socks, Flor. That's all you'll need.'

'I certainly know how to knit some if I ever get holes in these.'

John smiled and slipped an arm around his daughter's shoulder, pulling her in for a quick sideways hug. He peered at the contents of her suitcase. 'You're forgetting one thing, Flor.'

'What can that be? I've packed everything.'

'Take a pretty frock with you.'

'What for? You know I'm not one for dances or parties.' She felt the heat in her cheeks and guessed she was blushing. That he was still hoping for happiness for her touched her. 'And I have my uniform anyway.'

'Love, you'll be working as hard as any man. Take a pretty frock and some nice shoes. You'll want to feel like a young lady every now and then.' He smiled at her and Flora thought she would cherish this moment forever. 'I still can't come at the idea of you wearing those overalls.'

'What do you expect me to wear when I'm working? That pretty frock you insist I pack?'

John laughed. She threw her arms around him for a hug.

'We'll see you off at the train tomorrow. Me and Jack.'

'That'd be lovely, Dad.' She breathed out, hoping it would release the vice that had suddenly clenched at her ribcage, pulling tighter and tighter at the idea of being away from her father, the memories of her mother, her brother, this house, Melbourne.

'We're proud of you. What you're doing for the family. And your mother?' John sniffed. 'She'd be the proudest of all.'

Chapter Six

Lily

This would be their final party together before David left, and the knowledge of it weighed heavily on them both.

He arrived at Buxton Street in a taxi at eight o'clock, already in a sombre mood. He said a polite hello to Lily's parents at the front door, took her arm rather hurriedly and barely said a word as they made their way to Evelyn Wood's twenty-first birthday in Fitzroy. Lily had made a special effort that night. She'd had her hair done at Myer, and it was curled up and away from her forehead and brushed back over her ears in sweeping waves. Dangling pearl earrings matched the rope of them around her neck. And the gown she wore, the one she'd refashioned, looked rather lovely. Her sewing lessons had been a success.

She clutched her gloves and stared out the window into the warm summer night, trying not to fret over David's lack of attention to her frock or her hair. How should a young man act once he'd made the decision to go to war? Was he terrified? Was he feeling brave? His brother, Bill, was in hospital at Milne Bay in New Guinea, still too injured to be moved. How could anyone be jolly in the face of that?

When the taxi pulled up on Robe Terrace, a street filled with a row of Adelaide's finest mansions in art-deco brick and turn-of-the-century bluestone, David hopped out first and rounded the vehicle, opening Lily's door for her. She took his hand and stepped out. They stood together in silence as the dimmed headlights of the taxi disappeared into the parklands.

David pulled a pack of Woodbines and a matchbox from the inside pocket of his tuxedo jacket. He slipped a cigarette between his lips, struck a match and lit it, taking a long drag. His exhaled breath was a small cloud in the night air as if it were the middle of winter and not December.

Lily needed to make him happy. She needed to make this night a fond memory for him. 'This is going to be such a marvellous party. Evelyn told me her parents have turned the sunken garden by the tennis court into a Persian tent, with lights and overstuffed cushions and champagne. The waiters are all going to be dressed like genies. Doesn't that sound like fun?'

David smoked and looked out into the night. 'Lily, can we just wait a minute before we go in? Would you mind terribly?'

'Of course not. You want to finish your cigarette.'

He took another puff.

She waited a long moment before asking, 'Who knows that you're going?'

'Only my parents, my sisters and you.'

Lily adjusted her squirrel-fur cape and sat on the low brick front fence. She kicked out a foot, her pink dress draping elegantly from her slim leg.

'You haven't even noticed my new sandals.' Lily turned her ankle left and right. When David was like this it was best to distract him, humour him.

He glanced down and his eyes held on her ankle for a moment before he turned away. 'You're wearing new sandals.'

He took a puff and offered the cigarette to Lily. She pinched it between her index and middle fingers and watched the smoke rise. She didn't like it much but everyone smoked these days so she pretended to. She drew in and coughed when the smoke burnt her throat.

That made David smile. Finally. He came to sit next to her and she handed him the cigarette. They smoked and looked on as other guests arrived and began the long walk down the driveway, the soles of their shoes rustling the fine grey gravel.

'It's all a little bit pointless, isn't it?'

'What is?'

The end of his cigarette waved from side to side in the dark. 'Parties and tuxedos and champagne.'

'Champagne is never pointless, David.'

He looked at her, his gaze direct and serious. 'We're alike, you and I.'

'Not at all. I'm the life of the party and you'd rather sit out here and smoke. I detest coffee and it's all you drink. Not to mention that you like poetry and it bores me silly. I can't imagine why we're even friends.'

And you're so brave and I'm not in the slightest.

David looked across Robe Terrace into the darkness of the parklands. Somewhere past the trees and the newly dug trenches in the old playing fields, O'Connell Street would be filled with people. 'I mean, we're alike on account of my brother and your sister.'

'I suppose we are.' She smoothed her gown down over her thighs and her hand grazed David's leg. His head jerked to look at it, her gloved little finger against the satin stripe in his tuxedo trousers.

'Both our families have made sacrifices for the war.'

'Some more than others,' she replied.

'Do you think about Susan? Where she is? What she's doing this exact moment? The things she might have seen?'

Lily reached for the cigarette and took a good, deep puff. 'I tell myself she's on a grand tour, taking in the last of the seven wonders of the Ancient World, and she's been delayed in Egypt.'

'At the pyramid of Cheops?'

'Yes,' Lily said. 'Exactly.'

'You're lucky,' he said. 'To be able to think like that. Like there isn't a war.'

'It's not about luck,' Lily said, closing her eyes. She lowered her voice, almost whispered her confession. 'I work extremely diligently at it. It's my role to be the cheery one, don't you see? It takes an effort to keep everyone in my house smiling so they don't think about Susan quite so much. All this frippery, as my mother calls it … it's hard work. But if they're thinking about me and how frivolous I am they might not think about Susan with quite so much dread. I'm the naughty little distraction, don't you know.'

'Lil,' David sighed, his deep voice almost disappearing into the darkness.

'I can't listen to the radio. When Davina fetches the newspaper in the mornings so my father can devour every line of the news over his boiled eggs, I can't bear to look at it. It's full of Japan and Hitler and war bonds and battles in the Solomon Islands and other places I've never heard of. And if it's not that, it's demanding we girls be brave and go and work in factories making bullets or sign up for the armed services, for those girls who are good at typing. I can't even do that.'

A burgundy Dodge pulled up to the house and tooted its horn, and a clutch of young ladies stepped out, laughing. One called out to Lily and waved. It was Winifred Wills, a girl from her school days.

'Shall we see you on the dance floor shortly, Lily? Or are you staying out here all night with that handsome young man?'

'I'll see you inside,' Lily called back, and that seemed to satisfy them as they giggled their way into the party. Did they not know what was happening in the world? Or were they acting too, as she had been for so long?

'I think about Bill,' David said quietly. 'I dream about him. Sometimes I see him floating in the ocean. There's smoke and fire and planes flying overhead and it's simply horrific.'

'How ghastly, David.' Lily's heart shrank a little. She cast her eyes down into her lap, where her white-gloved fingers lay as limp as wilted flowers. 'In February, when the Australian nurses escaped Singapore before it fell and were killed on Bangka Island? That was such a dreadful day. I didn't think they'd go after our nurses. And then I realised that if they would go after our nurses, they'd go after our women doctors, too. That's when I decided not to read the papers any more. It's safer this way.'

David moved in and his arm slipped around her. She breathed deep and rested her head on his shoulder. When she opened her eyes, his tender face was close.

'You're too young to think like that,' he said.

'Eighteen doesn't feel especially young any more,' she replied.

'You are young. And so, so beautiful.' His voice was low and gruff and Lily stilled. Was this to be his confession of his love? Her gaze drifted to his mouth.

'May I kiss you, Lily Thomas?'

She held her breath. 'I've wanted you to forever.' His forehead dipped to hers, his nose gently brushed hers and his soft lips were on her cheek, kissing her there not once but twice. When he pressed his lips to hers for their first kiss, she slipped an arm inside his jacket and felt his warm skin under her palm.

A car horn honked and there was a shout from a passing car. David pulled his lips away and stared into her eyes, his breathing heavy. 'My lovely Lily.'

She shivered and it wasn't from the cold.

'Feel like a walk?'

She slipped a hand in his. 'Yes.'

They didn't care about missing the party. They walked hand in hand back through North Adelaide to David's apartment. They slowly took the stairs to the second floor and when he slipped his key in the lock, Lily stepped inside.

David flicked on the small lamp on the bedside table. Lily shrugged off her cape and put it on the bed. The room was small and plainly decorated. She'd never been there before. It wasn't the done thing for a young lady to go to a man's apartment but now she didn't care. The war had changed everything. There was a desk large enough for studying, a bentwood chair and a single bed pushed up against one wall. A dark wardrobe with two doors. A landscape paint-ing on the wall, featuring flat plains, a gum tree or two and a large flock of dusty sheep. A low bookcase was crowded with books. She ran her fingers along the spines.

'If there's anything you want to read.'

'No,' Lily replied, swallowing her nerves and the tightness in her throat. She went to the bed and sat, pulling off her white gloves one finger at a time. She slipped them in her purse, clasped it shut and held it in her lap.

'I have some sherry. I've just remembered. Would you like a glass?'

Lily said she would and David opened his wardrobe, rum-maged around on the bottom shelf and pulled out a bottle wrapped in a brown paper bag. There was a water glass on his writing desk and he filled it. When he handed it to Lily, she took a good slug before passing it back to him.

He emptied the glass and then poured another.

Lily savoured the sweetness in her mouth and waited for the heat and the kick of it to slip down inside her. 'When do you go exactly?'

David closed the wardrobe door and stood pressed back against it, slipping his free hand into pocket of his tux-edo trousers. 'Next Wednesday. Straight to Mildura for six months of pilot training at the RAAF base.' He cleared his throat. 'My parents and sisters are coming up from Millicent for a goodbye dinner on Tuesday night.'

'How lovely for you,' Lily said but she couldn't look at him. Everything from now on was too real, all this final detail. His final farewells to his family. This last night together.

'Would you like to—'

She shook her head. She couldn't meet his family. She wasn't brave enough. If something were to happen to him, she would be forced to bear their sadness as well as her own and she feared her heart wasn't big enough or strong enough for their grief, too.

If there was going to be grief, and that seemed inevitable, she was determined to make sure there was love first. She'd been thinking about the possibility of it all week and knew this was right. She could be brave. She could send him off with this gift, the memory of this night and perhaps even a promise.

She stood, walked to him, leant in to him so her stomach was pressed against his. His eyes flared and his breathing seemed to stop. She tugged at one side of his bow tie and it came loose. She slowly pulled it out of his collar and dropped it on the floor. She undid the top pearl button of his wing-tipped collar shirt. Then the next. And the next.

He stroked the curl of hair by her ear. 'I don't think I've ever told you how lovely your hair is. Like an angel's.'

'No,' she said. 'I would have remembered if you had.'

'You would have?'

'Of course I would have. You've barely given me a compliment the entire time I've known you.'

'That can't be true,' David said with a nervous smile as he sipped his sherry. She took it from him and drank some more. She was feeling rather lightheaded already, but perhaps that had more to do with David than it did the alcohol. He slipped off his tuxedo jacket and tossed it onto the chair by his desk. He took a hand and kissed her fingers one by one. 'I haven't told you how much you make me laugh?'

'No. Not ever.'

'Or what a terrible tennis player you are?'

She pulled his shirt out of his cummerbund, spread it open and splayed her fingers across his chest. His skin felt smooth and warm and her fingers tingled against it.

'Oh, yes, I distinctly remember that. But that hardly qualifies as a compliment.'

David freed his hand from hers and stroked an index finger down her face, slowly over the curve of her cheekbone, into the hollow of her cheek, before tracing the shape of her lips. Something tightened inside her.

'Then I probably haven't told you how I've longed to kiss you before tonight.'

'You do like to keep a girl waiting.' She held his gaze as she pressed her lips to his chest, as she kissed him right where his heart thumped, and she took in his scent, the soft heat of his skin. His breath hitched and she moved with him as his chest rose and fell. She looked up into his eyes. 'Why did you keep a girl waiting?'

His expression was pained and she thought he might be about to cry. 'I didn't want you to fall in love with me.'

'Whyever not?'

'Because I was always going to go off to the war. How could I do that to you?'

She brought her cheek to rest on his chest. His heart beat furiously.

'It's too late, David.'

'I thought it was better that we remained friends.'

'Not for me.'

He held her face in his hands and angled it up to meet his eyes. 'Do you know what I was thinking the entire walk back here?'

She shook her head. His thumbs stroked her cheeks.

His eyes gleamed in the low lamplight. '*She walks in beauty, like the night / of cloudless climes and starry skies …*'

He would always be her poet.

'Banjo Paterson?' she teased.

'Byron.'

She hesitated. 'I've never done this before.'

'Don't be scared,' he said. 'I won't hurt you. I would never hurt you, Lily.'

David undid his cufflinks and shrugged off his shirt. Lily ran her hands up and over his ribcage, smoothed them down over the curve of his shoulders and down his athletic arms to his wrists. She wrapped her fingers around them and lifted his hands to her breasts. She watched the way he cupped their fullness, and when her nipples tightened, so obvious to him even under her dress, the sensation was so unexpected and intense that she made a kind of noise she'd never heard herself make before, something between a sigh and a moan.

'Oh,' she sighed.

He leant down and kissed her. And she kissed him back, not caring if it was because he'd loved her all along or if it was because he was leaving. She wanted this. She wanted to send him off to war with this gift of her love, so he could hold it in his heart every day.

So it would keep him safe.

The bed in David's apartment was a single one but they fitted perfectly together in it. She'd loved the look of his naked body as he'd stripped off the rest of his clothes and later, wrapped in his arms under the tangled sheets, she loved the feel of it against her skin too. Its strength and softness and manliness. He'd been patient and impatient with her, all at once. His words had been whispers and his exclamations hushed and private.

As they lay silently together, breathing in time with one another, she pressed herself into the curve of his body and he wrapped his arms tighter around her.

'My beautiful Lily,' he whispered.

'Be safe, David,' she murmured.

This was living a life, she realised. They were living the lives her sister and his brother might not be able to. How could that be wrong?

This, with David, was the least frivolous thing she would ever do in her life.

'Be brave, Lily,' he whispered back.

Chapter Seven

Flora

January 1943

Flora checked her instructions for the tenth time that day. The Manpower Directorate paperwork was clear. She was to wait at the station upon her arrival to be met by a Mr Charles Nettlefold of Two Rivers at two p.m. She had been assigned to work for one month picking grapes on the family's property.

She'd memorised the name and the time, going over and over the details ever since she'd left Melbourne early that morning. Her anticipation for her assignment only grew as the train pulled into each station through the Mallee: Tempy, Gypsum, Bronzewing, Ouyen, Trinita, Nowingi, Boonoonar, Carwarp, Yatpool, Red Cliffs, Irymple.

And now here she was in Mildura.

Only it was now two-thirty and there was still no sign of her new employer. The train had left Mildura for Merbein and Yelta and the twenty or so people who had disembarked with her were now gone.

She hadn't made a mistake. She was definitely in Mildura. The white lettering on the railway building announced it clearly. She'd been employed by Mr Nettlefold to pick grapes on his property just outside the town.

If he ever came to fetch her.

Flora slipped a handkerchief from her pocket and patted her brow. It was blazing hot. The shade from the verandah, which stretched flat and wide from the ticketing office and waiting area to the edge of the platform, wasn't enough to keep her cool. The scorching breeze swept right under it and ruffled her Land Army uniform blouse.

She licked her parched lips. A glance at the water tower just outside the station made her feel even thirstier. She was sure she smelled of perspiration and her armpits were damp. Her feet must have swollen from all that sitting and her new regulation shoes felt tight. She'd swear it had never felt this stifling in Melbourne. And not that she would ever complain out loud, but she was hungry. The Vegemite sandwich and apple her brother had slipped into her handbag had been consumed hours and hours earlier. She would give her left arm for a cup of tea.

Above, the sky was a bright January blue with long streaks of snow-white cloud, not even enough to cast a shadow.

She cleared her throat, practising her introduction. 'How do you do, Mr Nettlefold. My name is Flora Atkins. I'm with the Women's Land Army and I'm here to work.' She'd repeated the words over and over on the train journey. She expected this Mr Nettlefold would want to see a confidence in his new worker and she didn't want to disappoint.

She checked her watch again. Fanned herself with the straw hat she'd carried with her on the train. Then sat on her suitcase.

This wasn't quite the welcome she'd been imagining. Her proud goodbye at Flinders Street station had buoyed her the whole journey. Her father wasn't an emotional man, never had been. If he could use three words to get his point across instead of twenty, three it always was. But she could see in his eyes that he was going to miss her, and not just because the Atkins household had lost its cook and cleaner and laundress.

'Look at you in that uniform. You look … well, you look like you're in the army. Work hard, love,' he'd said as he'd patted the epaulets on her shoulders and handed her suitcase to her. He'd carried it all the way to the station and right up to the platform. He had never been one for overly generous public displays of affection but this small gesture had touched her heart.

'I will, Dad. I'll do you proud. And Mum. And Frank.'

'Don't forget me.' Jack had slipped his arms around her for a hug.

'How could I ever forget you?' she'd whispered into his ear as they'd embraced. 'Be good and look after Dad, won't you?' She had felt the familiar ache across her chest. She hoped they hadn't heard the catch in her voice.

'I will. On both counts. I'm as proud as punch of you, Flor.'

Flora had let herself feel just a little bit proud of herself too. She'd only been away from home once before, when she'd gone to stay with her aunt—her mother's older sister—in Traralgon, the year she'd turned eighteen. Flora had nursed a sneaking suspicion that she'd been sent there to find a husband. She'd returned without one.

'Don't forget the tomatoes,' she'd called as she'd boarded the train. 'They're almost ripe. You'll have enough for sandwiches and supper for a month. And Mrs Jones likes them just the slightest bit still green. She fries them up with an egg on top for breakfast.'

'Noted.' Jack had smiled as he waved her goodbye. 'We'll look after your tomatoes and everything else in that damn Victory Garden of yours.'

'Goodbye then,' she'd called, finding a smile and a cheery voice as she stepped up into the carriage. She hurried to a seat two rows down, and claimed it before turning to find her father and her brother on the platform, waving. She slipped a handkerchief out of her skirt pocket and unfurled it, and the three of them waved and smiled until her father and her brother became small on the platform and then disappeared.

The Atkins family had been five for so long. Then four. Then three when Frank had been shipped out. Now there were two.

And there was only one of her stewing in the heat at the Mildura train station.

A fly buzzed at her mouth and she waved it away furiously, which was when she heard the shuffling footsteps on the railway platform.

An old man with a stooped back and a limp, wearing a broad-brimmed hat and a long-sleeved shirt, came towards her. Braces held up his sagging trousers and he was so slow that Flora wondered if he would be able to move at all with the crooked walking stick clutched in his gnarled hand.

At last. Mr Nettlefold. Flora made a quick assessment. Given his age and infirmity, it was no surprise help was needed on his farm. She felt immediately useful.

Flora sprang to her feet. The move seemed to take the old gentleman by surprise.

'How do you do, Mr Nettlefold.' She thrust out a hand at him. 'I'm Miss Flora Atkins. I'm with the Women's Land Army and I'm here to work with you on your property.'

The man stopped and turned a little, then lifted his chin. He seemed not to be able to straighten his neck.

'What's that?'

She was used to Jack so she leant in a little closer and spoke louder. 'I'm here from the Women's Land Army.'

'Are you now,' the old man grumbled and tapped his walking stick on the ground as a judge might bang a gavel. 'We've had a few of you out this way already. Younger lasses, mostly.' He looked her over. 'All the young blokes have gone, you see. Off fighting. More of our young men have enlisted than anywhere. Proud local boys, they are. My own grandson, too.'

'You have much to be proud of,' she shouted. 'I appreciate their duty and service. I have a brother in the AIF. That's why I'm here. To do the work of the men who've gone.'

'You? Help?'

'Why, yes.'

He huffed. 'I don't need help from girls like you. The ones who've come? They couldn't do the work. It's all over town.

They didn't last more than a couple of weeks. All went back to the city crying to their mothers, so I heard.'

Flora swallowed her confusion and tamped down the flare of anger. She was thirsty and hungry and sweltering, which didn't help. 'But Mr Nettlefold, you asked for some help. From the Manpower Directorate. Here I am.'

'Who?' The old man cupped his hand around his left ear and leant in closer to her. 'I'm Henwood. George Henwood.'

A horn tooted, three long sounds. Flora looked across the tracks in the direction of the commotion. A vehicle emerged out of a cloud of dust.

Mr Henwood followed her gaze and slowly lifted an arthritic finger.

'That's the Nettlefolds' Dodge. Don't trust it myself.'

The horn beeped again.

'Excuse me, Mr Henwood,' Flora said as she lifted a hand to shield her eyes from the sun. 'I believe that's for me.' She left Mr Henwood ruminating in her wake, lifted her suitcase and took the stairs at the end of the platform to cross the tracks. The Dodge's engine was still chugging and Flora jogged towards it, no easy feat with the weighty suitcase banging against her calf. The vehicle might have been black when it rolled out of the showroom but now it was covered in a thick layer of dust. There was a tear in its canopy and a long scratch and dent in the passenger door. The front passenger window was wound right down.

She looked through it.

'Are you Flora Atkins?' the driver asked.

'Yes. I'm expecting a Mr Charles Nettlefold?'

The driver was an old woman, judging by the tufts of grey hair that had come loose in wisps from the brim of her straw hat. She was fine-boned and sat propped on a pile of hessian sacks to help her see out the front window.

'Put your case in the back there.'

Flora did as she was told, then slid into the crinkled and ripped leather passenger seat. The door was heavy and stiff and it took two attempts to close it with a metallic crunch.

She held out a hand to the driver. 'Hello, I'm Flora. I'm pleased to meet you.'

The woman looked her up and down. 'I'm Mrs Nettlefold. Charles got caught up so he sent me to fetch you.'

'Thank you.'

Mrs Nettlefold considered Flora, studying her face, her physique and her shoulders, and even looking down into the foot well of the car to study her shoes.

'You're not a young lass, are you?'

Was she to be reminded of this by everyone she met? As if it were a miracle she was still alive. 'Not as young as some. But I'm a hard worker.'

'Mmm. Thought you'd be younger.'

The engine continued to chug. A fly buzzed at Flora's face and she flicked it away with her hand.

'You a spinster then?' Mrs Nettlefold queried.

'Yes. I'm not a widow.'

She heard the swallowed sigh of relief from the driver's seat. City or country, it didn't matter. Everyone knew someone who was fighting or missing in action or who had been lost. It didn't need to be someone close. People grieved for the loss of cousins and distant relatives and neighbours' grandsons or someone from church or the cricket club or the corner shop. Death was so close, always.

'All right then. Let's go.'

It was another half-hour journey in the clapped-out Dodge along rutted and dusty roads. On either side were paddocks filled with tightly packed crops swaying in waves as the wind swept through, making shapes like ripples on a pond, which then gave way to vines and orange groves as far as the eye could see. At a bend in the road, Mrs Nettlefold turned right, past a white wooden sign poking out of the red earth that said *Two Rivers* and *C.H. + A.M. Nettlefold* in black underneath it.

Mrs Nettlefold wasn't much of a conversationalist and Flora didn't mind the silence. It gave her time to think as she took in the view and observed the bluest skies she'd ever seen. She held her hat firmly on her head before leaning out of the open window to feel the wind flow over her. What had been a nervous excitement seven hours before at Flinders Street station now felt rather like two street cats clawing at each other in the pit of her stomach. She was a long way from home in a wholly unfamiliar place. She was to be billeted on her own in the middle of nowhere it seemed, with a suspicious old couple who already believed she wouldn't be up to the work.

She hoped she hadn't made a mistake.

At a turn in the track, buildings in the distance became clearer. A silver corrugated-iron roof shimmered in the blazing sun and it protected a stone cottage with a centre door at the front and a window on each side, behind which Flora could make out the pattern of lace curtains. The track curved around and behind the house and when Mrs Nettlefold pulled the Dodge to a jumpy stop, Flora leant out of her window and took it all in.

It was like nothing she'd ever seen.

A huge peppercorn tree on the other side of the house provided shade to a cow the colour of milk chocolate tethered to a post. A tyre hung from a thick rope, unmoving in the heat. Past it, a henhouse with perhaps a dozen chickens scratching in the red dirt. The rear of the house had been extended with a galvanised lean-to, and a set of wooden steps led to what Flora guessed might have been a pretty lawn in the middle of winter. Beyond the now-red patch of dust, there were shimmering apple-green grapevines as far as the eye could see, the rows dipping down slowly in the distance to a blue streak of river, and red cliffs on the other side shimmered like a mirage.

Two Rivers was an oasis.

'It's beautiful,' Flora said under her breath. Her shoulders released and her stomach stopped tumbling. She'd never been this far north in Victoria before. The Murray was something she'd learnt about in school but she'd never seen it with her own eyes.

'We have sultanas and currants for drying,' Mrs Nettlefold said. 'That's what we need you for. They're ready to pick. We don't have much but when they're ripe all at once, we need to move quickly. With the local boys all gone and the Italians locked away in that camp over the border at Loveday, we had to ask the Land Army for a girl.'

Mrs Nettlefold looked her over again. 'Girl,' she muttered, shaking her head. She opened the car door and slipped off her pile of hessian sacks. Before Flora could gather up her handbag, Mrs Nettlefold had slammed her door shut with a loud crunch and was striding up a stone path towards the back of the house. She might have been about the shortest person Flora had ever met but she was fast.

Flora quickly grabbed her suitcase from the back seat, slipped the strap of her handbag over her shoulder, and followed as fast as she could.

At the back door, Mrs Nettlefold stopped, turned and nodded her head towards the cow, grazing quietly in the shade. 'Ever milked a cow?'

'No. But I'm sure I can learn.'

Flora wasn't sure which was louder: Mrs Nettlefold's huff of indignation or the slam of the wooden flyscreen door after her.

Chapter Eight

'Here's your room then, Miss Atkins.'

The bedroom was situated at one end of the lean-to at the back of the house. The curtains had been drawn against the heat. Flora glanced inside, waiting for her eyes to adjust to the dim light.

'It's not much but there's a comfortable bed.'

'Thank you, Mrs Nettlefold.' Flora nodded, politely acknowledging her host. She'd been advised before she left Melbourne that she was to board in the Nettlefold's house as they only needed one Land Army girl. She had liked the idea that she would be staying with a family.

Mrs Nettlefold waved an arm in front of her impatiently. 'Go on then, in you go.'

The room was narrow but long. At the far end, a single bed with a dark wooden bedhead was pushed up against the wall. Two plump pillows lay on crisp white sheets pulled tight. To the immediate right of the doorway sat a small chest of three drawers with an oval mirror on a swivel on top of it. A lace doily had been prettily positioned with an opaque green vase on top, empty. Flora knew immediately that she would put her parents' wedding photograph there right alongside the picture of Jack to make the room feel more homely.

A single wooden chair sat next to the bed with a folded towel on it. Neat and tidy. Plain and practical. This would do.

'Thank you, Mrs Nettlefold. I'm sure I'll be comfortable here.' Flora gripped the handle of her suitcase. Her head felt itchy under her Land Army hat. She still wasn't used to it or perhaps it was slightly too small for her head. She had a big head for a woman. Frank used to tease her about it. 'Full of brains,' had always been her retort.

Mrs Nettlefold looked her up and down. 'You're tall for a girl.'

If Flora had known the woman better, she might have said that compared with her, everyone else was. But she held her tongue.

'My mother was tall,' Flora said.

Mrs Nettlefold looked up at Flora with narrowed and curious eyes. 'Your mother has passed?'

Flora hadn't been asked about her mother, hadn't had to tell anyone about her for so long, that the question came as a shock.

'Yes. Many years ago now.'

'Well.' Mrs Nettlefold averted her eyes. 'Who has a family untouched by sadness these days? Tell me that. Well, then. Put your case down and unpack. I'll put the kettle on.'

'A cuppa sounds lovely.'

Mrs Nettlefold closed the door behind her as she left. Flora set her suitcase down and tugged the curtains wide open, revealing louvre windows running the full length of her room. She'd leave them closed for now while it was still hot outside but guessed that at night they'd tease in the cooling breeze. When she pressed her nose up against them, all she could see was vines in a shimmering haze, like a million impressionist painter's brushstrokes. She lifted her hat from her head and tossed it onto the bed. When she sat on the crisp taut sheets, the bed squeaked, which made her wonder if she might keep the Nettlefolds awake with her tossing and turning. She hadn't slept a full night through since Frank had enlisted.

She swivelled, lifting her legs onto the bed and dropping her head on the pillows, trying them out for size. Yes, her feet would hang over the end of the bed but needs must and how could she grumble about that when she'd landed in such a beautiful place for her first Land Army posting? She was already planning how she would describe it to her father when she wrote her first letter home. *Red earth and green vines and blue skies, Dad. It's heavenly.*

Flora knew she should find the kitchen and accept with thanks the cup of tea Mrs Nettlefold had offered, but she needed a moment. It had been quite a journey to Two Rivers and an even longer two weeks since she'd enlisted in the Land Army and waited anxiously for her first posting. It felt as if she'd crammed ten years of adventures into a few short weeks.

Her breathing slowed and she laid her hands flat on her growling stomach. It grumbled.

'Hello there?'

There was a voice from far away in her ears. It sounded like Frank. His cheery face appeared behind her eyes and he was laughing in his uniform, his slouch hat rakishly askew on his head, and Flora reached out to tousle his hair.

'Miss Atkins?'

Her eyes shot open. She didn't recognise the white sloping ceiling above her or the small bulb hanging from a dark-brown cord. She jerked upright and gasped. 'Oh my goodness.' In the tangle of swinging her legs over the side of the bed, she almost fell to the floor.

'I'm sorry, I didn't mean to startle you.' Two solid footsteps on the linoleum. She righted herself and stood.

'You didn't. Well, actually … how rude of me …' Flora smoothed down her skirt and hoped her shirt was still tucked in. She looked up, tried to ignore the hot blush of embarrassment in her cheeks.

Who was this? The voice that had sounded like Frank was not Frank, she could see that now. The man was so tall he had to duck under the doorframe to step inside. He quickly lifted his wide-brimmed hat from his head, which revealed a damp and messy head of dark, almost black hair with streaks of grey at his temples. The sleeves of his collarless shirt were rolled up past his elbows, and he had the kind of deep tan she expected a man of the land would have.

He cleared his throat. 'I knocked but there was no answer.'

'I don't know what came over me. I must have fallen asleep.'

'That's no surprise. You've had a long day, I expect.' He held on to the brim of his hat and nodded a greeting. 'I'm Charles Nettlefold.'

Flora stared at him. 'I beg your pardon?'

'This is my family's fruit block.'

'Oh.' Flora shook her head. 'I was expecting someone older. Mrs Nettlefold. I thought she—'

If he'd offered her a smile, it had disappeared by the time he lifted his eyes from a quick glance at her shoes. 'My mother.'

'Oh, of course.'

'I'm sorry I couldn't meet you at the station. I got caught up here in the drying shed. A sprayer decided to stop spraying.'

'Please. There's no need to apologise.'

'You had a pleasant trip up from Melbourne, I hope?'

'Yes, I did. Thank you.'

'My mother is brewing another pot of tea if you'd care for a cup.'

'Thank you. I would.'

'We're in the kitchen. When you're ready.' Charles ducked under the doorway and closed the door behind him.

Flora stared up the ceiling, closing her eyes with a deep sigh. First impressions counted for so much, she knew, and she couldn't fight the distinct feeling that she had already failed with both of the Nettlefolds.

Too old for the mother and too lazy for the son.

She tucked in her shirt, straightened her tie and checked her hair, short and neat but somewhat misshapen from both the sweat of her hat on the car drive and the pillow that had provided her that welcome respite from her weariness. There was a brush somewhere in her suitcase but she made do with smoothing it into some kind of order and tucking it behind her ears. She ignored the flush in her cheeks as she checked her reflection in the mirror.

That's when she noticed the opaque green vase was no longer empty. It had been filled with a spray of grape leaves and sunshine-yellow paper daisies.

After Flora had washed her face and hands in the bathroom on the opposite side of the lean-to, which seemed to have been lately renovated with an indoor dunny, she followed the enticing smell of freshly baked scones to the kitchen. There she was greeted by not two Nettlefolds but four.

Mrs Nettlefold sat at one end of the table, Charles at the other, and in between, on the side nearest the sink, were two little girls. Charles pushed back his chair and stood, motioning wordlessly to the empty chair.

'Thank you,' she said. The aroma of freshly brewed tea made her almost giddy.

Charles waited until Flora was seated and returned to his chair. The scones sat in the middle of the table, plump and steaming.

'Miss Atkins,' Charles said. 'I'd like to introduce you to my daughters, Violet and Daisy. Girls, this is the lady I told you about from the Land Army who's come to help me pick our fruit.'

The girls giggled and dropped their chins, sneaking sideways glances at each other.

'Girls,' Mrs Nettlefold said. 'Manners.'

'Yes, Nan,' said Violet.

'It's very nice to meet you, Violet and Daisy.'

Violet's hair was as dark as her father's, almost black, and cut in a short bob quite similar to Flora's own. She had her father's eyes, too. Sky blue. Violet trained them on Flora and offered a friendly smile. The little girl's checked shirt, puffed at the shoulders, looked clean and pressed, and skinny little arms poked out of the sleeves.

Flora guessed the younger girl, Daisy, must be six years old or so. Her hair, almost white-blonde, hung in two thin plaits over her shoulders. With a smear of freckles across her nose and cheeks, eyelashes of the palest blonde and big blue eyes, she was like something out of a *Ginger Meggs* cartoon strip. She beamed at Flora.

'Miss Atkins?' Mrs Nettlefold offered the plate of scones to Flora. Steam rose from them in a tantalising cloud. A small glass bowl filled with chunky apricot jam sat on the table next to the teapot, along with a matching jug full to the brim with cream so thick the spoon stood up in it.

'They smell absolutely delicious, Mrs Nettlefold.' Flora took one and passed the plate to Charles on her other side. He gave his daughters one each.

'Dad,' Daisy whispered loudly. 'I'm so hungry. The lady took a long time to wake up and we've been waiting forever for afternoon tea.'

Flora felt hot all of a sudden. She studied her scone.

'One is plenty. You have to leave some room for dinner, Daisy.'

From the corner of her eye, Flora saw Charles reach across and tug his youngest daughter's ear.

Mrs Nettlefold poured the tea.

When Flora took that first bite of scone, loaded with glistening apricot jam and a dollop of cream, she decided the six-hour train journey from Melbourne had been entirely worth it.

'Would you like to see the block, Miss Atkins?'

Flora had just crossed her cutlery over her empty dinner plate when Charles had pushed his chair back and asked her to join him. She had struggled to finish Mrs Nettlefold's lamb chop, mashed potato, carrot and pea dinner, having earlier been urged to eat a second scone by Violet, and was glad of the offer so she could stretch her legs and help her stomach settle after all that food.

The girls looked up at her with wide eyes.

'Can we come too, Daddy?' Violet asked. 'Please?'

'We can show Miss Hadkins all the outside too,' Daisy added. 'Marjorie. And the chickens.'

'Miss Atkins does not need to meet our cow,' Charles replied with just the hint of a smile. 'You may both come if you don't get in the way. We have work to discuss.'

His daughters giggled.

'Off you go, then. I'll clean up here.' Mrs Nettlefold reached for the plates and Flora had to stop her automatic impulse to dash to the sink and help with the dishes. The rules were clear and had been repeated often: Land Army girls were to work, not to undertake domestic chores. Still, Flora felt a pang of guilt and sympathy for Mrs Nettlefold at having to keep her hands in the sink on such a lovely evening as this.

'This way, Miss Hadkins,' Daisy said as she tugged on Flora's hand. Charles led the little party to the back door and outside into the twilight. The sun was low and the sting had gone out of the heat. Charles led the way along the stone path, the girls chattering behind him. To the left of the house a loose rope was strung between two wooden posts that leant towards each other like lovers with outstretched arms.

The clothesline. They passed under the huge peppercorn tree and Flora felt the temperature change under its boughs.

The girls insisted Flora pat Marjorie, which she dutifully did, even though she'd never been that close to a cow in her life, and tried not to appear hesitant. The chickens had names, Daisy told her, including Dick and Dora and so many others Flora couldn't keep up. And then they were standing in the vines, the leaves flickering and dancing in the breeze as if they were waving to her.

Daisy hopped up and down on the spot. 'These make sultanas and Nan puts them in cakes and biscuits and they're scrumptious.'

Flora smiled at her. 'I can vouch for the fact that your grandmother is an excellent baker.'

The little girl pressed the flat of her hand on her stomach and rubbed. 'Yes, she jolly well is.'

'Are these all sultana grapes, Mr Nettlefold?' Flora turned back to Charles, who'd been lingering behind her. He'd slipped his hat back on before they'd come outside and his face was in shadow.

'Sultanas and currants. Here.' He reached right in among the leaves and with a tug pulled out a bunch that Flora hadn't even noticed was there. He plucked a single grape from the bunch and held it out to her. She cupped her palm and he dropped it there. When she bit into the tiny green orb, the taut skin exploded and sweetness flooded her mouth. 'Oh, goodness,' she sighed. 'I've never tasted anything like that from the corner grocer in Camberwell.'

Charles smiled proudly. 'It's difficult to get them to market when they're ripe, with us being so far away. That's why we dry them. Once they're picked, they're dried in the sheds over there on racks, or out in the sun, and then they're off to the local co-op for packing.'

Flora looked over to the drying sheds. A tractor was parked close by, its red canopy visible above the green. The branches of a few straggly gums hung over the sheds.

'Every wife and mother and sweetheart in the country seems to be baking fruit cakes to send off to the troops,' he said. 'Demand has never been greater.'

Flora smiled at the memory of her own hours in the kitchen doing the exact thing for Frank. 'Yes. In the Willow soldier's cake tin. They're not quite as tasty these days without so much butter, but we've learnt to make do. I'm sure our boys don't mind.'

Charles walked on ahead of her and looked back, and she followed.

'We're not a very big property, but there are just a few too many vines for me to do on my own. And the girls are far too young to help. That's why we need you, Miss Atkins.'

Flora straightened her shoulders. 'I'm pleased to be here to help you.' Flora hoped she sounded confident. *Be proud of your wartime calling. It will be hard and sometimes you'll want to quit*, she remembered being told at the induction session back in Melbourne, *but keep on smiling and carry on regardless, no matter how hard the work. Our troops and our country are depending on you.*

'Daddy, Daddy! We're hiding. Come find us.'

A small chuckle escaped Charles's lips. He slipped his hands into the pockets of his overalls and rocked back on his heels. 'It's the girls' favourite game.' He lowered his voice. 'They don't know it but I've twigged that they only ever hide in the same spot, right there behind that row.' He pointed towards the drying sheds and Flora followed his finger. She saw a flash of blonde hair and heard giggles in the distance.

When she was their age, Flora had loved to play hide and seek with her father but she'd never had a backyard this big to hide in. Their small house in Camberwell afforded only a few places to disappear: down the narrow side of the house, behind the water tank, or hidden in the leaves of the plum tree. Out here, Flora could easily believe that Charles's girls could disappear in one of a million spots all the way to the horizon and not be found for hours.

'We start early,' he told her. 'Before the heat of the day hits.'

Flora nodded, slipping her hands behind her back. 'Certainly.'

'Six o'clock. Will you need waking?'

'I'd appreciate a knock on my door,' she said.

'That's easily done,' Charles replied with a nod. 'Do you have a hat? I mean, something with a wider brim than your Land Army hat?'

Her hand went to the top of her hair without her planning it. His eyes followed. 'Oh yes, I brought a straw hat with me.'

'Good. Best not to get sunburnt on the first day.'

Practical. That's how Charles Nettlefold struck Flora. A practical, no-nonsense kind of a man. Her father was such a man. The fewer words they were able to use in a conversation, the better. That suited her just fine.

The girls continued to call after their father and the sound of it was playful and lovely. Magpies called from the gum tree by the drying shed, and a light breeze flicked and danced in the vine leaves. Flora stole a glance at Charles. His eyes were off somewhere in the distance.

'Mr Nettlefold, I'm not afraid of hard work. I'll be ready bright and early tomorrow. You have my word.'

He turned to her and smiled. 'Good to know. Now, Miss Atkins,' he said, and then he raised his voice in a dramatic fashion. 'I have to go and find my girls.'

There was more squealing and a lion's roar emerged from Charles's throat as he playfully loped off to chase his daughters. Flora's thoughts drifted to her own father. It was past dinnertime now. He would be settled in his favourite armchair in the living room, filling his ashtray with ash, listening to the latest news of the fighting before falling asleep in his chair, Frank in his uniform keeping watch from the wooden frame on the mantel.

Flora yawned and quickly covered her mouth. The setting sun, oranges and reds and purples in the sky, reminded her that the evening was almost gone. She turned to walk back to the house, but at the sound of a squeal looked back over her shoulder to see Charles striding after her, a little girl under each arm.

Chapter Nine

'Here are your secateurs, Miss Atkins.'

At six o'clock the next morning, the sun was almost up. The earthy smell of the red soil was fecund and Flora's early-morning hunger had been sated by boiled eggs on toast and a cup of sweet tea. Mrs Nettlefold had provided the hearty breakfast after rising early to milk Marjorie and collect the eggs from the chook house.

She and Charles were in the vines and Flora gripped her new tool in her right hand and squeezed the handles together, flexing her fingers, feeling their strength. The blades moved easily. On close inspection in the early-morning light, she noticed a shine on the curve of each blade, an indication they'd recently been sharpened. She'd pruned the roses at home and the plum tree in the back yard when it was bare-leafed, so this wasn't altogether unfamiliar to her.

'Righto,' she said. She adjusted her wide-brimmed straw hat.

'I see you have gloves,' Charles said. 'And ... overalls.'

Flora waved a hand in the air. 'Part of the uniform, Mr Nettlefold. It was all supplied by the Land Army.'

'Here are the buckets. We'll cut the grapes, put the bunches in there, and then I'll carry them over to the drying sheds and load them onto the racks. We'll keep going until about four.'

Flora looked down at the buckets on the flattened grass by her scuff-less boots. They were sheet-metal containers, about knee height, with a thin wire bowed from one side to the other. 'They've got holes in them,' she observed.

'That's so I can cold dip them in the buckets before the fruit is spread out for drying.'

'They need to be washed?'

Charles shook his head patiently. 'In an emulsion made from carbonate of potash, cold water and olive oil. The Greek method, we call it.'

'Is that because of the olive oil?' Flora had never tasted it herself but knew that some people in Melbourne bought it from the chemist.

'It's because the man who showed us all around here how to create world-class sultanas and currants is Greek. Kolios. Before him, all we had was shrivelled-up fruit. Now, they're plump and golden and in high demand. We have a lot to thank him for.'

'How fascinating,' Flora said. 'I don't mean to take up your time with so many questions. They're not important.' She waved her hand as if to bat her question away.

'They are, Miss Atkins. It's important you understand the process. Now, the grapes.' Charles leant down and reached into the vines. He gently cradled a bunch of sultanas in his hand. How did he know where they were hiding?

'The other important thing to remember is to keep the fruit clean. Too much handling spoils the drying. We also have to rinse out the buckets when they're emptied. We can't have dirt contaminating the grapes.'

'Righto.' Flora nodded, sure she'd taken it all in.

Charles adjusted his hat and she could have sworn he was hiding a grin when he replied, 'Righto, then.'

They got to work. As the sun rose higher in the sky, Flora worked the secateurs, searching and clipping. She'd managed to fill two buckets to every four of Charles's, but kept up her pace, hoping to improve on the impression she'd made the day before when she'd fallen asleep in the mid-afternoon. She still felt a flush of mortification in her cheeks when she thought about having to be woken.

She lifted her straw hat, ruffled her hair to cool it, and stretched out her back. That's when she heard it.

She looked up.

'What on earth is that?' she said to herself. Flora shielded her eyes from the bright sun but kept her eyes turned upwards. There was a buzz and a throaty, mechanical cough somewhere distant, but growing closer.

Charles walked over to her, tucking his secateurs in the pocket of his overalls. 'They're training pilots from the RAAF base at Mildura.'

'There's a base nearby?'

The plane was flying low in the distance, the engine roar getting louder and louder as it approached.

'He's coming in rather low, isn't he?' Flora took a step back into the vines, as if that might somehow protect her.

'They're young boys,' Charlies replied, shaking his head. 'Full of bravado. They like to have fun with us sometimes. They'll be off somewhere soon where they're going to need every bit of courage they can muster. I don't mind if they take a practice run here.'

The craft was so low coming in to its approach that Flora and Charles instinctively ducked.

'It's a Wirraway,' Charles said. 'A bomber.'

Flora wondered what it must have been like for the people of Poland and France and Czechoslovakia and Belgium when the Nazis invaded. For the people of Singapore when it fell. For every soldier strafed by bullets. Those final few minutes must have been terror. The approach. The sound. The pain. The oblivion.

Weren't they ripe for the picking, these pilots in their planes? How could one hide in the blue when even the clouds were no disguise for the noise? She and Charles followed the aircraft as it lifted, the sound of its engines fading, until it became a pinprick in the summer sky.

Three hours later, with the sun still high, Flora's back was about to break. The vines were low to the ground and she had to almost bend in half to fossick among the leaves to find the bunches. She was trying to be extra careful to handle the grapes as little as possible and to cut them at the top of the stem as Charles had shown her. More than one bunch had tumbled from her gloved and unwieldy fingers and she seemed to be getting slower, not faster.

She stood, arched her back and lifted her chin to the sky. Her straw hat toppled off and she breathed deep.

'Men to arms, women to farms,' she reminded herself, trying to ignore the ache between her shoulder blades and the burn in her thighs from crouching.

'Pardon?' Charles's low voice seemed to rumble.

She slowly straightened. Something in her lower back throbbed and she blew out a pained breath as she propped her hands on her hips. He held the handles of two empty buckets in one huge hand.

'I was talking to myself, that's all. It's something I read back in Melbourne when I signed up to the Land Army. It's something they say to encourage young women to join. *Men to arms, women to farms.*'

Charles suddenly seemed taller. His expression grew stony. 'Not every man can go to war, Miss Atkins.' He dropped the metal buckets at her feet and strode away.

They worked on in silence. Charles seemed to prefer it that way and Flora didn't object.

At two, Mrs Nettlefold walked down from the house with a vacuum flask of hot tea and two slices of fruit cake. Flora gobbled hers down hungrily, even though lunch had only been two hours earlier. Charles thanked his mother and took a moment to sit on the grass between the vines for a rest, slowly savouring the fruit cake and sipping his tea. Flora desperately wanted to flop down on the grass to rest her back but didn't want to create the impression that she was a shirker, so she stood, bending slowly from side to side to try to loosen her taut muscles.

Flora grew slower and slower as the hours passed. Her back was shot through with muscle spasms and her arms throbbed. Her only relief came when Daisy and Violet ran through the vines to find their father, announcing that it was four o'clock and they were to stop for the day. When he saw them coming, he dropped his secateurs to the ground, spread his arms open wide and grabbed the girls up in his arms for smacking kisses. They giggled uproariously.

Flora averted her eyes. It was another family moment that she should respect and keep her distance from.

'Miss Hadkins,' Daisy called.

She looked up. All three Nettlefolds were watching her. 'Yes, Daisy?'

'It's time for you to come home too.'

The spasm in her lower back pinched as she took a step and Flora heard her own sharp intake of breath as she moved to slip the secateurs into the pocket of her overalls. She felt a mess. Her hair had come loose from the pins she'd used to keep it back under her hat. She'd sweated through her cotton shirt and she was certain she had blisters at the back of both heels from her new elastic-sided boots. She wanted nothing more than a hot bath and to wash her hair. And then to sleep for a week. Why on earth had she thought she was capable of such hard work? Perhaps Mr McInerney back in Melbourne and the crotchety old man at the train station had been right.

'Righto,' she called and, struggling to put on a brave face, she followed the family back to the house.

The night before, her bed had seemed exceedingly comfortable. But that night it squeaked with every breath she took and her back complained with agonising stabs of pain every time she moved on the stone-hard mattress. It was going to be a long night.

When they'd come back to the house, she'd bathed, changed into a skirt and a shirt, and had joined the family for dinner. She'd barely been able to keep her eyes open and, after apologising that she had no room for custard and stewed apples for dessert, had excused herself to her room where she crawled between the sheets and moaned.

It was just seven o'clock. She'd drawn the curtains but the slanted louvres were open and the breeze drifted in, making the fabric float. Outside, Marjorie was softly mooing and the chickens were clucking lazily. Inside, two little girls were giggling and stomping up and down the hallway and a man's voice was growling like a bear. Not long after, silence fell and then there were soft footsteps on the other side of her door and a little knock.

'Yes?' Flora called. She tried to sit up but her back spasmed and she lay back, trying to find a position that didn't hurt.

'Miss Hadkins?' The door opened and Daisy's little blonde head peeked around it.

'Come in. Please.'

'Daddy said I should give you this.' The child tentatively walked towards her with her hands outstretched. 'It's a hot water bottle.'

Flora wanted to weep with gratitude. It was just like hers at home, dark green rubber with a white stopper. 'Thank you. That's very considerate.'

Daisy put it on the bed by Flora's shoulder and then looked about the room as if she hadn't ever seen it before. She took in Flora's suitcase on the floor, the gumboots next to it, her straw hat hanging from the swivel mirror on the chest of drawers and then, with an innocent lack of restraint, ran to the dresser and picked up the wedding photo.

'That wedding dress is very pretty,' she said, turning back to Flora, her eyes wide.

'Isn't it?' Her mother's dress had been Edwardian in style; high collared, lace trimmed, with puffed sleeves and a train. She hadn't worn a veil but a ring of flowers threaded in her hair.

Daisy carefully set down the silver frame and picked up the photograph of Frank. 'Is he an army man?'

'Yes,' Flora replied. 'He is.'

Daisy propped the image in front of the vase of vine leaves and daisies. 'Sweet dreams, Miss Hadkins.'

'And to you, Daisy.'

The door closed, but that didn't prevent Flora from hearing every word of Daisy's conversation. Daisy hadn't quite got the knack of whispering, it seemed. 'There's a photograph of a soldier, Daddy. And another one with a wedding.'

'Is there?' Charles asked.

'She looks like a princess. Just like Cinderella.'

Cinderella? More like Sleeping Beauty, she thought.

Flora tucked the hot water bottle under the curve of her lower back. The warmth brought instant relief, even if it did make her sweat.

She'd planned to write to her father that night, telling him all about the block and the Nettlefolds and her first day. She'd been composing it in her head as she'd cut and held the grapes carefully in her gloved hand, loading them into the buckets with great care.

'Dear Dad. All is well here. It's so invigorating being out in the open air, feeling so useful ...'

She wouldn't tell him the truth. That she ached and she'd been slow. What did the children's fable say? Slow and steady wins the race? That's what she would have to do. Be patient, learn and try harder.

As she waited for sleep to claim her, Flora thought about the Nettlefold family. Were Mrs Nettlefold and her son sitting in the living room right now, listening to the entertainment on the radio, laughing behind their hands about how feeble their Land Army girl was after just one day at work? They'd asked for a girl and were sent a woman. Perhaps a younger woman might not ache so much after just one day.

The girls. Those playful and cheeky girls clearly adored their father. But where was their mother? Flora remembered that Mrs Nettlefold had hinted at something when she'd picked Flora up from the train station.

'Who has a family untouched by sadness these days?'

People had ways in which they hid their sadness and their grief. Flora knew that. Perhaps theirs was to remove any mention of Charles's wife, the girls' mother. And Charles— what grief had he endured? He'd shuttered himself after he'd overheard her going on about men bearing arms and women going to farms. She'd clearly offended him. She must learn not talk about herself and her family. That was safest. All in all, Flora had not made the best of starts to her career in the Land Army. The next day would be better, she resolved, as she drifted into a painful and exhausted sleep.

Flora and Charles worked their way into a routine. Flora had resolved not to chat, and Charles worked alongside her in silence. As she grew used to the work, she became more adept at finding the stalks in the vines and clipping them in just the right spot to snip the stem. She was filling buckets with more speed and the racks in the drying sheds were filling fast. Flora felt a growing sense of satisfaction as well as discovering, every day, muscles she didn't know she had. Her early back aches had eased as she grew used to the labour, but every night she'd fallen into bed early and exhausted with her hot water bottle almost directly after dinner.

On the first Friday, she'd taken to her overalls with the secateurs. Each day had been hotter than the one before, hovering near one hundred and fifteen degrees judging by the blazing sun and the still air, and she simply couldn't bear the stiff drill cotton of her overalls one minute longer. The sweat had been dripping down her back and down her legs since they'd begun work and she'd tossed her hat to the ground, clutched the stiff fabric in her fist and thrust the blades into the seam on the inside of her left leg. She squeezed hard and tight and tugged and in a couple of minutes, she was released from the constraints of the material in question. She tossed the secateurs on the grass, rolled the hems up to mid-thigh and stared at her handiwork. The relief from the heat was immediate and welcome

When Charles had returned with the empty buckets, he let them go so quickly they tumbled to the ground and clattered against each other.

'What have you done to your overalls?' Charles stared at her bare legs. When she'd looked up at him, she noticed his Adam's apple bob up and down under the growth of his salt-and-pepper beard. His gaze lingered on her legs before drifting to her face.

'I know, I know, they're a little pale. But it's too damn hot for long trousers.' The heat made her feel cross and frustrated and anyway, she didn't need his permission to make herself more comfortable in the heat. She challenged him with a return glare. It didn't escape her attention that his utterance was the first thing he'd said to her all week, other than 'It's time for a cuppa' or 'That bucket's got room for more grapes'. She'd been working so hard, trying to prove something to him and to herself. She'd worked through her aching back and bleeding blisters and if he appreciated it, he hadn't taken it upon himself to mention anything to her.

'You'll burn,' he'd said and turned his back to her. He lifted four full steel buckets—two in each hand—and stomped off to the drying shed.

On the second Monday, Flora was working her way down the vines and, stepping in close to clip a stem, she stepped on something that moved. She jumped and shrieked all at once and Charles was by her side in a moment.

'What is it, Miss Atkins?' He hunched to peer into her eyes. 'You look white as a sheet.'

'I think I stepped on a snake. It was soft and it wriggled and ...' She shivered at the thought of it.

He dropped to his knees and his fingers gripped her legs above the edge of her work boots, pressing into the skin there and searching every inch. 'Do you think you were bitten?'

That made Flora shriek again and she took off, running so fast she didn't stop until she was by Marjorie's side, her lungs shrieking with effort and terror. That started up the chooks in a cacophony. Marjorie mooed and swished her tail. Flora leant over, her hands on her knees, trying to catch her breath.

The back door slammed and Mrs Nettlefold rushed to her. 'I heard screams. What the devil's going on out here?'

Charles jogged towards them. 'Miss Atkins saw a snake in the vines.'

She bolted upright. 'Saw a snake? I stepped on the bloody thing.' She shivered involuntarily, goosebumps breaking out on every inch of her.

'You're not bitten?' Mrs Nettlefold asked.

'I would have felt that, wouldn't I?'

'You most certainly would have,' Mrs Nettlefold said with a definitive nod. 'Probably a lizard. No need to panic. I'll go fetch you a cold drink. Sit there on the grass and calm your nerves.'

Flora nervously looked around her. She walked to the tyre swing and sat in that instead.

On the second Wednesday, Flora filled a bucket so quickly she decided to take it to the drying shed herself, where she could hear Charles spraying the fruit. She was keen to see the racks, how the grapes were draped over them, how the process worked. She wasn't sure how it happened, but on the way over she tripped, the toe of one boot catching on the dirt, and she tumbled, falling on the bucket, its angular corner digging into her hip and scraping her shin as she met the trampled grass with a thud. It took her a moment to orient herself and when she opened her eyes, blinking against the blazing sun, Charles was looking down at her.

'Miss Atkins, what the blazes …' He lifted the bucket away and flicked squashed clumps of grapes from her legs and her stomach.

Flora caught her breath, and went to speak, but what came out of her mouth weren't words but laughter. Pure, joyous laughter. At the ridiculousness of tumbling like a clown, at the wide view of the sky above her, as azure as the ocean, and at the face staring down at her, frowning at her incompetence. It was all so ridiculous as to be hilarious.

The waves of laughter made her stomach ache and she brought her knees up to her chest and clutched them there. And when Charles tumbled backwards onto the grass, he joined in, and it was one of the happiest times Flora could remember.

On the next Saturday afternoon, the girls came down into the vines to call their father and Flora back to the house and Mrs Nettlefold greeted them at the back door.

'Supper's at six,' she said, her hand held flat over her eyes to shield them from the sun.

'Thank you,' Flora said wearily.

Charles was ahead of her, but he stopped and turned, his face serious. 'You've got time for a bath if you're inclined.'

Flora almost skidded to a stop. All week she'd washed over the handbasin in the bathroom filled with cold water. The house relied on rainwater and she'd quickly learnt they conserved it where they could.

'A bath?' she repeated, not quite certain of what she'd heard. The sheer excitement of such a thing, after two weeks of aching muscles and hard work, performed some kind of magic on her. 'Oh, yes, Mr Nettlefold. Thank you so much.' And the grin on her face, crinkling up her heat-parched cheeks, made her feel like someone else for the briefest moment: the new person she had been becoming since arriving at Two Rivers. She caught up to Charles and smiled up at him.

'A bath!' she exclaimed and rushed past him to her room to grab her towel and her toiletries.

When Flora sat down for supper, her hair was still wet. After soaking for an hour—such bliss—she'd washed her hair, scrubbing it so thoroughly the water looked pink afterwards from the red Mildura dirt. She'd towel dried it as well as she could though it still dripped on her floral dress. It was such a relief to feel so clean. After a week of sweat and dust, her hair had been so stiff it almost stood on end, as if she'd stuck her finger into an electric socket.

Charles had showered and was dressed in fresh clothes, too: a plain pale-blue shirt turned up to his elbows, and tan trousers. He was finished in the bathroom in ten minutes, which clearly included a shave as his jaw was smooth and she could smell some sort of men's cologne, nothing that she recognised from her father or brothers.

'This looks delicious, Mrs Nettlefold,' Flora declared as she looked over the spread of cold sliced ham, a green salad, a plate of hard-boiled eggs sliced in half and sprinkled with salt and pepper, a jar of homemade pickles and a loaf of freshly baked bread. Alongside the loaf was a china plate cradling a pat of butter an inch thick. It was the palest yellow and there were drops of condensation on it. Flora still marvelled at being able to have real butter, churned from Marjorie's own milk no less.

It seemed the perfect meal for a hot summer's evening.

'Eat up,' Mrs Nettlefold chided as she reached for the salad.

Charles poured their water glasses full. Violet and Daisy grinned at Flora across the table.

'Your dress is pretty,' Daisy whispered loudly.

'Thank you,' Flora replied. She was glad now she'd listened to her father. She was tired of her work clothes and the dress seemed just the right thing to wear for Saturday-night supper. It was short sleeved and knee length and had a matching belt. The V of the neckline and the blousy shape of the bodice were cool in the summer heat.

They ate in companionable silence, interrupted by the occasional murmur of appreciation from Charles or giggles from the girls. When their plates were empty, they still managed to make room for peach cobbler with fresh cream, which was devoured with great delight. Mrs Nettlefold might have been a little on the taciturn side, but she showed her love for her family—and an interloper—with her cooking and housekeeping and her kind attention to detail.

She worked harder than Charles and Flora put together, Flora was convinced. When Charles and Flora rose at five-thirty for breakfast, Mrs Nettlefold was already out with Marjorie, the sound of milk spurting against the sides of the milk tin now as familiar to Flora as the call of the magpies in the evenings. When they were out among the vines, the old woman was caring for and entertaining her two granddaughters. It seemed the only time there was a sparkle in her eye was when Violet and Daisy were in the room. Not for the first time, Flora envied them their closeness, for it made her miss her brothers even more.

Charles groaned, leant back in his chair and patted his flat stomach. 'That was just delicious, Mum.'

Mrs Nettlefold gave her son a proud little nod.

'Yes, it was,' Flora added. 'Thank you so much.'

Violet jumped up from her chair and began gathering bowls and spoons. 'Can we play cards tonight, Daddy?'

'I think we can. Who's up for a game of snap before bed?'

'I am!' Violet called out.

'I am, too,' Daisy whispered.

'You lot go and play cards,' their grandmother said. 'I'll clean up here and then I might walk to the drying sheds to see how those sultanas are getting on.'

Flora stood, too. 'Thank you again for dinner, Mrs Nettlefold. I'll excuse myself. I have some letters to write.'

'You don't play cards, Miss Atkins?' Violet asked, crestfallen.

'Oh, I—' She glanced at Charles. She didn't want to intrude.

'You'd be most welcome,' he said, his mouth a tight line. He didn't seem to want to disappoint his girls.

'Then yes, thank you. I'd enjoy that.'

Charles and Flora followed the bouncing girls down the hallway to the sitting room. It wasn't at all what she'd expected. A new three-seater lounge setting was positioned in front of a wide window with a lace curtain. Heavy burgundy drapes hung open on either side. It seemed strange suddenly to see open curtains in the twilight. She'd become so used to the blackouts, with darkened rooms and candles rather than lights. She glanced around for any photos and there seemed to be only one. Judging by the attire, it was Mrs Nettlefold's wedding photo.

The girls raced to the two matching armchairs that sat angled in the far corners of the room, their bare feet soft on the plush floral Axminster wall-to-wall carpet.

'Shall we put the radio on?' Charles asked, and when they clapped their enthusiasm he twiddled with the dial on the beautifully polished teak radio cabinet until he found something jazzy. He turned it up loud and Violet and Daisy jumped off their chairs and began practising what appeared to be ballet moves in the middle of the room.

Flora observed Charles watch his girls and marvelled at the transformation. There was a softness in his eyes when he was with them. If she'd formed a judgement of his character by the way he'd treated her, she might have a very different impression of the man. But standing there, his hands in his pockets, his head nodding ever so slightly to the beat of the music, watching his girls delight in their freedom, she judged him to be a wonderful father.

Flora felt a swell of something unfamiliar inside her. When Charles turned to her, she couldn't look away from his soft eyes and his smile, directed at her now too.

Her mouth was dry. Nervous, she reached a hand to the back of her neck where her thick hair was still damp and ruffled it. He crossed the room to her and stood by her side, watching the girls jiggle and move.

'They love to dance,' he said.

'I can see. Do they learn piano or take ballet lessons?'

Charles smiled at his shoes. 'There's not much of either around here, Miss Atkins. We're a long way from anything. I expect it's not much like Melbourne.'

'That is true, which is sometimes not a bad thing. Your family is safe here. A long way from the city. I think that's a good place to be these days.'

He searched her face, his brow furrowed. 'You must be missing your family.'

'Yes. I'm hoping to receive some letters soon. That's all people seem to do these days, wait on letters. Although I've been rather tardy and haven't had much time to write myself. I must get on to that tomorrow.'

Charles shifted, turned his body towards her. She'd only been this close to him when he'd crouched by her side demonstrating how to trim bunches of grapes from the vine on her first day. Now he was leaning in to be heard above the music.

'Didn't my mother mention it to you? We go to St Andrew's in Mildura on Sunday mornings and this weekend there's a morning tea afterwards in the church hall. The Country Women's Association are putting it on for all you Land Army girls. My mother's quite involved, has been for years.' He stopped talking and his breath was warm on her cheek. 'You'll come, won't you?'

'Yes, of course. Although …' She paused and wondered how best to say it. In the end, she was a practical, straightforward sort of person so she told him as it was. 'I'm sorry to disappoint you, but I'm not a regular churchgoer, Mr Nettlefold.'

He shrugged. 'I wouldn't go either if the morning tea wasn't so good. And …' He paused and glanced at his daughters. They were doing the Charleston, their hands on their waists like flappers, kicking their legs back and forth. 'It's an opportunity for the girls to play with other children their own age, especially during the school holidays when they haven't caught up with their friends for a while.'

'Of course it must be. They really are the most delightful girls, Mr Nettlefold.'

'You'll come then?'

Flora's cheeks felt hot and she put her hands behind her back so he wouldn't see her fingers fidget.

'Cards, Daddy. Cards!'

'Miss Atkins?'

'Yes. I'd be delighted.'

Chapter Ten

Betty

January 1943

After Betty Brower arrived at the Stocks' property just outside Mildura in north-western Victoria, she had cried herself to sleep every night for two weeks straight.

She'd spent each day on the verge of tears, rethinking every moment of her decision to sign up to the wretched Land Army. What had she done? With each step there were more grapes to search for and snip and place in the tin buckets, and then the tins kept arriving, more and more of them, and she felt like Mickey Mouse in that movie she'd seen at the Apollo, but here buckets kept arriving instead of brooms.

How on earth had she ever believed she was cut out for this kind of labour?

Her parents had been right and that realisation made her want to cry even more.

It was even harder to accept her own failings when every other girl seemed to be having such a jolly time. Of the twenty of them, she was the youngest by six months, something they'd figured out on that first day, when they'd played a fun game and lined themselves up in order of their birth. She was at one end and twenty-five-year-old Peggy was at the other. From then on, they'd called her the baby of the group. And she'd gone and proven them right by sobbing into her pillow each night.

Her sobbing could be heard by every single girl sleeping in the long corrugated-iron shed they called their quarters. Ten beds on each side, divided by makeshift hessian curtains, with a dining table at one end near the front door; her sobs easily carried from front door to back and over every cot in between.

Their work days were long. Picking all day then returning at supper time for a wash from the hot water in the always-boiling copper outside. Once they'd tidied up, they sat down to a meal prepared for them by the Land Army matron who had been assigned to the group. Betty had tried to keep her eyes open, listening in as the other girls chatted happily among themselves about the day, the rumour of a goanna in the vines, the incessant flies and the sunburn. After that, some of the girls laid outside on the grass to enjoy the cooler twilight and look up at the stars. Others sat around the dining table playing cards or listening to the wireless the Stocks had provided for them, and the rest went straight to their beds to relax for a while, to read a magazine someone had been sent from home or to write their letters. They worked six days a week, and they were long days, so there wasn't much time or energy for anything else. They hadn't even had time to make their temporary home feel like a home. Inside the bare privacy of their little bedrooms, each girl had a bed with a straw-filled palliasse to sleep on, a chair, a nail hammered into the frame of the shed for hanging a wet towel, and space under their bed for a suitcase. Most of the girls kept keepsakes to a minimum simply because there wasn't anywhere to put such sentimental things.

That night Betty was feeling her homesickness particularly keenly and it so overwhelmed her that she couldn't even find the strength to put on her cheery shopgirl face and engage in the banter flowing all around her. She was a long way from Woolworths now.

'Buck up, baby Betty,' Gwen in the next bed along called out, trying to sound cheery. She was from Griffith in New South Wales and had bright, coppery red hair which she tied up in a scarf when she worked, like Betty Grable.

'Think of something else, baby Betty.' Peggy, the oldest of them all, was a Land Army veteran with eighteen months and scores of assignments under her belt. 'Think about, I don't know. Think about what you're going to do when the war's over.'

There were exclamations and laughter from the other girls in the quarters. This was a popular and comforting conversation, in which they let themselves imagine that the war might really be over soon and everyone would return safe and sound.

'I'm going to make a home with my husband,' Nancy said. 'Back in Adelaide. Somewhere near the beach, like Grange. Or perhaps Semaphore.' She sat cross-legged on her bed, writing a letter to her beloved, which she did every night, even though she knew she wouldn't have enough money to post them all until payday and even then, considering Land Army girls didn't get special rates on postage like the troops did, she might not be able to afford to post them all unless one of the other girls donated a stamp.

'Oh, the beach,' Dorothy cried out from her bed. She tossed her latest copy of the *Women's Weekly* to the end of her bed. Betty heard the pages flap against each other like birds' wings. Dorothy's mother faithfully sent her every Saturday's issue and she shared it around once she'd finished. 'There are new bathing suits in the shops. Wait until you see the pictures.'

'What's the point of a bathing suit when we never seem to have time to swim? You wouldn't think the river was a stone's throw away, would you?'

'Maybe we can organise a picnic on our next day off?' Nancy suggested.

'A day off?' Helen laughed. 'What's that?

'When the war is over,' Gwen sighed, 'I'm going to kiss my fiancé for an entire year.' Gwen's Reginald was a soldier in the AIF and they'd been separated since July 1940. 'And then we're going to get married. Him in his uniform and me in mine. Gosh. I'm already twenty-two. Everyone will think I'm an old maid if the war doesn't end soon.'

'How many children are you and Reg planning, Gwen?' Nancy asked. She slept directly across the aisle from Betty. Her voice was always croaky, as if she'd smoked too many cigarettes.

'Three. Two boys and a girl. John and Peter for boys and Margaret for a girl.'

'Oh, Margaret. Now there's a name!' Peggy laughed.

Betty turned her wet face on her pillow. Her tears had created a damp patch, cool on her cheek in the stifling evening heat. The high windows in the shed didn't open, even if any of the women could have reached them, and the single doors back and front didn't let any breeze in at all. If there was any breeze. The nights so far had been still and stifling.

Betty tugged at the sheet that was wrapped around the straw-stuffed mattress and wiped her face.

'I'm never getting married.' Enid, a girl from Newcastle, leapt off her bed and stood at the foot of it. She held her hands together in front of her waist, as if she was holding a bouquet, and took one step, then another, then another. The girls around her hollered and clapped. Enid threw her imaginary flowers behind her into a nonexistent crowd. 'And give up all this? Three meals a day, luxury accommodation, a measly thirty shillings and you girls for company? Never!'

They were such terrific girls, Betty could see that. She just didn't feel like one of them yet. She missed home and she missed Michael. It had been a month since he'd left for the army. She'd kept the promise she'd made to him on their last night together, and had stayed home instead of going to the station to wave him goodbye. That last night. When he'd kissed her and she had, just slightly, a little bravely, kissed him back. It had been their last night as Betty and Michael from King Street, before they'd put on their uniforms, left home and were forced to grow up too fast.

His last words were imprinted on her.

'Don't get too lonely,' he'd said and kissed her, his lips full on hers, his arms around her and squeezing the air from her lungs and all sense from her brain.

She'd been so shocked that she hadn't uttered another word to him as he'd walked away, turning left through his front gate and up the path and the two steps to his front door.

Did he love her? Is that why he'd kissed her? Was it his way of showing her how much he would miss her? Or was she just there? She hadn't had the chance to be alone with him to ask these burning questions, even if she'd been brave enough. She'd given him his birthday present that next week, on the day he turned eighteen, surrounded by his family, and he'd smiled and said thank you for the Biggles book. 'I don't have this one,' he'd told her. She'd kept her promise to him to make that their farewell, and she'd hated that she'd agreed to it, for she'd never had the chance to give him a final wave. She wasn't there to see him step onto the train with a smile and a tip of his uniform hat.

That had been a month ago. And in a few weeks, on February fourteenth, it would be her eighteenth birthday and this year there would be no Valentine's card from Michael. There wouldn't be a birthday party with her mother and father, nor a celebration with the girls from Woolworths after work.

She was stuck here, in the hot middle of nowhere, with red and swollen eyes and hands full of blisters from the stiff secateurs and the work gloves that were too big for her shopgirl hands. All she had left of Michael was the memory of that surprise kiss and his lips on hers.

'I'll try not to get too lonely, Michael,' she whispered. 'I'll try.'

Chapter Eleven

Flora

The first person to approach Flora on Sunday morning in the street out the front of St Andrew's was Mr Henwood, the curmudgeonly old man who'd greeted her at the train station the day she'd arrived in Mildura. The man who'd told her she wouldn't last and that she would be back on the train to Melbourne within a week. She felt a little pop of pride that she'd proved him wrong.

'Mr Henwood.' Charles reached his hand out for a shake. He'd walked with Flora up the path to the front steps and they were standing in the shade of the portico. They were in the sun too long during the week to want to be standing in it on a Sunday as well. People were already milling about, women and children, high school–aged boys and girls, and older ladies and gentlemen, all wearing their Sunday best. When Mr Henwood had told her that Mildura had sent more than its fair share of men off to the war, he'd been right. About that one thing, at least.

'Charles,' Mr Henwood replied. 'How's your mother?'

'She's well, thank you. She's here, I believe talking with Mrs Hawkins and her daughter-in-law.'

The old man cast a sideways glance at Flora, studying her official Land Army uniform with rheumy eyes, taking in her smart skirt, shirt and tie and hat. She'd been determined to make a good impression on the local townspeople during her first official outing. She'd polished her regulation court shoes that morning although the dust had already dulled a little of their gleam. She looked smart. Like a real Land Army girl.

Mr Henwood lifted his walking stick to point it at Flora. She stepped back or it would have flicked her on the hip. 'That girl had enough yet?'

She sensed Charles stiffen. When he was cross, his shoulders broadened and he seemed to grow six inches. 'I beg your pardon?'

'Your girl. That one. She sick of the hard work yet? I bet she is. No, you can't trust this woman labour, not one bit.'

Flora bit the inside of her lip.

'And look at that uniform. Trying to be a soldier. The Land Army's not an army. It's a gaggle of city girls looking for husbands, that's what it is.'

Charles slowly adjusted his tie. He flicked her a quick look, as if to say *leave this with me*. A rage flickered and burnt deep inside her, an anger she hadn't felt since Jack had come home back in December with the white feather.

'As a matter of fact, she's working out just fine, Mr Henwood. As hard a worker as I've ever seen.' Charles stepped

forwards and pushed the old man's stick to the side so it
didn't hit anyone. Mr Henwood took a faltering step back
and poked the ground with it.

'If you ask me ...' Charles raised his voice and people turned
their heads. 'These Land Army girls are worth their weight.'

Charles tipped his hat to Mr Henwood and Flora felt his
hand on her elbow. 'I see the Kavanaghs. Let me introduce
you, Miss Atkins.'

Flora didn't hear a word of the service. She sat respectfully
at the back of the church—she wasn't any particular kind
of religion but this was Church of England and she had
been half-heartedly raised a Methodist by her mother—
and thought over every single word Charles had said to
Mr Henwood when they'd arrived.

As hard a worker as I've ever seen.

These Land Army girls are worth their weight.

So he had noticed how hard she'd been working. She had
believed he'd either ignored her limping from the blisters
on her heels, and the groans of agony those first few days
when her back was stiff and sore, or had been oblivious.
But when she thought it over, she started to put the pieces
together. When Daisy had brought her the hot water bottle
after her first back-breaking day, the little girl had whispered, 'Daddy said I should give this to you.'

Daddy said.

She was tall enough in the pew to see over the heads of the
parishioners. Charles was up in the second row. His short
hair was smoothed down with some kind of hair potion, so
different to its ruffled state at Two Rivers. He sat with his
arms around his girls, one on either side. She couldn't see

Mrs Nettlefold, no surprise given her size, but she knew she was there with her family, forming a tight little group.

After hymns had been sung and prayers had been whispered for those away fighting, the pews emptied and a low hum of chattering swept from the pulpit to the church doors. Flora waited for the Nettlefolds under the filtered shade of a ghost gum that towered over the stone church, its grey-green leaves swaying in the hot wind. It was a charming old building with sandstone walls and a corrugated-iron roof, rusty in spots but it looked well cared for. It might have been lonely on its own, with no other buildings close, but people had brought life to it. They'd tended the flower beds that ran either side of the stone path leading to the portico. In winter, they would cut the grass all around the church, which was dry now and dusty. It was loved, and when Flora saw what was behind it she understood why.

To the rear of the church building, on the left side, a low stone fence extending out a hundred feet or so was interrupted by a wrought-iron gate swung wide open. The crosses and stone columns of headstones inside the cemetery reached for the blue sky.

She felt her arms prickle with goosebumps in spite of the heat. How many new graves had been dug there for lost locals since 1939? And for the war before that? When she'd arrived she'd believed this part of the world to be a long way from danger but, in truth, war's ghastly tentacles reached everywhere.

A gust of wind caught Flora's hat and almost blew it from her head. She clamped her hand down on her head and repositioned it. Frank would blame her big head for the fact that it didn't sit tight. Full of brains, she thought to herself, brains that did too much thinking and worrying.

'Excuse me.' It was a girl's voice, tentative.

Flora turned. It was indeed a girl—another Land Army girl. 'Why, hello!' she exclaimed.

'Hello. I'm supposing you're in the Land Army too,' the young woman said, waving her hand up and down. 'The uniform's a clue.'

'Yes.' Flora held out a hand. 'My name's Flora Atkins. I'm so pleased to meet you.'

'I'm Betty Brower. Where are you from, I mean, originally?' Betty was a sweet-looking girl with brown eyes and a broad smile. Flora judged her to be perhaps eighteen. So many years younger than she was.

'I'm from Melbourne. You?'

'Sydney. I'm billeted out at the Stocks'. On the other side of Mildura. It's a huge fruit block. There's twenty of us there. We sleep in this enormous corrugated-iron shed, which is hot as anything.' Betty smiled weakly. 'But it's been fun, of course. Oh, and hard work.'

'I'm boarding with the Nettlefolds. It's a small place called Two Rivers. There's only me there to help.'

Betty's eyes widened and she laid a hand on Flora's arm. 'Oh, how lonely for you.'

'Not at all. The family has been very welcoming.'

Over Betty's shoulder, Flora saw Charles heading in her direction. He paused to tip his hat to a family, a young woman with a child and a matronly lady wearing a broad-brimmed hat with a garden of flowers on it, holding a plate draped with a tea towel. He glanced over and caught Flora's eye.

'Betty, will you excuse me for a minute? I'll be right back.'

Betty's hand on Flora's arm became a tight grip. 'You … you are coming to the CWA morning tea, aren't you?'

'Of course I am,' Flora said. 'You?'

'I wouldn't miss it,' Betty said, lowering her head.

Flora heard a sniff. 'I'll be right back.'

She quickly walked to Charles. She spotted Mrs Nettlefold talking to Mr Henwood, and Daisy and Violet were playing skip rope with three other little girls on the dry grass.

'Mr Nettlefold, I've met a girl from Sydney. A Land Army girl. She's rather homesick, so I think I'll take her in to the morning tea, if that's all right with you. Give her some company.'

'Of course,' Charles said. Flora turned to walk away, but looked back over her shoulder, and saw him stride away from the crowd of people towards the wrought-iron gate in the stone fence.

Chapter Twelve

The church hall was decorated with Australian flags and festooned with streamers cut from newspapers. Trestle tables arranged along opposite walls were laden with cakes and biscuits and sandwiches. As people crowded in away from the heat, they gravitated towards the display and eagerly began to sample the wares of the members of the local Country Women's Association branch.

Flora stood with Betty. They sipped tea from delicate china cups on matching saucers. Betty seemed rather nervous and her teacup rattled as she spoke.

'There's lots of girls at Stocks' and they're all lovely. It was such a long trip from Sydney but I chose Mildura because I didn't want to pick potatoes in Batlow. I don't even know where that is. Imagine what that's like? Digging in the dirt all day long. Did you know that some Land Army girls have gone to work in shearing sheds? I can't imagine how they put up with the language. You know what they say about shearers.' Betty seemed to shiver. 'Grape picking sounded more like my cup of tea.' She looked down at her cup and giggled. 'Look at me. Making funny jokes when I really am tremendously nervous about all this. Everyone's looking at us, don't you think?'

Flora's heart ached for this young woman, so young and clearly homesick and lonely. 'Have you found friends?' Flora asked, laying a comforting hand on her arm.

Betty's lower lip quivered. Flora was suddenly grateful for her maturity and her own nature. She was accustomed to her own company. She hadn't had the companionship of a best girlfriend or anyone close, really, other than her brothers and her father. Jack had once described her as a hermit crab. All the times he'd urged her to go out on the town, to see the latest Hollywood picture or to go to a dance, she'd had trouble convincing him that she'd rather stay at home. In Melbourne, she'd regarded that urge for quiet and solitude as a failure on her part, a hint of a chronic lack of some personality trait. In hindsight, perhaps it was a benefit, after all. Having never been the kind of woman to be out on the town, she could hardly miss it.

'Please don't misunderstand me, Flora. They're just ... it's not the same as the friends I had back in Sydney. The girls from Woolworths and my best friend next door.'

'How lucky to have your best friend living next door to you. What's her name? Tell me all about her.'

'Oh, no. It's not a girl. It's Michael Doherty. He's been my best friend since we were little ones. He's in the army. So is his brother.'

Flora breathed deep. 'My brother is in the army too.'

Betty blinked and tears rolled down her cheeks. 'Is that why you're in the Land Army?'

Flora nodded. 'Yes, it's exactly why. Tell me, Betty. How long have you been at the Stocks?'

'Three weeks.' Betty's tone made it sound as if it had been three months. The expression on her face hinted that it felt like three years.

Flora felt the urge to throw an arm around young Betty for a comforting hug, but she didn't want to draw attention to the girl being upset in case it might inadvertently support the theories of the Mr Henwoods of the community and their scepticism about the Land girls.

Instead, she leant in close and spoke quietly behind her teacup so she wouldn't be overheard. 'Buck up, Betty. If you've had the same experience as me, you'll have been working your fingers to the bone. When you're tired, things can seem a little out of proportion. Did your back ache when you first started?'

Betty nodded, clearly afraid that if she opened her mouth to speak a sob might blurt out instead.

'And did every muscle in your body groan at you as you slept?'

Betty's lip curled a little. 'Yes. It was agony.'

'Welcome to the Land Army then. Remember what we were told. We'll be hot and uncomfortable and yes, we'll get blisters and our backs will ache. But all those adversities will make us proper Land Army girls. You're one of us, Betty. Be proud. You'll be right, I know you will.'

Betty smiled and drew in a breath. 'Thank you, Flora.'

A bell rang and all around them the chatter quietened. A woman walked onto the stage at the front of the hall. It was the same person Charles had been talking to after the service, the owner of the immense floral hat.

She welcomed everyone and there was polite applause.

'The Country Women's Association takes a very special interest in the Australian Women's Land Army and both organisations welcome you all here today.'

The crowd burst into exuberant applause. 'I'm Mrs Turner, branch president of the CWA. With so many girls out in the country helping with agricultural production, we've been charged with ensuring every one of them who comes to our district is looked after. Girls, you may have left your own families, but you are part of our family now.'

Betty seemed to have recovered some confidence. She looked back at Flora and shrugged with a reluctant smile.

'Appreciation and self-esteem are among the more pleasant things in life and I hope you are all feeling it. You should take stock and enjoy the sensation of knowing you are pulling your weight on the vital food front. Even those farmers who were not in favour of the employment of women have had their minds changed by your endeavour and your adaptability in all the work that you do.'

There was a loud snort behind her and Flora didn't have to turn around to know it was Mr Henwood.

'And now,' Mrs Turner continued, 'those same people continually express their amazement at how well you have taken to farm work.'

Flora searched the crowd for Charles. There he was, twenty feet away, Daisy in his arms, his eyes on her. She felt a tug behind her breastbone. Perhaps she'd pulled a muscle the day before. She pressed a palm to her chest and felt her heart thudding.

'So, we thank you and we salute you. Moreover, our troops thank you too. You are standing by your sisters in the other services. You are standing by our troops. And you are standing by your country.'

This time the applause was thunderous and every head seemed to turn towards Flora and Betty to show their appreciation. This was so new to Flora, so overwhelming, that she swallowed the lump in her throat and laughed so she wouldn't sob.

Charles nodded at her and smiled and she didn't want to feel what she was feeling but it rose up in her, unstoppable and indescribable. He had noticed her, defended her, seen her. It was intoxicating.

A moment later, a group of young ladies in their Land Army uniforms surrounded Betty, tugging at her hat, patting her on the shoulder, joking and laughing with her. Betty was swept up with them and they moved off towards the refreshments.

Flora was overwhelmed. Mr McInerney had never once shown one-tenth of this appreciation for the work she'd done in his office and she'd worked for him for a decade. The praise she'd received for just two weeks of grape picking was almost incomprehensible to her.

Charles appeared at her side. Daisy smiled at Flora. She was tucked up in her father's arms, safe and so clearly loved. 'You look very nice in your special uniform,' the little girl said.

'Why, thank you.'

'I second that,' Charles added. 'It's quite a change from your overalls and boots.'

'Why, thank you too, Mr Nettlefold.'

'Daisy, would you like to go and fetch Miss Atkins and me a slice each of your grandmother's jam roly-poly?'

'Yes, Daddy.' Charles set his daughter on her feet and she snaked her way through the crowd and out of sight.

'Miss Atkins.' Charles met her gaze. He lowered his voice and, deep and raspy, it rumbled through her like a freight train.

'I can only echo the sentiments of Mrs Turner. I don't know what we would have done without you these past weeks. We've got so much fruit picked. You've been a godsend.'

'You and Mrs Nettlefold have welcomed me into your home and I couldn't be more grateful. I've learnt so much.'

'That's good to hear.' He paused and they shared a smile. 'We'll be leaving shortly, if that's all right with you.' Charles checked his watch.

'Of course, yes.'

'I'm sure we could both do with a restful Sunday afternoon.'

Flora sighed. 'That's very true. I can't wait to put my feet up and finally write my letters.'

'Oh, I forgot to mention it. Mr and Mrs Griffin have given me a bundle of them for you. They have the post office in Mildura. They came to church especially today to deliver the post to you Land Army girls.'

Chapter Thirteen

Flora held the letters in her hand. There were four of them, tied with a length of hessian twine. Above her, the dappled shade of the peppercorn tree in the Nettlefolds' yard gave her protection from the sun; beneath her, a blanket protected her legs from the dirt.

As soon as they'd arrived home from the CWA morning tea, Flora had politely excused herself to her room and changed out of her uniform. She'd slipped on her floral dress and her sun hat and hadn't even heard the back door slam behind her as she'd raced outside to sit in the fresh air and the peace and quiet to read all the news from home.

The letters were even more precious unread, she thought as she studied her father's handwriting on the letter at the top of the bundle. What promise they held, what threat too, of news she might not want to hear. She took a moment to relish the idea that her world was exactly as it had been when she left Melbourne. Flora closed her eyes and listened to the rustle of the wind through the vine leaves; Daisy and Violet's laughter drifting to her from inside the house; Marjorie mooing gently; the chooks cackling and scratching in the dirt; the call of a magpie in the peppercorn above her, seducing her with its trilling song. This really was a haven. This little property, so far from what she'd known, had already claimed a piece of her heart.

Flora slipped off her shoes, leant back against the rough bark of the peppercorn and found the courage to untie the knot on the string.

One of the letters was from her father, two were from Jack and—her heart almost burst out of her chest as she recognised his handwriting—there was one from Frank. She ripped the envelope open in such haste she took off a corner of the letter with it. She checked the date. It was from early December, before she'd left Melbourne.

Her hands were shaking so much she could barely read it.

2/11th Field Regiment
8th Division

December 12th, 1942
Dear Flor,
First up, let me apologise for not writing to you sooner. You know that letters aren't my favourite thing in the world, although I do like to get them from home, especially yours, filled with all the news from Melbourne. I'm sure all the boys you've knitted socks for have warm toes, although to be honest, no one here in the jungle needs to worry about cold feet.

I'll miss Christmas at home this year, the second year running I won't be there for your roast chicken with all the trimmings. I'll truly miss that. If I was there on Christmas Day, I'd make sure you and Dad and Jack all had presents specially chosen for you.

I think of you all every day and I hope you're keeping well. I wanted to say a tremendous thank you for the fruit cake you sent. The tin kept it safe from being nibbled along the way. I shared it with the boys in the regiment and three of them made sure I let you know of their offers of marriage. You always were a tasty cook, Flor.

You have spent too much time at home looking after 'your boys'. It's time you were getting married. You won't always have Dad and Jack for company and who knows when I'll be home. They say the tide is turning but we're still here. You aren't young but you're a wonderful girl. I reckon you should strike out for yourself and get someone who is worthy of you.

Don't worry about me. I'm safe and well. My best wishes for Christmas and a happy 1943.

I'll write again soon.

Your ever-loving brother, Frank.

Flora pressed her palm to her chest, breathed deep and tried not to cry. Frank was safe. At least he had been when he'd written back in December and that was enough.

She quickly read her father's letter and the two from Jack. Her father was becoming quite proficient at frying eggs, it seemed, and all was well with the tomatoes she'd left in his care. He seemed quite proud to tell her he'd managed to make himself a tomato and onion salad. She pictured him standing at the sink, a cutting board filled with juicy red tomatoes and thick slices of onion laid out in front of him. He'd probably scooped them all up with his calloused hands and put them directly onto his dinner plate. Another man of few words. She'd been around them her entire life.

Her father hadn't ever spoken of his loneliness, at least not to Flora or her brothers, but they all knew he suffered it. He'd been without their mother for so many years but had never looked at another woman. Flora wanted nothing more than for him to be happy, to perhaps find love again, but he'd not seemed inclined. She and her father were companions to each other, their loneliness a bond. Perhaps there was only one great love for each person in life, if you were very fortunate, and her father had had his in her mother. Now he had his work, his children and his house. And the war meant he had the wireless too.

Jack's letters were filled with humorous details about the pictures he'd seen and the dances he'd attended and there was more than one mention of a young lady called Jane, whose name she hadn't heard before. Had he slipped it in by accident or was she already so important to him that he didn't need to explain? Flora chuckled. Jack would never be lonely. She knew he would find someone who would love him for the kind and considerate man he was, and not judge him by his deafness or the fact that he wasn't able to serve, not in a uniform anyway. It was a great comfort to Flora that the men in her life were thriving without her. The war had forced every Australian to make sacrifices and they were bearing theirs with good humour and their sleeves rolled up. If they missed her, they wouldn't show it.

Flora looked out into the vines and breathed in the scent. She shuffled her letters and read Frank's again. One part in particular.

You aren't young but you're a wonderful girl. I reckon you should strike out for yourself and get someone who is worthy of you.

Tears welled and tumbled down her cheeks, spilling onto the precious pages before she could catch them, smudging the loops and strokes of Frank's handwriting. Mortified, she frantically waved the papers in the air, flicking them back and forth, hoping the motion and the heat would dry them, and then she felt for the hem of her dress, dipped her head and pressed the fabric to her cheeks. She felt sad and foolish all at once and hated herself for it. What point was there in feeling so melancholy about her situation? Time had passed her by. Water under the bridge, as her father would say when asked about something that had happened in the past and he couldn't change. He didn't like to look back but it was all Flora could think about after reading Frank's imploring words.

How on earth could she strike out for herself and find someone who was worthy of her? She couldn't conjure love like Mandrake the Magician might conjure a rabbit out of a hat.

She had never met a man who might look at her as a wife, as someone worth loving. Oh, but she had loved. Once. He was a clerk in Mr McInerney's office. Jonathon Carmichael. He was a handsome devil and he knew it, and somehow Flora had let herself be carried away by his flirtatious behaviour and into thinking it was directed solely at her. One day he'd brought her a bunch of flowers and she'd convinced herself that he must have been taken with her. She'd believed herself to be in love with him. She'd prickled with anticipation before his arrival in the office each day. She'd made a habit of arriving at work early, even catching an earlier tram, so she could ensure she was already at her desk when he arrived. She knew the particular sound of his stride on the wooden steps and in the corridor outside the office, and when he would burst in like a jack-in-the-box she had melted. He always had a smile and a wink for her before he hung his hat and his suit jacket on the hat stand near the glass front door. But she discovered the hard way that it had only been some kind of manly pride at having a young girl so enamoured of him, after he turned his flirtations to a new girl in the office one day, a girl who giggled at his humour and batted her eyelids at him like a silent movie star.

The shame and humiliation of her affections had been a heavy weight she'd borne in all the years since. She had long been resigned to her status as a confirmed spinster. A girl unmarried at twenty-one was suspect, at twenty-five unfortunate, and at thirty just sad. She had tried to reconcile herself to the fact that she would never know the joy of a family of her own, the satisfaction of comforting a sad child with a mother's warm affection, the love of a husband who loved her as much as her father had adored her mother. She'd seen the best of what marriage could be between two people. She wished it for Frank when, God willing, he returned home, and for Jack, who had the kind of friendly demeanour that women were attracted to.

She would have to be a devoted aunt to all their children. She might knit them some socks. At least she was able to do that. And anyway, she had the Land Army now. A boss who appreciated her instead of overlooking her work, and a workplace that was definitely an improvement on her old office with its view over a dank laneway.

She sniffed, rummaged inside her dress for the handkerchief she always tucked inside the cup of her bra and blew her runny nose.

She heard him before she saw him, clearing his throat. She would know the timbre of his voice anywhere. Ignoring the prickle under her skin, she hurriedly tucked the handkerchief away.

'My apologies for interrupting,' Charles said quietly. 'If you'd rather ...' His voice trailed off.

'No, you're not interrupting at all.' Flora looked up. His eyes were shaded by the brim of his hat. She wished she could see them, see what was in them when he looked at her. Had he been observing her from afar? How long had he stood there waiting before he finally spoke? Had he seen her tears?

Frank's letter was loose on her lap and she clumsily stuffed it back in its envelope, her fingers fumbling.

'I hope there's no difficult news from home.' The kindness in his voice rumbled right through her.

'No. It's happy news, Mr Nettlefold. Everything and everyone is fine.'

'Well. That is something to celebrate then.' She hadn't noticed he was holding a wooden tray, the type with fold-out legs that a patient might have if they were ill in bed, and he hovered for a moment, as if he was looking for a place to set it on the ground. He glanced over his shoulder at Marjorie, busy chewing, and then he turned back to look out to the vines and beyond to the river. He'd changed out of his suit into cotton work trousers and a shirt, the sleeves rolled up to the elbow as always.

'I was wondering, Miss Atkins, if you might like some company? The girls are about to have a lie-down after their adventures with their friends at church this morning. My mother has squeezed some fresh juice and baked a batch of honey drops. She thought you might like one.'

'How thoughtful of her.'

Charles lowered the tray onto the rug by Flora's legs and sat down on the other side of it. The peppercorn tree threw enough shade that they were both protected from the sun, and Charles slipped off his hat, tossing it at his feet. He poured two glasses of juice, almost overfilling one of them, and passed one to Flora. She took a sip of the cold and sweet liquid and licked her lips to savour the taste and the coolness.

'It's thirsty work reading your letters, I see.'

'Yes,' Flora smiled. The heat wasn't the only thing causing her throat to feel parched. 'That and the heat.'

'It's hotter here than Melbourne in the summer, I expect. Doesn't rain as much, either.'

'No?'

Charles lifted the plate of biscuits and held it towards her. She took a honey drop and bit into it, slowly, luxuriating in its buttery taste. How she missed the creamy taste of real butter. Having Marjorie certainly had its advantages, even if one had to wake at sparrow's to milk her. Luckily for them all, Mrs Nettlefold was the early riser.

'This whole area was desert before irrigation. The vines wouldn't survive without water from the river.'

Charles took two biscuits for himself and settled on the rug, leaning to the side on an elbow, one knee propped up. Flora swallowed hard. She'd never seem him this relaxed and comfortable. There was a reserve to him that she respected. She was a Land Army girl and he was her employer. Thirty shillings a week and board for her labour, and a polite distance between them.

But something was on the verge of changing. Flora leant back against the rough trunk of the peppercorn, let her eyes drift closed, and tasted the honey drop still on her tongue. She didn't feel like a Land Army girl in this moment, the hot breeze in her hair, her cotton dress cool on her legs, her feet bare. She breathed deep and wiggled her toes. She felt like a version of herself she had perhaps never been. This felt a little like freedom.

She looked across at Charles. Who was this man, out here at Two Rivers, living in a house full of women? There was no sign of what had happened to his wife or any mention of a sweetheart. He didn't seem to go into Mildura much, except to pick up supplies and the post. He had dinner with his family every night and hadn't once missed reading his daughters their favourite stories before they went to bed. It was Flora's favourite part of the evening. Once the girls had washed and were in their pyjamas, they would race to Charles sitting in the armchair and each claim a knee. Charles would pretend they were getting too big for his lap and they would both plead that no, they weren't. Flora always managed to be in the sitting room to witness this scene, with her cup of tea and whatever biscuit Mrs Nettlefold had baked that day.

She knew that Daisy liked 'Clancy of the Overflow' while Violet preferred *The Magic Pudding*. She'd listened in so many nights that she was sure she knew them by heart.

'He had written him a letter ...' Charles always began, his deep voice undulating with the rhythm of the poem, and Flora found it mesmerising. She stared at his mouth as he recited. As he turned the pages, he always twirled a lock of Daisy's hair around his left index finger, or brought his hand to rest on Violet's hand.

He was a loving father and a dutiful son.

But who had loved him?

'Would you like another?'

Flora's eyes sprung wide open.

'If you don't, I might eat them all myself. They're my favourite, I have to admit. And with the girls asleep I don't have to share them.' His eyes, so blue, were trained on her, the smile in them creating wrinkles in the smooth skin just above his cheekbones. 'Except with you, of course.'

'Perhaps just one. Your mother's baking ...' Flora sighed.

'I know what you mean.' Charles left the plate on the tray this time. He picked up another honey drop and passed it to her.

It tasted even better than the first one. 'I know there are sacrifices to be made for the war but doing without butter has been the hardest,' Flora told him. 'Back home, I mean. Lots of people have chooks so we always had eggs, but you can't make a really lovely cake or a batch of biscuits without butter.'

'Enjoy them while you can, Miss ... Hadkins.' He laughed, and she laughed too.

'Your mother does look after you all very well. She's absolutely devoted.'

'To all of us, don't you mean?'

She paused, thinking over the implications of what that simple word meant. Us. 'Why, yes. She's been very kind to me. More than I could have expected.'

'She's always loved baking,' Charles said. 'When I'm in Mildura, I often pick up a copy of the *Women's Weekly* in case she's of a mind to try out some new recipes or see what the latest fashions are. But she sticks to what she knows. And what she does best.'

Flora crunched on her biscuit, and swept crumbs from her dress. 'The whole of Melbourne has gone mad for apple pie,' she murmured, gazing out over the vines, a wave of calm sleepiness washing over her. 'It's the Americans. They want things to feel like home, at least that's what some people say. So we now have hot apple pie and Coca-Cola and hamburgers everywhere.'

'I've never had a hamburger,' Charles said.

'I have. It was all right. Did you know that the Yanks prefer their apple pie with ice-cream but not on top, on the side? Apple Pie a la Mode, they call it.'

'I've tasted that.'

'You have?' Flora asked, surprised.

'At the milk bar in the Astor Theatre, in Mildura. The Spot Sundae Parlour, it's called.'

'Well,' Flora stammered. 'I didn't think …'

Charles laughed loud and deep. He dropped his elbow and flopped flat on his back. He propped his hands under his head and stared up into the drooping branches of the peppercorn. 'You didn't think we had all the latest things up here in the country, Miss Atkins?'

Flora shrugged. 'Well, yes. I am a little surprised.'

'Who needs Melbourne when we have it all here? Sodas. Sundaes. Milkshakes. I took my mother and the girls there for Daisy's sixth birthday in August. Mr Raftopoulos is quite the milk-bar entrepreneur in Mildura.'

'Daisy would have loved that, I'm sure.'

Charles turned his head to her. 'She did.' He paused, frowned a little. 'Perhaps you might like to come along next time I go to Mildura. Taste a banana and cream sundae for yourself.'

'Oh,' Flora said. 'That sounds quite delicious.'

'It's my favourite,' he smiled.

There was so much she wanted to know about Charles Nettlefold and she found the courage to begin to ask.

'Mr Nettlefold, has Two Rivers been in your family for a very long time?'

Charles breathed deep. He moved his hands to the flat of his belly, the stretch of his long body untucking his shirt from his trousers. There was a sliver of skin exposed near his belt and she found it impossible to look away.

'My father was a soldier settler, after the first war. My parents met in Melbourne but mum's from Wentworth. They compromised and ended up here. That's where the name comes from. Two rivers. The Murray and the Darling meet at Wentworth. My father surprised her one day with the sign out by the main road. He painted it himself.' A small chuckle escaped his lips.

'It's C and A Nettlefold. What was his name?'

Charles smiled sadly. 'Charles was his name, but everyone called him Charlie.'

The only child, the only son, carrying on his father's name and his legacy.

'That's why I'm Charles, not Charlie. And my mother is Alice.'

Flora considered it and decided that Charlie wouldn't suit him. 'When did your father ...?'

'Twenty-three years ago, coming up in June. In 1920. He never really recovered from the mustard gas from the first war. It damaged his lungs. The winters here were just too cold.'

Flora struggled to find the right words to say and when she spoke, she almost whispered her condolences. 'How dreadful for you and your mother. You must have been just a boy.' If she had been closer she might have placed her hand on his as an act of comfort. Instead, she twisted her fingers together in a knot in her lap.

'I was thirteen,' Charles said quietly. 'My mother didn't want to leave this place, even though we hadn't been here all that long. We've done our best to muddle along, the two of us. It's not a huge block and we've usually hired some local men over the years to help with the picking but they've been hard to find lately. The Italians are interned and every other young man in the district has up and left for the war.'

What losses Charles had borne in his life. When she'd seen him walking towards the gravestones earlier that morning after the church service, had he been intent on visiting his father's grave? Or his wife's? Or both?

The vines seemed to speak to Flora. Their rustle was like a love song, the summer breeze intoxicating. Or perhaps it was something else entirely, but the thought of leaving Two Rivers when the harvest was over suddenly tore at her. She could understand why his mother loved it so. The air, the sky, the river, the smell of the red earth and even the heat. Flora had never felt so alive in her life. And soon it would all come to an end. When the vines were bare of fruit, she would be assigned somewhere else.

'I apologise for mentioning the war if it makes you upset,' he said.

'No, it's all right. It's all everyone talks about these days, isn't it?'

'I hope you don't mind if I ... I've been wanting to know,' he said then stopped, his forehead creasing in a frown. 'I hope you don't think it rude of me to ask but is your sweet-heart serving, Miss Atkins?'

'Pardon?'

'Your letters.' He sat up, his frown hardened now. 'Are they from someone very dear to you?'

Flora blinked. 'Oh, yes, but no. I don't have ... no, I don't have a sweetheart.'

'I'm sorry,' Charles said, looking startled. 'Daisy mentioned the photographs in your room. The wedding. The soldier.'

She exhaled deeply, feeling skittish and hot. 'The wedding was my parents' and the soldier is my youngest brother, Frank. He's in the AIF. I was reading his letter when you walked over.'

'Your brother,' Charles repeated slowly.

'I have two. Frank and Jack. Frank's the baby and Jack's in the middle.' Then the story tumbled from her lips, much to her surprise. She'd gone so long without saying their names that she needed her words to bring them back to life. 'Frank's a charmer. Everyone loves him. He's younger than me by four and a bit years, so that's twenty-six at his next birthday. Then there's Jack, who's twenty-eight. He's exceptionally kind and considerate. When he was fourteen years old he contracted meningitis and he lost the hearing in his right ear. Medically unfit for the war, he was told.' Flora held her breath, wondering if this was too much of a story to tell, but it felt so wonderful to be talking about her beloved brothers that she kept on going. A glance at Charles revealed she had his rapt attention.

'He would have enlisted. He honestly would have.' She breathed deep. 'Back in December, a woman handed him a white feather right in the middle of Swanston Street.'

Charles muttered something under his breath. 'I thought that only happened to people in my parents' years.'

Flora straightened the hem of her dress across her knees. 'I was furious. The only thing I knew to do was to join the Land Army. I could do my patriotic duty in my family's name even if Jack couldn't.'

Charles studied her face. A smile crept up on him. 'I find it hard to imagine you being furious with anyone. You have such an even temper.'

'I fought back with my deeds, if not my words.'

'I've wondered why you put your hand up to leave your life in Melbourne and your family and come out here to help us. I presume you worked, Miss Atkins, before you joined the Land Army?'

'Yes, in an insurance office, typing invoices for Mr McInerney.' She hesitated. 'As a matter of fact, I did more than that. I ran the office. I trained up all the new girls. I made sure there was a pot of tea brewing every morning when he arrived for work and I was always the last to leave.' An exhilarating feeling welled up inside of her. 'And I was still paid less than the most junior male clerk. So I didn't have much to leave behind in the way of work, Mr Nettlefold.'

She couldn't read his expression but remembered what he'd said earlier to old Mr Henwood.

As hard a worker as I've ever seen.

These Land Army girls are worth their weight.

'Good for you.' His gaze softened. 'My mother mentioned that you lost your own mother many years ago. I was very sorry to hear it.'

The ache rose up, still, after all these years. 'She died of pneumonia when I was fifteen. And,' she said, hesitating, 'I've just realised it was fifteen years ago. She's been gone half my life.'

'That's a terrible thing for a young girl to bear.'

'It was. I do miss my family, my father and Jack. And Mrs Jones next door. But I didn't really have any dear friends or anything like that. I answered the call, proud to be able to do my duty. I promised myself that as long as Frank is serving, I'll serve, too.'

Charles whispered something under his breath.

Flora looked at him quizzically.

'*Men to arms, women to farms.* That's what you said to me that first day we were out in the vines, picking.'

'Oh yes, I remember,' she replied. 'I read it in the paper or a magazine, I'm not sure, and it stuck with me. Rhymes are meant to do that, aren't they? Stick in your head until you believe you might have made them up yourself?' And then, a jolt of awareness. 'You must have thought I was aiming those words at you.'

Charles glanced down at the blanket. 'I must admit I did. I was angry about it, at the slur I believed you'd sent my way. I apologise for that.'

'You don't have to, Mr Nettlefold. Honestly. You're doing your duty here, too. The farm. Your girls and your mother. You're responsible for so much here, for so many.'

He reached for the last honey drop, held it between his thumb and index finger and held it out to her.

When she took it, their fingers touched and held.

'It's yours, Miss Hadkins,' he chuckled and Flora followed with a laugh that came freely and fully from deep in her belly.

Then, 'Can I ask you something?'

'Of course.'

He paused, met her gaze. 'Will you call me Charles?'

Something seemed to blossom inside her. 'Only if you call me Flora.'

'Flora,' he said, and the sound of his voice, saying her name, was enchanting. 'I've always thought it to be a beautiful name.'

She'd said his name in her head a thousand times. 'Thank you, Charles.'

Chapter Fourteen

Betty

On Saturday evening, the girls from Stocks' had been allowed an early knock-off as they'd been invited as special guests to a Red Cross ball in Mildura.

They were all beside themselves with excitement. The weeks they'd toiled picking fruit had seemed like an eternity and they were not going to miss the chance to powder their faces, slip on their stockings and go out for the evening. Nancy had had it confirmed by Mrs Stock that there was going to be dancing, and that caused a giggle of anticipation.

As they rushed back to their quarters, Dorothy elbowed Betty playfully in her side and whipped off her straw hat to fan her face.

'You know what dancing means, baby Betty?'

Betty felt a little too flummoxed to answer. What else could it mean besides music and dancing?

Dorothy threw her hat into the air and whooped. 'It means men, baby Betty! Men! Real men!'

'It does?'

Dorothy ran ahead of her, her tanned brown legs long and slim, and looked back over her shoulder with a laugh. 'Didn't you know there's an RAAF training unit right here in Mildura? And that means pilots, baby Betty. Pilots!'

They'd all learnt quickly that twenty women, one copper full of hot water and one outside dunny meant patience, just the tiniest bit of sniping, and a long time waiting in line. Oh, and the occasional red-back spider. Gwen always shrieked the loudest, but not as loud as Helen had when she'd been convinced she'd seen a snake among the vines. Peggy had assured her it was most likely a blue-tongue lizard and that she needn't worry unless it bit her, because once a blue-tongue got hold of you it never let go. Helen had gone white at the thought.

Betty stood fifth and watched with good humour as the other girls lingered by the copper outside under the dappled shade of a copse of straggly gum trees. Each girl sudsed her hair with soap, washing away a week's worth of dirt and sweat, and bent over while another girl tipped a saucepan full of cold water over her hair for a rinse. Mrs Stock had brought her iron out to the shed so the girls could press their uniforms, and Betty took longer than everyone said she should, which caused some good-natured ribbing about her homemaking skills.

'Steady on. I was a shopgirl, not a laundress,' she'd tossed back at them with a grin.

At their induction, they'd been reminded that every woman privileged to wear the Women's Land Army uniform should respect it. For social occasions such as the one they would attend that night, they were to wear full dress uniform, including their hat, at all times. Betty, and all the girls, had taken those instructions very seriously.

On two flatbed trucks, twenty hats bobbed up and down as the rutted and bumpy roads created a rough journey. Betty felt herself buck up a little when she looked around at her new chums, dressed so neatly and proudly. While they were full of laughs after hours, they were hard workers in the vineyards and, right now, they looked smart and proud. She had to pinch herself to believe she was really one of them.

A Land Army girl.

She wished there was a camera to record this moment. Her mother and father had made sure to take her to a photographic studio in Sydney's Strand Arcade before she left for Mildura. She'd waited in line with, it seemed, half of Sydney, so many of them in uniform, the other half weeping. She hadn't yet seen that photograph but was certain that her expression had been one of stricken panic. She'd asked her mother to send her a copy so she could put it in her next letter to Michael, but only if she looked pretty in it and not fearful. She didn't want Michael to think she was scared when she was right here at home in Australia doing farm work. He would have been facing much worse, she knew.

Perhaps it was getting used to her work or perhaps it was being around the other girls, but their attitude and energy had rubbed off on her, and Betty was glad of it. She thought back to her meeting with that older Land Army girl at the church-hall reception.

'Remember what we were told,' Flora had advised her, a reassuring hand on her arm. 'We'll be hot and uncomfortable and, yes, we'll get blisters and our backs will ache. But all those adversities will make us proper Land Army girls. You're one of us, Betty. Be proud.'

Betty let herself feel proud as they pulled up to the hall in Deakin Avenue. Would Flora be there tonight? Betty hoped she would be, so she could tell her new friend in person how much those words of comfort had helped her. Would Flora be able to see in the set of Betty's shoulders and her confident smile how much had changed in just a few short weeks?

'Here we are, girls,' Enid called out. She was the first to jump from the flatbed, then she reached up to help the shorter girls jump down. The hall was a hive of excitement and the twilight made everything look more glamorous. From inside the hall, lights gleamed, spotlighting bosomy ladies wearing elegant gowns and hats adorned with feathers and flowers. There were a few older gentlemen in dark three-piece suits and white bow ties, wearing sprigs of flowers in their boutonnieres. Some were escorting the older ladies and others were gathered in small groups, smoking and talking earnestly through their thick grey moustaches. Younger local ladies stood in clutches, talking effusively with their friends, every so often casting glances up and down the street. Betty quickly understood that Dorothy wasn't the only girl there eagerly awaiting the arrival of the RAAF pilots. School-aged boys in suits that were too short for them talked loudly and cheered when one boy acted out, with waving hands, a plane crashing and an explosion, complete with sound effects.

'Line up then,' Peggy said, and with a nod the others fell into two lines, just like Betty remembered doing at school assemblies. The crowd fell silent. At first there was a whisper and then a chatter and when people began to applaud, Betty's heart swelled.

There were calls of 'hear, hear' and 'well done, girls' and 'welcome' and 'thank you', so many that it sounded like a chorus.

Gwen was at her side. 'Buck up, baby Betty,' she whispered in her ear. 'We're going to have a wonderful time.'

They were stopped at the doorway by two women in Red Cross uniforms but they couldn't resist looking past their shoulders. The room was festooned with streamers on each window and across the ceiling. The stage was set with vases of chrysanthemums, vine leave and sheaves of wheat. Behind them a poster was decorated with the letters AWLA in green and gold glitter, and beside it a wheelbarrow was filled with fruit and vegetables. Even at a distance, Betty could spot the bunches of pale green sultana grapes.

She gasped and clutched at Gwen's arm. 'How terrific.'

The special guests were guided through a guard of honour, made up of local children holding sheaves of wheat aloft, to a chorus of applause. The girls ducked enough to make it through the tunnel and out the other side, smiling proudly at the warm welcome.

'Isn't this grand?' Gwen whispered.

Betty was almost speechless. 'Very grand.'

'Wait until you taste the supper.'

Gwen took Betty's hand and led her through the appreciative crowd to an array of tables at either side of the theatre. They were groaning with cakes and biscuits and sandwiches, pitchers of cordials and lemonades. Before Betty and Gwen had a moment to wonder where to begin, they were surrounded.

'Please allow us to thank you girls,' a woman told them. 'I don't know what we'd have done without you all coming from the city to help.'

'You're very welcome,' Gwen said with a dip of her chin.

An older gentlemen hurried towards them, his jittery hand extended in greeting, and he wouldn't rest until he'd heartily shaken Gwen's and Betty's hands until they were almost sore. 'I've found you all very solid and conscientious workers. You little ladies have such a cheery disposition. You've brightened up the whole district. Well done.'

'It's never a chore to do our bit for the country,' Gwen said.

'No, indeed it isn't,' Betty added.

'Hear, hear,' the man replied before shuffling away.

There were so many congratulations that Betty was overwhelmed. When she had the chance to peel away, she examined the trading table and bought herself a small notebook and a bar of Lux soap. She held it to her nose and sniffed its scent through its wrapping. She ate four lamingtons and the most delicious chicken sandwiches and, for a time, struck up a conversation with two young girls of the district who seemed quite keen to know about her life back in the city. When she told them she worked at Woolworths before joining the Land Army, their eyes widened.

'What's Sydney like?' one asked, almost quivering with excitement.

'It's very exciting but ...' She paused, thought for a moment. These girls were perhaps fifteen years old. How protected had they been from the realities of the war? How much should she tell them about how Sydney had changed? 'I'm very pleased to be out here in the fresh air and working hard. And I'm sure you are both doing your bit on your family's properties, too.'

'We are doing our best and—' The young girl was suddenly silent and her mouth gaped. She leant in to whisper to her friend, 'Here they are.' Betty looked over her shoulder. Mrs Stock's piano playing was suddenly lost as a raucous burst of spontaneous applause erupted to welcome the pilots into the hall. Betty glanced around. A couple of the older gentlemen wiped tears from their eyes. In a corner, a man comforted a woman as she buried her face into his suit, away from onlookers.

They were smiling, confident young men. Uniforms could do that to you, Betty thought as she glanced down at her own. The pilots wore forage hats, all tipped at an identical jaunty angle, and their deep royal-blue jackets and trousers were smart and elegant, as handsome as anything Betty had seen at the pictures. Clark Gable didn't have a patch on those blokes, she thought with a smile. They came in as a group, perhaps twenty of them, and began to mingle, politely nodding to the ladies and shaking hands with the gentlemen.

Dorothy was quickly by her side, with Nancy and Helen trailing behind.

'Oh, my,' Dorothy almost moaned. 'I used to go dancing twice every week back home. I think I'm rather out of practice.' She looked back at her friends with a sly wink.

Mrs Stock resumed her playing with a renewed gusto and couples began to crowd the dance floor. Pilots with the Red Cross committee members. Elderly gentlemen with their wives. The young boys in the too-short trousers with older girls who rolled their eyes in embarrassment at having had to say yes to a local youth. Betty looked for Flora but could find no sign of her. Perhaps she hadn't come along that night after all. Dorothy quickly found herself in the arms of a tall pilot with a wide grin, and when Betty saw a smudge of blue in her peripheral vision, she turned.

'May I have this dance?' A handsome man with a friendly smile and olive skin was at her side, his hands behind his back. He gave her a little sort of bow as he asked. Betty was still chewing a chocolate and coconut encrusted lamington and hurriedly set it on a plate. She brushed away any stray flakes on her mouth and cleared her throat. 'Thank you.' She let herself be led to the middle of the crowd and the pilot took her in his arms, his hand politely guiding her in the small of the back without pressing.

'This is a lovely party, isn't it?' Betty asked. She could make small talk with anyone. It was her special skill, developed from all the years she'd spent with customers at Woolworths, answering questions, cajoling them into buying an extra lipstick, dealing with complaints and steering people away from their anger. She could find something to say about almost anything, and this man appeared as if he desperately needed distracting. Behind his smile, there was a sadness in his expression, in the dark shadows under his eyes, in the droop of his broad shoulders.

'Yes,' he said. 'It's quite a pleasant change from the base and being surrounded by all the other chaps, I have to admit.'

'I'm Betty Brower. I'm very pleased to meet you.'

He met her eyes with a distracted smile. 'I'm David Hogarth. Or should I say, Flying Officer David Hogarth, 2nd Operational Training Unit, Mildura. At your service.'

'We heard you RAAF boys were coming. Everyone was very excited about it.'

David chuckled. 'You Land Army girls have been the talk of the base for a good few days too.'

'Yes, I expect so. Boys will be boys and girls will be girls, as they say.'

'That is true.'

They danced to the pounding piano for a while, David's smooth rhythm making him an excellent dance partner. Betty knew that finding a partner with rhythm was not something to be taken for granted, wartime or not. Across the crowd, Betty saw Dorothy flirting outrageously with another of the trainee pilots and, if she wasn't mistaken, he was flirting right back.

'How are you finding it, working on the land?'

'I'm loving it.' This was not the time to tell the truth to a man in a uniform who would soon be facing far worse than a sore back and a few weeping blisters. 'I'm working on a fruit block, picking sultana grapes. There's a whole lot of girls, all of them here tonight, too. So, Flying Officer Hogarth, when you're abroad and you receive a fruit cake from home, think of us. We're the ones who picked the sultanas and currants.'

David perked up. 'Well, there you go. I hadn't thought about it that way. That's a cheery thought.'

'We're proud to be doing something for the war. For Australia. To support you boys.'

'A man can't fight a war on an empty stomach. So good for you, Betty. And all your girlfriends. We'll all need to be fed when we're assigned to our operational squadrons. Thank you.'

'How's your training going?'

David smiled. 'Very well, thank you. I expect you've heard us buzzing overhead as we get our hours up.'

'Yes, we have. When we hear you coming we all stand and salute,' Betty laughed.

That made David laugh, too. 'I'm halfway through. Only eight weeks to go. I've flown the Wirraway, the Kittyhawk and the Spitfire.'

'I've heard of the Spitfire,' Betty said. 'They're made in England, aren't they? By women.'

'I hear they are. They're just as good as all the others.'

'Do you know where you'll be going? When you finish your training, I mean?'

David shook his head, casting a quick glance down. Perhaps she shouldn't have asked. It must be on their minds all the time, mustn't it? Training in Mildura and dances and applause were one thing, but the idea of being sent abroad to fly in battle must have been terrifying. She decided to change the subject.

'I'm from Sydney,' Betty said. 'You?'

'Adelaide.'

'I shouldn't be dancing with you. You stole Bradman.'

David let out a belly laugh. 'That was almost ten years ago! And anyway, we're not giving him back.' David seemed to relax a little and Betty let him go on. Talking about home was clearly what this young man needed. 'I've missed the cricket. Used to go to Adelaide Oval every summer when I was at university. Saw Bradman score a century in the Shef-field Shield in the summer of '38, '39. Marvellous.'

'Do you play cricket yourself?' Betty enquired.

'No, tennis.' And she saw his focus shift. 'I played it at school. I'm quite good, actually, but I never could quite get the hang of teaching Lily.' His eyes gleamed at a memory.

'Lily?'

'Yes, my Lily.'

'She sounds very special.'

'She is special indeed. Do you have someone, Betty?'

'Oh, I …' She didn't yet understand exactly what she was to Michael or exactly what he was to her now, other than her best friend in the whole world. That wouldn't change. Not in a million years. But she had a feeling that one kiss had changed everything.

'I have a good friend, a dear friend.' She felt heat in her cheeks. 'He lives next door. Michael. He's in the AIF, 2/23rd Field Battalion, 9th Division.'

They shared a long look for a moment, an unspoken acknowledgement of all that might be lost.

'Godspeed to Michael,' David said in her ear.

'And to you,' Betty replied.

When the music stopped, David let her go. They nodded to each other and he drifted away into the crowd. Suddenly Gwen was at her side, cheeks ruddy, her smile wide and happy. She seemed a little out of breath.

'May I have this dance, miss?' Gwen bowed and held out a hand to Betty.

Betty giggled behind her hand.

'Do a girl a favour, will you? There are too many women here and not enough men. I saw you dancing more than one with that nice-looking young man. I think you might have sneakily stolen my turn.'

'I did not! He seemed sad. We were just chatting, that's all.'

'We'll be lucky to get a man to dance with us after tonight or anywhere else for that matter until the war is over. Let's show them.'

Betty and Gwen laughed and twirled around the dance floor, bumping pilots and Land Army girls; Enid and Daphne; the two young girls who'd asked Betty about Sydney; and an older gentlemen beaming as he guided Nancy who, by any measure, was the most beautiful one of the group, around the hall.

The laughter and the music and the dancing made it easy for Betty to forget, for just a little while, her homesickness and her growing sense of dread about the war.

Chapter Fifteen

Lily

'I think I saw him.'

Lily Thomas peered through the branches of a cherry tree at the girl with the white-blonde hair. She was as tall as any man Lily had ever met, which made her the perfect height for reaching the highest fruit on the Norton Summit trees. 'Who did you see?'

'The Premier. That Mr Playford. A big black car drove in yesterday and there he was driving it himself. Tom Playford!'

'He owns this place,' Lily said matter-of-factly.

'I know. I heard the manager, Mr George, talking about it yesterday but I didn't think we'd be seeing him right here, did you? I've only ever heard him on the radio. He seemed very tall, although I suppose it's hard to tell since he was sitting down. Do you think he's tall, Lily?'

It was the kind of conversation two people had when they didn't know each other and the work they were engaged in was repetitive and monotonous. At least Lily found it to be repetitive and monotonous. She hadn't wanted to tell the young Amazonian that she knew full well that the Premier of South Australia was the owner of the orchard. If she'd wanted to she could have also confirmed that he was quite tall, not very tall, as she'd met him once. But she didn't want such tittle-tattle to spread through the group of Land Army girls. She didn't want them to know that she had what some might call connections. She hadn't known any of the nineteen other girls when she'd arrived at the property for the cherry season. They most definitely weren't from her set. They hadn't gone to the best schools or played tennis in the clubs her family belonged to and they'd probably never holidayed in the cooler Adelaide Hills or even seaside Victor Harbor during South Australia's stifling summers.

Her other life.

How quickly it seemed as if she was now living someone else's.

Her father had arranged her first posting in the Land Army. She didn't know who he'd called or what strings he'd pulled, but once Lily had declared to her mother that she was determined to quit Miss Ward's Training College for Young Business Girls, where she'd failed spectacularly to learn typing and shorthand, to enlist in the Land Army, her mother had immediately phoned her father, who had apparently made a call.

To say her mother had been horrified at her pronouncement was only a little shy of the truth.

'What on earth are you talking about? Girls from good families don't sign up to work as … as common labourers.

It's for the girls with no prospects, who think a little time in the country and a free uniform might be a lark. Shopgirls. Cleaning girls, secretaries, that kind of … person. Girls like you go into office work and then get married, Lily. Or … or if you're bored silly at that typing school, you could become a Red Cross volunteer or work at the Cheer Up Hut on King William Street.' For the first time, Lily realised there were limits to how much the Thomas family was willing to sacrifice for the war. And their daughter's reputation was clearly not one of those things.

'I'm determined, Mother,' she'd replied. 'You can't stop me.'

'Lilian.' Her mother's angry shout across the front reception room had stunned Lily into silence. She'd never seen her mother so upset. Her cheeks were puffed and red and the cords of her throat strained against the high collar of her buttoned shirt.

What would you do, Susan?

Lily had looked up to the framed portrait of her sister on the marble mantel. So serious and smart in her Australian Army Medical Corp uniform. Why, she was probably saving a young soldier's life right that moment as Lily had been arguing with her mother about how common it was to pick fruit or dig potatoes or pluck oranges from groves.

Mrs Thomas had quickly glanced at the door and then lowered her voice to an angry whisper, in case their maid Davina could hear. 'What's got into you?'

The war had finally got into her, that's what. The people she loved the most—Susan and David—were away. If they were willing to sacrifice everything for king and country, the least she could do was get her hands dirty.

A week later, enough strings suitably pulled by her disapproving father, Lily had found herself picking cherries at Norton Summit in the Adelaide Hills on Mr Playford's forty-acre property, in the five square miles of what was known as cherry country.

The high winter rainfall, undulating landscape and cooler climate of the hills made for the perfect topography for cherries. And it was just close enough that Lily's mother could keep an eye on her.

Lily hadn't given her parents an option, really, in the end. She'd discovered in herself a kind of wild spirit, an unleashed energy, and quitting Miss Ward's had only further emboldened her.

Her mother had escorted her on the ten-mile taxi trip from North Adelaide up Magill Road and through the winding hills to the Playford property. Lily chastised herself for thinking her mother's real motive was to run into the Premier himself.

They'd turned off the road onto a precarious winding track with cherry-clad hillsides all around them. It took a few minutes to arrive at Lily's quarters, and when the stone cottage came into view she had sighed in wonder at how pretty it was. Nestled in a valley, the cottage was decorated with climbing roses and weeping bright purple fuchsias in stone urns at the stone steps. There was a large holly tree on one side of the cottage, and a carpet of daisies and purple sweet peas in the lush garden.

'Look, mother. Isn't it beautiful?'

Her mother had clutched her handbag on her lap, quickly glancing out the window before turning back to glare at her daughter. 'It won't be a picnic, you know.'

'Mother …'

'You'll be out in the orchard working all day and night, you know that. In the sun. Your complexion.' Mrs Thomas shivered at the thought. 'At least the accommodation seems acceptable. I have to admit I half-expected you to be put up in a packing shed. By that measure, it looks pleasant enough.' Lily's mother gripped her arm. 'You may change your mind if you wish, Lilian. You're not bound to this ridiculous idea. If you want to, we can ask the driver to turn right back around and drive us home. Your father and I won't think any less of you if you do.'

Lily's throat had tightened. She so desperately wanted to get the words out in the right order, in the right way. 'Mother, please. I know it will be hard work.'

'You've had people do for you your whole life. You don't know what you're in for.'

How could Lily explain to her mother that that was exactly why she'd signed up for the Land Army in the first place?

'I promise I will tell you if I change my mind.'

Her mother had frowned. 'I'm going in to check where my daughter is to be accommodated. Please, for heaven's sake, let there be running water and toilet facilities. And a private room. You don't want to be sharing with those girls from who knows where.'

'Ouch.' The prick of a sharp twig interrupted Lily's thoughts. She sucked on the soft pad of her palm until the stinging stopped. She was learning that scratches and grazes were part and parcel of cherry picking. She tried to be more careful this time, manoeuvring a hand through the dark green leaves and the branches. She pinched a stem between her thumb and forefinger and was careful to pull it from the branch, not the cherries from their stems. She lowered the fruit into the bucket that was tied around her waist with a wide leather strap. It was half full again and she repositioned it so it didn't pull on the small of her back.

During her first week, she'd gorged herself on the ripe fruit, indulging in their juicy sweetness like a young child devouring their favourite sweet. Mr George had told the girls they could eat as many as they liked.

'Go on,' he'd said with a knowing smile. 'You'll soon get over it. Can't eat the fresh ones myself. The wife stews them up and then I'll have them with fresh cream. You'll see. You'll be sick of the sight of them before too long.'

Lily wasn't quite at that point yet.

When it was full, she trekked to one of the wooden cases that had been positioned at the end of each row of trees and emptied her bucket. Soon after, one of the orchard men would carry the cases off to the packing sheds. They were a little too heavy for the girls, so the task was reserved for the experienced and trusted men who had worked on Mr Playford's orchard for decades. Lily also suspected it was a way for them to keep watch over the workers.

To her immense surprise, Lily was happy with the repetitive work. She had never worked so hard in her life, and never worried less. Her days in the orchard were pleasant and quiet. The gully breezes kept the hills cooler than the plains and the suburbs, and she had grown to enjoy the comparative solitude of picking. It gave her time to think, something she hadn't had much of a chance to do before. Some of the other girls sang to pass the time, taking turns with the chorus and verse of 'White Cliffs of Dover', or one of the other tunes from the popular radio shows. She listened, picked, carried, emptied and did all those things over and over in a peaceful routine that lasted all day. Here, she was untroubled by the busy whirr of the complicated social life she'd had when she was living in Buxton Street. The dances and concerts and piano practice and sewing classes and the expectation that she should be seen in the right places by the right people, to entertain, to distract, to be a diversion for her parents.

That was over and she'd never been happier.

Now, when Lily looked up into the summer sky between the cherry trees she saw bright blue. When she took in a deep breath she smelled earth and fresh air. The sounds were the rustle and occasional curses of the other pickers as they scratched themselves or fell off their ladders; or the more diverting call of birds in the trees around them, or in the natural bush surrounding the block. The Norton Summit mornings were cool, and when the Land Army girls trooped out of their quite pleasantly furnished old two-storeyed home and made their way to the packing shed for their instructions for the day, they breathed in eucalypt and damp earth and cherries.

There was no need for pretty frocks and making do with remade outfits and hair pins and make-up and stockings out here. It was boots and overalls and hats under which to hide all kinds of frizziness.

Lily glanced down at the ring on her wedding finger.

She still felt a tremble in her stomach at the idea that she was married. As she picked, her memory worked its magic.

It had happened the night after Evelyn Woods' twenty-first birthday party.

The night after she and David had made love in his rooms at the Greenways Apartments.

The night after she'd irrevocably fallen in love with David Hogarth.

Lily had been up in her room after dinner, sitting at her dressing table composing a letter to Susan, when Davina had knocked on her door and announced that she had a visitor.

'That lovely Mr Hogarth is here to see you,' she'd told Lily with a raised eyebrow.

Lily hadn't had time to point out Davina's impertinence and, anyway, she didn't care any more who knew about her and David. She'd quickly checked her reflection in the mirror above her dresser, kicked off her slippers and put on a pair of court shoes, and had skipped downstairs, her heart in her throat.

David had shot to his feet when she burst into the room.

'David,' she'd cried out, and she had stopped, suddenly finding herself out of breath at the sight of him. He'd looked so sad and handsome all at once that she'd wanted to rush to him and throw her arms around him.

'Lily.' He'd crossed the room to her in three long strides. She'd held out her hand and he'd taken it in his.

She'd wanted to tell him how glad she was to see him, that she wanted to kiss him again, to do more than that, but the sombre look in his eyes had stalled her outburst. She'd seen no point in pretending she didn't feel these things, these desires for him and how he made her feel. Time was short now and Lily felt the pressure of it, propelling her, squeezing in on her.

David had lifted her hand to his mouth and kissed the back of it. The press of his lips caused her heart to race.

'I didn't know you were coming. You didn't say,' Lily had managed.

He'd searched her face. 'How could I not come? After last night?'

'I'm glad you did.'

'I asked you to be brave, didn't I?'

Lily had nodded. 'I am brave. I've had to be that way since Susan went away.'

'Of course you have.'

Lily had held his hands in hers, pulled them towards her beating heart. 'We don't have much time left. It's racing away from us, I can feel it. I can feel it pulling you away from me.'

'I've been wandering the streets of North Adelaide all day,' he'd whispered. 'Trying to convince myself that what I'm about to do is foolish and ridiculous and unfair to you.'

Lily had waited.

His eyes gleamed and she noted the faintest quiver in his bottom lip. She kissed it still.

'Oh, David.'

He'd pulled his hands from hers and got down on one knee. 'Lily, dearest Lily. Will you marry me?'

Lily hadn't had to think before she answered. 'Yes.'

He'd stood and gripped her shoulders, searched her eyes, perhaps looking for facetiousness there. There was none. She knew this wasn't a game and she didn't feel like a child any more. Could he see that in her eyes?

'You don't have to think about it?' he'd asked, laughing at the speed of her reply.

'No.' She'd been sure. 'Of course not.'

'Are you absolutely certain?'

'Yes, David Hogarth, I am absolutely certain. I will marry you.'

He had closed his eyes and breathed out all the tension that had been in his face. 'You'll marry me.'

'If you love me, that is. You haven't said it yet.'

He'd kissed her, quick and fierce. 'I don't want to love you, you know. I don't want to break your heart or mine by declaring it now. But it's too late for that. I do. I have for a very long time.'

'And I love you too.'

'After last night,' he said, and his eyes had softened. 'After being with you that way, I didn't want to leave without making my intentions clear. Why should we wait? We don't know what the future holds, for either of us.' He'd paused a long moment. 'For me, in particular.'

'I'll wait for you. When the war is over and you come home, I'll be here in Adelaide. We'll make a life together, the two of us, no matter if it's next Christmas or the one after that or the one after that. How does that sound?' It was her responsibility now to give him hope, to give him a reason to try all that much harder to be safe. To stay whole. To fight to come home.

It was impossible to think about the war being over, although it was wished for more than anything on earth that Christmas, the fourth Christmas of the war.

'It sounds perfect. I want you to know that the thought of you here, waiting for me, will be enough to keep me going. It'll be enough, Lily, to remind me what I'm fighting for. And if I don't come back …'

She'd kissed him before he could finish and they hadn't stopped until they were breathless.

In the cool nights at Norton Summit, Lily's dreams about David always ended the same way, with that kiss in front of the marble fireplace in her parents' sitting room in Buxton Street.

When Lily told her parents that she and David had walked into the Births, Deaths and Marriages offices on King William Street the day before and were now married, her mother had fainted dramatically onto her favourite tapestry sofa. Her father had blustered and threatened all kinds of things with solicitor friends but David's father was a solicitor and they had spoken by telephone and come to the decision that it might be best to announce it publicly rather than hide it, because the scandal of a discovery would be worse than the romantic elopement of a good Adelaide girl and a good Adelaide boy heading off to the war.

And so it appeared in the Births, Marriages and Deaths page of *The Advertiser* on 19 December, 1942.

Thomas-Hogarth—On Dec 17, Lilian Elizabeth, youngest daughter of Mr and Mrs F.H. Thomas of North Adelaide, to David (R.A.A.F) youngest son of Mr and Mrs W.B. Hogarth of Millicent.

She'd been so excited at the idea of seeing it in the newspaper that she'd woken early and instructed Davina to rush out to O'Connell Street first thing in the morning to fetch a copy.

'Two copies,' she'd called as Davina rushed to the front door. 'I'll have to send one to Susan.'

When Davina had returned, breathless from the rush, Lily had flicked through the pages impatiently until she'd reached the Marriages column, peering at the fine print and searching through the Andersons and the Arnolds and the Browns until she'd seen her name there next to David's.

This made it feel real. She read it over and over with a sense of giddy excitement tingling her fingertips as she traced her name in the fine print.

That elation drained like water from a bath when her eyes drifted to the next column: Died on Active Service. There were too many entries, too many names to read, too much grief to absorb.

Dumas, Charles John (R.A.A.F.)—Killed in action in Middle East, the beloved eldest son of Mr and Mrs E.R. Dumas.

Griffin, Pte J.—Our dear pal Jimmy killed in action in New Guinea. His duty notably done.

Holman, Charles—Killed in action, Egypt, husband of Irma and father of Ron and Colleen.

They'd spent their wedding night together in the fanciest room at the South Australia Hotel on North Terrace, drinking champagne on the top balcony, leaning on the balustrade to wave to people on the footpath below, trying not to notice the railway station down the road, from where David was to leave Adelaide and his new wife early the next morning. She'd tried not to cry but had lost that battle, and David had cried too, with happiness at having married her, and with fear at leaving her.

He had already arrived in Mildura to commence his pilot training at the RAAF base when the announcement had appeared in the paper. Lily had snipped it out and placed it between the pages of her diary, which she carried with her everywhere.

Lily had been relieved to already be at Norton Summit in the week before Christmas and there had been plenty of work to do to distract all the Land Army girls from being away from home.

'Cherries wait for no man when they're ripe for picking,' Mr George reminded them. 'Not even Father Christmas himself. We've had a late start to the season because of the cool spring so we have to keep cracking on. I don't want to be the one to tell all the ladies of Adelaide that there aren't enough cherries at the markets for their Christmas tables.'

The girls had worked on Christmas Eve but had a free day on the twenty-fifth. Mr Playford generously provided a delicious lunch of roast chicken with all the trimmings, hot Christmas pudding with pouring custard and as many fresh cherries as the girls could eat. Being away from home at such a family time somehow made Lily's meagre contribution to the war effort feel important. Her sorrow for the absence of her loved ones was a way for her to share in the honourable pride of their sacrifice. She hoped Susan might by now have received the Christmas cake she and Davina had baked back in November. It had been rather a sad and sorry thing—with no eggs, and lard instead of butter—but once they'd added the sugar and raisins, sultanas and currants and baked it, it looked slightly more appetising. Together they'd packed it into the Willow soldier's cake tin ready to be shipped off.

Lily hoped the next letter from Susan might mention how delicious it was. She didn't know when that might arrive though. Susan's letters had been sporadic since she'd been away in the Middle East. Sometimes there was nothing for two months and then three letters all on one day. She'd been sure to write to Susan about her wedding. Had she received the news yet? Would she be excited and proud of her younger sister?

Lily was still surprised to see the wedding band on her finger. It felt unfamiliar and strange, as did calling herself Mrs David Hogarth.

Her mother had tried to convince her to leave the ring at Buxton Street.

'You don't know who those other girls are. It might not be safe. I know it's not much of a wedding ring but if it truly means that much to you, for goodness sake leave it behind here for safekeeping.'

She would grow used to it. She hoped she would have the chance to become familiar with being a wife as well. She had tried to imagine when that might be and what married life with David might be like, but it was unimaginable. She and David had shared a bed but never a house. Was he the kind of man who left his socks on the rug when he undressed? Would he hang his suits at night or leave them for her? Did he prefer eggs or porridge for breakfast or nothing at all? And where would they live? She blinked away all those thoughts of the future. The only certainty they had was their marriage, her ring, and the letters they had promised to write to each other for as long as he was away. David had already written to Lily from Mildura, where he was training. All she knew was that he was safe for now. He loved flying—his favourite was the Spitfire—and he'd told her how pretty the River Murray looked from high up in the clouds, edged by vines and fruit blocks and orange groves.

It sounded picturesque—and safe —but Lily knew that David wouldn't stay safe there forever. As much as she'd been able, she had prepared herself for the reality that it might be years until she saw him again. Their life together hinged on a bullet or a bomb or a mortar missing him, over and over and over. It was predicated on his plane staying in the air, on him landing safely, on his equipment not failing, on other people saving him if he was injured. So many variables that neither of them could control.

She had vowed to keep the home fires burning in her heart for him, and her home for now was Norton Summit. It would take another three weeks before the Playfords' orchard would be stripped of all the different varieties of cherries.

That meant more picking.

Lily blew out a breath to distract a fly from landing on her lip. Her basket was full once again and she trekked up to the top of the hill to empty the fruit into one of the wooden cases. The way down was always easier and when she reached the spot she'd left, ready to finish the tree, she saw that Kit had got there first.

'What are you doing up there?' The ladder they called King Dick was still flat on the grass in between the trees. Lily was still scared of it. It was twenty-five feet long and she feared if it wasn't positioned properly on hard ground it would topple over, leaving her dangling in midair from boughs that could snap in the wind. Kit had clearly decided she didn't need it at all. She'd unfastened the bucket from her waist and hung it on a strong bough, and had climbed right up the tree where they had just picked from the lower branches. It must have been more than thirty feet tall but Kit didn't seem to mind in the slightest.

'Looking for bananas,' Kit laughed. 'Don't worry. I've been climbing trees with my brothers since I was a wee thing. I'll be fine.'

'But you might fall,' Lily exclaimed.

'Then you'd better get ready to catch me, hadn't you?'

Something bounced on her head. Its soft plop made her laugh and she propped her hands on her hips. She reached for a cherry, tugged it free and then threw it up the tree at Kit.

'Missed!' Kit called back and Lily breathed in the orchard and the earth and the blue sky and her freedom.

Chapter Sixteen

That night, after a dinner of meatloaf and salad, Lily politely declined the offer of a game of cards downstairs in the sitting room of the old stone house. She left some of the other girls listening intently to 5CL for the latest news from the war, and wearily took the steps upstairs.

She wanted to go to bed so she could be alone and dream about David.

There wasn't really any privacy on the orchard. She missed the quiet solitude of her room at Buxton Street. She was with all the other girls all day, from their early breakfast in the kitchen downstairs to dinner at night and picking every hour in between. The Land Army matron who'd been assigned to cook and look after them, Mrs Holland, hovered in a motherly fashion whenever they weren't busy. They shared a bathroom that thankfully had running water, a dining table of a trestle with folding chairs all around it, a living room featuring four worn tapestry sofas, a ping-pong table and a wireless, and they all shared bedrooms upstairs, which were situated on either side of a long and wide hallway running the length of the building.

Lily lay between her crisp sheets, staring out her window to the night sky. The gully breeze cooled her bare shoulders and she shivered a little. While the war was still raging in theatres unknown and far away, she would work. She'd promised herself that. For every day that David was away, she would toil and labour and remember that wherever he was, and wherever Susan was, she was better off by a country mile. Lily could do more than sew and host functions like her mother, or make pretty gowns for events she didn't want to attend. She wanted to make a difference. She would do her bit alongside the shopgirls and the secretaries and the hairdressers because no matter the differences in their manner of speaking, their social skills or their background, death, if it came, would touch them all just the same.

The next day when the girls trooped in from the orchard in the evening, Mrs Holland met them at the front door with a cheering smile.

'I have good news for you all.'

'Are there letters?' Edith called out eagerly, pushing her way to the front of the crowd.

'Please tell us there are letters,' Bernice begged.

'Yes, there are letters. The post—'

Mrs Holland's announcement was drowned out by whoops and cheers, which echoed through the cherry trees and down the valley and back to them. She held up a hand to quieten her girls, which took a moment or two. 'The post arrived today and there are some parcels too. I dare say Father Christmas has come late for some of you. Perhaps he couldn't find his way up and down all these winding roads through Norton Summit, hey? Anyway, dinner's ready. Tonight it's lamb chops and veg, and we have some fresh bread, too. Clean up and I'll see you at the dining table.'

There had been no discussion about it, but a collective consensus had developed among them that their mail always waited until after dinner. Perhaps it had been Mrs Holland's idea, Lily wasn't sure, but they'd slipped into that routine as easily as they might have put on a pair of slippers back home in their old lives. They always came in from the orchard starving hungry, and letters needed to be read slowly and repeatedly in a considered fashion. This was especially important if there were words of love handwritten on the pages. Who would want to rush through such a missive?

'Thank you, Mrs Holland,' Lily said as she filed past. 'That sounds just delicious.'

'Hard work means a big appetite, Lilian,' Mrs Holland winked. 'There's plenty of food.'

The young women formed a line and went inside, chatting as they waited impatiently in line at the bathroom door to wash up for dinner. Some were trying to guess how many letters had arrived, others were silent. Lily expected some were wary of receiving any news, and she could understand that. No news was good news, as people said. Some of the other girls in the house hadn't received any letters at all in all the weeks Lily had been there at the orchard. She wondered if they didn't have family or weren't close.

Lily fought hard not to feel like an outsider. The other girls were from a different world, she had realised. One of them had left a job as a cleaner in a factory to join the Land Army. One had been a hairdresser. Another had been the lift operator in David Jones on Rundle Street. Lily had looked closely at Mavis, trying to remember if she'd ever noticed her announcing 'first floor, Ladies Wear' during any of the hundreds of times she'd visited the store with her mother. Two of the girls had worked in houses just near Buxton Street. Waiting in line for the bathroom the first week after she arrived, Lily had overheard them talking about the families they'd worked for. Lily's ears had pricked up: she knew both.

'I'm earning three times as much here picking cherries as I was working in that house,' Noelene told Annette.

'Tell me about it,' Annette had replied with a huff. 'Ten shillings a week to fetch and clean the house from top to bottom and polish shoes and wash dishes and everything else. Cup of tea, miss? Like the paper, miss? Hem needs stitching? I don't have none of that any more. Here? Thirty shillings a week and no one to tell me what to do all the live-long day. And there's sunshine and fresh air. I know where I'd rather be.'

Lily had thought of Davina and turned away.

The post didn't come quicker for her than it did for the other girls because of who she was. She waited in the queue for the bathroom, just as everyone else did. Here, they were all in the same boat.

'Who are you expecting a letter from?' Lily looked over her shoulder and asked the question of Nora, a curvaceous girl with a button nose and a wide smile.

'My mum and dad,' Nora replied happily. 'They're up in Gawler. They've got a drapers shop but my three other sisters work behind the counter so they didn't stir up too much fuss when I told them I wanted to join the Land Army. And I wish I could say I was waiting on letters from a sweetheart but no such luck.'

'You? No boy who's crazy about you? I can hardly believe that,' Lily said.

Nora laughed. 'I expect when all the boys come home they'll be desperate for some good old Aussie girls, don't you reckon? I'll have the pick of the crop.'

Lily joined in with Nora's laughter, her hands in the pockets of her overalls, her fingers crossed for luck. What news was waiting upstairs for her?

'And what about you, Lily?'

'You mean my letters?'

'Of course.'

'Oh. I would love to hear from my sister, Susan. She's in Egypt.'

Nora gasped. 'What's she doing there? Is she a nurse or something?'

Lily cleared her throat nervously. 'She's a doctor, actually.'

'A lady doctor? I've heard of those but I've never met one. My doctor went off to the war too and now we've got some old coot who should have retired before the first war.'

And before Lily could explain about her family and about David, Nora had nudged the girl on her other side and Lily heard the words 'lady doctor' and they both glanced over their shoulders at her, looking her over.

Lily looked away. Perhaps they weren't all in the same boat after all.

Later, with clean hands and faces, the young women gathered around the dining table downstairs and Mrs Holland served dinner. There was chatter all around her, but Lily didn't feel in the mood to say much of anything that evening. She ate her lamb chops in silence, declining the offer of more mashed potatoes, suddenly feeling more tired than she'd ever been. She watched the other girls and played a guessing game. Who would get letters? And how many would bring bad news?

When dinner was done, Lily went upstairs, taking the steps two at a time, good-naturedly racing Edith, Kit and Bernice to the top of the landing and the door of their room.

They all ran to their beds and on hers Lily found a pile of mail. She clutched at it, tugged the string away and dropped the letters on her blanket. One. Two. Three. Four. Five. Six. Six letters! She scanned the array. When she saw her name in David's handwriting, her heart leapt in her chest and she had to blink back the happy tears.

Mrs David Hogarth.

She smiled at the surprise she still felt at thinking of herself as his wife. Lily slipped off her shoes and climbed up on her bed, making herself comfortable with her back pressed against the cool stone wall. Her mother had forwarded on a Christmas card from Clara, her acquaintance from Miss Ward's, which was rather sweet. Lily set it on the windowsill by her bed. Her mother had written twice, dated just a few days apart. Lily stilled. She checked the post marks and opened the oldest one first. She tried not to scan ahead, tried to calm herself for any news.

'We've received a letter from Susan, dated late November but it only arrived here today, in which she wrote of seeing the pyramids and a Bedouin camp, of all things. She says she is well and very much looks forward to our letters so,

Lily, you must write to her again. I've almost forgotten to say that Susan was thrilled to receive the cake you made. She says it arrived safe and well but sadly didn't last very long. It's hot, apparently, but she is still finding time for some entertainments among all the hard work.'

Lily began to daydream. What did a Bedouin camp look like?

'Oh my,' Edith exclaimed from across the room. She giggled behind her hand and then burst into laughter. 'Listen to this, girls. It's a letter from my Ernie. Or should I say, Lance Corporal Ernest Harmon, AIF.' A proud smile lit up her face. 'He says he saw a monkey!' She bit her lower lip as she read on, her eyes squinting at the pages. 'He's in Malaya somewhere, I think. He says here that it came out of the jungle and took some food from his hand. How's that?'

Kit rolled over on her stomach and propped her chin in her hands. 'How long's he been away, Edith?'

'Ern's been away since February 1940. He was in the Middle East first and then he came back to Darwin and now he's in Malaya.' Edith's bottom lip quivered and she bit it. 'Wherever he is, it's too far away. Honestly, it feels like forever.'

'That's almost three years, Edith. I'm not surprised it feels like forever.'

Edith wiped her eyes. 'Sometimes I think I've forgotten what he looks like.'

'Wait, let me guess. Tall, dark and handsome?' Kit suggested.

'He's short, blond and handsome and that'll do me,' Edith replied. 'What about you, Kit? Do you know anyone who's abroad? A young man or two?'

Kit frowned playfully. 'No. And with all the blokes away, my chances have gone from Buckley's to none, don't you reckon?'

Edith looked across the room at Lily. 'What about you, Lily?'

'Me?' Kit, Edith and Bernice were all looking at her, waiting for a reply.

'We know you're married,' Kit said. 'It's not half obvious the way you play with the ring all day and night. What's his name then?'

'His name is David. Hogarth. I'm Mrs David Hogarth.' Lily's cheeks were suddenly hot. She pressed her cool hands to her face.

'Well, well, well. Mrs David Hogarth,' Kit said.

Lily had the distinct feeling Kit was mimicking her voice, her diction, her North Adelaide accent. Her cheeks flushed even deeper.

'Tell us all about him,' Bernice called out. 'Is he tall?'

'As tall as me?' Kit laughed.

That made Lily smile. 'He's quite tall. A head more than me.'

'And is he a looker?'

'Yes, he is quite. He's very handsome.'

'Which service, Lily?'

'The air force. He's in Mildura at the moment, training.'

'How long you been hitched?' Bernice asked.

'Did you have a honeymoon? I hear Victor Harbor is where all the fancy young couples go these days.'

Lily's throat tightened. She missed him so much she wanted to cry.

'David and I married just before Christmas. It was in the paper. Would you like to see?'

Kit, Bernice and Edith scurried to Lily's bed. She leant down and pulled out her suitcase from underneath her bed, reaching for her notebook. She flipped it open and the girls crowded around. Lily pointed to the classified ad pressed between the pages.

There was silence as the girls read it.

'You're from North Adelaide?' Kit asked, propping her hands on her hips.

'Yes.' Lily's heart cracked. She wanted nothing more than to be one of them, just like any other Land Army girl.

'What in heaven's name are you doing with us in the Land Army? Places I've been, girls like you don't do work like this.'

Lily heard the challenge in Kit's tone. 'My husband's serving so I'm doing my bit too. Isn't that why you enlisted, Edith? Because of Ern?'

Edith glanced at Kit and Bernice. 'Yes.'

'Well, I'm no different. I get the same wages as you do. I'm trying to work just as hard. David will be abroad soon and I'd much rather be up here being useful, doing something, than being home and …' Lily struggled to find the right words. 'Than being home and waiting.'

Edith's hand was on her shoulder. 'I understand, Lily.'

'And my sister is serving too.'

'In the AWAS?'

'No. She's a doctor. She's in the Army Medical Corp in Egypt at an army hospital.'

Edith's fingers tightened on her shoulder. 'Cheers to her, Lily. She'll be patching up our boys and we should thank her for it.'

'I'll pass that on. I'm going to write to her tonight.'

'Good for you, Lil,' Kit said as she walked back to her own bed. Edith and Bernice followed.

Lily picked up David's letter. She held it to her mouth, pressing her lips against it, inhaling deep to see if it smelled like him. There was nothing. She carefully tore open the envelope and pulled out the letter.

Four pages.

My dearest Lily,

Just a few lines to let you know that I'm still here in Mildura, safe and well. My training is going very well and I'm getting my flying hours up. A few more to go until I reach seventy-five, but I'm up in the skies over Mildura and the surrounding towns every day. Lord knows what they think when they hear the Kittyhawks and Mustangs flying overhead like giant blowflies.

Training is focussed and quite intense but surprisingly fun, Lily. I've flown Spitfires and Wirraways so far, and I've spent quite some time taking off and landing, flying the skies of Mildura and the river. It really is like a snake, the Murray, as it loops and curves through the red earth here. The countryside is surprisingly green, filled with orange groves and grapevines for miles and miles and miles. I'm enjoying while I can the quiet and the blue skies. Last week I spotted a house and some sheds and I flew in quite low to have a look around and was surprised as anything to see a man and woman in the vines. I waved like mad so they knew I was having a little fun but I was in and out too quick for me to see if they waved back. I expect that people here would be used to us flying overhead by now, as familiar to them as the blowflies that are rather relentless at this time of year.

I expect they know why we're flying. I've joined up with some of the other fellas—terrific blokes all—and we've gone into Mildura for a meal and pictures at the Ozone. I can highly recommend This Gun For Hire *with Veronica Lake. The boys came out and searched high and low up and down Langtree Avenue for a girl as pretty as her, but all I could do was think of you.*

Lil, I'll be shipping out at the end of training, which I figure is the end of April. We have plenty of time to write letters before then, don't we? For now, I console myself with the fact that, at least for the time being, I am close to you. When I'm flying, I sometimes imagine that I might one day keep going and not stop until I fly home to you.

Please write to me as often as you can. I know you'll make a go of the cherry picking. You're a sensible girl. You married me, so you must be.

Lil, I love you with all my heart and it will be a comfort to me to know that I'm in yours.

You be brave and I'll be safe, remember?
Ever yours,
David

Chapter Seventeen

Flora

The trip into Mildura had been Charles's idea. He mentioned it to Flora one Thursday evening at Two Rivers, in the living room after dinner. The girls were on the rug, drawing pictures on scraps of butcher's paper. Mrs Nettlefold sat on the sofa embroidering a handkerchief, her needle threaded with cotton the colour of a Two Rivers bright orange sunset. Charles sat in one armchair skimming the pages of the latest edition of the *Sunraysia Daily*. The wireless was on in the background, Bing Crosby crooning and a smooth announcer's voice drifting over them between the songs.

Flora sat in the other armchair, a few feet away from him. She'd managed to find time in the evenings over the past week to read a little before sleep and was in the final few pages of her Agatha Christie novel. When the killer was revealed, she closed the book, laid it on her lap and sighed.

'You're finished?' Charles asked, his newspaper rustling as he lowered it into his lap.

'It's taken me a while but yes.'

'You like reading,' he said.

'Definitely,' Flora replied. 'It's almost my favourite thing. Who doesn't love a good book to carry you away into the thoughts and minds of other people? Their crimes and misdemeanours, their loves, their adventures?'

'Was it good?'

'Oh yes, Agatha Christie is my favourite author. She's so clever and I never see the endings coming. I'll have to find another, now I've finished this one.'

'Our library has a good collection, but that won't be much use to you, will it?' He paused, dropped his gaze for a moment. Perhaps she wasn't the only one who'd been thinking about her imminent departure. One more week and she would be gone.

'No. I don't believe I'd have enough time to finish it before I leave, unfortunately.'

Charles glanced at the girls, colouring quietly, and his mother, silently stitching. He lifted the paper, as if he might be using it as a shield from his children and his mother, and leant towards her. She moved in close in response. He smelled of soap. For the first time she noticed the length of his eyelashes and the flecks of sapphire in his eyes.

'There's a bookshop in Mildura, on Hiscock's corner. You might find something there you like. Perhaps we could go in on Saturday afternoon?' he said quietly.

Not quietly enough, it seemed. On the floor, the girls erupted. 'Can we come too, Daddy?'

Charles rolled his eyes and pulled his lips together in a frown, before transforming his features into a happy, fatherly smile. 'Of course. Maybe we can see what's screening at the Ozone.'

Flora felt her cheeks warm and blush. Is that what he would have had in mind for them? A little shopping and a picture? Perhaps dinner too. She thought the world of the girls but let herself feel a flare of disappointment in that moment, at the chance that she and Charles might have had some time alone. She blinked the thought away as the girls squealed their delight and climbed up into their father's lap. The newspaper was crushed in the commotion and Charles's laughter echoed around the room.

A tut-tutting Mrs Nettlefold interrupted. 'Girls, don't go and get all excited when it's so close to bedtime. Speaking of which, I think it's time for you both to go to bed.'

'Come on, Daddy,' Violet said, tugging on Charles's little finger. 'Time for stories.'

Charles flicked a glance at Flora.

Mrs Nettlefold watched them both. 'I'll do the stories tonight.'

The girls knew better than to protest, so after quick kisses for their father, and goodnights and sleep-tights from Flora, Violet and Daisy went to bed.

Daisy whispered loudly to Violet behind her grandmother's back. 'Do you think we'll get to have a soda from the soda fountain?'

'Sssh,' Violet replied, holding a finger to her lips. 'Don't jinx it.'

Flora and Charles sat together in the peaceful quiet. A warm breeze danced in the lace curtains and another song started on the wireless. Flora thought it might be Glenn Miller. She turned to Charles to mention it only to find him staring her.

He had such a handsome face. She'd grown to know it during the past weeks; the sky blue of his eyes, the fullness of his lips, the messy thatch of his black-and-grey hair and how it stuck up in all directions after it had been pressed down under his straw hat. She was familiar with the sound of his footsteps, the long loping stride of his boots in the dirt. When he lifted four buckets full of grapes he breathed out as if he was bracing himself, and when he was about to begin 'Clancy of the Overflow' he always cleared his throat. Twice. He murmured his appreciation at the end of every meal and nodded his head in time to the music on the radio, especially if it was jazz.

Was it any surprise, given how closely they'd been working together, side by side in the grapevines, that they'd created a routine which now flowed seamlessly like the river beyond the block?

Flora had also come to understand things about herself. She understood that she had made a difference at Two Rivers, that she had helped them continue making a living from their land. She'd taken a leap of faith in herself when she'd enlisted and her confidence in herself had grown, buoyed by the swell of pride she felt every morning when she walked down the back steps of the Nettlefolds' house with Charles to head out into the vines. She could comment with some authority now about how hot it might be in the mid-afternoon, and knew exactly which row of vines she had to return to after leaving the afternoon before. Under Charles's patient and expert tuition, she'd even been trusted with the task of spraying the drying sultanas with the emulsion of potash and olive oil, and could pick out the drying stages of the fruit by its colour, from greenish to gold to amber to light brown to brown and blackish.

'Flora.'

She would always remember the way he said her name. 'Yes, Charles?'

He stood and came to her, lowered himself on the wide armrest. His calf brushed against her knee and she looked up into his eyes.

'I had hoped that you and I ...' He shook his head and chuckled. 'But the girls have other ideas, clearly.'

'I'll miss them terribly,' Flora said, her voice catching in her throat.

'And they will miss you. Having you here has been ...' The door to the sitting room swung open. Charles stood abruptly.

'Daddy.' It was Daisy, tears welling, a brown teddy bear under her arm. 'I want you to tell me my story.'

The muscles in Charles's jaw flinched. 'I'm coming.' He strode across the room, swept Daisy up into his arms and left.

Charles pulled the dusty Dodge to a stop in the middle of Langtree Avenue in Mildura. The wide street meant that there was room for parking in a strip in the middle, if you were lucky to get there in time before all the spaces were full.

'Saturday afternoons get pretty busy,' he'd explained on the bumpy journey to town and now Flora understood the rush of the morning's work in the vineyard, the quick wash, the hurried lunch and Mrs Nettlefold fussing over the girls to get properly dressed. They were in the back seat, their hair neatly brushed, and in Daisy's case twisted into two plaits. They wore the same cotton sleeveless dresses they'd worn to church the weekend before, and were fizzing with excitement about their outing. The whole journey had been filled with a discussion about which sweets they were going to buy at Coles.

Flora was just the slightest bit excited herself. She looked out at the footpaths groaning with people jostling for space, cars hustling for parking spaces, and shop doors opening and closing like swinging doors in a cowboy picture with customers coming and going with parcels and bags.

Charles was out of the car quickly to open Flora's door. She took his hand and stepped out, feeling slightly anonymous in her civilian clothes. This was her free time, and the rules were that she was able to wear whatever she liked. Her trusty floral dress and a pair of tan sandals saw her blending in with all the other shoppers.

'I'll see you in half an hour?' she asked Charles. 'I'm off to the bookshop and you're off to the Coles sweets counter, is that right?'

The girls giggled and took their father's hands to drag him towards their bounty.

Flora quickly found the Agatha Christie novel she wanted, *Evil Under the Sun*, and after purchasing the book and some stamps and envelopes, she sauntered down Langtree Avenue, past the Hit Cafe and Smiths Dry Cleaning Laundry, which seemed to be doing a roaring trade, and then the window display at Lapin and Blass caught her attention. The drapery store was crowded with ladies and Flora resisted the urge to go in. She didn't want to spend what little money she had left on something new, and anyway, she wouldn't have any room in her suitcase to lug it to her next posting. But that didn't stop Flora pressing her nose up against the glass and imagining that she might indeed spend ten shillings on one of the floral linen frocks so prettily displayed on the mannequin in the window.

Wishing she could walk away with a new straw hat trimmed with ribbon, lace and flowers.

Wishing she had the courage to buy a silk princess slip and silk hose and that Charles might one day caress his fingers up and under the sleek fabric on her thigh.

She closed her eyes. Her most fervent wish was that there had never been a war and she'd wouldn't have had to come to Two Rivers in the first place.

But she was there now, and she didn't want to leave.

'Flora.' Charles was by her side, his girls bouncing on the spot on either side of him. She swallowed hard, a sudden thirst drying her mouth. The girls were a useful distraction.

'Did you get your sweets?' she asked them.

Violet and Daisy held out white paper bags tied with string.

'Bullets,' said Violet.

'Jaffas,' announced Daisy. 'But Daddy says I'm not allowed to roll them down the aisle at the pictures.'

He tugged one of her plaits. 'All I said was that if you do, you won't have any left to eat.'

Flora looked into the shop window, trying to distract herself by concentrating on the display of tea towels and white pillowcases.

'Flora?' Charles asked. He reached for her, a gentle touch on her arm. The gesture created an ache deep in the pit of her stomach.

'Is everything all right?'

She found a smile. 'I'm all done. I have my new book. Did someone say something about a banana and cream sundae?'

Their table at the Spot Sundae Parlour was pushed up against one wall on the left of the long narrow space, to leave an aisle for customers in front of the wooden counter on the right. Behind it, shelves of sparklingly clean soda glasses were in neat rows and above them was a stained-glass window with the words *soda fountain* etched in a glass panel.

Charles had given his order to a waitress in a white uniform and cap and it wasn't long before Violet and Daisy were spooning ice-cream into their mouths. Flora's chocolate malted milkshake and Charles's banana ice-cream soda sat untouched. Their shoulders pressed up against the dark wood panelling as they gazed at each other.

'You don't like it?' she asked.

'I'm sorry?' He was distracted.

'Your soda.'

'Oh, yes.' He stirred it around in its tall glass and then took a long sip. Beside them, the girls were deep in conversation.

They caught the pictures at a quarter to six. Later, Flora tried to remember what announcements had been made in the newsreels or the name of the film but all the details escaped her. All she remembered was that, in the dark, the lights flickering on the faces from the screen at the front of the theatre, she had been sitting next to Charles, their shoulders had touched and his leg had brushed against hers until the final credits rolled.

The last of the grapes had been picked by the first week of February. The dried fruit had been boxed and delivered to the local co-op. Charles had come home with payment, a cheerful grin and some surprises for his family.

For the girls, a bag of the sweets they liked. For his mother, a bottle of perfume from the pharmacy, which she insisted was far too frivolous, and a bottle of brown Muscat for the adults to share over dinner. He handed over Flora's final pay—thirty shillings a week as agreed by the Manpower Directorate for a girl who boarded at a property—and over dinner, proposed a toast to her to thank her.

'To Miss Atkins,' he'd announced, holding a sherry glass in the air. 'I don't know what we would have done without you.'

Mrs Nettlefold looked at her son and then at Flora. The girls whooped and they all ate their dinner hungrily.

Their final week together had slipped by in the blink of an eye. Flora had taken every chance to watch Charles, to study the ropes of muscle on his arms, the breadth of his shoulders, the shape of his strong jaw and the wrinkles around his eyes and mouth. She knew his scent, sweat and dust and, after he'd washed, soap and wet hair.

On their last day, when they'd walked together deep into the block after lunch, he'd caught her by the arm, and said, 'Taste this.' He waited for her to open her mouth and when she met his gaze and parted her lips, he'd squeezed a sultana and rubbed it over her lips, its juice sweet. When it dribbling down her chin, he swiped it with a finger and then sucked on it. Her craving for him was so unfamiliar and so insistent, stronger and stronger every day they were together.

She'd already received her instructions from the Land Army for her next posting and that night's farewell dinner was to be her last with the family. There was an early train to catch in the morning, and she would have to leave before the girls were out of bed.

After dessert, vanilla custard with stewed plums, the girls began to stir. Finally, Daisy whispered loudly, 'Daddy, can we give it to Miss Hadkins now?'

'Yes, you may.'

The girls scurried out of the room and returned a moment later, grinning from ear to ear. 'We made you a gift. To say thank you,' Violet announced confidently. She passed the present across the table to Flora. It was thin and light and wrapped in old newspaper.

'That's very kind of you. May I open it?'

The girls nodded vigorously. Flora turned it over, untied the string that fastened it and the pages of the newspaper fell away to reveal a drawing on a piece of butcher's paper. In one corner of the page, a sun with rays like sticks. There was a little house. And a cow. A chicken coop, grapevines and a shed. Two children, one with yellow hair and one with black. A woman with her hair in a bun holding a plate of biscuits and a man with a tractor.

And there, in the middle of it all, was a lady with short brown hair and brown eyes wearing a khaki Land Army uniform.

The next morning, in the early-morning light, Charles pulled the Dodge into a dusty parking area at the Mildura train station. It was a bustle of activity, with cargo and sacks of mail and parcels being offloaded and replaced, people milling about and fussing over their suitcases, soldiers embracing lovers, children waving grandparents goodbye.

Wordlessly, Charles unloaded Flora's suitcase from the car and they walked across the tracks and up onto the platform. Flora bought a ticket and tucked it inside her handbag. She checked her hat to ensure it was straight. Charles watched her.

The train horn blew, signalling that it was time to board.

'Thank you for everything,' she said, holding out her hand.

Charles gazed down at it.

'You're most welcome,' he said, taking her hand. His touch sent tingles through her.

He stepped closer. 'I need to ask you something. Before you go,' he said gruffly. He seemed to be fighting with some instinct about what he was going to say, and Flora waited.

'Yes?'

'You've never asked about the girls' mother.'

She shook her head. 'No. I haven't.'

'Why is that?' Charles's brow furrowed.

'I can't say I haven't wondered, Charles, but I didn't feel it was any of my business.'

He breathed long and deep. 'I want you to know, Flora. I've been a widower since Daisy was born.'

She gripped his fingers between hers. It was all she could do in so public a place. She had expected death, but not this way, the cruellest way for a mother to leave her family behind.

His voice was brittle, hoarse. 'I had almost given up hope of being happy again. I'm such an old man now.' He chuckled with a sad and self-deprecating laugh. 'Who would want to have me?'

I would, in a heartbeat. And she almost said it out loud.

'You have given me hope. I wanted to tell you that before you left. You've made me happy and I haven't been happy in a long time.'

'I've been happy here, too, Charles.'

She let go of his hand, averted her eyes from his. There was so much to say but suddenly she had no words to describe how she felt. How much she had changed since coming to Two Rivers. When her duty was done, when her family was whole again, she might tell him.

But not now.

He cleared his throat. 'May I write to you?'

'Please,' Flora replied. 'I'd like that very much. As you well know, I only receive letters from my father and my brothers, and Frank not that often, so they'd be most welcome.'

He tipped his hat to her and she stopped herself from reaching over to lay her hand on his bare forearm.

'Goodbye,' she said.

'Bye, Flora,' he replied.

It was only when a waving Charles became a speck in the distance through the dust-covered window that she let herself sob.

Chapter Eighteen

Lily

'Lily.'

Lily blinked her eyes open. It still took her a moment or two in the mornings to remember where she was. This wasn't her bedroom. Davina hadn't set a cup of tea on the table by her bed. Light was pouring in but Davina hadn't opened the curtains.

Dark green walls and three other girls standing by her bed in their overalls.

A skitter of nerves jolted her awake and upright. 'What is it? What's happened?'

Kit rolled her eyes. 'You need to get up and have breakfast or we'll all be late for the softball game.'

'I don't want to watch any game.' Lily flopped back down in her bed and covered her eyes with her arm, push-ing the inside of her elbow hard against her brow to block out the bright light. One day off a week and she was being bothered about watching a game?

Kit tugged at her arm. 'We're not watching the game, Lil. We're playing it.'

Lily's eyes were wide open now. 'I don't know how to play. I'm not sure I even know what softball is.'

Bernice whipped Lily's sheets back. 'I didn't either but it's tremendous fun and there's afternoon tea, too. Everyone comes from miles around and applauds. It's like being a movie star.'

Edith laughed. 'Come on, Lily. You'll have fun. We promise. And it'll give you something to tell David when you write to him next. I don't know about you, but I've plain run out of ways to talk about picking cherries.'

They were including her, she realised. Perhaps she'd been a little too sensitive about being so different to these girls. When her feet hit the floor, she turned to them. 'I have to warn you. David tried to teach me to play tennis and I was absolutely hopeless. I can't promise I'll be any good at all.'

Kit and Edith held out a hand and when Lily put her hands in theirs, they tugged her to a standing position.

'It's a hoot, that's all. We don't play for sheep stations or anything.'

Sheep stations? As Lily pulled on her Land Army overalls and tied the laces on her work boots, she reminded herself to ask David what sheep stations were.

The sky above the football oval in the next little town was bright and South Australian—summer blue and it made the leaves on the surrounding gum trees shimmer in its light. When the twenty Playford girls arrived, having walked an hour from the Playford's orchard in two merry rows like soldiers, they'd been welcomed with rousing applause and whoops from the hundred or so people milling around a small clubroom with a wide verandah. The local ladies had brought along plates of sandwiches and cakes, and sliced lemon floated in the jugs of lemonade.

'You ready?' Kit nudged Lily.

'Ready as I'll ever be.'

'First we play, then we get to eat.'

Lily reached for Kit's arm and Kit turned back. 'You all right, Lil? You look like you're going to be ill.'

'I meant it when I said I was no good at games. I'm hopelessly uncoordinated. I'm like a newborn baby giraffe, except not as tall. If I'm really terrible we could lose and then I'd let everyone down. Edith and Bernice and Mavis and … even Mrs Holland!'

'She's gone home to see her mother today. You don't have to worry about her. Look, Lil. Let's have some fun. It's for laughs. We all need a laugh, don't you think?'

Lily understood what Kit meant.

'Follow me up to the plate. I'll explain it to you.'

Lily skipped after Kit and listened intently to every word as they watched the rest of the girls in their team throw the ball and catch it over and over.

'Right. It's like a diamond. See? That's home base. And those other three markers out there are first, second and third base. The object is to hit the ball as hard as you can and make it home here. That's called a home run. You can take it one base at a time, too. That person over there who looks like *The Man in the Iron Mask*—remember that film with Joan Bennett?'

Lily shook her head.

'Anyway, she's like the wicket-keeper in cricket. You do know cricket?'

'Of course. My father's a member—' Lily stopped.

'Okay. The girl pitching at you is the pitcher. And there'll be a girl on all of the bases and out in the spaces in between waiting to catch the ball. Got it?'

Lily felt the nerves flip-flopping in her belly. She held a palm there to calm down. 'Right. Hit the ball and run as fast as I jolly well can.'

Kit laughed. 'Why didn't I say it like that? I'll bat first, so you can watch for a little bit before it's your turn. Okay?'

'Okay.'

Kit was magnificent. Lily watched on in awe as she swung the bat from behind her shoulder around in a perfect arc, dropping it like a hot potato as soon as she heard the crack of the ball against it, and then sprinting like an Olympian to first base and then second and, while the opposition's girl was still chasing the ball in the distance, dancing over third base and jumping on the home-base plate when she reached it.

The crowd erupted and so did the Land Army girls. Lily watched on with increasing terror as, one by one, her team-mates took their turn at bat, a few being caught out but most making it back for a home run.

It was her turn. Kit handed her the bat. Lily walked to the plate, as she'd seen all the other girls do, and gripped the bat tight. It was heavier than she imagined. She positioned herself side on, swung the bat over her shoulder and waited, her heart in her throat and a throbbing in her head.

She watched the pitcher and her arm and suddenly the ball was sailing towards her and she closed her eyes and swung and ... missed. She opened her eyes and looked around, unsure of what had just happened. She turned back to Kit.

'Does that mean I'm out?'

'You've got two more strikes. Hit it, slugger!' The Land Army girls were behind her, encouraging her, and she heard 'You can do this, Lily' and 'Eye on the ball, Lily', and a wag exclaimed, 'Just like Bradman, Lil', and she had to swallow a laugh at that preposterous thought.

The pitcher stared her down, swung her arm, Lily swung and ... missed again. She had overbalanced and almost toppled off her feet. She felt foolish. David had been so patient with her when he was trying to teach her tennis but she hadn't been able to run and swing the racquet at the same time.

Hang on, she thought. This is standing in the one spot. This is swinging then running. A surge of confidence puffed up her chest. She took a deep breath.

'Two strikes,' announced the lady in the iron mask behind her.

'Rome wasn't built in a day, Lil. Keep your eye on the ball,' Kit shouted.

Her third attempt. The ball flew through the air towards her. Her eyes were on it like a hawk on a mouse. She moved, she swung, and there was a crack and she ran and then the girls shouted, 'Drop the bat, Lil', and she did and ran to first base and then second and kept going and the ball seemed to have disappeared and she ran right over third and then as she was coming into home base, she tripped over her feet, stumbled and then fell right on top of the plate.

There was a roar in her ears, and hands slapping her back, and when she lifted her face from the dirt, Kit and Edith and Bernice and Mavis and all the other Land girls were squealing their excitement.

'You did it!' Kit said with a gleeful exclamation and Lily was hauled to her feet and hugged over and over and over.

The other team struggled valiantly but couldn't reach the Land Army team's score and the girls from Playfords were declared the winners, but both teams were serenaded off the oval with cheers from the locals.

The swell of pride and joy filled Lily up more than anything in the lunch spread put on by the ladies of the district and, on the walk home, she was allowed to lead the group, marching like a band leader, and someone began to sing and the strains of 'It's a Long Way to Tipperary' accompanied them all the way.

That night, after a supper of soup and sandwiches, the girls sat together in the living room, music softly playing from the wireless in the corner, going over the victory.

'And Lily was trying to warn me about how hopelessly uncoordinated she is.' Kit slapped her thigh. 'And look what she did! Her first game and a home run, no less.'

'She whammed 'em,' Edith announced as she leapt out of her chair to salute Lily.

'You're a star, Lil,' Bernice laughed.

And as they sipped cups of hot tea and talked about the afternoon all over again, Lily leant back in an armchair, hearing that distinctive crack of ball on bat over and over again, and realised that she hadn't thought about the war all afternoon.

It was a blessed relief.

Lily starred in two more softball games before the cherry season was over. It didn't matter to the girls in her team that she was caught out both times; they cheered her anyway. They were the type of people, she realised, who shared in your successes as well as your failures. A strike-out at softball was not the end of the world that she'd imagined it might be and the rest of the team had rallied and they'd won, ending the season as the Norton Summit softball champions.

She'd had more letters from David during those two weeks. In each of them, she'd tried to read between the lines to understand if he was feeling scared but he didn't give anything away. The food was good, it was hot, the skies were big and blue and seemed to go on forever, he'd said. The lads he was training with were terrific chaps and he'd even come across someone he grew up with, from down the south-east. He was spending much of his time in the skies now, as his training was drawing to a close, and he'd declared with a flourish on the page that he had absolutely fallen in love with flying. There had been a Red Cross ball in Mildura, designed to brighten the spirits of the pilots. 'There was a group of Land Army girls there,' David had written, 'and we danced with them all night. I thought it was our patriotic duty to only dance with the young ladies who were serving their country, too.'

Lily had closed her eyes then, casting her memory back to how it felt to be in David's arms, dancing with him at the Palais Royal and at smart parties. She couldn't help the stab of envy that pierced her at the thought that someone else was dancing with her husband. But then she read the next line.

'Don't worry, Lily. They were terrific gals, but none so lovely as you. As I was twirling around the dance floor, for as you know I'm a dancer of some renown, all I could think about was you.'

His war had already begun. He wouldn't be coming home until it was all over.

She had read David's precious letters every night, until they were packed up in her suitcase, which now stood in a line with every other girl's in the driveway outside the old house that had hosted them for the past month. The girls were dressed in their official Land Army summer uniforms, their hair neatly at their collars, their hats just so on their heads. Mr George was driving them in small groups into Lenswood to wait for the bus down the hill to Adelaide.

Lily had received instructions via a telephone call to Mr George that she should wait for her mother to come and fetch her. She looked back at the sandstone house that had been her home these past weeks, and then along the eager and excited faces of the girls who had been her colleagues. She might never have met them but for a stubborn determination on her part to do something more practical for the war than raising funds at church stalls and tea parties. Her mother's work was important, she knew that, but this work felt more real to her than popping pennies and pounds in a tin. She had fought for her freedom to choose this path, and had no doubt that being Mrs David Hogarth had helped. With her husband fully supporting her decision, she had been emboldened to stand up to her parents. All she had to do now was decide where to go next. There was more work to be done. She'd heard the girls talking about it almost every night.

She turned to Kit. 'Have you finally decided where you're going next?'

Kit shrugged. 'I've been thinking. Shall I go back to the shearing sheds in the mid-north or maybe pea picking in Moorook?'

Lily swallowed hard. 'You've worked in shearing sheds?'

Kit grinned. 'Oh yes, and it's just as tricky as you can imagine.'

'The swearing?'

Kit winked and began to sing in a voice that was melodic and beautiful. '*Click go the shears boys, click click click. Wide are the blows and his hands move quick. The ringer looks around and is beaten by a blow, and curses the old snagger with a bare-bellied yoe.*'

When the girls applauded and cheered, Kit bowed deeply.

'So it's true about the language?'

'You haven't heard swearing until you've seen a shearer get kicked by a sheep. I don't know if I'll go back. The blokes don't like a woman in the shearing sheds. They say it's bad luck.'

'Really?'

'True. The wives aren't even supposed to go in. But they didn't have much choice in the end. There aren't enough blokes left who know shearing. My job was to walk up and down the race branding the sheep after they'd come out of the shed, with some of the worst haircuts I've ever seen. Tar streaks on their white bodies where they'd been nicked by the shears. They don't much like keeping still, the sheep.'

Lily's mind raced at the idea of such a thing.

'But I think I might head to Port Noarlunga for the flax.'

'What's flax?' Lily asked.

'It makes linen for thread for parachutes and it's turned into canvas for field hospitals. Pretty darn useful.'

Lily stilled.

Mr George's truck chugged down into the small valley where their cottage was nestled and pulled up in front of the group of girls. With the motor still running, he opened the door and stepped out. 'Who's coming in the first run?'

There was a scramble all round Lily, of hugs and kisses on suntanned cheeks, and tears, promises to write and calls of 'I hope I don't see you next year!'

Kit threw her arms around Lily, and Lily held on tight. She was a smashing girl. Lily would miss her terribly.

Linen thread. Field hospitals.

'You've turned out to be a real chum, Lil,' Kit whispered into her ear.

'You too, Kit,' Lily replied, swallowing her own tears.

'I've got your fancy address in Buxton Street. I'll be sure to write and tell you about all my new adventures.'

Kit grabbed her suitcase and hauled it into the back of Mr George's truck and it took off down the bumpy dirt track towards the main road. As Lily watched it chug up the track and out of the valley, she waved frantically to Kit and the other girls inside. A horn sounded twice. Lily peered into the distance. It was a taxi and her mother was perched in the back seat, the net of her summer hat slowly coming into focus.

Lily breathed deep, preparing herself for the battle. The taxi pulled up and the driver got out to open one of the rear passenger doors. As he loaded her suitcase in the boot of the vehicle, Lily knocked on the window. Her mother wound it down.

'Mum. How good to see you.'

'Hello, dear. Time to say goodbye to the girls over there and hop in. You're coming home.'

Lily's nerve faltered as she ran to the other girls still waiting for their ride into Lenswood. She was hugged by everyone.

'All the best, Lil,' Edith said with a hitch in her throat. 'It's been a real hoot sharing a room with you.'

Lily squeezed her hand. 'All the best for Ern. I'll be thinking of you both.'

Edith wiped her tears. 'And for your husband, too. He'll be in my prayers.'

Bernice wrapped Lily in a huge hug. 'Go well, young Lil,' she whispered. 'David will be safe. I just know it.'

'Thank you, Bernice. I'm hoping to come back next year if … what I mean is, I hope the war will be over but if it's not, I'll see you here next December?'

'Definitely,' Bernice said, and she and Edith and all the other girls waved as Lily got inside the taxi and kept waving until it turned a bend in the winding track and they were out of sight.

'How are you, Lily?' her mother asked. The driver stopped at the end of the track before he turned onto the main road. Lily looked ahead. A horse and cart was approaching from the other direction, piled high with hay bales, and the driver waited for it to pass.

'I'm very well, Mum,' Lily said. 'How's everything at home?'

'I've been busier than ever with the Red Cross and the Cheer Up Hut. The Americans are so terribly homesick for Kansas and Minnesota and California. Especially so over Christmas and New Year. Poor boys. There's nothing they like more than anything resembling a home-cooked meal. They're so polite, always so "Yes, ma'am" and "No, ma'am".'

'I expect they are missing their families,' Lily said.

'Yes. As I expect you have too, being so far away up here in the hills. It's felt quite like a summer excursion coming up to see you today, but there's no time for picnics or rowboats. Are you glad to be coming home, Lilian?'

'Yes.' Lily answered in the affirmative before she could even think. She was so practised at saying yes to her mother in every matter that counted.

'Davina is very much looking forward to seeing you. Everything's just as you left it.'

'Is it?' Lily said, her mind wandering. She remembered her room with the pretty floral curtains and the soft rug. Her freshly laundered sheets, always starched into stiffness by Davina. Her dressing table with her silver hairbrush and mirror. All her gowns and her sewing in the corner. Her books in a small pile on her writing desk.

Lily watched the soaring gums rise into the sky on either side of the road. 'I've been playing softball.'

Her mother turned to her. 'What is softball?'

'It's similar to baseball. You strike the ball with a long bat held over your shoulder.'

'Was there no tennis?'

'No, and you know I'm hopeless at it anyway.'

'You are?' David knew that Lily was hopeless at tennis. He'd laughed when she'd tripped over her feet on the court and had leapt over the net rather dramatically to sweep her up into his arms. Perhaps that's what it meant to be married. To know each other's secrets, each other's strengths and weaknesses, and love them regardless. She would love him always, no matter what happened. She knew that in her heart.

Lily was thankful for the bathroom in Buxton Street. For the hot water that sprayed from the shower; for the fact that she felt clean, really clean, for the first time in a month; for fluffy towels and clean clothes that weren't her bib-and-brace overalls.

But she wasn't used to the elegant silence of the big house anymore. Her mother had dropped her off and shortly after left again for a fundraising meeting somewhere or other. Her father was at the office and Davina was in the kitchen preparing a feast for dinner. Lily lay on her bed with the heavy drapes pulled closed, revelling in the soft mattress and the darkness. The bedroom at the stone cottage in Norton Summit was bare of curtains and it had been bright until the sun went down.

In the dark, she tried to sleep but it wouldn't come. Her mind was in a million places and her thoughts in a million pieces. All she could think of was David. She couldn't go downstairs into the sitting room because that was where he had proposed. How would she cope standing in the very same spot where they'd declared their love when he was so far away and his future so uncertain? It should have made her happy, shouldn't it, to think of him and what that night had meant. But she couldn't drag her thoughts from the darkness, and for the first time since they'd become husband and wife she let herself cry. In the dark of her room, she wept.

'Isn't it nice to be home?'

Lily sipped the sherry her father had just poured for her. The overhead light caught the patterns on the cut-crystal glass and it sparkled. Davina had probably spent all afternoon polishing as well as cooking.

'Yes,' she answered politely. 'Especially when the dining table looks like this.' Lily feasted her eyes on the meal laid out before them. Glistening roast potatoes and carrots and peas. A lamb roast and mint jelly in a silver serving dish. There were fresh bread rolls on their side plates and Lily knew that stewed fruit and custard was for dessert, as Davina had asked earlier if Lily wanted her favourite now she was home and Lily had thanked her and said yes.

'Now you're home, with your adventure in the Land Army out of your system, the Red Cross committee could certainly do with another volunteer. Things are still looking quite dreadful abroad and we're wrapping bandages next week. You'll come along and help.'

Lily wondered if her mother realised she hadn't asked but instructed.

'There's an opening at the firm,' her father said as he reached for another slice of roast lamb. 'It's a part-time position as a secretary to one of the other partners. Between those two things, you'll surely have enough to fill your days, Lilian. Married women can work too these days, I understand.'

Linen thread for parachutes.

'Your little summer holiday is over and it's time to be serious now, Mrs Hogarth,' her father said with a wink. 'Who would have thought. Susan is doing her best work tending to the troops abroad and Lilian is already on her way to fulfilling her destiny as a good Australian wife and mother.'

Canvas for field hospitals.

'Have you heard from Susan?' Lily asked.

'Not since the last time I wrote to you,' her mother answered, suddenly quiet.

'And even then, that letter was two months old.' Mr Thomas crossed his cutlery on his plate and the clatter of steel against china echoed in the room.

'She must have seen some terrible things,' Lily said quietly.

'Our Susan is smart and capable. She'll be fine. She'll come home and have a distinguished career in medicine.'

'Of course she will, Mum.'

And Lily would become a wife and mother. When David came home. If David came home.

Linen thread for parachutes. Canvas for field hospitals.

Lily ate in silence while her parents discussed the affairs of their neighbours and the fine people of Adelaide, trying not to feel that the walls were closing in on her. She was already a wife. What was she doing here back in her parents' home in her schoolgirl bedroom? She thought of playing softball and the faith the other Land Army girls had shown in her, even when she was filled with trepidation and the horror of potential embarrassment. They had become her friends, those girls. They had shown her what she was capable of.

Lily breathed deep. She pushed her plate aside, lifted her glass, threw her head back and swallowed her sherry in one gulp.

'Lilian, some decorum please,' her mother chastised.

'I've made a decision.'

'You can do both, dear, the Red Cross and working in your father's firm.'

'Thank you for the kind offers of assistance. I do appreciate you thinking me capable of being useful in your charity fundraising and Red Cross events. They're very important. But what I've been doing is important, too. I signed up for a year to the Women's Land Army and I'm going to see that commitment through.'

Her father chuckled. 'You don't have to worry about that, Lilian. I can ensure you're eased out of it, no questions asked. All it will take is a phone call.'

Lily steeled herself. 'I don't want to be eased out of that commitment. I'm going to head down to Port Noarlunga for my next posting.'

'Port Noarlunga? Why, that's in the middle of nowhere,' her mother exclaimed. 'Whatever is going on there that they need labourers for?' She flinched at even saying the word.

'Flax production. My new friend Kit is going to work there and I'm joining her.'

'Flax?' Mrs Thomas leant forward in her chair, intrigued.

'Flax makes thread, dear,' Mr Thomas explained.

'And the canvas used for field hospitals,' Lily told them.

Her mother's face drained of all colour.

Her father cleared his throat. 'The government can't source it from Russia or Belgium any more, obviously, so the Brits sent stocks of flax seeds over here for agricultural production. There are big quotas to meet. I've done some work at the firm for one of the fellows here in Adelaide who's investing in the industry and we discussed it in great detail over lunch at the club, as a matter of fact. It's growing so well here that he's exporting tonnes and tonnes of it back to England and there are mills now in three other states. When it's spun, the flax fibres are turned into linen thread for uniforms and boots and parachute harnesses. Canvas ropes for the navy. Hose pipes for the fire brigade. And tents and tarpaulins for all the services. I have to say I had no idea before having lunch with that chap just how important it was to the war.'

Mrs Thomas pressed her linen serviette to her mouth. 'You're leaving again, Lilian?'

Lily reached across the corner of the table to cover her mother's hand with her own. 'I must, Mum. Imagine if the flax I help harvest helped keep Susan and David safe?'

Mrs Thomas pulled her hand away from her daughter's and burst into tears as she ran from the room.

Lily blinked and sat frozen in her chair. She had never seen her mother cry. Not once. Not even when Susan had left.

'Dad?' Lily asked softly. 'Is there something I don't know? Has something happened to Susan?'

He rubbed his eyes and leant forward on the table. 'We don't know, Lily. Your mother finds that very difficult, not knowing from one moment to the next if she is alive or dead.' His shoulders sagged and he found a sad smile for his youngest daughter. 'I think it's a wonderful thing you're doing. It will help, I know it.'

Chapter Nineteen

Betty

On Sunday morning, each of the girls at Stocks' rose at their leisure. It was a free day and the dry summer heat and a hard working week made most of them feel languid and lazy. After a breakfast of soft-boiled eggs, toast and tea, some of the girls tried to find a cool spot outside under the gum trees to lie in the grass and read new magazines sent from home. A couple of girls rode bicycles into Mildura to go to church. Nancy had her nose in a book and Dorothy pored over all the latest news from Hollywood, which she then relayed to the other girls. Betty was lying by her side, watching the grey-green gum leaves dance in the breeze.

'Mickey Rooney and his new wife are off on their honeymoon,' Dorothy announced.

'Who did he marry?' Helen perked up at the news. 'Was it Judy Garland?'

'They've never been sweethearts.' Dorothy spoke with such an air of authority about all things Hollywood that no one doubted her.

Except Helen. 'They were so. You can see it in their faces in all the Andy Hardy movies. Mickey and Judy were made for each other.'

Nancy rose up from the grass, sunglasses covering her eyes, waving her Ponds cream in one hand. 'Don't forget *Babes on Broadway*. I saw it last year at the Tivoli with a fella called Rex. He kissed like a lizard.' She grimaced and wiped her mouth.

'Oh, and look at this.' Dorothy splayed a hand to her heart and held her trembling lips together. 'Clark Gable is "crushed by grief" about Carole Lombard. Even President Roosevelt sent a condolence message. A plane crash in the mountains with her mother. Can you imagine? What a terrible thing for a husband to have to bear. She was flying all over the country getting people to buy war bonds when she died. She was so beautiful. It says here that Zeppo Marx was one of the pallbearers.'

'Which one's Zeppo?'

Betty closed her eyes and let the rest of the conversation flow over her. She didn't want to think about plane crashes and Clark Gable's grief because all it did was remind her of Michael and the sad man she'd danced with at the Red Cross ball. The pilot, David from Adelaide. She would never forget the way his face lit up when he mentioned his girl. He seemed so in love with her.

What would it feel like to be truly in love?

Betty opened her eyes to the blue skies, squinting into the brightness and the heat. Was she in love with Michael? She wasn't sure and if she wasn't sure, didn't that mean no? Was he somewhere thinking about her, mentioning her name to a complete stranger with a sigh and a crooked smile? It was hard for a girl to know and she couldn't ask her mother what love felt like because her mother would ask who the boy was and she didn't want to say Michael's name in case she wasn't and he wasn't. Perhaps he'd kissed her because he wanted to kiss a girl one last time before he left for the army and she was the one who had happened to be standing right there, next door. It was all so very confusing.

Thinking of King Street brought a kaleidoscope of memories flickering behind her closed eyes. Her mum and dad who'd looked at her with a patronising disbelief when she'd told them she'd signed up for the Land Army. She would never tell them how much she'd cried and missed them, how much her confidence had faltered, how close she had been to coming home. If it hadn't been for the girls she'd met, she might have. Flora's kind advice, Peggy's leadership and Gwen's friendship and, yes, even Dorothy's endless reports about the movie stars had kept her going. And even poor Clark Gable had played a part in her turnaround. Betty found it strangely comforting that being rich and famous was no protection from loss and sacrifice.

She stretched and got to her feet. It was still hot and she felt lazy but she wanted to write some letters that afternoon. She sauntered past two of the girls washing their smalls and pegging them up on a line strung from their quarters to a post dug into the ground. She passed some of the girls on their beds, dozing in the heat, or lying quietly listening to the wireless.

Betty retrieved her notepad and pencil from her suitcase. She sat cross-legged on her mattress, her pencil poised over her new notebook, thinking about what to tell her mother and father. How could she put into words all that had happened since she'd arrived in Mildura, what she'd learnt about picking grapes, about living with nineteen other girls and, most importantly, what she had learnt about herself?

Dear Mum and Dad

She stopped, sucked the end of her new pencil.

Where to begin?

She'd learnt she could cry for two weeks straight and not run out of tears. She'd learnt that no matter how much your body ached, you got up again the next day to do it all over again because every girl around you was feeling the same aches and pains and smiled through it and did her best. She'd learnt that women had left happy homes and sad ones. Gwen missed her fiancé terribly but June never talked about home or her family, other than saying once, in a rather off-handed way, that she didn't miss one single thing about it and she wouldn't be going back when the war was over.

And as she thought about how to describe all of this to her parents, Betty realised she had learnt something powerful. Sometimes, it's not telling the truth that is kinder.

She put her pencil to the page.

I'm simply having the most marvellous time imaginable out here in the country among the grapevines with the finest girls you can imagine.

On Monday, a north wind throttled the vines, sweeping up dust and topsoil and swirling it around like a dervish, trapping it in everyone's ears and hair, inside the collars of their shirts and down into their underwear. It was a miserable day. Every time Betty opened her mouth, she tasted dry red earth. The sky wasn't blue but a swirling dust storm full of reds and pinks. The buckets seemed heavier, the vines pricklier, and the heat scorched the girls as if it were trying to turn them into sultanas, too.

By day's end, there were choking sighs of relief and a weary tussle about who would get to the copper first for a wash. They'd all been getting on marvellously well until that day, when the dust and the heat seemed to sap every bit of their strength. For the first time since coming to Mildura, Betty felt cross. With the girls who'd complained, with the damn heat, with her secateurs that had become stiff with sticky moisture from the branches and clinging dust, with the sweat that drizzled from her like honey from a spoon, and other aggravations she couldn't name as she stomped back up to the quarters. Gwen was back too, tugging off her boots and socks and thumping her clothes with her palms to get rid of the dust before dragging her feet up the steps into their quarters.

Betty moved to the shade of the gum trees. She lifted her straw hat, bent over and shook out her hair, scrubbing her scalp with dirty fingers to flick the dust out of it. Then she moved to the tap, yanked it on and cupped her hands until they overflowed, splashing her face, gulping the warm water down, over and over, for what seemed like minutes, until she wasn't tasting dust any more. It was a blessed relief. She turned off the water and stood, blinking her eyes against the grit that still scratched under her lids. She couldn't see more than fifty feet ahead of her.

There was a scream.

The hairs on Betty's arms prickled.

'Who's that?' It was Peggy, suddenly beside her, frantically looking around the group of girls to see who was missing.

Betty did too, and realised with a sinking heart that it was Gwen.

Peggy ran for the door of their quarters, Enid, Nancy and Betty running fast behind her. Their boots stomped on the wooden floor as they ran to reach Gwen, halfway up the room.

She was clutching a telegram, shrieking and shaking, her eyes closed tight but tears falling anyway, streaking the red dust on her cheeks like stage make-up under hot lights. Betty was shaking too, so she wrapped her arms around herself, trying to be still.

Not Gwen. Not her Reggie.

Peggy took the lead, stepping forward to gently slip an arm around Gwen's shoulder. Then Enid was by her side, too, prising the crumpled pink telegram from Gwen's fist.

They all watched Enid as her eyes skimmed from right to left, her lips moving almost imperceptibly as she read. Enid's expression became grim. She exchanged a look with Peggy who seemed to know what it meant even though no one had said a word out loud

Betty didn't know what to do, what to say. I'm only seventeen, she wanted to explain. I'm just a shopgirl from Woolworths. She stepped backwards, away from the rest of the girls who'd gathered around to create a cocoon of comfort for Gwen. Their sobs and words of comfort were drowned out by the thunderous thudding of her pulse in her ears, as loud as the Spitfires that had flown low over the block the week before.

The next thing Betty knew, she was running into the vines, the dirt kicking up behind her feet gritty against her bare calves, and she ran and ran until she couldn't find a breath. She collapsed into the dirt, cowering in the vines. She pulled her knees up to her chest, crossed her arms on her knees and dropped her forehead. And when she was sure no one could hear, she sobbed.

It was Peggy who found her.

'Baby Betty. What on earth are you doing out here in the dirt?'

Betty lifted her head. She made a fist and rubbed her eyes, which spread the grit and made her cry even more.

Peggy sat next to Betty. She brought her knees up too, mirroring Betty's crouched pose. She was silent for a long while before reaching behind her to pluck a bunch from the vine and picking the tiny grapes off one by one. She popped a few in her mouth, chewing slowly. Then she offered one to Betty.

Betty shook her head. She couldn't eat. She felt sick. 'No, thanks Peggy,' she said, her voice croaky.

Peggy popped another grape in her mouth. 'Don't blame you. Don't reckon I'll eat another one as long as I live after being here.' Slowly, she picked the grapes, eating them one by one.

Finally, Betty summoned the courage to ask. 'It's Reggie, isn't it.'

Peggy nodded. 'He's been reported missing. He's an RAAF boy, just like the ones we were dancing with on Saturday night.'

The thought made Betty want to weep all over again. But she clenched her teeth together and willed herself not to cry. Not in front of Peggy.

'That's dreadful,' she whispered.

'No one wants to get that telegram.'

Betty thought she heard Peggy sniff.

'But there could still be hope, couldn't there? If he's missing they might find him. It doesn't mean he's …' Poor, lovely Gwen. Betty thought of the children called John and Peter and Margaret that Gwen and Reggie would never have if he didn't come home.

Peggy didn't answer Betty's question. 'The Stocks have taken Gwen up to the main house. They'll look after her for a bit.'

Betty could only nod to acknowledge their kindness.

'They're good people. I didn't know until just now but they lost their only son in Palestine in 1940 and a daughter in Darwin last year when it was bombed. She was a telegraphist in the army.' Peggy paused, wiping her cheeks. 'Who would have thought answering the phones could get you killed, hey?'

Peggy got to her feet, dusting off her shorts and any hint of the emotion that had made her cry. 'You coming, baby Betty?'

Betty followed Peggy back to their quarters.

On February fourteenth—Betty's eighteenth birthday— the girls did their best to help her celebrate but Gwen's news had cast a pall over them all. No one wanted to talk about the telegram and what it meant, and Gwen's bed sat empty, a reminder to them all that grief and loss had snaked their way into their quarters and would never leave.

That evening, the women found ways to distract themselves. Nancy took to her bed and read all of her husband's letters over and over. Dorothy read the *Women's Weekly* magazines in her collection from front cover to back and, if she was inclined to share the latest titbits of news from the home of the movies that she might have previously missed, she held her tongue. Enid whittled a piece of wood with a pocket knife, the slick sound of the knife blade against the wood rhythmic and calming, and left a perfectly formed little cat on Gwen's bed. And no matter how much Peggy tried to jolly them up with a rousing call for a game of cricket or an impromptu dance around the dining table to *Australia Sings* blaring from the wireless, there were no takers.

Betty sat on her bed, with a pencil and her notepad on her lap.

Dear Michael,

Today is my birthday and I'll admit to being a little cross with you for not sending me a birthday card or a Valentine's card. I hope you see that I'm pulling your leg. As I sit in the quarters here on the fruit block near Mildura (that's on the River Murray) with my pencil scratching out my thoughts, I can't help but think how different things were just one year ago. I remember well our little party at home for my last birthday, with your mother's delicious sponge cake with jam. I promise you I can still taste it. Things were a little bit more gloomy then, don't you think? I mean with the war, not the blackouts. Not that I know all that much but from what we hear on the radio, Churchill and MacArthur seem to be turning the tide against the Nazis and the Japanese.

I miss our park and the Moreton Bay figs and Columbines and Cherry Ripes and the sound of all the boys in the street playing cricket at night.

Be safe.

Yours always,

Betty

Chapter Twenty

Four days before the girls were to pack up and leave the Stocks' fruit block, Mr Stock knocked on the door after supper and handed over a box of letters, each bundle wrapped in twine. Peggy thanked him and assumed the role of lady postmaster.

The girls gathered around the table as she did a rollcall of names and passed on the bundles.

'Dorothy. Enid.' Peggy looked up from the box and handed a collection of letters to Gwen. 'There are quite a few there.' Gwen snatched them up and ran through the open door of their quarters and out into the twilight.

'Betty. Well, you have a parcel of some kind. And some letters.'

As Betty walked to her bed, she tugged on the twine and let it fall to the floor. One from her parents. One from Mrs Black. One from Jean, her friend from Woolworths. And two from Michael.

A tiny grey envelope was stamped with a diamond shape and the words *Passed by Censor* on the front.

Pte MX Doherty
2/23rd Bn
AIF
Abroad
January 16th, 1943
Dearest Betty Boop,
Just a few lines to let you know that we have left country and are out at sea. We left camp and caught the train to ————— ———— and had an excellent supper at ——————————. We then embarked at ——————————. The cabins on board are great and there is plenty to eat, with the food as good as you'll get at any hotel in town. There is not much I can tell you about the ship or tell you its name but I'm sure you quite understand that.

All the boys are looking forward to getting to ——————.
We're all up for an adventure and determined to do our best for Australia.

When you write, Betty, use the address at the top here and it will find me no matter where I am.

Don't forget to write. I will very much look forward to hearing from you.
Yours,
Michael

Betty snatched up his second letter and tore open the envelope. A folded letter was inside and when she opened it, a little post card fell out too, small enough to fit into the palm of her hand, with *Be My Valentine* printed on the front, the red words set among roses and carnations and a lace garland. She flipped it over. There was an X and nothing else.

Betty's pulse raced. He hadn't forgotten. She flipped open the wafer-thin pages.

The address on it was King Street. Home. And the date in his neat handwriting was the day they'd said goodbye. The day he'd kissed her on the footpath and said, 'Don't get too lonely.'

Through her tears, she tried to focus on his words.

Dearest Betty,

Happy birthday!

I bet this is a surprise. I don't know when I'll get to write to you after I leave and how long it will take for you to get my letters, so I have written this tonight after my birthday party. It really was a good night. Thank you for the Biggles book and the Cherry Ripes. Boy, do you know how to get to a fella. You won't be surprised to know that I've already eaten them all.

I will ask Mum to post this to you wherever you are 'soldiering'. I'm sure she will find out from your mum so will have the proper address. It didn't want to miss your birthday or Valentine's Day so also, happy Valentine's Day.

Well, well. Betty Boop is eighteen. All grown up, as they say. I hope you are having fun working the land and that you are sorting out those cows and pigs. Or maybe you're picking peas or carrots? I don't know. I hope you'll write me many letters telling me all about your adventures. It must be a big change from Woolworths, hey.

I know your mum and dad will miss you terribly, as will my own mum. You know you are like a daughter to her.

*With so many sons, she has always treasured your company.
As have I.*

*That's about all the news from here. Cheerio and happy
days,*

Yours,

Michael

*P.S. I hope you like the Valentine's card. I'll be thinking of
you on the 14th, wherever I am.*

Betty flopped back on her pillow, clutching the little Valentine's card to her chest. There was a sound in her ears that felt like ringing and she was suddenly hot and shivery all at the same time.

'I'm thinking of you, too, Michael,' she whispered.

Two days later, the harvest was finished and the vines were bare of fruit. The wind blew as hot as the first days of summer. The dry red earth was as hot first thing in the morning as it was in the middle of the blazing afternoons, water from the tap was always warm enough to have a bath in, and they'd almost got used to the flies. Gladly, there had only been one snake sighting, and it was still unconfirmed.

The girls were stronger than when they'd arrived. Leaner, too. Those with olive skin tanned as if they'd been on holidays on a tropical island, while those with fair skin, Gwen especially, constantly had peeling sunburn.

Betty had eaten well but worked hard and she'd had to ask Peggy to work a new notch on her belt as her uniform's skirt had become loose.

The last night, all the girls were invited up to the Stocks' for a special farewell dinner. There wasn't enough room for them all to sit at a table, so the twenty girls filled their plates with sandwiches and cream cakes and biscuits adorned with glacé cherries and sat wherever there was a space in the large living room.

Enid had dubbed the girls a flying squad, and Betty smiled at the thought of that. They may not be up in the skies like the local trainee pilots in their Spitfires and Boomerangs, or like the lads abroad keeping ships and troops safe, but they were flying off nonetheless, to who knew where. Six weeks earlier, Betty had sobbed over being away from all she knew, all that was familiar, so far from the loving embrace of her family.

Deep down she knew that it wasn't her birthday that had changed her. It was the girls and the hard work and the independence she'd discovered being away from home, something she now relished. She couldn't wait to decide on her next posting. How much had changed. How much she had changed.

As the girls ate and chatted, relived adventures and misadventures, teased Dorothy about the snake she'd supposedly seen, taunted Enid about her pledge never to marry, Betty listened on. For an only child, this was the first experience of what it might have been like to come from an enormous family of sisters.

For they felt like sisters now. Even if there had been squabbles about who needed to wash their smalls first and who was spending far too much time in the lav, they were quickly forgotten. If one girl was suffering with her monthlies and needed to stay in bed to deal with cramps and headaches, the others worked harder. When Gwen had received her news and spent two days up at the main house, as many grapes were picked as if she were still in the vineyard with them.

Protective Peggy. Gossipy and glamorous Dorothy. The quiet Daphne and dreamy Helen, who always seemed to be two steps behind in any conversation. And dear Gwen, who'd looked hollowed out since she'd received the telegram about Reggie. The night Gwen had gone up to the main house, the other girls had shared their stories, murmuring quietly in the dark. Nancy told them about her husband, who'd gone from packing biscuits at Mottram's in Grote Street in Adelaide to the jungles of Malaya. Nancy had four brothers away, all in the army. Enid had two. Others had cousins and uncles and neighbours and sweethearts. Someone's father was in Darwin, too old to go and fight but still young enough to stand guard duty with a rifle. There were boys from school and from their street. Sisters and friends were in the AWAS or the AWAAF. One had gone to school with one of the nurses killed by the Japanese at Bangka Island.

'You have to bounce back,' Peggy, wise as ever, had told them, and they did their best to, for Gwen's sake. For all of their sakes. They may have been a long way from blackouts and bomb shelters and beaches strung with barbed wire, but they had all brought the war with them to Mildura and, sure as anything, it would hunt them down too if there was more bad news.

'I don't know if I want to pick any more grapes,' said Helen. 'I might try oranges instead.'

'If you're keen to do more of this work, there's more grapes down Shepparton way,' Peggy said. 'The season's longer there with all the different varieties.' Peggy knew as much as any farmer about the seasons and when crops would need harvesting come February and March and April and May. 'Or there's apples, pears and peaches until about April. Or who wants to go up to New South Wales to pick cotton?'

There wasn't a taker for that option.

Daphne piped up. 'There's potatoes in Berri, just over the border in South Australia. They're dried into flakes. I've got family there. My great aunt.'

'Or there's peas in Oberon,' someone else added and Betty couldn't keep track with the conversation going so fast.

'Portarlington needs pea pickers, too.'

'My friend Mary's at an orchard near Leeton. I can't remember where exactly, and she's permanent. Wouldn't it be nice to not be sent here, there and everywhere?' Nancy asked.

'Couldn't stand it,' said Enid. 'I like the change. If one place doesn't turn out so good, or the blokes who run the place give you the heebie-jeebies, you can always go somewhere else. Last year I worked on a pig farm for a while.'

'Don't pigs stink?' asked Betty.

'Not more than a houseful of brothers,' Nancy piped up and everyone laughed and then looked away from Nancy's wistful smile. Everyone sat for a moment in silence, leaving her in that memory for just a little longer.

'What about working in a cannery?' Peggy suggested.

'That could be all right,' Nancy replied. 'Wouldn't it be nice to be working inside for a change instead of outside in the stinking sun every day?'

'Your tan would fade,' said Dorothy. 'And maybe those wrinkles will, too.'

'What wrinkles?' Nancy exclaimed.

Dorothy tapped her index fingers to the corners of her eyes and cocked her head at Nancy. She then leant over to inspect her friend's face. 'Gosh, how dreadful. Girls, I think we should all chip in a few shillings to buy Nancy some Pond's cream next time we're in town. Who'll ever want to marry her when her face looks like a sultana?'

The girls burst into uproarious laughter. Betty looked across the room at Gwen. She was smiling, too. Finally. It hurt Betty's heart to see it.

'I think I might go to Batlow,' Gwen announced, and the room fell silent, every head turning to her as she spoke. 'It's closer to home in case … well, in case I need to get home. It's coming into apple-picking season and I like apples.'

Dear Gwen. Betty had thought she might find a special friend in Gwen and they'd been growing close until she'd received the news about Reggie. Since then, Betty had felt herself unprepared, naive even, about what to say to her friend. She hadn't been able to find the right words of comfort. She wanted to tell Gwen how brave she was to keep on going the way she had, to even think about continuing in the Land Army when she was still waiting for the second shoe to drop. That's what Betty's mum used to say, when one bad thing had already happened and you were waiting for the next bad thing. Or perhaps when you didn't want to think positive thoughts just in case. Betty had laid awake at night in their quarters, the soft sounds of snoring and sleep chatter all around her, thinking about Gwen—and how she herself would react if such news were to arrive about Michael.

Was it better to know or be in the dark? What if Reggie had already been dead for weeks? Was it better for Gwen to keep hope alive in her heart for him or think the worst?

Betty didn't know. She'd never had to think about such things before.

But she knew this much was true. She could be a friend to Gwen and, in that moment, she realised exactly how she would be that friend.

'I'll go to Batlow with you, Gwen. I like apples.'

From across the room, Gwen smiled happily. There was a pat on Betty's shoulder. Peggy. And then murmurs and *hear, hear*s and someone was proposing a toast.

They all raised their glasses of lemonade.

Peggy got to her feet. 'Isn't this a funny turn of events? Who would have thought that we shopgirls and secretaries and hairdressers would all know so much about the land?'

There was laughter and cheering.

She lifted her glass. 'To those who serve. To those who have been lost. And to those we keep in our hearts.'

The girls fell into a thoughtful reverie. Heads dipped. Prayers were uttered and one or two of the girls crossed themselves. Betty stole a quick glance at Gwen, who seemed to be praying the hardest of all.

'To the Stocks, who've been marvellous hosts.'

'Hear, hear.'

'And finally, to the Mildura sultana and currant season of January 1943. May you fill the fruit cakes of people all over Australia and every fruit cake shipped to our troops. And to you girls.' Peggy stopped. Every Land girl could see her eyes filling with tears. 'You've been absolutely smashing.'

Chapter Twenty-One

Lily

March 1943

'I bet you're glad you came, hey?'

Lily looked across the field at Kit. Kit was standing, her hands braced in the small of her back, stretching backwards and moaning. This was nothing like the cool valleys of Norton Summit. Port Noarlunga was flat plains and burning sun and sweat drizzling down her back all day. Their overalls were hot and the rubber boots on their feet made Lily's feet swell. They needed to wear gloves for protection and by the end of the day her hands were like prunes from the sweat.

But she was happier than she'd ever been. She was with Kit and a whole group of new Land Army girls in a hostel near the beach and they seemed to laugh all the time, despite how hard they were labouring.

'I wish I had a cherry or two so I could lob them at you,' Lily laughed.

'You'd miss. I've seen you play softball,' Kit retorted.

Lily looked out across the flax field at the hundreds of women undertaking the same back-breaking work. Harvesting flax was labour intensive. There were no tractors or ploughs, as each plant had to be pulled from the ground by hand and laid flat in a bundle to preserve the length of the fibres for processing.

'That's the important part, girls.' Mr Ellis, the manager of the flax mill, had taken time to instruct them on their first day. 'The plants will need to dry on the ground, and then you'll be retting them with water to loosen the outer stalk. The next step is scutching, which removes the stalk. And then comes heckling, before it all gets taken off to the mill for spinning.'

As Lily tugged the plants from the dry earth, grasping and pulling, her head was still spinning from all the new words she'd have to learn. She knew that if she didn't remember, she could always ask Kit. Kit seemed to know everything.

Lily straightened, wiped her sleeved arm across her forehead, lifted her straw hat and fanned her face. In the orchard, there had always been a cool spot under a tree or in the afternoon shadows as the sun lowered in the west. Out here, there wasn't a tree to be seen. She looked east, where the Adelaide Hills rose up from the flat plains. She was a long way from Norton Summit now, working between the hills and the ocean.

Oh, how she longed for a swim in the sea. She had packed a swimsuit, knowing the flax farm wasn't too far away, but hadn't yet had a day off or the means to get to the beach.

The girls had worked for two weeks straight without a day off. Her arms ached in a way they never had when she had been employed in the relative luxury of picking cherries.

There had been talk that there wouldn't be a day off for another fortnight. She wondered how she would make it through, but when those doubts gnawed at her, when the pain twinged and burnt, she remembered David and Susan and parachutes and canvas tents and linen thread.

'Kit,' Lily called out.

Kit stood up tall and grimaced. 'What?'

'What are you going to do when the war's over?' It was a game they played to pass the time during the long hot days, to distract themselves from the dust in their eyes and ears and mouths, from the scratchy dried stalks that were prickly to handle, from the heat and the war. It was a way of imagining the end of the fighting, when life might return to how it was before the war.

'I'm going to catch the train to Semaphore for an ice-cream and a swim.'

'I'm taking the boat to Paris,' someone else called out. 'I want to see the Eiffel Tower and those dancers at the Moulin Rouge.' A wit working nearby began to sing the can-can. 'Da-da-de-dah de-dah-dah …'

'And drink French champagne!'

The talk could go on all day. After they'd exhausted exotic locations and foods they'd missed, men they hadn't kissed— and men they had—the talk became simpler, closer to home. There were wishes for children and comfortable beds and jobs in an office and silk stockings or a new frock.

Lily didn't talk about David. His training continued in Mildura, which she was thankful for. He was due to complete his seventy-five hours in the sky by late April and then he would be off to the war. For now, she could still hold him close. She could still wish for a miracle, that the war might miraculously be over before he faced any real danger. But there seemed to be no hope of such a thing. At night at the hostel, there were tussles over the radio between those who wanted to listen to news of the war and those who didn't. Someone would always crank the dial away from *When A Girl Marries* and Lily would catch snatches of what was going on in the Pacific or in Europe. The Americans had had a victory against the Japanese in a place in the Pacific called Guadalcanal, and the Germans had surrendered to the Russians at Stalingrad. The announcers on the radio hinted that the tide was turning, but the Japanese and Germans weren't defeated yet. Nothing was going to happen in two short months, she'd come to realise, no matter how hard everyone wished it.

'When the war's over,' Lily grunted as she tugged a flax plant out of the ground and threw it flat, 'I plan to devour an entire pound of real butter on a batch of freshly baked scones.'

'And sweets,' Kit added. 'I'm going to head into Haigh's on Beehive Corner and buy a whole bag full of toffees. I won't even care if I make myself sick.'

There was a grunt and a rustle and a thud, and when Lily looked over, Kit was flat on her backside, her legs splayed, clutching a flax plant in her hand.

'You all right?' Lily called.

Kit laughed and swore. 'That sodding thing was stuck.'

In a flash, Lily was by her side, holding out her hand. Kit took it and got to her feet, her smile brighter than the sun blazing from the sky above.

Two months passed and the flax harvesting continued. The war had been raging for three and a half years by March 1943 when the girls had three days off in a row over Easter. The temptation had been to go to bed and not leave it for the entire time, but a morning tea had been arranged for them, put on by the YWCA. Lily was well equipped to make small talk with strangers, and made up for Kit's reticence to engage by dragging her by the arm and introducing her around.

Lily was regularly cheered by letters from home, in which her father expressed his pride in her role in such an important wartime occupation. She had developed the distinct impression that he hadn't believed that cherry picking was real war work but he could now boast to his colleagues and acquaintances that both his daughters were doing something vital for the war effort. He had taken to slipping clippings from *The Advertiser* between the pages of his letters, featuring articles that he thought might be of interest to Lily, and sometimes a crossword. She hated doing the crossword but appreciated that he was thinking of her, even if he didn't seem to know her at all.

At the end of April, when autumn had well and truly arrived and the breezes blowing off the ocean were chilling, Lily received her last letter from David before he shipped out.

My Dearest Lily,
Let me first say how proud I am of my wife for how hard you're working on the flax, a vital commodity for our services and especially for us pilots. When I told my commanding officer in Mildura here what you were up to in the Land

Army, he slapped his thigh in delight at knowing about such a thing. The knowledge of it helps me now, as I pack up and prepare to leave Mildura tomorrow. Thinking that you might have had a hand in creating the items that will keep me safe fills my heart with a deep pride and love. When I pull on my flying boots, I'll think about the thread that binds the upper to the leather sole. When I strap on my parachute and climb into a plane, it will be as if your arms are wrapped around me.

Lil, I can't put into words how much I miss you. When I think about how hasty we were, I can't fight the feeling that I've failed you. If only we lived in a time when our marriage hadn't had to be so rushed. We should have had a celebration with the finest food and bottles of champagne, with your family and mine present. I imagine that if we were living in different times, we might have sailed off to London for a honeymoon. I hope we will have the chance, one day soon, to be the honeymooners our circumstances denied us. We are young and one day should have the chance to celebrate what that means.

Kit sounds like a real card. I'm glad you've found such a friend. Promise me, won't you, that you won't lose touch with her? You'll need a friend in the event you get the worst news. I feel I should be honest and not shy away from saying these things. If I can't express my honest thoughts with my wife, who else? Kit will help you, as will my own father and mother. You would always be welcome at Millicent if I don't come home. I am in a melancholy mood as I write. It can be no surprise to you, I expect, that the war feels very real to me now. If the worst should happen, my darling Lily, know that I love you with all my heart and soul. You are in my thoughts always and in my dreams. Remember the poem?

She walks in beauty, like the night
Of cloudless climes and starry skies …

You are my beauty, Lily. You are my love and my hope. I couldn't be happier that you married me and my most sincere wish is to come home and be your husband once again.

You be brave and I'll be safe, remember?
I remain, as always, your loving and devoted husband,
David

Chapter Twenty-Two

Flora

March–August 1943

Two Rivers, Mildura
March 2nd, 1943
Dear Flora,
I hope this letter finds you well and that you've settled in to your new posting. Life is quiet around here without you, and we miss you at our table at dinner time. I don't know if my mother has adjusted to cooking for only four of us again: we always seem to have so many leftovers. She sends her regards, by the way, as she is aware I am writing to you. Violet and Daisy ask after you often, and I have to remind them that there are no grapes left to pick now and that you're off helping another family. My answer always seems to make them a bit down in the dumps. It is wrong for so many reasons to wish you back here next year, because we are all hoping that the war might be over by then, but you would be so welcome.

Violet is making great strides with her reading and Daisy is a champion mathematician, according to her teacher. They're so young still and I've tried to keep them away from the truth of what's going on abroad; but that's a hard ask when children at school are being asked to collect rubber for the rubber drive and to do without because of rationing. It's a parent's instinct to keep their children safe, isn't it? I try to imagine a future for them, one that's lived in peace, but when the radio and the newspapers are full of such bad news from Europe and the Pacific, it's hard to be hopeful.

Still, we go on, day by day, doing our best.

Flora, I hope Frank is safe, wherever he is. The girls say a prayer for him every night, and for all the boys who are abroad. I hope to hear from you soon.

Fond regards,

Charles

Geelong, Victoria

April 4th, 1943

Dear Charles,

How lovely it was to receive your letter with all the latest news from Two Rivers.

Please encourage Violet to keep up her reading and Daisy to continue working on her sums. With that ability, she'll have every chance of securing a good job in an office once she's finished with school.

I'm safely here in Geelong with Mrs and Mrs Thompson on their farm. They're both getting on in years and with two sons in the merchant navy, they've needed some help with general chores around the farm. You'll no doubt laugh when I tell you that one of my jobs is to feed the chooks, something I managed to studiously avoid at Two Rivers. The best piece *of advice Mr Thompson gave me was to take a broom when I go into the chook shed. It's quite the scene when hundreds of chooks come at you all at once, flying and scratching, which was a bit frightening at first. Not to mention noisy! Making up the chook mash is another thing altogether. Your stomach will turn at the recipe: a boiled sheep's head, vegetable peelings, pollard and bran all mixed together in a sludge. If I wasn't so hungry at the end of the day I swear I might never eat an egg again, but there it is. Beggars can't be choosers, as they say. I've also learnt a new skill: chopping firewood. I have the muscles of a man now, you'll be shocked to know. Honestly, I've been so tired at the end of each day, that it's all I can do to write a letter or two before falling asleep. Still, it's good honest work and the Thompsons have been very welcoming. Just as I did at Two Rivers, I have a room of my own and a comfortable bed. There's not much more a Land Army girl can ask for.*

Well, I'm afraid there's not much else to report. Please say my hellos to your mother (tell her I miss her cooking dreadfully) and to the girls. I think about you all often, and I especially miss the evenings we spent in your sitting room, playing cards and listening to jazz.

With fondest regards,

Flora

Two Rivers

June 14th, 1943

Dear Flora,

I hope this letter finds you in good health and that you're staying away from those dangerous chooks. I know how hard you've been working so all of us here very much appreciate you making the time to reply to our letters and telling us how you're getting on.

The pruning is over and it feels like winter now, even though we are officially only two weeks in. As you can imagine, the nights are cold and the days short. It seems cruel that we've been in drought for as long as the war has been raging, but there it is, and there's no rain in sight. Without irrigation, Two Rivers wouldn't have crops and many of the growers around here are all in the same boat. We wish for peace and we pray for rain in equal measure.

I've been meaning to tell you that I've read the Agatha Christie book you left, Evil Under The Sun, *and I enjoyed it very much. The librarian at the Carnegie Library in Mildura is keeping an eye out for any others for me. Is there another you could recommend? There are many long hours to fill between dinner and bedtime these days. I often find I'm alone in the sitting room and I found reading the book you had loved a great comfort.*

My mother has been teaching the girls to bake and they've filled many hours when the weather is wet and cold outside. So far, they've presented me with jumbles, melting moments, and Anzac biscuits back in April, which were both appropriate and delicious.

I also have some sad news to share. You might remember Mr Henwood from your time here in Two Rivers? He was informed a few weeks ago that his grandson, serving with the AIF, was killed in Malaya. It has brought a pall of sadness to all of us here. I hope all the news of your brother has been good and I wish him godspeed and a safe return to Australia when the war ends.

Fondest regards,

Charles Nettlefold

It was raining steadily and heavily the day Flora and Jack Atkins buried their father at the Burwood Cemetery on 4 August 1943. Great grey clouds hung low and ominous over Melbourne and a chill wind buffeted all those who'd come to pay their respects: the Whites, the Craigies, the Plummers and the Tilleys from Waterloo Street; workmates of her father's from the council; relatives from her father's side of the family who she hadn't seen in a decade; and two of her cousins from her mother's side, the son and daughter of her aunt from Traralgon, who'd offered warm embraces and words of solace. It was the next closest thing to having her mother with her on such a terrible day, and she clung to them during the service.

For Flora the past five days had been a blur of tears and grief and coming to the heartbreaking understanding that she and her brothers were orphans now. With both their parents gone, Flora felt the immense weight of responsibility and duty, more than she ever had, to ensure that the ties that bound them would never loosen or come undone. She was the oldest, the girl, the one on whom the onus fell to keep the Atkins family together.

'Another cuppa, Flor?'

Flora looked up. Jack stood in the doorway to the living room in Waterloo Street. Outside, the rain continued to lash at the windows and the bare branches of the frangipani scraped against the glass.

'Yes, thanks, Jack.'

'Won't be a moment.' He nodded and went to the kitchen.

Flora sat back on the sofa opposite her father's favourite chair. His bakelite ashtray still sat on the table next to it, clean and empty, and a copy of *The Age* from the day he'd died, the thirty-first of July, was folded on the table, untouched since Jack had found him, cold and blue, in his chair.

She'd been feeding the chooks at the Thompsons in Geelong the next morning when the local superintendent from the Land Army arrived with a message for her. Mr Thompson had solemnly summoned her back to the house, telling her someone from the Land Army was there to see her. She barely remembered it now, that five-minute walk, her thoughts scattered and confused, fearing the worst about Frank, having imagined a thousand times that this day might come and being caught completely unprepared anyway. Was this how she was to find out about her brother's death? From a total stranger?

She'd stepped into the kitchen. A woman in a khaki uniform sat with Mrs Thompson, who was clutching a handkerchief to her mouth.

'You have news for me?' Flora asked, trying to be strong and capable and stoic when inside she felt nothing but dread.

The superintendent cleared her throat and stood. 'Your brother, Mr Jack Atkins, is urgently trying to get a message to you.'

Flora felt every limb turn to stone.

'Oh, Flora,' Mrs Thompson murmured. 'If only we had a telephone, you could call him right now.'

'It's your father, I'm afraid, Miss Atkins.'

The superintendent drove Flora in to Geelong to the office of the Manpower Directorate so she could use their telephone. Through his own tears, Jack told her that their father had died the night before, in his favourite chair by the fire.

'A stroke, the doctor said,' Jack had told her. 'I was out at the Tivoli and he was happy as Larry when I left him. When I got home …'

'I'm coming, Jack. I'm coming home.'

Flora's heart broke at the thought that her father had been all alone with the wireless, his son Frank and his wife, pictured at eighteen years old in her wedding dress, looking down over him from the mantelpiece.

Jack carried Flora's cup of tea to her and she reached out for it. The cup clinked on the saucer and she sipped the hot brew, trying to steady herself. Jack sat next to her.

'Do you think Frank got the telegram?' he asked. 'That he knows?'

'I'm sure he has,' Flora replied, although she had no sure knowledge that the telegram they'd sent from the Camberwell post office the day she'd returned home on compassionate leave had yet reached him in the jungle.

'He'll let us know, won't he?' Jack asked, sniffing, his voice far away. 'I can't think about how hard that'll hit him. Not being able to be here. For today, especially.'

Flora had thought the same thing, had obsessed over it during each dark and frigid night since she'd been back at Waterloo Street, sobbing under the blankets in her old room, having tried too hard to hold on to her grief until she could be sure Jack in the next room was asleep.

He would be alone now in this house full of memories, of ghosts. She would come back to him. Once the war was over, and her stint in the Land Army was complete, she would come back to Camberwell and be the family that he had lost.

'Mrs Tilley left some biscuits,' Jack said. 'You want one?'

Flora shook her head. 'I'm not really hungry, to be honest.'

Jack shrugged. 'Me neither.' And then he stood wearily, checking his watch. 'I'm going down the pub for a pot or two before closing. You don't mind do you? A few of the blokes from work said they'd be there.'

Flora reached for his hand and squeezed it. 'You go.' It would do him good to spend some time with his friends after having spent four days with his sister, helping her see to the funeral arrangements.

'Won't be long,' he said, before bundling himself into his heavy winter coat, jamming his flat cap on his head and closing the front door hard behind him.

When the house was quiet again, Flora found her note-paper and a pencil and went to the kitchen to sit at the table. She glanced around at all that was so familiar. The china sugar bowl. Her father's favourite teacup in the drainer on the kitchen sink. The floral curtains at the window. The Coolgardie safe that didn't need ice in this weather. Her father's map pinned to the back of the kitchen door that he'd marked with an X every time he'd heard news on the wireless about Frank's regiment.

Tears welled and she let them fall. She missed Charles. She missed the happiness that had bloomed inside her when she'd been at Two Rivers. She missed her mother and her father and her youngest brother.

She pressed the pencil to the page and started.

Camberwell
August 4th, 1943
Dear Charles,
We are all grief-stricken here at Waterloo Street. Today Jack and I buried our father. It was sudden, which was a blessing,

but that doesn't make his loss any easier to bear, as I'm sure you understand.

Jack and I have spent the past few days talking of our parents and our memories of the happy life they created for their children. There is some comfort in knowing that they are together once again. Jack will stay on in the family home in Camberwell and when I'm finished with my Land Army work, I shall come back to this house too. Frank's room will always be here waiting for him, exactly as he left it, and the three of us will muddle along as best we can when things go back to the way they were before the war.

I have one more week before my compassionate leave ends and I'm back to the Thompsons. I'm hoping the hard work will be a distraction from too many thoughts about those who are lost and far away.

I was very sorry to hear the news about Mr Henwood's grandson. It seems like death is stalking us all.

Please pass on my kindest regards to Mrs Nettlefold and the girls. Tell them I wish I was there to taste all those new biscuits, which sound delicious.

Charles, I wish you were here so I could borrow some of your strength. I need it now more than ever.

With kindest regards,

Flora

P.S. I hope you find the enclosed useful. I had become quite proficient at knitting socks before the Land Army and I've had some time in the evenings since I've been home. It was comforting to take up my needles again. I apologise for the colour. All I have is khaki wool, I'm afraid.

Two Rivers
August 10th, 1943
My dearest Flora,

I received your letter today and I couldn't wait a moment longer to write to you to express my most sincere sympathies to you and your brothers on the death of your beloved father. I wish I could offer more comfort to you than words scratched out in pencil on a page. I know, from the loss of my own dear father and my wife all those years ago, that you will come to a point where you will be able to think of them with a smile instead of tears. When you reminisce, you'll remember their best moments, not their last. It's an extra burden you bear being the oldest sibling, even more so because you have been like a mother to your two brothers. I don't believe a man ever gets over the loss of his father. It will take a toll for the rest of their lives, but it will be a reassurance to them both that they have you. I've told my mother your sad news and she also sends her deepest condolences. He must have been a very proud man indeed to have two of his children serving their country.

You are a caring and generous woman, Flora, and I know you will recover too. Will you allow me to distract you from your grief with some news from Two Rivers? It was my birthday last week and Mother and the girls baked a sultana cake. I have a piece of it, spread with a thick slice of butter, on the plate next to me while I write this letter to you.

I am in the kitchen, alone. Everyone else is long in bed. I enjoy the solitude, I must admit, when the rest of the house is asleep and I have time to think. Rain is loud on the roof overhead, such a welcome sound, and when I close my eyes I imagine it to be the percussion of a New York jazz band, the very one I last heard with you in the sitting room here at Two Rivers. The fire from the wood stove is warming and I'm not too far away from the kettle for a cup of tea, or the cake in the event I feel like another slice. The socks you sent with your last letter are warm and a perfect fit. You can't imagine my surprise when I opened the package and found them inside. You really are very generous.

My birthday, and indeed your sad news, has given me pause to look back and reflect on my life, which I have been doing in earnest these past few months. I have turned thirty-six years old, which is an age my father never had the good fortune to reach. It is a sobering thought. I do feel very fortunate to still have my mother and my daughters even though we feel his absence regularly, my mother especially.

Daisy celebrated her seventh birthday yesterday. Her grandmother knitted her a new cardigan, in the brightest of autumn grapevine orange with matching buttons, and Daisy didn't take it off, even for bed.

Flora, Daisy's birthday is also the anniversary of the death of my wife, Harriet. We spoke only briefly of her when you were here back in February, but tonight I'm of a mind to talk to someone about her and I apologise that it is you I am telling. I know you will understand.

As you might imagine, it is a day filled with both happiness and grief for me. She was very much loved and we had a very happy marriage. The girls, sadly, don't remember her at all. Violet was only eighteen months old when her mother died. As you would have seen for yourself, my mother has been their mother since then, a role she has carried out with the deepest love and affection. I don't know what we would have done without her.

I suppose what I'm trying to say is that life goes on, Flora. We have to bounce back after tragedy because there's no other choice, is there?

Things with the war are looking more positive, it seems, with the Allies making headway in the Pacific, island by island, but sadly there seems to be no end in immediate sight. This of course means your dedicated work with the Land Army will go on for the time being and your brother will continue to serve. I think of Frank often and feel very sad that he received such tragic news while he was so far away from home. You told me once that he is a cheeky young man. I hope his strength, courage and good humour stand him in good stead for a safe return. I should like to meet him when the war is over. From all you've told me about him, I'm sure we would be the best of mates.

Flora, my thoughts are with you always, especially at such a time.

I know you'll be returning to Geelong soon (you may already be there when you receive this letter) and to your farm work, but I hope you find the time to reply. I anticipate the post perhaps more than I ever have done before, in hope that every trip I make into Mildura delivers an envelope bearing your name.

Please know that any news, no matter how much delayed, can be a reassurance and very much appreciated and treasured by its recipient.

With fondest regards,

Charles

P.S. The pressed flower with this letter is from the front garden at Two Rivers. The roses continue to bloom, even in the drought. I hope it reminds you that life goes on, even when times are the toughest.

Chapter Twenty-Three

January 1944

Flora peered through the dust-streaked window of the train to check that she was only two stops from Mildura. She studied the timetable in her hands. This was Red Cliffs and there was only Irymple to go before she would be back.

It had been eleven months since she'd seen Charles and she was nervous and excited and cautious all at once. He had promised in his most recent letter that he would be waiting for her at the station and she didn't doubt his word. They had written to each other faithfully since she'd left Two Rivers the previous summer. Letters from Frank abroad were sporadic, and Jack wrote occasionally, but Charles had been a regular and faithful correspondent. Sometimes their letters to each other had been quick notes filled with good wishes; at other times, there had been pages and pages of sincere outpourings of sadness and grief. Flora had kept every single letter from Charles. They were packed in her suitcase in the baggage carriage; she hadn't cared about sacrificing a couple of books to fit them in. It had been worth it to carry Charles with her as she'd travelled the country.

Was she surprised to still be working in the Land Army? Unfortunately not. Progress in the war seemed to be glacial and to Flora it seemed everyone had become more reluctant than ever to wish it over for fear of being disappointed once again. All she could allow herself was the wish that the world was one year closer to the end of the war. Along with the 'Happy New Years' people had called to each other, there was a fervent wish to be strong, to carry on, with more perseverance and courage than they'd ever known.

She continued to wish for a victorious peace, for a time when the war was won, when Frank and so many other boys would be home, when order would be restored to her world.

When the war was won.

Flora had found herself looking both backwards and forwards since the New Year celebrations; back with a sense of pride in her work and grief at the loss of her father, but forwards with tremulous hope. When she'd arrived in Mildura the year before, she'd harboured naive expectations that the war would be over by now, and that she wouldn't be needed at Two Rivers again. But no one had come home from New Guinea, unless they were dead. Australian troops were still held in prisoner-of-war camps in Europe and through South-East Asia. And even though the Russians were driving the Germans out of the Ukraine and Italy had fallen and the Allies were closing in on the Axis powers, no one dared yet predict an Allied victory.

Flora had left the Thompsons' farm the week before Christmas to be home in Melbourne with Jack. She wouldn't be going back to Geelong. Mr Thompson had died suddenly of influenza in early November and Mrs Thompson had decided to sell up and move to Traralgon to live with one of her daughters. Flora had stayed until all the chickens had been sold off and she had written to Charles to let him know she'd be back at Two Rivers in early January if she was needed. His reply had been swift. 'Your room is waiting,' he'd written. 'As I am, with great anticipation.'

Christmas in Camberwell had been a sombre evening with a roast chicken and a dull-tasting Christmas pudding with no custard. She and Jack had exchanged presents, books and biscuits, and talked of their father and brother. They'd listened to the king's Christmas message and carols on the wireless with a glass of sherry and a toast to absent friends. There had been nothing fancy or generous about their gifts to each other. They'd had an unspoken understanding that they would be frugal, that they could only truly celebrate Christmas when Frank was home for good.

Flora had spent the week between Christmas and New Year scrubbing the house from top to bottom and clearing out the last of their father's clothes, something Jack had promised he would do but hadn't been able to face. She'd tidied up the long-dead Victory Garden and had visited Mrs Jones next door for afternoon tea, and the older woman talked for a long time about how much she missed Flora and Jack's father and then cried into her neatly pressed handkerchief.

New Year's Eve was hot and Flora and Jack had celebrated the passing of the year with a trip to St Kilda on crowded trams to eat an ice-cream and dip their feet in the ocean. Flora had refused to ride the Big Dipper at Luna Park, despite Jack's urging, and could barely watch it shoot into the sky and then plunge back down without feeling sick. Jack teased her about it good-naturedly, and after he'd ridden it twice he took off into the city to meet his latest sweetheart, Doreen. Flora hadn't minded going home on her own. It was only when she'd turned the key in the front door and walked into the empty house, still smelling of her father's tobacco, that she felt the urge to run to Two Rivers and all that was familiar there. The Camberwell house she'd grown up in didn't feel like home any more. Her father wouldn't be sitting in the kitchen with his newspaper when she got home from work. He would never sit in his favourite chair again, smoking into the evening, listening to the latest news from the war. And most heartbreaking of all, he would never know the fate of his youngest child.

When Flora opened her eyes in the mornings, she'd fought the sense of sad disappointment that she wasn't seeing the ceiling in the sleep-out at the Nettlefolds' house in Two Rivers. It had a hold on her now, that place, with its red dirt and its blue skies and its vines and its freedoms.

Back in November, Jack had posted a Christmas parcel to Frank, filled with a fruit cake, new socks, a comb, a toothbrush and toothpaste, some new pencils and a note-pad. Flora found herself obsessing over whether or not he'd received it. A distance seemed to be growing between them that was out of her control, and infuriating. Would he think his brother and sister had forgotten him? They'd exchanged quick telegrams to tell him about their father, but Frank's letters had become more infrequent during the past year, and with every week that passed without any news, Flora had battled with her thoughts about why. And then a letter would arrive, filled with jolly details about the heat and the rain and the hijinks Frank had been up to with Shorty and Johnno and Westie, and Flora had cried with relief and let herself believe the lie that he wasn't anywhere near the action. And then the wait would begin all over again.

On the second of January, Jack had announced to Flora that he and Doreen were engaged. They'd met at a dance at the Rialto and she'd been dazzled by his jazz foxtrot. And clearly much more, judging by the way she barely uttered a word and simply gazed at him all through dinner.

'But we're going to wait until after the war to get married,' Jack had told her as he'd reached across the table for Doreen's hand. 'I can't marry this lass without Frank as my best man, can I?'

To celebrate, the three of them had a special dinner at the Canton Tower Cafe on Bourke Street. Flora tasted dim sims and Chow Min for the first time and then cried with happiness for her brother and his fiancée.

The train chugged to a stop at a siding to unload boxes of cargo. Flora stepped into the aisle, stretching, staring out to the hot distance, crops of wheat tall and still in the heat.

As her destination grew closer, Flora thought over how much the war had changed her life in every conceivable way. What would she be doing right now if there was no war to fight, no enemy to defeat, no deaths to avenge, no country to protect? Frank wouldn't be abroad and in danger. Jack wouldn't have received the white feather and she would still be working at Mr McInerney's. There would have been no need for the Land Army and she wouldn't have met Charles. Guilt and happiness battled in her heart at the thought.

She had barely been able to keep a straight thought in her mind the past week, in anticipation of returning to the place she loved. Two Rivers really had spoilt her for any other posting. How had Charles and his family celebrated Christmas and New Year? She had some presents for them all tucked in her suitcase and then worried that it was presumptuous. Was it wrong to feel so elated about going back to Two Rivers?

The train slowed and pulled into Mildura station, its horn sounding as it screeched and came to a stop. She searched the crowd and her heart leapt when she saw Violet and Daisy shouting and waving at her and when she could focus through her sudden tears, she read the words on the piece of paper Daisy was holding above her head: *Welcome back Miss Atkins*. She replied with a happy wave and the girls hopped on the spot. Happiness bubbled up inside Flora and came out with a laugh and a cry. She gathered up her book and her handbag, set her Land Army hat on her head with a quick shove, and stepped off the carriage into a bustling crowd. A family was weeping over a soldier on crutches; postal staff unloaded bulky canvas bags onto a trolley; a pair of bosomy older ladies heaved their hold-alls along the platform; and a gaggle of Boy Scouts chatted excitedly about an adventure in the country.

And then, two little girls' spindly arms were around her waist, clutching at her, giggling into her skirt. She threw her arms around them, laughing and happy, surprised and overwhelmed by their reaction.

'Look, Daddy. Here she is!'

'Hello, girls. Oh, you look so well, both of you. And so grown-up! I can't believe my eyes. Daisy, where are your plaits?' Flora tugged at the little girl's new bob cut.

Daisy shook her head from side to side, flicking her hair out. 'Nan cut them off. I was tired of having long hair. And it looks just like yours, Miss Atkins.'

'Why, it does, too. And Violet. You're almost as tall as me. It must be all this fresh air.'

Violet peered up at Flora. 'No, I'm not!'

'You will be soon, I'm certain of it. Now, a little bird has told me that you've learnt to bake since I was last here. I can't wait to try some of your biscuits.'

Daisy's eyes widened and she looked as if she might faint. 'We baked some with Nan this morning!'

'Well, that's lucky, isn't it.' The girls didn't seem to want to let go of her and Flora found she didn't mind very much at all.

'The tooth fairy came lots of times this year,' Daisy tried to whisper as she pulled her lips back and tapped an index finger against her little white teeth.

Flora peered into her mouth. 'I can see. I hope you put all those pennies in your piggy bank.'

'We're on summer holidays,' Violet announced. 'I've had lots of time for books, Miss Atkins. I'm reading *Mary Poppins* for the second time. Have you read it?'

'No, I can't say that I have. Will you tell me all about it?'

'And we can't wait to hear what you've been up to.' Charles's deep voice seemed to echo right inside her. She lifted her gaze from the girls' beaming faces to discover Charles smiling at her. Looking as strapping as a eucalypt, he slipped off his hat and nodded, his smile creasing his tanned face. She looked him over with a quick glance. He'd barely changed. His face was as familiar to her as if she'd last seen him only the day before. The laugh lines at the corners of his eyes were streaks of tan and pale skin. His blue eyes matched the wide sky above and he'd pulled his lips together but it didn't stop them curving into the warmest smile. If anything, he looked happier than when she'd seen him last, his stance less hunched. Was it possible for a man of thirty-six years to have grown taller? Was he still as dear to her as he had been in January 1943? More than she had ever expected or believed was possible.

'Hello, Charles,' Flora managed. Something was buzzing in her ears.

'Welcome back,' he said.

'I'm so happy to be here.'

'Come now, girls.' Charles laid a hand on each daughter's shoulder and gently urged them away from Flora. And then he looked into her eyes. His expression transformed from fatherly approbation directed to his daughters into a broad smile just for her and she was suddenly holding her breath.

'Shall we go? I'll find your suitcase.'

'Let's.'

The girls raced ahead of them through the dissipating crowd, and were already across the tracks and inside the Dodge, bouncing up and down on the back seat. Charles came towards her with her case, and they ambled along the platform.

Charles scuffed a shoe along the bitumen. 'You look very well, Flora.'

'You too. Although I think you might have a few more wrinkles.'

He raised an eyebrow in a teasing glance. 'Do I now?'

'Perhaps just a few.'

He spoke to his shoes but his words were meant only for her. 'I'm flattered you noticed.'

She held her breath. 'Of course I did.'

Across the tracks, the girls waved to them.

'Is Mrs Thompson all settled in Traralgon?'

'Yes, just before Christmas. The timing worked out for the best, actually. I needed to be home with Jack for Christmas.'

'I'm glad for you that you were.' Charles repositioned his hat. 'You deserved to be with your family. Flora ...' He stopped suddenly and Flora did too. Charles's chest rose and fell on a deep sigh. He stepped closer to her, lowering his voice. 'Please let me say once again how sorry I was to hear about your father.' He reached for her, a hand resting on her shoulder and giving it a gentle squeeze. 'I wish I'd had the chance to meet him.'

Her heartbeat quickened at his touch, at the implication of what he was saying. 'Thank you. It's been months now but when I think of home I still imagine him there, listening to the radio, drinking tea at the kitchen table. We had a deal. I used to give him my tobacco rations and in exchange I got extra tea.' Fresh tears welled in her eyes and she swiped them away before they drizzled down her cheeks in front of everyone.

Charles's hand drifted from her shoulder to her elbow, to her hand, grazing her fingers. 'It will take time. More time than you've had.'

Of course Charles knew about overcoming grief. They exchanged a knowing glance and Flora closed her eyes for a moment to acknowledge what he'd said.

'Did Melbourne change while you were away? Is it still filled with Americans?'

Flora was happy for the change of subject. 'Still busy. Still full of uniforms. It's funny but it feels too crowded for me now. I've grown so used to space all around me and a big sky and the smell of the earth, and vegetable crops far more productive than my sad little Victory Garden in the back yard at home. After my father … well, Jack takes absolutely no interest in war cabbage and tomatoes. What hadn't gone to seed was dead. I took the hoe to it and cleared all the weeds out when I was home.'

'Have you heard from Frank?'

'Yes. He's not much of a writer these days, but just before Christmas we received a funny little thing. A field service post card. It was small and grey and all it had was our address on one side and then a whole series of lines on the back to cross off if they didn't apply. Like code or something. Frank had left untouched the lines that said *I am quite well*. And *I have received your letter*. Jack and I were very grateful to see he'd put a big line through the words *I have been admitted to hospital*. So he's safe, as far as we know.'

'I suppose there's not much time for writing where he is,' Charles said, and the meaning of his words hung heavy in the air between them.

'No, I suppose not.'

'And Jack? How is he?'

Flora's spirits brightened. 'Oh, I almost forgot. He's engaged.'

Charles seemed inordinately pleased for a man he'd never met. 'Well, that's terrific news. Congratulations to him. Who's the lucky young lady?'

'Her name is Doreen and she's very sweet. She's a typist in the AWAS. She's completely besotted and so, should I say, is he. She doesn't give a jot that he wasn't able to go to war.'

'She sounds like a very special young woman. Think she'll be good enough for your Jack?"

Flora laughed. 'If she tries very hard, I believe she might be.'

They crossed the train tracks and could hear the girls calling out to them to hurry.

'Charles, I hope your Christmas tree is still up. I've brought presents and I thought … I thought we might have a delayed Christmas dinner.'

'You didn't need to do that,' he said.

'I wanted to. I love seeing the girls happy. I couldn't help myself.'

'Hurry up, Daddy.' Daisy was leaning out the car window. 'I'm hungry.'

He lowered his chin and shook his head, laughing ruefully. Flora laughed back at him. With her suitcase packed in the boot, Charles slipped behind the wheel and started up the car. The girls bounced up and down on the back seat, causing a cacophony of metallic squeaks in the cabin.

'Can we tell her now, Daddy?' Violet asked, excitement pitching her voice up an octave.

'We have a puppy,' Daisy whispered loudly.

Violet and Daisy almost leapt over the seat and into Flora's lap.

'He's black but we didn't want to call him Blackie.'

'Or Charlie, because that's Daddy's name.'

Charles chuckled.

'And Daisy wanted to call him Fluffy but I thought that sounded silly.'

'His name is Frank,' Daisy announced. 'But we call him Frankie, don't we, Daddy?'

Flora caught Charles's gaze. 'Yes, we do. He's very cheeky. We thought the name was just right. He's our good-luck charm, isn't he girls?'

Flora looked out the passenger window so the Nettlefolds didn't see her tears. 'From your lips to God's ear,' she whispered as they drove home to Two Rivers.

Mrs Nettlefold greeted her at the back door with a warm embrace and a scrutinising once-over. 'Look at you. Are you sure those people in Geelong have been feeding you right? You look wiry, my dear girl. I have scones just out of the oven. I know they're your favourite.'

'Thank you, Mrs Nettlefold. That's very kind. I hope the past year has treated you well.'

She gave a reluctant smile. 'I can't complain. Come to the kitchen when you're ready.' Flora couldn't miss Mrs Nettlefold's long glance at her son. The girls had run off into the vines and Charles was carrying Flora's suitcase in one hand and his hat in the other and as he strode towards the house, Flora watched him. She remembered his pale-blue collarless shirt from the previous summer, its sleeves rolled up to his elbows and his work trousers and dusty boots were a sign that he'd been working on the block before he'd gone into Mildura to pick her up. He was a good man. A fine man, who'd made a life with his daughters and his mother there at Two Rivers. His letters had revealed to her that it hadn't been the life he'd expected, and Flora had immediately understood what he'd meant. If either of them had had the luxury of choice, they would never have wished to have met each other under these circumstances.

'Miss Atkins!' Violet emerged from the vines with a wriggling, furry, pitch-black bundle in her arms.

'So this must be Frankie,' Flora cooed. He looked as if he might have a touch of labrador in him, with his broad head and soft ears. His paws were already huge. She tugged on one of them and leant down to press her lips to the top of his head, and before she could jump back he'd licked her nose with a loud slurp and then wriggled free. When he gambolled off into the vines, Violet and Daisy dashed after him and he answered their shrieks of laughter and giggles with playful little barks.

Flora looked around and breathed in the scent of earth and fresh air and space. The chickens were scratching in the dirt of the hen house as they had the past January. Marjorie was right there in her usual place chewing cud under the peppercorn tree but there was something new under its weeping branches. A bench and a round table. Flora walked over to it and sat on the rough-hewn seat. From her vantage point, she could see the vista she'd dreamt about almost every night since January. Rows and rows of vines in lines that snaked away into a blur. The crisp and warm blue sky overhead, still cloudless. The river way beyond in the distance.

The back door slammed and she looked up. Charles was walking towards her, his long loping stride so familiar, his smile broadening the closer he came.

'I see you've gone and ruined my surprise,' he called to her.

'I have?'

He waved a hand. 'That is my Christmas present to you.'

'This bench?' Flora ran a flat hand over it, a slab of river red gum, its surface rough and old and as red as the earth.

He came to sit beside her, close enough that his arm brushed her shoulder. 'Merry Christmas, Flora.'

They sat in silence for a long while, taking in the quiet and the view. Flora took off her Land Army hat and ruffled her hair. Charles reached for it and she passed it to him.

'What would we have done without the Land Army?' He rubbed a thumb over the badge pinned to the crown of her hat. 'Me and all the other fruit blocks in the district.' He cocked his head to the vines. 'They're not far off being ripe. A couple of days, I reckon. You'll have plenty of time before then to sit here and look at the view.'

'That sounds just perfect to me. Maybe you'll sit with me, unless you have work to do.'

'I can make time.' Charles dropped her hat on his own head and raised his eyebrows in a question. 'What do you think?'

She laughed. 'I don't think it fits,' she said, and she tried to snatch it back from him but he was too fast and his fingers were around her wrist. Something shimmered deep inside her. Charles's breath seemed to catch. Then he loosened his grip, slid his fingers into hers.

'I found the tree down by the river. The drought, I reckon. It's taken a toll on the red gums along the banks. I hauled it up here behind the tractor. It gave me something do over winter. I needed something to distract myself, something to make the months fly.' His fingers entwined more tightly around hers.

It was too hot to shiver but she did. 'It's perfect. Although I'm not sure I'll be able to take it home in my suitcase.'

His booming laugh filled the air and Flora let herself feel truly happy for the first time in what seemed like forever.

Chapter Twenty - Four

'I don't like them.' Daisy sat on a leather bench in a shoe shop on Deakin Avenue in Mildura, pouting stubbornly. Charles, Flora and Violet stood at her side, staring down at the new pair of brown leather sandals that had just been strapped to her feet by the shoe fitter.

'It's not a question of liking them,' Charles told her, his expression stern. 'It's a question of size. You're back at school in a few weeks, Daisy, and your old sandals are no good.'

No one wanted to admit the truth: that Frankie had fossicked under Daisy's bed and chewed the straps apart. They couldn't bear to chastise the puppy so they ignored his misbehaviour entirely.

'They feel funny.'

'Mine feel fine,' Violet added, placing one foot in front of her as a ballerina might to admire the turn of her own ankle.

'You'll get used to them.' Charles turned to the shoe fitter. 'We'll take them. Thank you.'

Daisy burst into loud and frustrated tears. Charles frowned and Violet rolled her eyes. Flora gave Charles a subtle nod. 'Isn't Mrs Nettlefold after some brown shoe polish?'

He seemed confused for half a moment. 'Oh, yes. Violet, come and help me find some polish.' Violet dutifully followed her father. When they were out of earshot, Flora crouched down so she could look directly at Daisy.

'Can I let you in on a secret, Daisy?'

The little girl sniffled.

'When girls grow up big and strong, their feet grow, too. Your old shoes were already too small for your feet. Why, I saw you stub your big toe just last week when you were running back into the house from church on Sunday. Do you remember?'

Daisy nodded and slowly looked at Flora. 'Yes,' she sighed dramatically. 'It hurt.'

'You have a big-girl hairdo now and I think you need a pair of big-girl shoes. You'll be eight at your next birthday.' Flora guessed that reminding her of that fact might cheer her up and support Flora's somewhat flimsy argument. It seemed to be working. 'That's rather grown-up in my book.'

Daisy's lips began to curl into a smile. 'It is my birthday soon.'

Flora's heart clenched. Would this young girl ever have a birthday unclouded by the memory of her mother's death?

'That's right. Big-girl shoes for a big girl, don't you think?'

'Yes, Miss Atkins,' Daisy mumbled and hopped off the bench. She took three little hops, declared, 'They feel like real shoes,' and then raced after her father and her sister.

The shoe fitter gave Flora a thankful smile and, clutching a shoebox, followed Daisy to the counter and the till.

Flora swept her hair away from her forehead, letting herself feel a little bit proud of her achievement in calming Daisy. She hadn't had any experience with children before she'd come to Two Rivers but she seemed to be getting the hang of it. She heard whispering and stopped.

'She's one of those Land Army girls, isn't she?' It was said with a hiss of derision.

'Yes, she is, but where's her uniform?'

'Aren't they supposed to wear them when they're out and about? Look at her, in those worn trousers and that floral shirt. And what are those things on her feet? Plimsolls?'

'I swear that's the same girl I saw at the Red Cross ball last year. Interesting that she's come back to the Nettlefolds.'

Flora felt a surge of something she hadn't felt in a very long time. Her jaw tightened and her teeth ground against each other.

'Those Land Army girls say they're up here to work, but I think they're here to find themselves husbands. Charles Nettlefold is a catch, isn't he? A widower and all. One of the girls from Stocks' stole Mrs Geraghty's husband right out from under her last year. He up and left his poor wife and two children. Off to Sydney, they went. Utterly shameful.'

'Who knows what sort of work she's really doing out there on that fruit block.'

Flora's fingers clenched into fists. She breathed deep to stop herself saying something she would regret later. She was a Land Army girl, even if she wasn't wearing the uniform that day while she was out on her own time shopping. Being a member of the Women's Land Army meant she had a reputation to maintain and a standard to uphold in this community so she held her tongue and kept her head held high. She turned on her heel and strode past the two gossip-mongers. 'Good afternoon, ladies,' she said with a forced smile before leaving them in her wake and pushing open the door with both hands splayed on the glass.

She stood on the footpath, trying to collect herself. How could those women be so unkind? Land girls had left their homes, their other jobs and their families to come out to the country to work. Their labour had saved farmers in this dis-trict and no doubt hundreds of others around the country. Flora had never expected platitudes or parades but a little common decency and respect would have been appreciated. She'd put her whole life on hold while Australians fought in a thousand places around the world and those women could only believe that Flora and all the other Land girls had sacrificed their city lives just to find a man. She would have expected more from women. How many other people in Mildura thought the same? Had she been the subject of gossip last year too? She remembered old Mr Henwood and what he'd said, that she wouldn't last a week.

And then, in a flash, she remembered that Charles had written to her about him, telling her that he'd lost a grandson.

Her anger drained only to be replaced by a wave of despair. Perhaps those gossipmongers hadn't been touched by loss. How lucky they were when so many around them had. How could they not find it in themselves to be kind?

The bell above the door sounded and Violet and Daisy ran to her. She turned, quickly trying to find a smile for them. 'All done?' she asked.

'Daddy says we can have a banana sundae,' Violet said.

Daisy piped up. 'I'm going to walk there in my new shoes.'

'That … that sounds delicious.' Flora's voice faltered

'Is something the matter, Flora?' Charles murmured, bringing a comforting hand to rest on her shoulder.

She straightened. 'Nothing that some ice-cream won't remedy.'

The week passed in a blur. Flora and Charles had begun to work seamlessly together. During the hot days, they picked bucket after bucket load of fruit, and he had taught her how to properly mix the emulsion for spraying on the grapes to aid the drying process and provide Two Rivers with plump, luscious sultanas and currants to sell to the co-op. Although she worked hard and she still ached at the end of every day, nothing had felt less like work to Flora in her life. She was out in the fresh air doing something useful. She could see for herself how much she was contributing to the operations of Two Rivers and its income, and she felt part of a family. She'd almost forgotten what it was like to have a mother fuss over her, and liked that Mrs Nettlefold did. She washed Flora's clothes, although she wasn't supposed to, and made it a point to include Flora in the activities of the household. When Mrs Nettlefold wrote her shopping lists, she asked Flora what she might like for dinner. And when she had discovered Flora's favourite biscuits were melting moments, she'd baked a batch of them at least twice a week. Flora had devoured them with immense gratitude. She hadn't been able to make them back home since rationing had been introduced. It was only in the country, with ready access to a cow to make one's own butter, that a cook could even think of using six ounces of it on something for afternoon tea.

And the girls?

They were the sweetest, smartest little things. While Flora and Charles worked, Violet and Daisy carried glasses of freshly squeezed grape juice to them at all times of the day. They hid in the vines, imagining themselves to be pirates, and when Flora had turned some pages from an old newspaper into a buccaneer's hat for her, Daisy had worn it for two days straight until the thin paper ripped. Of course, everywhere they went Frankie gambolled after them but he quite liked a rub behind the ears every now and then from Flora. In the afternoons, after a day's worth of adventures, Violet, Daisy and Frankie collapsed from the heat and the exertion and slept peacefully on a blanket under the peppercorn tree.

It seemed an idyllic life, and when Flora looked up the rows of vines leading in straight lines to the peppercorn tree, where the little ones slept, and the house, which had become such a welcome home, she thanked her lucky stars that she'd come to such a wonderful place.

And then there was Charles. Their letters to each other had brought them closer, but the nearness of him now caused a physical ache. He was so close but she dared not reach for him, couldn't make that leap into the unknown, not now, not with so much up in the air.

Late on Friday afternoon, Charles and Flora strolled up to the house, satisfied with another day's labours. He was by her side and she playfully copied his stride length, which she was sure made her look like a clown, and when he realised, he stopped, leant over and belly laughed. The sound of it sent a flash of heat through her, into every finger and toe.

She loved that she could make him laugh and feel joy at such a simple thing.

'Flora,' he managed through his laughter.

'I'm glad you have the energy to laugh.' She chuckled. 'I'm exhausted. All I want is to strip out of these filthy clothes and soak in a hot bath until I wrinkle up like one of your sultanas.'

His eyes flared wide and he grinned. 'I'm sure that can be arranged.'

'Good. I'll feel like a new woman,' she sighed.

'I quite like the one you are now.' Charles moved next to her and peered at her face. 'You've got freckles.' He lifted a hand and slowly stroked a gentle finger across her cheeks and the bridge of her nose. Her heart beat faster at his touch.

'When I was a child, Daisy's age, I used to wish them away and took to scrubbing my face with Lux soap to get rid of them.'

He tugged at her earlobe and tucked a strand of hair behind her ear, studying every inch of her face. Flora swallowed hard. She tightened her fingers into fists to stop herself reaching out to splay her hands across his chest. Or run them down his muscular arms.

'I don't want you to change a thing.' His voice was little more than a murmur.

The sun was lowering in the west and there were shadows in the vines. A cooling breeze swept over them and Flora's shirt fluttered against her body. Charles's eyes dipped to the curve of her breasts and he took in a deep breath as he moved closer, a whisper away, and his lips parted on a word. She could almost taste him, he was that close.

'Daddy!'

Charles turned away and cleared his throat. Frankie was suddenly at Flora's feet, a black smudge, jumping up at her, barking, scratching her bare legs, his tail wagging wildly.

'Daisy.' Charles reached down and scooped his daughter up in his arms. She kissed him three times on his forehead and he laughed. 'Only three kisses?'

She giggled and gave him two more.

'That's better. Where's your sister?'

'She's in the kitchen. Are you finished working for today, Daddy?'

Charles met Flora's gaze. 'Yes. We were just on our way up to the house. Miss Atkins wants to have a bath. She's been working so hard all week and I think she deserves it, don't you?'

'Yes. I like baths. C'mon Frankie.'

Charles headed back to the house, Daisy in his arms, their dog trotting at their feet.

Flora turned in the opposite direction, striding fast over the red earth, walking deeper into the vines. She needed time to think about what had just almost happened. Charles had been about to kiss her and she had wanted him to.

She was thirty-two years old and no man had ever kissed her. The idea that Charles wanted to was so hard to fathom. Flora wrapped her arms around her waist and felt the hot pricklings of frustration shimmer up her spine. She bit her lip and stomped along the grass, thinking, thinking, thinking.

When she returned to the house, her head a rumble of contradictions and confusion, she opened the back door to the sound of the bath running.

'That you, Flora?' Mrs Nettlefold called from the kitchen.

'Yes,' Flora cleared her throat. 'It's me.'

'The bath's all yours. Charles said you were looking forward to a soak. He put the taps on a while ago, so you'd better check if it's full enough for you.'

Flora ducked her head inside the small and practical bathroom. The water was steaming and the claw-footed bath was already half full. She quickly fetched her robe and a fresh bar of soap from her room, and when she closed the bathroom door behind her, she pressed her back to it with a contented sigh.

After dinner, the family retired to the sitting room. The girls were bathed and in their pyjamas, lying on the rug playing a fiercely contested game of snakes and ladders. Frankie, despite Mrs Nettlefold's objections about him being in the house, was curled up on one of Charles's old jumpers in the corner of the room. The girls had fashioned it into a bed of sorts by tying off the arms and stuffing the body with rags. Charles was reading the newspaper, freshly shaved, smelling clean and crisp from a cologne Flora hadn't noticed before, and Mrs Nettlefold sat in her favourite armchair, knitting. She'd pulled apart a couple of the girls' old jumpers to make a bigger one for Violet for the coming winter.

Flora had a book in her lap, but truth be told she hadn't absorbed a word. She and Charles were a playing a silent game, exchanging surreptitious glances at each other when they were sure his mother and the girls were too distracted to notice. When Charles put the paper down to turn on the radio, she watched him walk, studied his broad back as he leant over to twiddle the dial on the radiogram, the fabric stretching across the muscles in his legs, his tanned forearms revealed by the turned-up cuffs of his shirt.

She had never been a nail biter in her life but she nibbled on a thumbnail now in frustration.

'Miss Hadkins.'

She hadn't noticed Daisy in front of her, clutching a book. Flora recognised the cover. It was a book of Banjo Paterson's poems. Flora closed her Agatha Christie and put it on the side table next to her. She smoothed down the skirt on her cotton dress.

'Daisy.'

'Yes, Miss Hadkins?'

'I'm wondering if you might do something special for me.'

The girl looked up in awe.

'If it's all right with your father, perhaps you might like to call me Flora.'

Daisy's head spun to her father. 'Can I, Daddy?'

Charles's soft eyes creased in a smile. 'That's fine with me, if Miss Atkins approves.'

'I do. When you call me ...' she said, pausing and stifling a smile, 'Miss Hadkins, I feel like your teacher.'

'What about me, Miss Atkins? Can I call you Flora, too?' Violet piped up from the rug, her hand poised in the air to roll her dice.

'Of course you can.'

'In that case, Flora ...' Daisy dragged out the name as if she was getting used to the sound of it in her mouth. 'Can you please read me "Clancy of the Overflow"?' Then she yawned. It was close to bedtime for the playful little thing.

'I certainly can. Hop up on my lap here.'

Daisy opened the book to the right page.

Flora began.

*He had written him a letter which he had, for want of better
Knowledge, sent to where he met him down the Lachlan
years ago ...*

And as she read, Flora saw Charles from the corner of her
eye, sinking back into his armchair, looking on at the scene
with hooded eyelids, his chin in his hand. And as Flora listened
to the words of the poem she'd read so often, she had a new
clarity about her time at Two Rivers. Just as Clancy loved the
murmur of the breezes and the vision splendid of the sunlit
plans extended, the red Mildura earth was as familiar now to
her as the bitumen of dusty and dirty Melbourne's streets. How
on earth would she be able to go back to working for Mr McInerney in a stingy little office after the adventures she'd had?

Was her voice jittery or was it the pounding in her ears
that made it sound so?

*And I somehow rather fancy that I'd like to change with
Clancy,*

Like to take a turn at droving where the seasons come and go,
*While he faced the round eternal of the cash book and the
journal—*

Daisy sat up for the last line, her little voice a sing-song,

But I doubt he'd suit the office, Clancy, of The Overflow.

Flora closed the pages and Daisy leant back into her. She
smelled of soap and such pure, innocent loveliness that, without thinking, Flora nestled her nose in Daisy's hair and inhaled,
before planting a kiss on the top of her head. When she looked
up, Mrs Nettlefold and Charles were staring at her, wide-eyed.

'It's probably bedtime,' Flora said quickly, lifting Daisy
from her lap. She must have been drowsy for the little girl
already felt heavy.

Charles stood. 'Come on girls, I'll tuck you in. Say good-night to … Flora.'

The girls waved and Flora waved back. 'Sweet dreams,' she called after them and sat back in her armchair. Had she crossed a line? It had felt so natural to snuggle with Daisy, to kiss her, but perhaps she had gone too far. She moved to the edge of her chair, her hands folded in her lap.

'Mrs Nettlefold?'

'Yes?' Charles's mother looked up from her knitting, her face inscrutable.

'I apologise for cuddling Daisy the way I did just now. I saw how shocked you were. I shouldn't have been … so familiar. Next time, I'll remember my place here.'

Mrs Nettlefold's knitting needles stopped their clicking and her face softened. 'You don't need to apologise, dear girl. Someone else used to sit in that chair and read to Violet. That's all it was.'

'I'm so sorry.'

'You don't need to be. I promise.' Mrs Nettlefold tucked her knitting in a quilted bag at her feet and then rose slowly from her chair. 'I think I'm going to warm up some milk and then head to bed myself. Can I get you a cup?'

'No, thank you all the same. Sleep well, Mrs Nettlefold.'

'You too, Miss—'

Flora held up a hand. 'I'd like it if you called me Flora, too.'

'Flora.' And with a knowing smile, Mrs Nettlefold left the room and closed the door behind her.

Flora picked up her book but couldn't concentrate and slapped its pages closed. She nibbled at her thumbnail and then chided herself for it.

When the door opened, she looked up.

Chapter Twenty-Five

Charles softly closed the sitting-room door and stood across the room. He slipped his hands into the pockets of his trousers and watched as Flora stood and walked to him.

'Charles,' she whispered. 'I shouldn't have kissed Daisy. I'm so sorry.'

His gaze dropped to her mouth before returning to her eyes. 'Why shouldn't you have?'

'I'm here to work. This has become very confusing. I never expected to feel so welcome here in your home, with your family, and I forgot for a moment who I am.'

'Flora.' Charles rubbed the back of his neck. 'The girls adore you, you must know that. Why would I want to get in the way of that affection?'

'But I'll be leaving soon for my next posting. I should have thought about it more. I should have been more careful not to get too close.'

She no longer knew who she was talking about. Was it the girls or was it Charles?

'It's too late.' He brought a hand to her cheek, cupping it, caressing her lips with a thumb. She fought the urge to open her mouth and take it inside her.

'What are we going to do, Charles? About this?' She moved close, pressed her hands across his chest, right where his heart was, and felt it beating.

'I know what I want to do, Flora. Can't you tell? I've been a lonely man for so long. I'd given up hope of happiness in my life. And then you turn up in your uniform, so beautiful and determined and serious.'

Flora moved closer to him. 'I wanted to make a good impression. But I was nervous, too.'

'And you cut off the legs on your overalls.' He exhaled. 'And you were sad, too, I think. I recognised that in you because I carried it in me. But I don't feel that way any more. I see a light at the end of the tunnel for me, when I used to see and feel nothing.'

Flora held a breath and went up on tiptoe as he bowed his head and kissed her. His lips were unexpectedly soft and tender and he tasted like sherry. There was jazz on the radio and his shirt felt soft under her fingertips and she closed her eyes to remember it all.

On Saturday, Charles took the girls with him into Mildura to pick up groceries and items from the agricultural store. It was part of Land Army rules that her food-rations booklet was passed over to the family hosting her so, along with eggs from the chooks and the supply of milk from Marjorie, which also meant butter and cream, there was plenty of food. While it was true that Flora missed chocolate, sometimes quite desperately, she ate sultanas for her fix of something sweet and relished Mrs Nettlefold's fresh scones, which she was now learning to bake.

Flora missed cooking. She wasn't terribly accomplished in the kitchen, but it had felt like years now since she'd nourished her own family. Back in Camberwell, there had always been a Sunday roast and Frank and Jack knew never to miss it. Flora had worked hard to maintain their mother's tradition. It was so important to gather together at the table, to share stories, to laugh, to learn about each other's days. That was one of the things she treasured most about living in with the Nettlefolds.

Although she wasn't expected to help with household chores, that morning she'd asked Mrs Nettlefold for a refresher lesson in baking scones. Truth be told, she needed some distance from Charles, to think about what had happened the night before in the sitting room.

After that first kiss, and the second, he'd led her to the sofa and they'd kissed each other over and over. She'd been bolder than she'd ever imagined she could be. She taken Charles's hand and covered a breast with it and, when she'd unbuttoned her blouse, Charles had kissed the swell of her flesh there before revealing a nipple and slowly drawing it into his mouth. He'd whispered intimacies to her, low and private, and the combination of his words and his touch and his body on hers had created new and overwhelming sensations in her.

But they knew where they were, in his house with his daughters and his mother close, so they'd stopped and breathed and kissed again before Flora had stumbled to her room.

That morning, they'd said quiet hellos to each other over breakfast and when Charles had excused himself, saying he had work to do in the drying shed, Frankie had galloped after him, with the girls hot on their puppy's heels. Flora had taken a notepad and pencil outside to the bench Charles had made for her, and had written letters to her brothers.

So much had happened yet there was so little she could say to them. She gave them each a quick update about the sultana picking and the weather. She playfully chided Frank for his tardiness in writing, suggesting he might be too busy pulling pranks to put pencil to paper. The idea had made her feel lighter for a moment.

She'd signed off as she usually did, 'With much love from Flora', folded the flimsy pages and slipped them inside an envelope, on which she affixed a green four-penny stamp featuring a koala sitting in a gum tree.

How important letters had become in the war years. Would she one day tell Charles that she had saved every one he'd written to her in the eleven months they'd been apart? Could she admit that she had read them over and over to herself at night, closing her eyes to take herself back to Two Rivers to hear his voice narrating them, instead of her own in her head?

'Does this need to be thinner, Mrs Nettlefold? I can't for the life of me remember what my mother used to do.'

Flora pressed a rolling pin into the scone dough, which formed a ragged shape on the kitchen table. She blew a wisp of hair from her eyes.

'A little, yes. Keep rolling it.'

Flora did as she was instructed. The radio played in the background as they worked. Mrs Nettlefold had just finished listening to *When A Girl Marries*. The serial was dedicated 'to all those who are in love and all those who can remember'. Flora had never enjoyed it when she was at home before the war. She'd thought herself to be in love once, but in the end it had been nothing more than a silly girlish crush, and she would rather not remember anything about it. Joan Field's romantic adventures only served to remind her of that fact. But now, things were so very different.

A song began to play on the radio and Flora was distracted by it as the crooning voice of Frank Sinatra dragged her head back to thoughts of Charles and the night before.

'He's very fond of you, you know, Flora.' Mrs Nettlefold stopped kneading. She rubbed her hands together and a drift of flour fell into her pottery mixing bowl. 'I've always been a plain speaker, dear, and I'm going to speak plainly to you now. I don't know what happened between the two of you last night and it's none of my business.'

'No, Mrs Nettlefold,' Flora stammered. 'Please don't …' Flora's thoughts flashed back to the two women in the shoe shop and the unkind things they'd said about her and all the Land Army girls. Flora shuddered at the thought that Charles's mother might think the same about her.

'Charles is a grown man and you are a mature woman. But I have to say this. My son lost his wife in the most tragic of circumstances. I can't see him go through any such heartbreak again.'

Flora rolled her patch of dough, up and down, forward and back, blinking back her tears.

'I know you and Charles have been writing to each other. And now, well, I've noticed what's going on between you two. You'd have to be blind not to see it.'

'Please don't think that I came here to … I know what people are saying. I've heard them. That's not why I joined the Land Army, Mrs Nettlefold.'

She huffed. 'I take no notice of what those busybodies in Mildura say. I, and many others, have seen how hard you all work. Flora, I don't disapprove of you and Charles. It's been a long time since I've seen him so happy. He hasn't been this cheery since … well, since Harriet was alive.'

Flora dropped into the chair next to her, clutching the rolling pin. She needed to hear every word.

'They were so excited about having another baby, you know. Violet was such a sweet little thing, just walking. They talked of a big family and, of course, Charles wanted a boy, like every father does. Harriet was a lovely girl. They went to school together. High-school sweethearts, is what everyone said. Her parents blamed Charles, you know, for a long time. They'd cross Langtree Avenue rather than talk to him. At Harriet's funeral, they walked right over to me and told me that Charles should have waited, that Harriet hadn't recovered from having Violet.' Mrs Nettlefold sniffed and wiped a flour-streaked forearm across her face.

'He took it to heart, how could he not? None of it was true but it was cruel. Sometimes mothers are lost in childbirth. It used to happen much more than it does now. But it still happens.'

Flora found her voice. 'He's had to be so very strong for his girls.'

'They're the light in his eyes,' Mrs Nettlefold replied. 'If it wasn't for them, I don't know where he'd be.'

Flora reached a hand across the table and held Mrs Nettlefold's in her grasp. 'And if it wasn't for you. I know you lost your husband young. I saw what that did to my father.

It broke his heart and he never loved again. You've been a grandmother and a mother to Violet and Daisy. I know a little of what you've gone through, too.'

Mrs Nettlefold met her eyes and a new understanding passed between them.

'Please believe me when I say that I would never hurt Charles. You're right. I'm a mature woman. And I'm a sensible one. Whatever I feel for your son, it's impossible to imagine a future at the moment. Until Frank comes home from the war, I can't make any plans. I helped raise him after our mother died. And Jack, too. We're a very close family ourselves. In that respect, I see similarities with yours, Mrs Nettlefold. When there is grief over the loss of a loved one, the natural thing to do is to turn in, to shut out the world. That's what we did when my mother died. But the world came to us anyway. I couldn't protect Jack from losing the hearing in his ear when he was fourteen. I couldn't stop the taunts he received about not going to war. And I couldn't stop Frank from wanting to do his duty for the country. But I will be there when he comes home, to see to it that the Atkins family will endure, that we won't lose each other. We're all we have left now.'

Mrs Nettlefold looked up suddenly and her lips drew together in a tight line. Flora turned to see what had startled her so and saw Charles in the doorway, a paper bag filled with groceries in each arm. She hadn't heard his footsteps. Hadn't heard the back door slam.

How long had he been standing there? How much had he heard? He put the groceries on the sink and strode out of the room without saying a word.

Flora spent her Sunday reading in the dim light of her room, avoiding everyone. She'd pulled the curtains closed to keep out the heat but because the windows beyond were open, the fabric floated and swooped as the north winds outside tried to reach their tentacles inside. It was almost impossible to feel cool when the harsh winds were whipping up dust on the block and swirling it around the house.

She couldn't read, couldn't think, felt unable to string a coherent thought together. Where was Charles? Flora cocked her head, listening, hoping to hear the girls' giggles or the sounds of play. There was nothing but silence. Perhaps the Nettlefolds had driven off somewhere, for a picnic, or perhaps a swim in the river. Would they have done so without inviting her? Of course they would have, especially after she'd made it clear the night before at dinner that she'd planned to stay in on Sunday and rest. It had all been a ruse. Her conversation with Mrs Nettlefold—and knowing Charles had overhead her—had deeply upset her. Had he heard her say that she had feelings for him but that she couldn't do anything about them until the war was over? Is that why he'd been so taciturn the night before, and why they'd left her to her own devices that day?

She had barely been able to think of anything else since Friday night after what had happened between them. Charles's attentions had stirred something deep inside her. For the first time, she ached with a heat, hotter than any north wind.

Why could she think of nothing but him? What was she supposed to do out on the block the next day when they were working side by side, their well-oiled process familiar and fast now. Would they speak of it? And what would they say to each other?

Flora turned on her side, closed her eyes and let sleep overcome her.

Sunday-night supper was egg sandwiches, thanks to a fresh loaf baked that morning by Mrs Nettlefold and the chooks' bountiful supply. Violet and Daisy chatted away about their visit to the Stewarts in Mildura. The mystery of their absence that day was solved. Charles had bought another sprayer from Mr Stewart and the rest of the family had gone along for a ride to see their old friends whose daughters went to school with the Nettlefold girls.

After slices of fruit cake for dessert, Mrs Nettlefold began clearing the table. Violet went one way down the hallway to her room and the slam of the back door revealed Daisy had run outside.

Flora sat at the table sipping her tea. Charles had unfurled the local newspaper and seemed intent on page three. She watched him as he read. His brow furrowed and there were two vertical lines right there above his nose. At one point, he rubbed his hand over his jaw and then sighed as he turned a page. There was a hint of growth on his chin, white like the grey hair at his temples.

Mrs Nettlefold dropped a plate in the sink and apologised for it with a dramatic mutter. The clatter made Flora look over at the sink for a moment and when she turned her attention back to Charles, she found to her embarrassment that he was watching her intently. Discovered, he lowered his eyes to the newsprint.

Mrs Nettlefold walked over to the table for the jug of milk and put it back it in the Coolgardie safe to keep it cool in the heat.

Flora felt the awkward tension in the room and she wasn't sure what to do or what to say to dispel it. Before she could decide, the back door slammed and there were running footsteps into the kitchen.

'Daddy, I can't find Frankie.' Daisy tugged insistently at her father's turned-up sleeve.

Charles lowered the newspaper, his attention firmly on his youngest daughter. 'Did you call him, Daisy?'

'Yes. Ten times,' she insisted. 'I counted. I called and called and he didn't come.'

Flora leant her elbows onto the table. Watching the tears welling in Daisy's eyes tore at her.

'He'll come back,' Charles said reassuringly. 'He's probably found something delicious to eat. Like a blue-tongue lizard.' Charles pulled his daughter close and flicked his tongue in and out.

Daisy giggled. 'Your tongue's not blue, Daddy.'

He ruffled her hair. 'Why don't you go and get Violet and see if she'll help you find him. Perhaps you just need some help looking.'

'Wait, Daisy.' Flora tore a chunk of bread from the loaf on the table and passed it to her. 'See if this helps.'

'Thank you, Flora.' Daisy ran outside with an excited smile.

Charles waited until the back door slammed before he spoke low. 'When did you last see the dog, Mum?' Mrs Nettlefold came to the table; drying her hands on her apron.

'He barked like a mad thing when we came back from the Stewarts', didn't he? Violet and Daisy hopped out of the car and chased him back to the house. I gave him a bone to chew and last time I saw him he was running off into the block with it in his mouth. To bury the thing, I expect. What kind of silly dog is he to bury it for later when he could chew the thing to bits right there and then?'

'He's never done this before, has he?' Flora asked, fear skittering up her arms, goosebumping them. 'Run away, I mean?'

Charles shook his head. He folded the paper. 'He stays close to the girls. And the house.'

'Do you think he's lost?'

Charles pushed back his chair and stood, reaching for his hat on the nail on the back of the kitchen door. 'I'll go for a walk and have a look.'

'Wait,' Flora said without a second thought. 'I'm coming with you.'

Chapter Twenty-Six

For two hours Charles and Flora listened to the echo of their calls, from the house to the drying sheds, until their throats were hoarse from shouting. Frankie was nowhere to be found. When twilight fell, Charles sent the girls and their grandmother back to the house—the girls' sobs had been on the verge of hysterical—but still he and Flora searched, up and down each row of vines, searching under the leaf canopy, hoping the dog was hiding somewhere, playing with them or guarding his bone.

They lost their battle against the light. It was pitch black now, with only the stars to guide them, and Flora couldn't think straight any more. Every rustle in the leaves had filled her with hope and then heartbreak as exploration after exploration proved fruitless.

'A rabbit trap?' she asked desperately.

'I don't use them,' Charles told her. 'Not with the girls so young.'

Flora peered into the darkness. Charles was by her side, and she didn't need to see his face to feel the tension prickling his skin.

Frankie couldn't be missing. He was supposed to make the girls happy, not heartbroken. He was their good-luck charm, too. Frankie and Frank. The charming man and the lucky charm. During the past weeks, the two had become one in her mind. Each stroke of Frankie's pitch black fur reminded her to say a silent prayer for her brother. From her lips to God's ear.

Hot tears welled in Flora's eyes and she sniffed over and over, wiping her nose and her cheeks. She didn't want Charles to see her cry. Not about Frankie. Not about Frank. But with each step, the little pieces of hope she was holding on to drained away, replaced by a sense of foreboding so ominous it choked her. And finally, when she could no longer hold in the sobs, panic and fear caught her like a vine leaf in a storm and she took off, her boots crushing the grass underfoot, running blindly; crashing into the corded and twisted vines, their soft leaves no protection, as she ran. She had to find him.

'Frankie!' she called. 'Frankie. Frank … Frank … Frank.'

Her chest heaved and her throat burnt and she slowed, bending over to catch her breath, her hands on her knees to keep her from falling into the dirt. Her heart thudded, her sobs unbidden and uncontrolled. Two years of dread burst from her and she collapsed onto the grass, hot tears streaking and dripping into the collar of her shirt, chest burning, eyes scratching. *Let me cry. Let it hurt. Let me feel it, finally, all of it, so when it happens I'll be immune. Frank. My beloved brother. Where are you? Are you safe? Are you dead?*

'Flora!' Charles crouched at her side on bended knee. His voice was close, panicked, his breath on her face. 'Bloody hell, Flora.'

'Frank,' she cried out in a high-pitched wail. When Charles pulled her up into his arms, she clung to him. He pulled her into his lap and pressed her face into his chest and there, in the dark, in the dirt, among the vines, Charles comforted and whispered to Flora until she finally calmed.

When she could open her eyes, Charles's shirt was wet from her tears and her fingers ached from gripping the fabric so tight in her fists. His hand was stroking her hair. Her heart felt broken.

'Flora.' Charles's voice was hoarse.

It felt as if there were razor blades in her throat.

'Sshh now. We'll look for him in the morning. Maybe he's back at the house already. Asleep on Daisy's bed, just the way he likes it. He'll be as exhausted as the girls are.'

Flora knew that couldn't be true. If it was, the girls would have shouted from the house and come running to find their father. She burrowed her face into Charles's neck and his arms tightened around her. She inhaled the scent of him and her lips brushed his warm skin. She needed that comfort of his skin, his scent, his sure strength, to say what she was going to say.

'What if Frank's dead? What if he's been killed and I don't know it yet? What if he's lying in the mud somewhere in a place I've never heard of and he's already gone?'

'Darling Flora,' he murmured into her hair, into her heart.

'I told my mother I'd look after them all. When she was sick, she made me promise that I'd keep the family together.'

All she needed was to say it aloud, to have someone listen to her deepest fear. Charles kissed her forehead and held her. It was all he could do.

Flora blinked her eyes open at the knock on her bedroom door. It was already light. She'd had a fitful night's sleep, filled with dreams, snatches of horror from newsreels she'd seen at the pictures, mud and death. Had she slept late? What time was it?

'Flora?' Charles's voice was so quiet she barely heard it.

'Come in.' She pulled the sheet up to her chin.

He opened the door enough to poke his head through the gap. After a quick glance at her in bed, his attention shifted to the fluttering curtains. 'Can you get dressed? I need your help.'

'Give me a moment.' Her morning voice was croaky. Her throat still felt ragged from the night before.

Last night. She knew immediately what Charles would have to tell her. But she had no more tears. She was cried out, spent. She'd done all her grieving in the dark.

'I'll be out in the yard.'

Flora wearily dropped her feet to the floor and stood on shaky legs. She dressed in a shirt and her overalls, tugged on her boots and went outside, taking care to hold the back door so it didn't slam and wake everyone in the house.

She stepped out into the day. The sun was just up in the sky in the east, casting long shadows over the block. The air was already prickly hot and smelled like dust. She sniffed against the dryness. Charles stood under the peppercorn tree, his hands clasped behind his back. As she approached, she spotted the mound of freshly dug red dirt. She pressed a hand to her chest and dread filled the pit of her stomach. When she was by his side, she slipped an arm through his. He shifted his weight, leant towards her a little to acknowledge her comforting touch.

'A snake bite, I reckon.' He paused, looked up to the cloudless sky through the wafting leaves of the tree. 'I got up at sunrise to have another look. I swear I searched that same spot six times yesterday.'

'Oh, Charles.'

'I didn't want the girls to see him like that.'

'No,' Flora said quietly. 'Of course you didn't.'

'I thought … at least I was hoping you might help me tell them.'

'Of course.'

He sniffed. 'What was I thinking, agreeing to let them have a puppy.'

'You were being a good father who wanted to make his daughters happy.'

His chest rose and fell. 'They'll be very upset. I'll need you there with me.'

Flora rested her head on his shoulder. 'Whatever you need, Charles.'

He reached for her hand. 'About your brother.'

How could she explain to him what had happened the night before? She barely understood it herself. 'I apologise. I don't know what came over me.'

'I understand, Flora. More than you know. I also know that the only thing you can do is wait and hope.' He turned towards her, made sure she was looking at him when he spoke. 'And if the news is the worst, you will have me to comfort you. You won't be alone. I promise you that.'

He kissed the top of her head, gently pressing his lips to her hairline. She wanted to throw her arms around him. Instead, she gripped his forearm tight.

'Family comes first,' he said.

'Yes.' He had heard her talking with his mother and he understood.

'When the war is over ...'

'Yes,' she replied. 'When the war is over.'

They went back up to the house and woke the girls. Their single beds were a mirror of each other in the dark room, except one pillow cradled blonde hair and the other a dark spray of messy curls. Charles sat on Violet's bed and Flora on Daisy's.

When they stirred, their father told them what had happened. Violet climbed into her father's arms, sobbing. Daisy clung to Flora like a limpet on a rock. The little girls were held and comforted, their heads were stroked and soft words of support were uttered until there were finally no more tears.

As Charles cradled Violet in his arms, he looked across at Flora. His soft, loving gaze was an invitation.

Stay and be a part of this family.

Leeton, New South Wales
April 15th, 1944
Dear Charles,
Firstly, thank you for all your letters. A big bundle of them finally found me here in Leeton. I so enjoyed hearing about all the goings on at Two Rivers, the latest with the girls and your mother. Please pass on my fondest regards to all of them when you get this.

This is a pleasant property and there are eight of us girls here. We have little sectioned-off rooms on the verandah of a big farmhouse, which are all enclosed, thankfully. The other girls are so young, one only seventeen, so I do feel rather like their spinster aunt. I especially feel the difference in our ages when they chatter about the latest popular crooner and their plans to head into town for the weekend dances. It's quite a social spot. The girls have convinced me more than once to go the pictures with them. It's a lovely art deco cinema, rather like the Ozone in Mildura, and we've seen so many movies I can't honestly say I can tell one from the other. All I can report to you is that there has been dancing, swash-buckling pirates, and a little too much of Douglas Fairbanks and Jeanette McDonald. I can't bring myself to stay for the war movies, which seem to be very popular, especially among the younger men, who stream out into the foyer afterwards clutching their empty boxes of Jaffas and yelling 'Bonzai', which I find rather unsettling.

All these excursions help the time pass and stop me from thinking about Frank quite so much and from missing you. As I'm hoeing weeds in the potato fields, I imagine I'm back at Two Rivers picking sultana grapes, looking out across the vines, anticipating your mother's dinners and more time spent with you.

Charles, you've been so understanding about my Land Army work and what drives me to keep going. We're not the only ones making sacrifices for the war, are we?

We haven't heard from Frank for a month and as every day passes, I fear for him more and more. All I can do is cling to the hope that all this will end and, when he is home, we will all look back on these years knowing that we displayed an enormous sense of courage and sacrifice, even in the midst of such despair.

Hug the girls for me and let your mother know that I'm saving all her recipes to my notebook so that when I go home for good, I might add them to my vast repertoire.

With fondest regards,

Flora

Chapter Twenty-Seven

Lily

April 1944

'I can't believe it.'

'Can't believe what?' Kit asked as she flopped her head forwards and wrapped a towel around it like a turban.

'Susan is married.' Lily's hands shook with excitement at the news, so much that she could barely read her mother's handwriting. She was sitting on her bed in Land Army quarters on a farm in Athelstone, in Adelaide's foothills. She and Kit and a dozen other girls were picking turnips and beans and pulling onions for a farmer with a military contract. There was plenty of work, seven days a week of it, and they were into their third month of hard scrabbling in the dirt, but Lily was still with Kit and that made everything easier to bear.

'She still in Africa somewhere?'

'The Middle East, in the Australian Army Medical Corp. Last time we were told she was in an Australian General Hospital in Egypt. Oh my goodness.'

'Who did she marry?'

'An English doctor.' Lily scanned her mother's letter quickly, looking for details among the complaints about it being done abroad, her daughter being married in her uniform, in a registry office, with a man the family hadn't even met, much less heard of until the announcement. 'He's a major in the Royal Army Medical Corp. Colin Wells. They had leave a month ago and were back in London. They decided on the spot to get married. She's now Mrs Colin Wells.'

'Or should that be Mrs Major Colin Wells? Or Mrs Major Doctor Colin Wells.' Kit laughed. 'Such a fancy-pants name. He's probably a duke too, isn't he? Or a prince!'

Lily stared at the letter and tried not to feel guilty about the wave of melancholic sadness that engulfed her. Of course she was happy for her sister. She mourned the loss of not having been there for such a moment, and for her sister not having been able to be in Adelaide for her own wedding. Wars tore people apart in more ways than she could count. There was a surprise too in hearing that someone as intellectual as Susan had even considered giving her hand to anyone. She must love Colin very much. Perhaps she'd lived through some experiences that had led her to change her mind when it came to marriage and settling down?

You should grab happiness when it's close. Lily knew that. What was the point in waiting when no one knew what tomorrow, or the next hour or even the next minute, would bring?

Lily thought back to her simple registry-office wedding and glanced at her plain wedding band. Had Susan had a real honeymoon? Was London still too much under siege to let a couple celebrate? Lily remembered her own honeymoon, as much as it was, her one night shared with David as husband and wife. They had made love precisely three times and that was now nearly eighteen months ago. She'd been apart from him three times as long as she'd known him.

'Lil,' Kit called, and Lily looked up from her letter.

'Yes?'

'Write to David. You'll feel better.'

Lily rummaged through her suitcase for David's most recent letter. The envelope was so small, his writing so neat, and the stamp *Passed by Censor* was imprinted in it in a blue diamond. She needed to read it again, to feel him close, to create in her mind's eye a picture of where he had been when he'd taken pencil to paper. Had he been in a barracks? A tent? Sitting in an aircraft? Safe somewhere or on guard? How would she ever know?

May 1st, 1944
Abroad
Darling Lily,
Just a few lines to say that I'm well and being well looked after. I've received so many of your letters, which are such precious and wonderful reminders that you are waiting for me at home. I thought I might keep it a secret and surprise you but I have plans for a huge party when I return. What do you think of all the champagne we can drink and a Persian tent erected in your parents' back yard? Do you remember that night, when we decided not to go to Evelyn Wood's twenty-first

birthday party in Fitzroy, and walked back to my apartment instead? The only thing I regret about that night is that we didn't sneak down the driveway and see it for ourselves. I recreate that wonderful evening every night in my dreams, Lily. I'd love to give you such a party, as a way of celebrating my return and announcing to the world in a way we didn't get the chance to, that you are my wife and I love you with everything I have.

I continue to be so proud of you for your Land Army work. Who would have thought I'd chosen a girl with such grit and tenacity?

I can't tell you exactly where I am but please know that I am safe. I can rest more easily at night knowing you are so far away from things and I pray you remain so.

I'm very much looking forward to your next letter in which I hope you'll tell me all about your latest horticultural adventures in Australia's wide brown land.
Your ever-loving husband,
David
P.S. I love you with all my heart.

Lily lay back on her bed, staring at the ceiling of the old farmhouse that was their quarters, and clutched David's letter to her chest. She had lived her entire life in the same house in Buxton Street until she'd joined the Land Army and since then she'd lived in so many different places. Not one of them had been her marital home. She'd picked cherries, harvested flax and potatoes, and now onions and turnips. Her latest horticultural adventures indeed. Her fingers and hands were a farmer's now. There was always dirt in the fine lines of her knuckles and she'd developed protective callouses on her palms. She'd had to order new Land Army shirts, as she'd broadened in the shoulders since she'd been working manually. Would she be better at tennis now she was stronger? The thought made her smile. She must talk to Kit about heading back to Norton Summit for the cherry season. She would have a better softball swing now, that was for sure.

She sat up, found her pencil and wrote her reply to her husband. Before she signed off, she remembered to add, 'I'll be brave and you be safe, remember?'

Weeks and weeks of work went by until winter arrived in the Adelaide foothills, bringing with it cold mornings and an occasional frost. The Land Army girls rugged up in extra jumpers, wrapped their heads in scarves and their feet in extra pairs of socks to bear the cold and, at night, needed extra blankets to keep them warm in the unheated quarters.

The crops were so abundant that year, and the need for labour so great, that the government in Canberra had decided to allow some Italian prisoners of war to work on local farms. Their employer, Mr Norris, had gathered the girls together one morning to explain the changed arrangements.

'Now that Mussolini and his mob have been defeated, the government has decided to let some of those POWs work. I'll keep them away from you girls as much as I can. They'll be over on the other end of the property picking the celery. Don't talk to them and if any of them get familiar, you let me know right away.'

Kit had whispered to Lily. 'Too late. I've already been familiar with an Italian. Enzo Zocchi, back in primary school. He kissed me behind the shelter shed at Campbell-town Primary School.'

The Italians kept their distance and the girls continued to work long days in the fields. Lily had found comfort in the evenings in sitting by the radio with a cup of hot Milo, a blanket over her knees and her friend Kit for company. They'd long ago exhausted their game of what they would do when the war was over, and now could sit in companionable silence, listening to the radio, humming along to songs they recognised.

On the night of Wednesday 7 June, 1944, it wasn't music they were listening to in their quarters. The Allied invasion of France had begun and every girl was absolutely silent, hands clenched in prayer, hanging on every word being broadcast from the wireless.

The announcer spoke quickly, urgently. 'Under the command of General Eisenhower, Allied naval forces supported by strong air forces began landing Allied armies this morning on the northern coast of France.

'Four years later, almost to the hour of the evacuation of Dunkirk, we go back to the same Normandy coast which saw the closing chapter of the battle of France. The Allied invasion of Europe from the west is launched. Today is D-day, the second front and the second battle for France. This is the last great act of liberation of the war. Four years ago, Europe was Hitler's and the lights of the free world went out. Now the world of free men strikes in all its assembled might at the weakening chains of bondage. The great curtain of secrecy is still drawn but the first of a series of landings is in force, sustained by eleven thousand first line aircraft.'

And then General Eisenhower said something too but Lily and Kit were dancing and whooping and crying at the news, and every single girl there joined in until they were all laughing and letting themselves imagine the tide really had turned.

The next day, Lily's mother arrived in a taxi with a picnic basket full of cakes freshly baked by Davina. One of the farm managers came to find her and after the initial panic of being called out of the field, Lily was relieved to have the respite. She was cold, her fingers were stiff and her back ached. Her mother was waiting in the dining room for her, and there was hot tea, and delicious treats to eat, and for a moment Lily listened while her mother once again tried to convince her to come home.

'Did you hear the news yesterday? I've brought you the paper so you can read it for yourself.'

Lily unfolded *The Advertiser*. Right there on the front page was a large map of Europe. England, Sardinia, Corsica, Russia and half of Italy were shaded. Allies. Those countries left white were still under Nazi control. An arrow marked out Normandy on the French coast.

Allies Slash Way Into North France, Cherbourg-Le Havre Beaches Stormed the headline announced in capital letters. It was reassuring to see it in print, that an armada of four thousand ships had sailed across the English Channel, that tens of thousands of troops had stormed ashore. The Allied forces had sent eleven thousand aircraft into the invasion, strafing miles of Normandy beaches, dropping thousands of tonnes of bombs on enemy positions, and flying inland to break communication lines.

'We're on our way to victory, Lily, and I've never felt happier about a headline in my entire life.'

Lily sighed, studying her mother's face. It wasn't just husbands who were away fighting. It was sisters and daughters too. Lily felt a wave of sympathy for her mother, something she'd not been gracious enough to feel before.

'I'm so excited and happy for Susan, Mum. Have you heard any more details of the wedding?'

Mrs Thomas opened her purse, found a handkerchief and dabbed her eyes. 'Only the telegram, which I wrote to you about in my last letter. How wonderful for her to have fallen in love, don't you think?'

'Yes, Mum,' Lily said, leaning in to kiss her mother's cheek. 'It really is. I'm sorry for what I put you through with David. Our impulsive marriage, I mean. I don't regret it one bit, but I realise now that you've been robbed of two daughters' weddings. I'm sorry you weren't there for either of them.'

'Oh, Lilian.'

'The war really has turned everything upside down, hasn't it?'

Lily's mother stilled, and tears rolled down her face. She didn't bother to mop them up this time. 'Yes,' she said quietly.

'I haven't understood until now how hard this has been on you. I apologise for that.'

Mrs Thomas stared off into the distance a moment. 'I received a letter from my cousin yesterday. Her son, Archie, died in New Guinea. It was malaria.'

'How awful,' Lily whispered.

'To go all that way and be so brave, and to be killed by a mosquito. It's rather appalling.'

Lily poured them both another cup of tea and sliced another piece of Davina's cake.

'I came here today to ask you to come home, you know.'

Lily couldn't fight the feeling that her mother was seeing her for the first time. 'I thought as much.'

'Your father isn't sleeping. The house feels too empty and I said I would try to convince you. But I see how you're thriving and I'm not going to ask you. At the end of the day, you're a married woman who can do whatever she chooses.'

'Oh, Mum,' Lily sighed. 'What say I come home on my next day off? It won't be for a couple of weeks but I'm sure I can arrange a Sunday. I'm not too far from home after all.'

'He'd like that. So would I.'

Davina had whipped up a celebratory spread that had Lily's eyes watering. A platter in the middle of the dining table was filled with a glistening roast chicken, surrounded by honeyed baby carrots and new potatoes garnished with parsley. A boat filled with gravy next to the platter called to Lily. Her father had brought up a bottle of his finest French red wine from the cellar and had decanted it into a crystal bottle to breathe. Lily sat in her chair, wearing a pretty dress she hadn't slipped on in the longest time and, just for a moment, was able to pretend the world wasn't at war. Her parents seemed excessively happy to have her home and they talked about Susan's latest letter and played a guessing game about who her husband might resemble: Churchill or the king. Lily hoped, for Susan's sake, that he was more like Errol Flynn or Cary Grant.

'It's a pity they weren't able to have a honeymoon,' Mrs Thomas said with a sigh, before glancing at Lily and remembering that her youngest daughter hadn't had one either. 'And you too, Lily. Your father and I had the most wonderful trip to Paris not long after we were married.' She hesitated, her expression suddenly bereft. 'It's dreadful to think of what Parisians must have endured during all these years of occupation.' Her mother shivered. 'And to think that a swastika flies from the Eiffel Tower now ...'

'It won't be long now,' Mr Thomas replied. 'The Allies are on their way to Paris and before long they'll liberate all of France. And then they'll be on to Berlin. Hitler's men don't stand a chance with the Russians coming from the east. And General MacArthur's troops are moving through the Pacific, island by island. Some are saying we could have victory by Christmas but I—'

'Christmas?' Lily's fork was suspended midair and the peas on its tines tumbled back down to her china plate. December? That was still too long to wait. It was June. Six more months? There were too many battles that would be fought before then in which young men would die. 'You don't think it will be over by then, Dad? There were so many troops and ships and planes ...'

Mr Thomas paused, staring at his dinner for a moment. 'I don't think so, Lily. There are still many battles ahead.'

'Can't we hope for the best at least?' Mrs Thomas said, trying to bring some cheer back to the evening.

'Yes, let's hope and pray,' Lily replied. 'That by Christmas, Susan and David and everyone else will be home in the arms of those who love them.'

On Sunday morning, Lily woke from a deep sleep in the comfort of her bed, with clean sheets and soft pillows and a woollen blanket so warm and soft it felt as if she was enveloped in clouds. For the first few moments she half-dozed, turning to the window to judge by the sliver of light leaching through the gap in the curtains what time it might be. Had she slept in? Or had so many months in the Land Army changed her habits so completely that she would rise at five forty-five without even trying? She was about to roll over to the wall and close her eyes again when she heard the commotion outside her door. She pushed herself up to sitting and listened. Had the doorbell sounded? There were galloping footsteps up and down the stairs and a whispered conversation in the hallway outside her bedroom door. She threw back her blankets, pushed her feet into her slippers, draped her dressing gown over her shoulders and tiptoed to the door. Her hand on the brass knob, she pressed her ear against the small crack between the door and the frame.

'Let her enjoy the sleep of an innocent just a little longer.' It was her mother but her voice was hoarse and rough. 'Please.'

Lily threw open the door. Her shocked parents turned to her and gasped. Her mother's hand flew to her trembling mouth and she clutched at her husband's arm.

Her father cleared his throat. 'Lily ...' he started and then stopped and his face contorted in a moan, his eyes filling with tears.

He held a telegram in his hand.

When he reached out a hand to pass it to his daughter, she stared at him, the buzzing of a thousand bees suddenly in her head.

Chapter Twenty-Eight

REGRET TO INFORM YOU THAT YOUR HUSBAND FLIGHT LIEUT DAVID WILLIAM HOGARTH IS REPORTED MISSING AS A RESULT AIR OPERATIONS ON 8TH JUNE 1944 STOP ANY FURTHER INFORMATION RECEIVED WILL BE IMMEDIATELY CONVEYED TO YOU ... AIR BOARD

For two days, Lily was mute. It hurt to talk. It hurt to cry. Her throat was raw and pain pricked all over, a physical pain that had struck her like lightning. Her mother and father had knocked on her door, gently trying to prise her from the dark, but she'd not answered. Davina had opened her door quietly and brought in soup and toast on a tray but it remained untouched.

She was twenty years old but felt older. Was she already a widow? How could she hold on to her dreams for a life with David when she didn't know if he was dead or alive? Would she always be Mrs Hogarth even if he was dead?

She closed her eyes, tried to hear his voice. His laughter at her silly attempts to hit a tennis ball across the net at Memorial Drive. Calling out to her to go faster on their bike rides up in the hills. The sadness when he'd told her that his brother was missing. The desperation in it when he'd told her he was enlisting.

And the love, the adoration, the joy in the words he'd spoken and the promises he'd made on their wedding night, for safe return, for a future together, for happiness, for children. For a time when duty and honour wouldn't take him from her.

In the dark, in her room, she could hold on to his voice and the press of his lips on hers and the weight of his limbs as he moved inside her.

For the five days after that, Lily moved about the house half awake, weak from crying, her appetite having completely abandoned her. Her mother had arranged an appointment at their doctor's surgery, and old Dr Carmichael had prescribed pills to help her sleep, and recommended she resign immediately from the Land Army.

A week after receiving the telegram, Lily put on her uniform and went back to work.

Kit was the first one to throw her arms around Lily, knocking her hat off in the rush, and she held on for what felt like hours. Lily had barely stepped out of the taxi at the farm in

Athelstone when a group of girls in bib-and-brace overalls and woollen hats had run towards her, clomping across the paddock in their rubber boots. But her dear friend Kit got there first, her long legs able to outrun everyone.

'Oh, Lil,' she cried. 'The matron told us the news about your husband. Your mother called her and we were all so devastated to hear it. I'm so, so sorry.'

Lily clutched at Kit, her greatcoat crushed against her friend. 'Thank you, Kit.'

'He'll come home, you'll see,' she whispered into Lily's ear.

'I'm trying to think the best. I truly am.'

Lily was then engulfed in hugs and showered with whispered commiserations from the other women until she gave them a little smile of thanks. Together, they marched in formation back into the turnip field.

Kit slipped an arm through Lily's and they walked slowly back to their quarters in the old farmhouse. Lily found it hard to keep up. Her suitcase knocked against her leg, which she was sure would cause a bruise, and she had to stop and put it down. She'd lost some of her strength in the past week, it was obvious. Kit quickly took the case.

'We're all here,' Kit said quietly. 'You're not alone, Lily.'

And then she remembered what David had written to her about Kit.

You'll need a friend in the event you get the worst news. Kit will help you, as will my own father and mother. You would always be welcome at Millicent if I don't come home.

'Thank you, Kit.'

When work was finished at Athelstone, Lily followed Kit and some of the other girls to Hectorville, where they picked olives in a grove. They laid sheets under the trees and beat their branches, loosening the fruit to encourage it to fall to the ground. When that didn't work they hauled out tall ladders and leant them against the trunks, which made Lily think of summer and cherry picking at Norton Summit, her first Land Army posting, the place she'd met Kit. After picking, they pickled and packed the olives until the grove was bare. Then they moved to a potato dehydration plant not far away and worked side by side on a fast-moving production line. The spuds were peeled in a mechanical tumble, but each one had to be checked for flecks of skin and each eye had to be gouged out with a knife before they were returned to the line to be shredded and then dehydrated. Kit joked that she felt like a scientist, in her white coat and hair net, but Lily couldn't laugh at it. The work was repetitive, their hands were wet all day and the whole place was loud. The droning noise of the machines and the tumbling potatoes sounded like bombers.

One night, as they were drifting off to sleep, excited at the arrival of spring after a warm and sunny day, Lily asked Kit about what they would do next. She'd ceded her future to her friend, to her strength, to her confidence, having somehow lost the will to make decisions for herself. She would do anything but go home because going home was surrendering, not fighting. And until she knew where David was, what fate had befallen him, she had to fight to keep him alive in her memory, in her fingertips, on her lips and her body and in her heart.

'I've been thinking about cherries,' Kit replied in the quiet of their room. 'I've been thinking about Norton Summit. Feel like going back there in December?'

Lily turned to stare at the ceiling. She remembered how hopeful she'd been, after D-day in June, that the war might be over by Christmas. Surely all those boats and ships and planes would steer the Allies to victory? Her father had been right to temper her expectations. There had indeed been many more battles to fight. It wouldn't be over by Christmas. She would stay with Kit in the Land Army.

'Cherries it is,' Lily replied.

Chapter Twenty-Nine

Betty

July 1944

Betty and Gwen huddled under their four blankets each, their breath clouding in front of their faces.

'Is the fire out?' Gwen called.

From across the quarters, the reply came. 'Of course it is. Someone forgot to bloody well chop the firewood, didn't they?'

'It wasn't me.'

'Wasn't it Betty's turn?'

'No, Betty did it yesterday. Almost chopped her foot off with the axe.'

'It was Elaine's turn.'

'It was not my turn at all,' Elaine answered, her insistence muffled by the blankets covering her head.

No one liked chopping wood but it was a necessity in July in Batlow, a small town nestled in the foothills of the Snowy

Mountains, two hundred and seventy-five miles west of Sydney. It meant sawing the big logs with a cross-cut saw and then splitting the sections with an axe, which always seemed to be blunt. And given they had to be up in the dark at six-thirty the next morning, the Land Army girls chose to stay in bed and gripe, rather than search outside for any wood.

Their accommodation was clean but primitive. The long building was divided into six rooms on each side of a long hallway, two to a room. There was a verandah at the front of the building that afforded them some protection from the rain. The laundry served as their bathroom, with metal tubs instead of a bath, which they had to fill with water heated in a copper. When the taps froze, they had to fetch water from the tank outside, crack the ice on top of it, and wash themselves with that instead.

There was a matron's room and a mess hall next door with bare tables and stools, but it had the advantage of having a stove in it for warmth, and a kitchen, in which they had to volunteer one day a fortnight. There was always a race to put one's hand up for that duty when rain was forecast.

Their days were long. The women would be out in the orchard in the dim early-morning light at seven-fifteen and work until twenty past four. Monday, Tuesday, Wednesday, Thursday and Friday. And then half a day on Saturday too. The weeks were long. The work was hard. It was freezing cold.

Why on earth had Betty and Gwen made the decision to return to Batlow for the apple season of 1944?

'Gluttons for punishment, that's what we are,' Gwen had decided. You only needed one good friend to survive the Land Army, Betty knew, and Gwen was her one friend.

'It's an adventure, Betty. That's what it is. And we Land Army girls can do anything. We've proved that, all right.'

Betty reached inside her sheet to check the warmth of the brick she'd slipped into her bed a few hours earlier. The girls had learnt a practical tip: to put a brick in the fire and then wrap it in a cardigan to slip between the sheets. Betty's was already stone cold. Under her four blankets, she wore a pair of men's pyjamas, winter underwear, a jumper sent from home and two pairs of socks, but she still shook from the cold.

She closed her eyes and wished herself back in her bedroom in Sydney. Their quarters were rough, and that was a polite way of putting it. Betty played a game with herself, counting the rafters overhead, and in the morning she counted the shafts of weak sunlight that shone in like spotlights through holes in the corrugated-iron walls. The girls had given up pretending their breath clouds were elegant cigarette smoke. What had been fun the first night, walking up and down pretending sophistication, their fingers in a V as if they were holding a cigarette between their fingers, was now a tedious reality.

More than once, they'd eaten a breakfast of rolled oats and hot tea and then trudged outside to see snow blanketing the ground. The first time, it was delightful and beautiful. Now, it made the days more miserable.

'Psst.' In the next bed, Gwen peeked out from under her blankets.

'What?' Betty asked.

'Perhaps after the war we'll to Queensland. Somewhere way up north. Where the sun shines all the time, hey?'

Betty had invented this game for Gwen when they were in Mildura, after Gwen had found out that her fiancé,

Reggie, had been reported missing in action over Germany. A year later, and Gwen still hadn't heard anything more. His parents had sent letter after letter to the Red Cross, to the Minister for Defence, had even asked their local mayor to help, all to no avail. Reggie was still missing and Gwen was still heartbroken. Betty tried to distract her whenever Gwen appeared to be feeling low. They'd been playing the game a lot lately.

'I wonder what fresh pineapple tastes like?' Betty wondered. 'I'm sure it's nothing like what comes out of the tin.'

'I bet it's sweet as sweet.'

'When Reggie's back, I just know you'll take John and Peter and Margaret for the trip of a lifetime. Perhaps you'll have a new car, maybe one of those Chevrolets, and you'll pack everyone inside and head off for an adventure.'

Gwen laughed. 'That sounds marvellous. Fresh pineapple. Imagine that.'

Betty shivered and pulled the blankets in close around her. She wished someone had done their fair share of the chores. She wished the fire was roaring. She wished she was anywhere but here in this shed, sleeping on a straw-filled mattress with a fruit box for a dressing table and a suitcase for a wardrobe.

The freezing temperatures had made her disheartened. The weather and the hard work had combined to make this the toughest posting she and Gwen had endured since they'd joined up.

They been to lots of places. They'd picked peas in Oberon, which they'd agreed was the most back-breaking work of all the agricultural jobs one could do. They'd debated which was worse there: the back aches from the constant bending or the brown snakes.

They'd both agreed it was the snakes.

From Oberon, they'd gone to Turramurra to work on a poultry farm and then, in January, they'd gone back to Mildura, to the Stocks for the sultana harvest.

From there, they'd come full circle, back to Batlow. When they'd arrived back in February to pick apples in the local orchards, the autumn weather had been a much-welcomed respite from the blazing summer heat and dry winds of Mildura. They'd worked for three months on a variety of properties, picking juicy apples for dehydrating or canning or to send to the city. There had only ever been Granny Smiths in the fruit bowl at home, but here she had picked Jonathons and Red Delicious and Sundowners, right into June. When the picking season was over, she and Gwen had decided to stay on for the pruning season—heaven knows there was enough work—but it had tested them. The work was tough. The ladders were heavy and balancing on them was precarious, especially when leaning over to find the main leader to cut that to a bud, to open up the inside of the tree.

'Shape it out towards the sky,' the orchard's foreman had shouted at her when she'd been learning the year before. 'And don't cut the spurs. That's where next season's fruit comes from.'

Next year's fruit. It was such a cruel thought. Wouldn't the war be over by next season? Surely all the boys would be home by then and all the girls could go back to the city and be the wives and mothers they'd always hoped they'd be? That was her dream, to be Michael's wife and mother to his children.

It was the dream that every Australian girl had, wasn't it?

Michael wrote regularly, but the vagaries of the wartime postal service meant that since he'd been away, there had sometimes been months when she wouldn't hear from him, and then, to her great delight, twelve letters would arrive at once. She'd never made a big fuss, out loud at least, about the troubles and delays with the post. It felt unfair when Gwen didn't receive anything from Reggie. So she'd waited and read her letters in private, purposely not recounting any of his news to Gwen. If she asked, Betty would simply say that he was well and safe.

But when she could, she pored over Michael's words. She laughed behind her hand at the news of the hijinks that he and his friends had got up to. He always passed on regards from his parents back in Sydney and even filled her in on what he knew of his brother Patrick. He never once mentioned any fighting or that he'd been in any danger, which Betty always took as a good sign. If he wasn't near the fighting, he would always be safe, wouldn't he? In her letters back to him, she had filled him in on her adventures all over the country and the fun she was having with Gwen. She hadn't written to Michael about Reggie and how he was missing. Some things were perhaps best left unsaid.

'Betty?' Gwen called. 'Is your brick still warm?'

'As cold as ice, I'm afraid. In fact, hold on, it might even be ice.'

Gwen giggled and Betty laughed with her. They'd made their beds and they were going to lie in them. Even if they were cold as charity.

After their work finished on Saturday morning, there was a tussle about who would get the first lot of hot water so they could wash their hair. It had been the same battle every Saturday for months now. Betty figured it was the difficulty of the weather and the work that was causing such aggravation between the girls and she hoped that the dance that night at the Batlow Literary Institute would help ease the tension that had been brewing among them.

The two-and-a-half-mile walk helped as well. By the time they reached Batlow that night, they were too tired to argue and too excited about the occasion. The institute was a rather grand-looking two-storey building, with its name set in plaster along the top and a portico with columns and the date 1935 above it. The wooden double doors were closed to keep the cold out but when the girls pushed them open, there was party music from a live band and laughter and a delicious supper of hot soup and sandwiches. Almost immediately, their aggravations were forgotten. The hall was filled with local people—farmers, orchardists, those who worked in the packing sheds—and the Land Army girls were welcomed with open arms. When they shrugged off their heavy coats to reveal their winter uniforms, they received a round of applause that bucked them all up considerably.

Betty figured that if the girls hadn't arrived to pick that season's apples, there would have been no jobs for locals in the packing sheds. She could understand why they were so grateful.

'Excuse me, miss. May I have this dance?' A boy who looked no more than twelve stood in front of Betty, bowing, one arm bent behind his back and the other crossed over his stomach. His hair was parted in a crooked line and smoothed down with cream. He wore a white shirt and a tie, and what looked like an older brother's trousers. They bunched at the ankle and almost covered his shiny brown shoes.

Betty smothered a giggle of pure delight at his eager manner. 'Of course you may.'

The boy, a head shorter than Betty, slipped an arm around her waist and held out a hand. She was impressed he knew that much, but three steps in she realised that was all he knew.

'To whom do I owe the pleasure of this dance?' she asked his two left feet.

'What's that?' He looked up at her, his mouth curled in a question.

Betty looked down. 'That means, what's your name, young man?'

He lifted his chin. 'Roger.'

'Very pleased to meet you, Roger. My name's Betty.'

'My sister's name is Betty,' Roger replied with a smile. 'At least we call her that. Her real name is Elizabeth.'

'My name's Elizabeth, too, but I've always been Betty.'

He stomped on her feet and she tried not to gasp too loudly. 'Here, Roger, let me show you something. Try this. Two steps to the right and one to the left.' Betty guided him to the left, then one step back. They tried it again. 'You'll always impress the young ladies if you at least know this dance.'

They moved around the floor for a few minutes, Roger earnestly mumbling *one, two, one* to himself and staring at his feet. He really was sweet and the people of Batlow had put on a wonderful dance but Betty longed for a Sydney boy, one who knew the foxtrot and the waltz and the twostep, one who would whirl her around the dance floor and sing along if they knew the words to the tune and make her feel like a movie star.

'That's it, Roger. You're really getting it now.'

'Thanks, Betty. This is pretty easy, actually.' He glanced down at his shoes.

'How old is your sister, Roger?'

'She's twenty. Six years older than me. She works up in Sydney in a munitions factory making bullets.'

'You must be very proud of her. Her work is helping to keep our boys safe.'

'I asked her to send me a bullet once but she's not allowed to.'

'I can see why. Our troops need every single one.'

Roger stepped on her foot again. Betty turned a wince into a quick smile.

'Sorry,' he said quickly. 'My mum made me come tonight. She said you Land Army girls need partners and, well, all there's left around here are boys from school and our dads and grandpas.'

Betty glanced around the hall. He was right.

'I hope the war goes on a little bit longer so I can go. I want to fly bombers and drop bombs on the Japs. Take that for Darwin, Tojo!'

'Oh,' Betty managed to say but her heart wasn't in her reply.

The band ended the song with a cymbal crash and Roger bowed to thank her. She nodded her head in return, complimented him on his dancing, and then moved off to the side of the hall where the refreshments table was being refilled with trays of sandwiches and jugs of cordial.

Gwen sidled up to her. 'I saw you dancing with that young local boy. He very sweet.'

'Couldn't dance for toffee,' Betty whispered and rolled her eyes at her friend. She feigned swooning and held the back of her hand to her forehead. 'Oh, for a partner who can foxtrot.'

'Or waltz.' Gwen smiled sadly and wrapped her arms around her waist. 'Reggie's the most beautiful dancer. That's how we met, you know. He really did sweep me off my feet. I went home that night and waltzed around the kitchen. I told my mother right there and then that I'd met the boy I was going to marry. And I was right. Two months later, Reggie proposed. It was the night before he shipped out. He gave me a ring and everything but I left it at home. It's sitting right there in the little wooden jewellery box on my dressing table. I didn't want to lose it when I was away in some apple orchard or potato field or crop of peas. It's safe at home. It'll be waiting for me when all this is over.'

Betty's heart ached for Gwen. Could the agony of not knowing be worse than the truth? She slipped an arm through her friend's.

'I just happen to know an excellent dancer.'

'Oh no, Betty. Don't make me dance with that boy.'

'I mean me, silly. Shall we?'

The next morning was Sunday, their only day off. A couple of the girls had volunteered to chop some more firewood in exchange for being let off kitchen duty, so the stove in their quarters was glowing red and radiating warmth, which was a blessed relief from the night before. The young women spent most of the day sitting by the fire, with blankets wrapped around their shoulders like capes, writing in notepads pressed against their knees, or leafing through old magazines and newspapers that had been sent to them by their families.

On Sundays, Betty wrote to Michael, to her parents and sometimes to Jean, her old friend from Woolworths. She missed her fun friendship but Jean's letters had become sporadic since Betty had joined the Land Army and they'd begun to lose touch. Back in February, just as Betty and Gwen had been packing up to leave Mildura, Jean had become engaged to her American soldier, Kevin from South Carolina. That's how Jean described him in her letters. 'Kevin from South Carolina has a funny twang in his voice and a good heart. He's going to send me to America to live with his family until he gets home from the war.' Even if Betty thought the engagement rather rushed, she didn't say that to Jean. She simply congratulated her friend on her good fortune and wished her all the best.

'Don't forget to send me your new address in America,' Betty had replied. 'And be sure to send me photos of all your American children!'

When all the American troops had begun pouring into Sydney after Pearl Harbor back in 1941, rumours had begun to spread about what Australian girls were willing to do for silk stockings and pretty orchids and a one-way ticket to Hollywood. A customer at Woolworths had turned her nose up at a young lady buying a red handbag, scowling, 'Yank catcher' at her. Betty didn't know what to think but Jean liked the Americans. They were polite, they had money to take girls out to dinner and dancing, and as Jean had said, there were so many of them to choose from. Betty supposed that moving a long way away from your family would be very hard, but on the other hand it seemed quite romantic and glamorous to be waiting to be whisked across the sea to

South Carolina or California or Kansas. Some people said outright that the girls were being disloyal to the Australian troops by going after Americans. Some of the local boys were nothing but jealous, Betty thought. But there was lots of talk.

'Wait until the Yanks go home,' she'd heard a customer say once. 'Those girls will be hunting for those self-same Australian boys who weren't good enough for them when the Americans were here. Those girls should be blacklisted, I reckon. And anyway, they'll never make good Australian wives once they've chased after a Yank.'

Betty hadn't understood the sentiment. If you were lucky enough to fall in love with someone, did it really matter where they were from?

She adjusted the blanket wrapped around her shoulders. She was close to the fire and she was finally feeling almost warm. On the notepad on her lap, she'd written, *Dear Michael.* The rest of the page was blank. What more could she say about picking apples? And how to tell him how much she'd changed since he'd gone? She was no longer the young girl he'd kissed on the path outside her house in Sydney, who loved Columbines, who was happy to sit in the park across the street in which she'd played pirates with him and stare up at the stars. They had only been children back then, really, but she was no longer a child. Perhaps it was her friendship with Gwen, watching on as she struggled and survived with the knowledge that Reggie was missing. She'd soldiered on, kept working, kept smiling, but there was a light in her eyes that had gone out, and Betty wondered if it would ever come back. The war had stolen from them too, even if they weren't holding a rifle or flying a plane or stoking coal on a ship.

'Dear Michael,' she whispered to herself and her pen hovered over the page, hesitantly.

The door to their quarters flew open and when a freezing gust blew in there were howls of complaint from around the fire. Their friend Mary slammed the door behind her as she came in and turned to look at the girls with a gleeful expression.

'Where on earth have you been?' Gwen asked, shocked. Mary slipped off her coat and hung it on one of the nails on a beam by the door. Her winter uniform was rumpled, her shirt untucked. Her hat was crooked on her head and when she whipped it off, they could see her hair was knotted and unkempt. 'In Batlow.' She pulled her lips together to supress her smile.

'We waited for you last night,' Betty said. 'The taxi driver was about to leave without us but no one fancied the walk home in the cold at that hour of the night. Are you all right?'

'I'm perfectly … oh, I feel just terrific.' Mary beamed.

Gwen and Betty exchanged glances. A murmur rose among the other girls. 'Those Sydney girls are fast,' someone said under their breath.

'Country boys are so grateful, aren't they?' Mary sighed and sauntered to her bed at the end of the shed.

By the fire, Doris stood hurriedly, the blanket in her lap falling to her feet. The gold cross around her neck glinted in the light of the fire. 'I'll pray for you,' she called to Mary. 'For your sins.'

Mary stilled and spun around. 'I don't want your prayers, Doris. I wanted a man's arms around me and, yes, I wanted sex.'

Some of the girls gasped. Betty shrank in her chair.

'Is that so wrong? Do you know how long my husband has been away?' Mary's voice cracked, her hands were fists. 'Since May 1940. May the sixth 1940, to be precise. That's more than four years, Doris. Four bloody years. So, Doris, don't waste your prayers on me. Send them all to New Guinea, will you?'

Mary covered her face with her hands and began sobbing, wailing, stomping her feet in her rage. Betty moved to go to her, but Gwen was there first, an arm of comfort around her, leading her to her bed. Doris crossed herself over and over and over, her eyes closed, whispering to herself.

Betty snatched up some of those prayers for Michael.

Chapter Thirty

August 1944

That August in Batlow, it was colder than July. The apple-tree pruning continued. The Land Army girls' routine of Friday-night dances and Saturday nights at the pictures continued through those winter months, small windows of respite from the hard physical work and the incessant cold. They'd sung along to *Babes on Broadway* with Mickey Rooney and Judy Garland and been scared out of their wits by *Apache Trail* starring Donna Reed. When the newsreel relayed the latest news from the war, of further Allied gains in France and American bombing in the Philippines, everyone in the theatre stood and sang 'God Save The King' and cheered.

The girls had marched out of the cinema exhilarated, singing the Andrews Sisters' 'Boogie Woogie Bugle Boy' until they forgot the lyrics and botched the harmonies but they didn't care as they walked the two-and-a-half miles home in the cold.

On the sixteenth of August, Gwen received word about Reggie. A telegram from his parents came with the mail and she'd almost fainted before ripping it open. It contained the best of news. Previously reported missing from operations over enemy-held territory, Reggie was now listed as a prisoner of war. The word had come from the air force, via the Red Cross in Geneva. Gwen had sobbed happy tears for days and their friends had celebrated with an impromptu dance around the fire that night, with the wireless turned up as loud as it could go.

On weeknights after supper, the girls had grown used to sitting around the radio, listening to *Australia Sings* and then the news on the ABC. When the familiar orchestral music played, everyone knew to hush, put down their cups of tea or their books or magazines, and listen intently to the sombre tones of the announcer broadcasting from Sydney.

'The Red Army is within one hundred and thirty miles of the frontier of Germany proper and the road in the heart of Germany is open.'

'That's good, isn't it?' asked Doris, clutching her Bible to her chest.

'Yes, it's definitely good news,' Gwen replied, her eyes bright. 'The Allies are in France and the Russians are taking the east. In no time, the Germans will be squeezed in the middle and they'll have no choice but to surrender. And then it'll be all over for the Japs, too, won't it? And then our boys will come home.'

The next Saturday night the girls climbed up onto the back of a flatbed truck and hung on for dear life for the forty-minute drive to Tumut in the north-west of the Snowy Mountains. They'd been invited to a dance and euchre party in aid of the Red Cross at the Oddfellows' Hall. Gwen had been particularly keen to go along as a way of thanking the Red Cross, which had helped get word to her about Reggie.

They'd all happily paid their admission of three shillings and had bid on items in the silent auction. Betty had come home with six embroidered handkerchiefs and a pair of thick woollen socks. Gwen had won a pack of notebooks, envelopes and stamps, and Doris had been pleased to bring home a new knitted woollen cap.

The social life in the region was almost too much to keep up with. Grand Balls sponsored by the Patriotic and War Fund in Brungle. Football dances. Hospital dances at Adelong in the local parish hall. Cheer Up reviews organised by the Tumut Comforts Fund, featuring tap dancers, yodellers and a two young ladies doing an Irish jig, which finished with tearful renditions of 'There'll Always Be an England' and 'Advance Australia Fair'. Betty would have enjoyed them all the more if she hadn't had to work so hard during the day, but the social occasions and the warm welcomes certainly helped time pass.

In September, just as the weather at the foot of the Snowy Mountains had begun to thaw and orchard pruning work was coming to an end, Gwen received news that Reggie had died and had been buried in a prisoner-of-war camp in a place in Germany called Weinsberg.

She'd quit the Land Army that day to go home.

Betty missed the 1944 Batlow Apple Blossom festival. She went home for a few weeks. She'd never met Reggie, but his death had been as devastating to her as if she'd known him all her life. Betty had admired Gwen so much for the calm restraint she'd shown when she'd told the rest of the Land Army girls. Was it easier to come to grips with the death of someone you loved when you'd already imagined them dead? Betty had never let herself think of Michael being in danger and it was only after Reggie's death that she realised how naive she'd been. Michael's letters had been filled with humour and reminiscences and tales of local people and his mates. Shouldn't she have guessed that anything more wouldn't have passed the censor's pen? She'd seen the stamp on all his letters—*Passed By Censor*—but hadn't twigged what that really meant. How could the news on the radio and the newspapers be full of the war every day and letters home not mention it?

Reggie's family couldn't have a funeral as there was no body to bury, but Gwen had stood by his parents' side at a memorial service at their church. She was nothing to them now, the almost daughter-in-law they barely knew who was now a reminder of the son who would never be coming home.

A month after the service, Gwen wrote to Betty. She was working in a munitions factory near home and trying to find a new life for herself. Although she would never wear it again, she told Betty that she would keep Reggie's engagement ring forever.

Betty's parents met her at Central Station on the day she arrived home on leave, bearing a posy of daisies and a box of chocolates. They splashed out and paid for a taxi home to Rozelle and when she walked in the door, the first thing Betty did was strip off her Land Army uniform and soak in a hot bath. As the water cooled, she pulled the plug a little and topped it up afresh, and repeated the procedure for hours and hours. She wondered how long it would take to completely thaw after her winter in Batlow.

When she was as wrinkled as a prune, she dressed in the new pyjamas her mother had kindly left on her old bed, wrapped herself in her soft and comforting dressing gown and sat down at the kitchen table for a cup of tea and a piece of fruit cake. It was golden and dense, full of sultanas and currants and orange peel and, as she slowly savoured it, she was reminded of Mildura and her two seasons there.

'Betty?' Her mother sat opposite, staring at her. 'Did you hear what I said?'

'Sorry, Mum?'

Her father sat at the head of the table, a folded newspaper in front of him. He'd asked the deputy headmaster to look after things at school so he could take the day off to meet his adventurous daughter. 'Your mother asked what you'd like for dinner.'

'Anything,' Betty sighed. 'As long as it's not macaroni cheese. I think I've had enough of that to last a lifetime. Our matron at Batlow was not the best of cooks and, well, none of us wanted to appear ungrateful and at least it was warming. I'm sure whatever you've prepared will be delicious, Mum.' Betty didn't bother to stifle her yawn. It had been a long trip home from Batlow and the bath had made her even sleepier. 'I thought I might pop next door before bed and see Mrs Doherty too. She's well?'

Betty's mother dropped her teaspoon with a clatter onto her saucer. Her father cleared his throat.

'What is it?' Panic rose up in Betty's throat and she sprang to her feet, adrenaline coursing through her veins like an electric shock.

'Michael? Is it Michael?'

Suddenly, her mother was on one side and her father on the other, each with a hand on her shoulder, urging her to sit down.

'It's not Michael,' her mother said quietly. 'It's Patrick.'

Betty felt her legs give way and she splayed her hands on the table to keep herself upright. Her breath came fast and short. It hurt to breathe all of a sudden.

'Tell me everything,' she said quietly as her eyes welled.

Her mother went to the stove to boil the kettle for another pot of tea. Her father covered a hand with one of his. 'He was killed in Bougainville two weeks ago. Mrs Doherty found out yesterday.'

'Is … is he coming home?' Betty stammered.

'Betty, listen to me. Patrick has died. He won't be coming home.'

She closed her eyes and thought of Gwen without even a body to mourn over. 'No, I mean, are they going to bring his body home? Will there be a funeral?'

'We don't know, Betty.'

'And Michael. Does he know? Will they send a telegram to him? He'll want to know, he'll want to know.' And then she could speak no more, as the tears came and sobs wracked her chest. She sat with her parents at the kitchen table until she fell asleep on her crossed arms.

The next morning, when Betty knocked on the Dohertys' door, there was no Michael calling out to her, 'Don't you knock any more, Betty Boop?' but she let herself in anyway. The curtains were drawn in the living room at the front of the house and she stepped quietly past Mrs Doherty's china cabinet in the hallway. Its shelves full of trinkets and her best china were familiar and comforting but something was different. The top of the polished cabinet had been cleared of its bone-china figurines and in their place were two framed photographs of her sons in their uniforms. Patrick and Michael. How proud she was of her only children.

Betty had lived a life untouched by death, until the war. Both sets of her grandparents were still alive and she had three girl cousins on both sides of the family from aunts and uncles she saw a few times a year. What would she say to Mrs Doherty? She tried to think back. What had she said to Gwen?

'Mrs Doherty? It's me, Betty.' When she reached the kitchen door, Betty found her, sitting at the table, her shoulders slumped, a creased handkerchief in her fist.

She looked up. Her eyes were red raw, her cheeks flushed, her lips trembling. 'Betty?'

There was nothing to say. Betty pulled up a chair next to her neighbour, opened her arms wide, and they cried in each other's arms.

'Here are all his letters.' An hour later, after three cups of tea and some fresh scones, Mrs Doherty slid a shoebox across the table to Betty. 'Michael's, I mean. Not Patrick's. I thought you might like to read them. I know he's been writing to you as well, but here they are. We share him, Betty. We always have.'

'Thank you, Mrs Doherty.' Betty understood her need to feel close to her only living son. By studying his handwriting, by reading his words, his stories, they could bring him back for just a moment. Betty wanted nothing more than to feel his presence in this house. Simply sitting in the kitchen, it was easy to imagine the sound of his footsteps, the way he devoured his mother's cakes, his sheer physical presence in every room.

'How long are you back for?'

'The Land Army has given me four weeks' leave.'

'Four weeks?' Mrs Doherty sniffed, and Betty suddenly felt guilty for having the luxury of a holiday.

'Mum and Dad have promised to pamper me while I'm home. I'm quite looking forward to it, to be honest. I've worked hard this year.'

'So I hear. They played a newsreel about you Land Army girls at the pictures. I can't remember what the film was, but there they all were in their overalls just like those ones you have, Betty. I think they were growing potatoes, I can't be sure. There was a girl on a tractor, driving it just like a man. Imagine that, I said to myself. When your mum told me you were in Batlow for the apples, I thought of you every time I went to the green-grocer's. Good on you, I thought. What a good girl you are for helping all those people out in the country. And our boys.'

She clasped Betty's hand.

Perhaps talk of her adventures might distract Mrs Doherty for just a moment from her grief. 'I've met girls who've worked in shearing sheds.'

Mrs Doherty gasped and smiled sadly. 'I can't believe that's true.'

'It's true. They told me themselves.'

'My goodness me.'

'And the farmers everywhere are saying we've worked just as hard and done just as good a job as the boys. How about that?'

'You're a good girl, Betty. I'm so pleased that Michael …
well, it's all in his letters.' Mrs Doherty nodded at the shoebox and wiped her eyes with her handkerchief. 'You go
ahead and read them. Take the box home. Just bring them
back when you're done.'

Betty reached for the box, hesitating. 'Why don't you
come home with me, instead of being here on your own?
You know you're more than welcome.'

Mrs Doherty's lips trembled once more. 'Thank you, dear
girl. My sister's coming from Lismore to stay with me. You
go home and see your parents. They've missed you terribly.'

Betty rose from her seat. She lifted the box, heard
Michael's letters rustle inside it.

'I'll pop in tomorrow for a cup of tea. See if there's anything you need.'

Mrs Doherty nodded and as Betty closed the front door
behind her and walked home, the unmistakable sound of
weeping followed her for every one of those thirty-five steps.

Chapter Thirty-One

Betty woke to a sunny and perfect Sydney spring morning, the sweet scent of jasmine wafting through her open bedroom window and the tweets of the New Holland honeyeaters reminding her she was home. She gave in to the luxury of lying in bed for as long as she wanted.

She needed time to figure out everything that had happened in the past week. Gwen's Reggie dead in Germany. Patrick in New Guinea. Death had come too close, as if it were stalking her. The weight of that terrible news was counterbalanced with the things she'd read in Michael's letters to his mother. She'd been a little perplexed when Mrs Doherty had insisted she read his letters home. She couldn't imagine what things he might have told his mother that he hadn't told her.

Now she knew, and she could barely put into words how she felt.

*Mum, I can tell you because I know you'll keep it
a secret, but when the war is over and I'm home,
I'm going to ask Betty to marry me. Yes, that's right.
Betty Brower. Now I know what you're going to say
about that, that you were right all along. And, gee,
were you ever. When I left for my training back in
'43, you were right when you said that I was in love
with Betty. I don't think I knew it really myself at the
time, but all this time away and I haven't thought of
any other girl but my dearest Betty Boop. Thoughts of
her have helped me get through the days when things
are a bit tough around here. I can't say much more
than that but I'm sure you know what I mean. Why
did it take the war for me to realise that the girl for
me was the one living thirty-five steps away?*

Betty pressed her head back into her pillow. How was it possible to feel so heartbroken and so happy all at once? Death was close but happiness was close too, and Michael was still alive and, with that awareness, there was hope for Betty's dreams for the future. He wanted to marry her. How on earth could she keep that a secret until he was home?

Sydney had changed while Betty had been away. The buildings seemed taller, the ups and downs of the streetscapes from Circular Quay were more undulating, and there were so many people everywhere that she felt the need to duck into shops whenever she could to escape the crush. She was on her way to Woolworths to see the girls she'd worked with, after having spent the morning with Mrs Doherty. Michael's mother had alternated between sobs of despair and elation at the realisation that she had lost a son but would be gaining a daughter-in-law. The war was full of such paradoxes, Betty was beginning to learn. She only had a job she loved because there was a war. She had made perhaps the best girlfriend she'd ever had because of the war.

She shook off the thought as she walked into her old workplace. At her old counter, she discovered new girls she didn't recognise. When she introduced herself, they stared at her blankly, and told her, no, they had never heard of the Betty Brower who'd left to join the Land Army.

Betty ambled to the bus stop, watching people as they passed her in the streets. Uniforms everywhere. Children in school uniform laughing and licking ice blocks. Mothers with their babies in perambulators clogging the footpaths. Businessmen scurrying from place to place. Office girls clutching bundles of papers and files. She wished the years back to 1939 when she was innocent about the damage the war would inflict and the changes it would bring.

Betty's mind whirred. She'd been a part of this world but now felt a stranger. The noise of the streets was an assault. She didn't like the way people bustled up beside her and scowled at her when she didn't move out of the way. By the time she stepped off the bus at the end of King Street, she had a throbbing headache.

When she turned her key in the front door and walked into an empty house, she was glad of the silence and the peace. She boiled the kettle, made a cup of tea, and took it out into the back yard. The blooms on the jasmine at the side of the house perfumed the whole garden, which comprised a strip of lawn, a clothesline, and lemon, plum and nectarine trees. Two pink hibiscus bloomed by one of the side fences, their branches long and spindly from a lack of attention. She sat on the back step, sipping her tea, thinking about the garden and the war and Patrick and Reggie and her dear Michael. She thought about Jean off with an American and Mary in Batlow whose husband had been gone for four years.

She found a pair of garden clippers in the small shed by the water tank. They weren't as sharp as those she'd used for all those months in Batlow, shaping the apple trees as she pruned them, but they would do. She changed into her Land Army overalls and rolled up her sleeves to let her arms feel the sun. And she got started.

By the end of her first week home, she'd transformed her parents' back yard. She'd not only pruned all the trees and bushes into manageable shapes but she'd dug out a square of grass and planted potatoes, carrots and war cabbage. She'd fashioned a sign from an old fencing pale and painted *Victory Garden* on it in wonky lettering. She would be home for three more weeks before she was assigned to her next posting, which would be more than enough time to see the seeds germinate, take hold and send their roots deep into the soil, to encourage her parents to come out into the garden and dig the earth and tend to it, just as their daughter was doing so far away.

Her garden was a piece of her new life that she'd brought to her old. She didn't have to explain it to her mother and father that first day when they came home and found her tilling the soil.

It was her way of telling them, 'This is who I am now.'

Chapter Thirty-Two

Flora

Melbourne
September 4th, 1944
Dearest Charles,
I write to you today with a heavy heart.

Frank has been home, having been granted two weeks leave on very short notice, but today we farewelled him again and I can hardly bear it. I'm so grateful to have been granted leave myself from the Land Army. I wasn't quite due my holidays but my matron in Leeton put in a good word for me and I was able to hop on a train and head home as soon as I knew Frank was on his way.

It was so marvellous to have the three of us together again. Jack arranged a special dinner so Frank could meet Doreen and everyone got on like a house on fire, which was wonderful. We shared a toast to our father and then said nothing more about death and loss and grief.

Saying goodbye to Frank was the hardest thing I've ever done. Jack and I stood on the docks at Port Melbourne, chilled by rain and a southerly wind, trying to be strong. Frank smiled and said, don't worry, you two, I'll be fine. Then he hugged Jack, kissed me on both cheeks and I clutched at him like a child might squeeze their favourite teddy bear. We've had so much luck keeping him safe and now all I feel is a growing dread that we might have run out of it. When it was time to board, he gave Jack and me a salute, his fingers tapping the side of his slouch hat, and then he threw his kit back over his shoulder and walked up the gangplank onto the ship. He didn't look back and I'm glad he didn't, because I was trying so hard not to cry but failed miserably.

I've felt rather low since he left and the monotony of work back here at Leeton has kept me in a sad daze. It's only thoughts of being back at Two Rivers again that have kept me going. I want nothing more than to be sitting around the kitchen table with you and your mother and the girls, laughing at their stories and eating some of your mother's scones. In a world that is unpredictable and full of sadness, that thought has been like a beacon to me.

Please wish your mother all my best for her continuing improvement from pneumonia. I'm relieved to know that the warmer weather and sunshine have helped.

Charles, your letters mean so much to me. Please keep them coming. I haven't forgotten our promises to each other about the life we might have when the war is over. In my dreams, I see your face and I wake up happy.

With every best wish for Christmas and the New Year.

Your Flora

Two Rivers
November 1st, 1944
My dearest, Flora,

I was out among the vines today and saw the first signs of life, of new leaves on those gnarled old vines that my father planted so many years ago. Even in the drought somehow they survive and thrive. There must really be something in the water here at Two Rivers.

When I saw those new buds, my first thought was to share my excitement with you.

I can't wait until you return.

Violet and Daisy have grown so much since you were last here that you might not recognise them and let me assure you that they will be thrilled to have you back, although not more than me.

My mother's health took a long time to recover and the doctor believes her lungs still suffer. She has a cough that won't seem to go away, but the warmer weather has helped. She's able to sit outside in the sun and looks out to the view that she loves. I believe that's made a big difference to her recovery.

I have some news I've been waiting to share with you. I've decided to expand Two Rivers. Mrs Northcott decided to sell up when her husband died in August and offered it to me at a good price. It makes sense being neighbouring blocks to consolidate. We shook on it and the deal is done, which means there will be more grapes to pick this summer.

I think of Frank often and I'm so happy for you and Jack that you were able to see him. I wish him godspeed and a safe return to Australia when the war is over. And for you, I wish you the courage and strength to keep going and serving your country in the way you do.

It won't be long until you return to Two Rivers and I find myself counting down the days.
With fondest regards, Charles

Chapter Thirty-Three

January 1945

Flora wanted to run. She wanted to race down the platform like a puppy chasing a cat, not caring if she bowled over every other person in her path with her flailing arms and her flying suitcase. She had seen Charles and she wanted to throw herself at him, to be held and to feel his lips against hers. But she was a Land Army girl and she had a reputation to uphold and a job to do. And, in truth, she didn't need grand displays of affection. She'd had his words, had held them in her hand these past eleven months. Every letter had been like a promise to her, she could see that now. She'd borne witness to a gentle unfurling of this man, all he thought and hoped and wished for.

She didn't need anything else at this moment. For now, his smile was enough. His handsome face was enough. So instead of running, she strolled and he ambled until they were close enough to touch.

'Flora.' He tipped his hat.

'Hello, Charles.'

'I have the car.'

'I have my suitcase.' She glanced around. 'Where are the girls?'

'At home.'

'They didn't want to come to meet me?'

He stepped in closer. 'I wanted some time alone with you.'

'You did?'

'I wish you weren't wearing that damn uniform.' He looked Flora over, from the polished leather of her Land Army shoes to the top of her hat, her AWLA badge gleaming on its crest.

'Why is that, Mr Nettlefold?' Flora asked, cocking her head to the side as if she didn't understand his meaning. The train sounded its horn and people shuffled and bustled all around them but all she could her was the deep timbre of his voice and her heart beating fast in her ears. It was so wonderful to see him. Without a photo, she'd had to recreate him anew each night in her dreams, but this was so much better.

He took a step closer. 'Because people will be shocked and you'll probably get into trouble if I kiss you when you're on duty.'

Flora's cheeks were suddenly hot and she fought the urge to reach out to him, to touch the tanned skin on his forearm exposed by his rolled sleeves.

'Charles!'

Charles looked over Flora's shoulder and tipped his hat politely. 'Bert.' A man about Charles's age positioned himself in between Charles and Flora and held out a hand. 'Good to see you. It's been a long time,' Bert said.

'It sure has been. How are you?' There was a tone in Charles's voice that pricked Flora's attention. When his eyes briefly flickered to Bert's chest, Flora realised that the fabric on one sleeve of his white shirt had been sewn closed at the shoulder.

'Can't complain.' There was a forced cheeriness in Bert's voice that Flora immediately recognised. She'd heard it in Frank when he'd been home in September. A brittleness, a nervousness.

'The missus sure is glad I'm home. I'm here to meet her sister. She's come up from Melbourne to help with the kids for a bit. You?'

'I'm here for Miss Atkins. Our Land Army girl out at Two Rivers.' Charles raised his eyebrows in a question, extending a hand to encourage her to come forward. 'Miss Atkins. This is Bert Williams. I went to school here in Mildura with his brother, Terry.'

Flora smiled warmly at him. 'Pleased to meet you, Bert. My brother's serving in the AIF.'

Bert's ears pricked. 'Good on him. Which division?'

'The 8th. He's in the 2/11th Field Regiment. He was just home in September on leave.'

'I wish him all the best for a safe return,' Bert said as he tipped his hat to Flora. 'Well, Charles, it was good to see you. All my best to your mother.'

'You too, Bert. Say hello to Sheila.'

Bert ducked into the crowd and Flora turned to watch him go. There was a limp in his step too, not enough to need a walking stick but obvious all the same. When she was sure he was out of earshot, Flora asked Charles, 'Where was he?'

'New Guinea. He came home six months ago. Medically discharged. As you can see.'

Flora followed Charles and they walked in silence to the car. Charles quickly put her suitcase in the back and guided her into the passenger seat, and they drove off.

The Dodge was covered in red dust, inside and out, but Charles had thoughtfully put a blanket on the seat for her to help keep her uniform clean. As soon as they were out of the streets of Mildura, she wound down her car window and leant her face into the wind. It played with her, tugging at her hat and teasing her ears, creating a little echoing whistle that she hoped might drown out the thumping behind her breastbone. She closed her eyes and took in a deep breath, trying to hold this memory close, this precious moment in time. She could do nothing else about the war than endure it, work hard and imagine a life after it.

Was the man sitting next to her, driving with careful concentration, going to be a part of that future?

After the war. That was the promise they'd made to each other.

The route to Two Rivers was familiar to Flora now, as familiar as her walk home to Waterloo Street from the tram stop in Camberwell. The straight stretch of road, then a veer left and a turn right over the dry creek bed. A copse of gum trees that had survived clearing and a stone house in the distance behind an orange orchard.

Australia had been at war for more than five years. Frank had been away for nearly four. Thousands of young men had already been sacrificed, nurses had been killed at Bangka, and citizens in Darwin—and in a hundred thousand small towns and cities around the world—had been bombed and killed, too. But change was in the air and people let themselves imagine, for the first time in a long time, that victory was within reach. Every day, the news Flora heard on the radio seemed more positive. The Americans were winning in the Pacific and the Japanese were reeling. In Europe, the Allies were pushing back against Hitler from every direction. But Frank was still fighting. The young men of Mildura she'd heard about when she'd first arrived, who had signed up in higher proportions than boys from any other town in Australia, were dead or injured or abroad. Farmers still needed labour and there were more girls in the Land Army than ever before.

She pulled her head inside the cabin, smoothed back her hair. 'I can't wait for a tour of the new block.'

Charles smiled, finally, and she breathed out. 'I can't wait to show you. It's now officially ours.' He looked at her for a long moment, the implication of the word *ours* hanging in the air between them. 'My dear old dad used to say that war is good for business.' Charles paused, ruminating over what he'd just said and how it sounded. 'And the terrible truth is that he was right about Two Rivers. Things were tough for us before the war, when the drought hit.' Charles's revelation had embarrassed him. She could hear it in the resigned tone in his voice

'An army marches on its stomach,' Flora said with a sigh. 'It's the same for me. I've only had work in the Land Army because of the war. I've thought about that more than once.' She shook off the melancholy. 'So, the new block. Is it all sultanas?'

He nodded. 'They delivered a good crop last year so I'm hoping for the same this summer.' The truck jumped over the ruts in the dusty dirt road and Flora and Charles bounced on the front seat. In three years, the old Dodge had slowly become more rickety but Charles had clearly been investing his earnings in something far more important: a future for his family.

'There are more grapes than you and I will be able to pick on our own, so I contacted the Manpower Directorate. We have a couple of new Land Army girls coming to help us this season.'

'Really?' Flora was immediately delighted at the thought.

'Is that all right with you?'

'Of course. But where are we going to put them?'

'I've thought about that. My girls will sleep in their grandmother's room and the two from the Land Army can have the twin beds in Violet and Daisy's room. It's only for a few weeks. Mum says she doesn't mind. The girls love the idea of top-and-tailing in the double bed, although my mother thinks she might wake up with feet in her face.'

Flora laughed at the idea of it.

'They have all sorts of things planned for her, including a night of ghost stories, I'm told.'

'It might lift her mood, do you think? If she's still recovering, I mean.'

Charles glanced across at her. 'That was my plan.'

'I'm sure they'll be smashing girls. I've met so many these past couple of years. They're all so hardworking and adventurous and brave. They'll put up with anything you can think of.'

Charles tipped back his hat and grinned. 'I can vouch for that. I've been pretty happy with my Land Army girl.'

Flora laughed and gripped the door handle as Charles turned right off the main road at the sign saying Two Rivers.

No more than a hundred feet after the turn, he pulled over to the side of the road and cut the engine. When he turned to Flora, she knew what he wanted because she wanted it, too.

He slid across the front seat and kissed her. Flora didn't need words. They had shared thousands of them in the eleven months they'd been parted and now she wanted his mouth and his arms around her. He kissed her lips, her cheek, and down her neck to the collar of her uniform. She pressed her palms to his face and met his urgency with a need of her own, tasting and searching.

He finally pulled back, breathing hard, searching her eyes. 'I wanted to do this at the station. Right in front of everyone.'

'So did I,' she replied. 'So much.'

'Do you know how much I've missed you, Flora?'

She pressed her hands to his chest and cuddled into his neck. He swung an arm around her shoulder and pulled her in close. She had fought her nerves about seeing him again all the way since Flinders Street station very early that morning. She'd been unable to think about anything else other than this moment, about this reunion, about what her time in Two Rivers might bring this year.

She took in every detail of his beloved face. It was now two years since she'd first met him and she tried to find any signs of alteration in his appearance. Perhaps he was greyer, a little more wrinkled about the eyes, but she hoped that was from laughing with his daughters and smiling at her letters. That first time they'd met, when he'd walked into her room and woken her, he'd taken off his hat and given her a passing smile. She'd thought he might have been taciturn. But she'd been so wrong.

She couldn't help it. She kissed Charles again, throwing her arms around his neck, tasting him, holding on to his strong shoulders, breathing in his scent, finally letting herself imagine that this month at Two Rivers might change everything.

Flora feigned enormous surprise at seeing Violet and Daisy when they raced over to the truck to meet her.

'Flora!' Daisy called out as she ran, delight in her expression. Flora's cheeks were still flushed from kissing Charles and she slapped her hands to them to hide the blush. She looked Daisy over, from bare feet to her white-blonde hair.

'I don't believe we've met,' Flora said, deadpan.

Daisy jumped on the spot. 'Yes we have. It's me! Daisy!'

'No, you can't possibly be Daisy. She was only this big when I was here last January.' Flora held her hand out flat at hip height. 'You must be an imposter. Or a vagabond.'

Daisy flung her arms around Flora's waist and giggled into her shirt. It was so good to have these little arms around her again that Flora had to blink away her tears. 'Hello, Violet.' Charles's oldest daughter had hung back a little and Flora wondered if she already thought herself too grown-up for such displays of childhood affection. How old must she be now? Ten years old?

'Hello, Flora,' Violet replied. 'Nan made afternoon tea. Would you like to come inside?'

'I would love to. The train journey was so long and I had already devoured my Vegemite sandwich a half-hour out of Melbourne.' Daisy released Flora and entwined their hands as they walked to the back door. Violet waited, walking behind Flora and Daisy. Flora looked to Charles with a questioning glance and he gave her the slightest nod, which she understood to mean that he'd seen Violet's reluctance. Flora filed it away to discuss later when the girls were asleep.

Later, after Flora had unpacked her things and washed and changed clothes, after a shared supper of meatloaf and vegetables, the family gathered in the sitting room. Flora had missed its comfortable familiarity. Mrs Nettlefold sat on her armchair quietly. She seemed to have shrunk since the previous January. There were hollows in her cheeks where there had previously been the blush of rude good health and country air and, instead of knitting or sewing or darning, she watched the girls with a distracted expression.

Violet and Daisy had set up a game of snakes and ladders and were lying on the rug, rolling their dice and disagreeing with good humour about the precise square that captured the end of a snake's tail. Charles was reading an Agatha Christie novel.

When Flora stood at the doorway and cleared her throat, four pairs of eyes turned to her.

'I hope you don't mind,' she started, suddenly nervous. 'I know I've missed Christmas by a good few weeks but I have some presents for you all.'

The girls' eyes widened and Daisy shouted, 'Presents?'

'Father Christmas accidentally left these for you at my house back in Melbourne,' Flora said in an exaggerated fashion.

Charles winked at her and played along. 'How did he get so confused about where the girls live?'

Flora shrugged, gripping the handle of her calico bag with both hands. 'It's a mystery to me.' She reached inside it. 'This one has … your name on it, Daisy. And, Violet, this one's for you.'

The girls hopped up from the rug and accepted their gifts with gracious thanks and smiles of excitement. Daisy impatiently ripped at the newspaper in which Flora had wrapped her gift. '*Blinky Bill*! *Blinky Bill*!' She hopped on the spot.

Violet was more considered. She unwrapped her gift carefully. Flora sensed that Violet was on the cusp, sitting on the verge of wanting to be a young woman herself, desiring to cast aside childish things, but secretly longing for them at the same time. Flora remembered that her own confusion had set in when her mother had died. Dear Violet, she thought. The world will come to you all too soon. Enjoy these last innocent and golden moments.

'*Seven Little Australians*!' she exclaimed, looking up at Flora with eyes wide and her mouth agape. 'I've borrowed this from the library over and over but I don't have my very own copy. It's my all-time favourite ever.' She sat back on the settee, staring at the cover.

'Isn't Father Christmas clever?' Charles asked.

Mrs Nettlefold sniffed and patted her cheeks with a handkerchief. 'He certainly is.' She smiled warmly at Flora, who thought she saw a little spark in the old woman's eyes.

'You might want to thank Flora for bringing those gifts all the way from Melbourne,' Charles added and the girls went to her and kissed her on the cheek. 'Perhaps next year he won't get so mixed up and he'll send them to the right place.'

He and Flora exchanged a look. She had understood what he meant.

'I have something for you too, Mrs Nettlefold.'

'You shouldn't have,' she said quietly. 'Flora, really ...'

'It's not much, I promise.' Flora walked to her, bent down and pressed her lips to Mrs Nettlefold's pale cheek. She gave her a small parcel. Mrs Nettlefold held it on her lap and slowly unwrapped the paper. Inside, was a selection of embroidery thread wound around cards, from a lush apple green to a pale pink.

'They belonged to my mother and somehow got pushed to the back of the linen cupboard in our hallway at home. I know you embroider things so beautifully, and although I can knit, I'm completely hopeless with a needle. I thought you might be able to use them for something.'

'What a lovely gift,' Mrs Nettlefold said, running her fingers along the threads, shuffling them to arrange them in gradations of colour.

Any nervousness Flora had felt at anticipating Charles's mother's reaction disappeared in the flash of a smile. For a moment, she watched the girls and Mrs Nettlefold examine their presents. The girls began silently reading, their stomachs pressed to the floor and their legs kicked up behind them. Mrs Nettlefold took a single thread and rewound it on its card. They were too distracted to see Flora mouth the word *Later* to Charles or to see him nod in return. He didn't return to the pages of his book but leant back on his chair, his head on the headrest, one leg crossed over the other. He and Flora allowed themselves the luxury of staring at one another for as long as they wanted.

Later that night, when the rest of the household was asleep and the moon was high in the sky, Charles knocked on Flora's door. She had been sitting on the edge of her bed, twisting her fingers around each other in frustrated knots, waiting for him. She opened the door as quietly as she could and he entered wordlessly, immediately reaching for her, wrapping his arms around her, lifting her off her feet and kissing her.

'I thought you'd never come,' she whispered, her lips pressed to his cheek.

'You doubted me?'

'No, never.' He lowered her feet to the floor and she took his hand, guiding him to the edge of her bed, where she pushed him to sit down. Despite his reluctance to let go, tugging at the pocket of her trousers, the puff of her sleeve, he released her and gazed at her with loving eyes as she disentangled her fingers from his. She went to her chest of drawers and found something in among the soft rustle of her clothes. 'Here's your gift.'

Charles took it, darting his hand to her shirt to hold the fabric and pull her close. When he spread his legs wide, he pulled her into the space he made between his thighs, pressing his face into her breasts. She moved against him, kissing the top of his head and holding his face in her hands. His stubble grazed her palms and made her shiver. In the dark of the night they were operating by touch, not sight.

'You're all I want and all I need.'

'Open it,' she teased.

'You haven't been knitting again, have you?' He let go of her long enough to rip the paper open.

'I can always knit you more socks if you want them.'

The rustle of paper stopped. Perhaps his eyes hadn't adjusted to the dark for he sat silently, staring at the small sphere in his open hand.

'Do you like it? It's from the Atkins family Christmas tree this year. It's a decoration. I know it's not much but it's something that's hung from our tree at home since I was a little girl. I thought you might like it for your tree. The girls might like it, too.'

She heard him swallow. 'I don't want to wait any more. I can't, Flora.' He pulled her closer, wrapped his arms around her waist and held tight. There wasn't an inch between their beating hearts.

'I'm here now.'

'But you'll go.'

'I made a promise. Until Frank is home safe—'

'I understand. I do. I know how much your family means to you. I had hoped the war would be over by now, you see?'

'So did I,' she said quietly.

'I don't just want your Christmas bauble on my tree. I want you here, always.'

'Charles ...'

He pulled Flora into his lap and she dropped her head onto his shoulder. She pressed a hand to his chest to feel his heart beating beneath her fingertips. He stroked her hair as he spoke. 'I'm not a young bloke any more, Flora. Years seemed to go by so fast until I met you. Now, they go so slow I can hardly bear it.'

'I'm here now.'

'Could you love me?' Charles asked, his voice gruff.

'You need to ask me that?' she replied softly, kissing his forehead, his neck, his mouth.

'I need to hear you say it.'

'Yes,' she said softly into his lips. 'I could and I do.'

She felt for the buttons of his shirt, slipping them through their buttonholes, one by one.

Chapter Thirty-Four

'Miss Atkins!'

Flora wiped her brow and turned. She was hanging her wet clothes on the drooping clothes line by the chook shed, squeezing wooden pegs onto the thick cotton fabric of her overalls. She peered across the yard.

'I thought it was you. It's me! Betty Brower. Don't you remember? Back in '43. We met at the Red Cross ball here in Mildura.' And before Flora could place the face, the young woman who had raced across the yard had whipped off her hat and thrown her arms open wide for a hug.

Flora remembered. Betty, the young woman from Sydney who'd been scared and teary all those years ago. Look at her now. A young woman, strong and confident, wearing her uniform with pride instead of apprehension. 'My goodness me. Of course I remember!'

The two women exchanged a warm embrace, then Flora held her at arm's length. She looked her over. 'It's your hair. It used to be longer.'

Betty laughed and took off her hat. 'People say I look like a boy with hair this short but I don't care in the slightest. When you can only wash it once a week, who wants to fuss with anything longer than this?' Betty ruffled a hand over her black locks, perhaps only two inches long all over.

'It's perfectly practical. I approve. I'm so pleased to see you here, no matter now long or short your hair is. How are you?'

'I'm very well, thank you. And all the better for seeing you here. I didn't want to go back to a place with lots of girls this time. It wouldn't be the same without my dear friend Gwen. We met here back in '43 and travelled all over. She's retired from the Land Army now.'

'Is she married?'

Betty pulled her lower lip between her teeth. 'Her fiancé was killed. She was too broken-hearted to go on. She needed to be back home with her family, which I understand. I didn't want to go back to the Stock's place without her.'

'Of course. And what about you? If I recall, you had someone special serving abroad? How is he?' It had become a habit to connect one who was serving with one who was left behind. Everyone was linked to someone away in the war: brother, sister, husband, fiancé, sweetheart, neighbour, cousin, uncle, mate.

Betty clapped her hands together. 'I do. Michael Doherty. But he's no longer just a friend.'

Flora gasped. 'You mean …?'

'He's going to ask me to marry him when he comes home. Can you imagine?' Betty jumped up and down on the spot in her excitement, and Flora was struck by how like Daisy she seemed. By just how young she was.

'That is the most wonderful news!'

Betty linked an arm through Flora's and together they walked towards the house, past the chooks and Marjorie the cow and the weeping peppercorn tree and the bench seat that Charles had made for Flora the year before.

'Are you excited about being a bride?' Flora asked.

'Of course, who wouldn't be? I'm not exactly supposed to know but when I was home, his mother, Mrs Doherty, obviously she's Mrs Doherty! She showed me his letters, and he'd told her everything. His whole plan! But, oh dear, I forgot to say. This all happened when I was home on leave, when Michael's brother, Patrick, was killed. Oh Flora, it was just awful. Gwen's Reggie, then Patrick not long after. It was very hard. And I think that's why Mrs Doherty was so excited by Michael's news and told me everything. She needed to feel some happiness, you see?'

'I understand,' Flora answered.

'For her to know that there would be some happiness at the end of all of this? That I'm madly in love with Michael and he's madly in love with me? That was what she needed to keep going. And I did, too.'

Flora understood implicitly that gritty determination to hang on to the idea of a better future, so Betty's words didn't sound naive or unrealistic. They sounded like a way to survive.

Charles shut the boot of the Dodge and the sound caught Flora's attention. He looked up suddenly, straightened his shoulders. Had he sensed her gaze on him? He lifted his hat from his head and ruffled his hair, jamming his hat back down firmly. And smiled. Her heart leapt against her ribs. Madly in love. Was that what she was, too? A low tingle sparked in her belly. She hadn't been able to sleep after Charles had left her room the night before, too exhilarated about making love with him—with anyone—for the first time. She'd never felt a naked man's body before, the smoothness of his skin, the fine hair on his chest and stomach, the weight, the desire. In a sense, nothing had changed for them. They were both in a kind of limbo brought on by the war and their roles in it. But everything was different. They were both aware that they'd opened a door that could now never be closed.

The war had changed almost every single thing about Flora's life and who she was. It had liberated her from her expectations about what a woman should desire for herself and for her own life. She might not jump up and down on the spot now or declare it so publicly as Betty had, but she loved Charles in a way she had never thought possible. It was deep within her, this knowing. It was in the way she breathed, in the way she trembled when he looked at her, in the way she softened at the tender way he held her hand, and in her visceral reactions to the way he spoke to the women in his life, his daughters and his mother. How could she not love a man who understood her obligations to her brothers? It was in a look, a smile, in the spaces between the words in his letters to her and in his expression now that they were reunited.

'Two Rivers seems a lovely place.' Betty sighed and leant in to Flora's shoulder. 'I can't believe there's a cow. Please don't tell Mr Nettlefold but I hate chooks. We don't have to do anything with them, do we?'

'They're Mrs Nettlefold's responsibility, you'll be relieved to know. And yes, it is a beautiful place. This is my third summer here and I've never been anywhere so quiet and peaceful. Sometimes I swear it's so still you can hear your own thoughts racing around in your head.'

'I don't know if that's a good thing. I have way too many for any sensible girl,' Betty laughed. 'You know, I always thought I was a city girl, a Sydney girl, especially. But I think that after all this time away, the country has got under my skin somehow.'

Flora understood more than Betty knew. They were quiet for a moment, watching Charles manage the suitcases, one in each hand, another under one arm.

By Charles's side was another young woman. Caught up in her chatter with Betty, Flora had almost forgotten that two Land Army girls were arriving that day.

'What's your friend's name?' Flora asked. They watched as the young woman held a hand on her hat and tipped her head up to the sky, scanning from east to west, from north to south. Flora wondered if she might be searching for birds. She was tall and slender, with straight blonde hair sitting on the collar of her Land Army shirt.

Betty came in close to whisper. 'Her name's Lily Hogarth. She's from Adelaide and that's about all I got out of her. She was very quiet in the car. I didn't even know we were on the same train until I was on the platform and Mr Nettlefold turned up to meet us. She seems, I don't know. Lost.'

Betty stepped up inside the house as if she'd visited it a hundred times before, but the other young woman, Lily, was apprehensive. She was quite thin. Her shoulders drooped, and there was a distant look in her tired eyes.

'Lily?' Flora asked.

The young woman turned to her. 'Yes?'

Flora wanted to stop everything and throw her arms around this sad girl. 'Follow me and I'll show you to your room. Mine is just here off the back lobby. The bathroom is over there and your room is off the hallway this way.' Flora led the way. 'Mr Nettlefold's two daughters have moved in to their grandmother's room so you'll both be in theirs. Here we are.'

The two single beds had been freshly made with clean sheets and the curtains were open wide, brightening the room. The view from the window was filled with vines.

Charles had followed and set their suitcases down just inside the door.

'We're very pleased to have you here at Two Rivers, Mrs Hogarth and ...'

'Miss Brower,' Flora added.

'Please, call me Betty.'

'Betty.' Charles gave her a polite smile of thanks before tipping his hat. 'Flor—Miss Atkins— here knows the lay of the land. If there's anything you need, please ask me, Miss Atkins, of course, or my mother, Mrs Nettlefold. She's in Mildura with the girls and I'll be going to pick them up shortly.'

'Thank you, Mr Nettlefold,' Betty said with a cheery smile. She took off her Land Army hat and patted down her black hair. 'It's nice to be in a family home, I have to say.' She looked around at the plain space. Cream coloured walls. Two beds. A dresser. 'And it'll be a fine change to share with one girl instead of being in quarters of twenty.'

'I know the feeling,' Flora said with a smile. 'You won't know yourself to have such peace and quiet.'

'I hope you find it comfortable,' Charles said and turned to go.

Lily followed Betty's lead and removed her hat, setting it on the bed nearest the window. The gesture revealed the loveliest blonde hair, cut short and stylishly, and pale blue eyes the colour of an early summer morning.

'Do you mind if I …?' she asked quietly, glancing from Flora to Betty.

Betty stepped forward. 'Of course not. I'm perfectly happy to sleep here.' She turned and sat. When she leant back, pressing her hands into the mattress, she asked, 'What's the family like, Flora?'

Flora sat beside Betty. Across the room, Lily seemed to be moving in slow motion, her face pale, her eyes glazed.

'Mrs Nettlefold is very kind and her food is delicious. Charles's girls—I mean, Mr Nettlefold's two girls—Violet and Daisy, are the sweetest little things. Violet is smart and a little reserved but when she gets to know you, she's darling. And Daisy is a little livewire. Wait until you meet them.'

Betty jabbed Flora in the side with her elbow. 'Did you say *Charles*?'

'That's his name,' Flora replied.

'I'll pretend you're not blushing, Flora.'

'It's not …' What was it? Not anything she could talk about just yet. 'I've grown to know the whole family. Who would have thought the war would go on so long?'

'I'll be twenty soon, in February. It does seem hard to believe.'

'Where have you come from, Betty?' Flora asked.

'Batlow in New South Wales. I picked all kinds of vegetables. It was hard to get back in the swing after four weeks' holiday back in Sydney, I'll have to admit. It was so wonderful to spend time with my parents again but … you know? I thought it would be heaven being back in my old bed with all the creature comforts. But I missed the freedom of being in the Land Army. Does that sound strange?'

'Not in the slightest, actually,' Flora said. 'I'm a Melbourne girl, born and bred. But I've grown to love these big skies and the quiet of the mornings out here. Just me and the magpies warbling overhead.'

'I promised myself I'll stay until Michael comes home and that's what I'm going to do.'

Flora's expression softened. 'I have a brother serving abroad. Frank.'

'Which division?' Betty's face lit up.

'Frank's in the 2/11th Field Regiment, 8th Division.'

'Michael's in the 2/23rd Field Battalion, the 9th.'

The three women were quiet. Flora and Betty exchanged glances and looked across the room. Lily sat with her hands in her lap, her eyes downcast.

'We're very pleased to have you here too, Lily.'

She looked up. 'I was still at school when Hitler invaded Poland.'

'Oh, Lily,' Flora said. Lily's tears made her want to cry too.

'My husband's abroad, too. That's why I joined the Land Army.'

'There's something we all have in common, then,' Flora said, and a familiar motherly instinct swelled inside her.

'We're all doing our duty. While Frank is away and all our boys are still fighting, I vowed to do the jobs they can't.'

'I thought the Land Army would be fun,' Betty grinned. 'A lark. If only I'd known. It's been the hardest work I've ever done, but I don't think I can ever go back to Woolworths. My days as a shopgirl are over, I reckon. If only we were paid the same as the boys doing the same labouring work, I might have been able to save some money for after the war and my married life. But once you've bought a few stamps and a movie ticket or two and a magazine, not to mention the train fare out here and a woman's essentials, there's not much left.'

'So, Lily,' Flora prodded gently. 'You're from Adelaide?'

Lily nodded. 'Yes.'

'How long have you been in the Land Army?'

'Two years. My first post was in December '42, just before Christmas. I picked cherries in the Adelaide Hills. I've just come from there actually. I almost forgot.' She moved in slow motion to her suitcase, laid it flat and rescued a cardboard box from within the rumpled layers of her overalls.

'Norton Summit cherries.' She flipped open the lid and Flora and Betty were met with shining orbs of fruit that were begging to be tasted.

Betty sighed. 'I love cherries.'

Lily's mouth curved in the slightest smile. 'Taste one. Or two.'

Betty selected one, picked off the stem and popped it in her mouth. The sweet juices dribbled from the soft flesh and she moaned. Flora followed and immediately understood the reaction.

'I picked them with my own hands.'

'Which clearly makes them all the more delicious,' Flora added with a smile.

'We should probably save some for the Nettlefolds, don't you think?'

'Definitely,' said Flora as she scooped up another.

'Absolutely,' added Betty, grabbing two up in her hand.

Flora was heartened by the smile on sad Lily's face. She hoped her time at Two Rivers would encourage it to appear all the more.

'I know that Mrs Nettlefold has made scones for you both. Are you hungry?'

'How do you think they're settling in?'

Two days later, Flora and Charles were working on the far side of the block. The fruit there was ripe and ready. Charles didn't say it, but Flora guessed he'd separated them for a reason. So they could be alone to talk, to touch each other when they wanted, to enjoy the feeling that there were only two of them under that azure sky.

'Quite well, I think. Betty's a bundle of energy, as you well know having heard her at the table.' Flora tucked her hands into the pockets of her overalls. They were the same pair she'd had two years earlier when she'd taken the secateurs to them. She let herself enjoy the fact that Charles looked at her legs every single morning when she turned up to breakfast bright and early. It gave her a swagger in her step she'd never had before, although, if she was honest, it wasn't the only thing giving her a swagger.

'She's quite the chatterbox, young Betty, isn't she? There's some competition for Daisy at last.' Charles tipped back his hat, shifting his weight, his shoulder brushing Flora's. Since they'd made love that first time, since they'd opened the floodgates to each other, he took every opportunity to touch her in some way. When they were standing alone together like this. When they passed buckets of grapes to each other. He snuck a kiss if they were at the drying sheds working alone. And this far away from his girls and his mother and Lily and Betty, Flora studied him; the way his body moved, his smile, the bunching of the muscles in his forearms and his calves above his thick socks and elastic-sided boots.

He kissed her, long and soft. 'I like that I can do that whenever I want.'

'So do I,' she replied. She looked into the distance, where she could see the two young women picking, their straw hats disappearing in the leafy vines as they bent and stood to search for bunches of grapes among the leaves.

'I'm worried about Lily. She's still so very sad. I haven't dared ask her why but I think I might. She looks like she needs someone to talk to.'

'That might not be you, Flora. She has Betty.'

'They didn't know each other until two days ago. They're strangers, really. Although I suppose I'm a stranger to her too.'

'Betty has a friend serving?'

'Yes, Michael's in the army. She's going to marry him.' Flora glanced at Charles and she knew there was doubt etched in her face. How could anyone know anything these days what was for certain and what could disappear in the blink of an eye, in the sight of a gun, in a bomb or a bullet?

'And what about Lily's husband?'

'David's his name. To tell the truth, I'm surprised she's in the Land Army at all. She seems quite well-to-do. I wondered if she was British at first but no, she's from Adelaide. Born and bred. In all the places I've been, I haven't met any posh girls working in the Land Army. I've watched them plenty of times watching us do all the hard work while riding past on their ponies in their fancy riding clothes.'

'True?' Charles furrowed his brow.

'True.' Flora sighed. 'I'll see if I get the chance to talk to Lily. I forget how young they are, how much of life they've yet to experience.'

Charles scuffed the dirt with a boot. 'Maybe they've experienced too much, Flora.'

Flora reached for Charles's hand. He gave it a squeeze and then went back to work.

Chapter Thirty-Five

Lily

After a long, hot day, Lily was in bed before the sun had fully set. She had waited her turn at the bathroom to wash, ignored her lank and sweaty hair, half-eaten a dinner of cold meat and salad, and then politely said her goodnights.

From across the hallway she could hear music playing on the wireless and the squeals of the two little Nettlefold girls. They must have been playing a game of some kind. Lily thought of the fun she'd had with Kit in all the places they'd worked together and never would again. Six months before, Kit had married a potato farmer in Naracoorte and the last Lily had heard, she was expecting. Lily thought of her sister, too, of the times Susan had let her win at checkers, giving her the chance to feel triumphant and smart. She missed her so dreadfully. Her idol, her guide, her role model, had been away so long now. Susan, of all people, would understand about David. Was everyone Lily loved to be torn from her?

She pulled the bedsheet up to her neck and turned away from the window. She didn't want to wait for the stars tonight, couldn't look at the sky. The warm evening breeze made the curtains dance and her mind drifted back to 1942, to the Palais Royal, to before her war, when she'd worn her pale pink chiffon shoestring-strapped gown and danced with David. The night he'd told her he was signing up. The night after that, they'd gone back to his apartment and made love for the first time.

Lily curled in on herself, wrapped herself up in a ball under the soft sheets. She craved her husband, ached for the memory of him. The few days they'd spent as lovers and as husband and wife were as elusive in her mind as last night's dreams. His hands on her body, his mouth on hers, the tender ache of her first time. But it was all so far away now, as if it had been a story she'd read in a book, the words floating on the page, not close enough to hold on to and remember clearly.

What did David's voice sound like? How had he said her name? *Lily. Lily.* She reached for the memory of it but it wouldn't come. He'd teased her when she'd tried to learn tennis. He'd whispered poetry to her. He'd cried in her arms on their final night together.

Why couldn't she feel him any more? Why couldn't she remember his voice? She'd chosen to come to Mildura to be close to him, to the last place he'd stood on Australian soil, to the place where he'd learnt to fly the plane he was piloting when he'd gone missing. She needed to find a piece of him somewhere in this wide brown land, to breathe the same air as he had.

But he wasn't here. Was he anywhere? Was he ground into dust and mud in a foreign field? Was he alive somewhere on the Continent, trapped with no chance of escape? She wondered if she would feel it in her heart the moment he died. Would it be possible, over such a distance, to know the exact moment? He could have been dead for months and she wouldn't know, because surely missing meant dead, didn't it?

'Lily?' Betty had slipped between the sheets of her own bed across the room. Had Lily been asleep? She hadn't noticed Betty come in.

'I'm awake,' she replied, but she didn't feel like talking and she knew how Betty liked to chat. During the long days, at work, she didn't mind it, but here in the dark, in the privacy of her own bed, she craved the silence to dream of David.

'Just wanted to say goodnight. Sleep tight. Don't let the bed bugs bite.'

'You too, Betty.'

Lily found something comforting about the dry heat of Mildura. She stopped, closed her eyes and breathed it in. It reminded her of Adelaide, this crisp and parched air, the scorched earth underfoot. Mrs Nettlefold had mentioned something about the drought at dinner the night before and she tried to imagine the block lush with grass, but she couldn't picture it.

She snipped another bunch of grapes and placed them in the metal bucket at her feet. She'd performed so many tasks in so many different places that it hadn't taken very long to become familiar with this one. Nothing had been as arduous as tugging flax from the ground, that was for sure. She would survive her five-week stint here and then she would choose somewhere else to go to forget.

A fly buzzed at her face and she swatted it away. Once. Twice. Three times, but to her surprise the buzz didn't disappear, instead growing louder. She looked up to the sky. She felt a sudden ache in the back of her throat. She tried to swallow but couldn't. In the distance, a plane roared and she watched it growing closer, its engines throbbing, until it grew larger and larger and roared overhead, leaving a streak of smoke behind it and her heart thumping like a bass drum.

'Look at that,' Betty exclaimed from a few feet away.

For a moment, Lily didn't remember where she was, didn't recognise the young woman with the black hair talking to her.

'It's so close.'

Every bit of strength drained from her limbs and Lily stumbled backwards against the vines, dropping her secateurs into the dirt.

Betty was immediately at her side. Lily looked up at her new friend, tried to focus and breathe.

'Lily. Lily … are you all right?'

'It's the plane,' she managed.

Betty chuckled. 'There's an RAAF base in Mildura. The pilots train there and get a kick out of buzzing us. When I was at Stocks' a couple of years ago, we used to salute them. I think a couple of the girls used to flash them too, if I remember.' Betty laughed at the memory and lifted her hand to wave.

Lily heard a moan and realised it had escaped her mouth.

Betty came close, peered into her eyes.

'It's one of ours, Lily. It's okay.'

Breathe. Her hands shook uncontrollably. 'My husband is a pilot. He trained here before he went abroad.'

Betty reached for Lily's shoulder, gripped it hard, steadied her and stared right into her eyes. 'You're all right. I've got you.'

Lily closed her eyes, waited for the noise of the plane to disappear, for the sky to clear. Betty stayed with her, a firm hand on her arm to keep her from shaking. When Lily found her feet and a steadying breath, she knew in her heart she had also found a friend.

After lunch, Flora had walked over to the drying sheds to spray racks of the grapes picked that day. She had first checked that Lily and Betty were set, reminding them to keep their hats on and to take drinks regularly to keep up their strength. Flora was kind and Lily liked her. There was a steadiness in her manner, in her calm demeanour and in the way she seemed to take responsibility for the two new girls at Two Rivers, just as the matrons had done at many of the other places Lily had worked during the past two years.

When she'd received the news about David, many people had visited the house in Buxton Street to commiserate and bouquets of flowers had arrived with cards attached expressing condolences, as if David were already dead. She'd experienced a different sort of kindness from Flora since she'd arrived at Two Rivers. Her attentions and words weren't offered out of a sense of politeness but out of a genuine sense of caring. Lily wasn't the only one at Two Rivers to see that compassion and admire her for it. The Nettlefold girls clearly loved her. They fought for her attention, beamed at her when she ruffled their hair, bounced up and down on the spot when she called their names. Lily understood the adoration. It was easy to feel calm in Flora's presence.

Lily had fought so hard to be calm. Inside, she was coiled as tight as a spring under pressure, and she coped with it by trying to feel nothing, to smother any thought that wanted to burst out of her. She reasoned that feeling nothing was safer than feeling everything.

Susan had told her that it was to be expected. Her sister had written as soon as she'd received the news about David. 'Screw your courage to the sticking place, my dear Lily. You must find the strength to go on, even when it's a struggle. The war has forced us all to be heroes, hasn't it? No matter where we are. I'm counting on you to be bold. David will do everything he can to come back to you, you must know that. You must believe that.'

Perhaps that was why she'd taken to Flora so quickly. In many ways, she reminded Lily of Susan. Was she the same age? Perhaps older. Thirty perhaps, or thirty-two?

The heat beat down on Lily and sweat ran down her back inside her shirt. She wiped her forearm across her forehead and arched her back to stretch it.

'Hooroo, Lily.' Betty was working the other side and bobbed her head up above the leaves.

'Mm-hmm?'

'I've been thinking about something. Did you say your husband's name is David?'

'Yes.'

'So ... let me get this right.' Betty's expression was curious. 'Your husband is David Hogarth from Adelaide?'

'Yes. Well, not quite. His family is from the south-east but he was studying at the University of Adelaide when we met. He lived near me in the city so, yes, I suppose he would probably say he was from Adelaide.'

'Did you go to university too?'

'No, but my sister did. She's a doctor.'

'Well, there you go. A doctor for a sister.'

Lily felt a warmth spreading in her chest. Yes, she could feel proud of Susan. That was safe. 'She's in the army. She's been helping all the chaps injured in the war. She was in Egypt but she's in London now. She got married this year to an Englishman.'

'Good for her,' Betty nodded adamantly. 'Listen, Lily. I was thinking about your David. You said that he trained here and I know this might sound silly but … I think I met him.'

Lily's arms goosebumped. 'You did?'

'I'm sure of it. It was two years ago, back in January '43. It was my first few weeks in the Land Army and the Red Cross had put on a ball in Mildura. You know the sort, to welcome us to town and raise money for the troops. You've probably been to a hundred.'

'I've been to one or two,' Lily replied impatiently. 'Tell me more. Please. Tell me everything.'

'You see, all of us at the Stocks' were besides ourselves because word had got around that a group of pilots from the RAAF base were coming to the ball. We were thrilled at the idea that we wouldn't have to spend all night dancing with young boys and all the old men.' Betty chuckled. 'Or each other. I hope you don't mind me telling you but he asked me to dance.'

Lily felt her heart picking up speed. 'Was he tall with blond hair? Blue eyes?'

'Yes, I think so. And he was a terrific dancer. Very confident on his feet. I distinctly remember him saying he had a girl back in Adelaide. I was telling him all about Michael, you see, and he told me about, well, you, as it turns out. He seemed quite smitten with you. At least that's the way it seemed to me.'

Blood rushed to Lily's head. David was real. She hadn't imagined him. He had truly existed somewhere beyond their wedding night and the train station from which she'd waved him away, sobbing inconsolably.

She felt a smile crease her face and it was a strange sensation after so many months when she wasn't sure if she would ever smile again. She reached up with both hands and felt the curve of her lips, the creases in the corners of her mouth.

'He wrote to me, telling me about a dance, I'm sure of it,' Lily said. 'I'll find the letter tomorrow and show you.' Happy memories flooded through Lily like heat from the best sherry. 'He told me he danced with a girl. I'm so glad it was you, Betty.'

'Isn't it funny,' Betty said. 'I danced with your husband and now I'm working side by side with you. When did you two get married? Tell me all about him.'

As the day wore on, they filled bucket after bucket as Lily talked about her life before the war, of falling in love, of being loved, of David's proposal and their marriage. And in that moment, she was able to pretend that he was up there in the skies over Mildura and the winding Murray River, safe, instead of missing somewhere over Europe.

Just saying his name had been enough.

Chapter Thirty-Six

Betty

'May I have this dance?' Betty bowed low and held out a hand to Lily, who splayed a hand on her décolletage and giggled.

'Me?'

Betty looked across the sitting room at her audience. Mrs Nettlefold was sewing something fine on a linen place-mat. Violet and Daisy were at her feet with their books, and Charles and Flora sat almost side by side on the settee, watching on. The wireless was turned up nearly as loud as it could go, and Bing Crosby and the Andrews Sisters were crooning about the Yanks marching into Berlin.

It was Saturday night. Work was finished for the week and Betty needed to dance. She needed to do something with all the restless energy that brewed inside her like bubbles in a bottle of champagne. She stood before Lily, tapping her foot on the rug and swinging her hips.

'Hop up, Lil. Show me how you danced with David back in Adelaide.'

That was the trick. Lily beamed as she reached up and grabbed Betty's hand. Betty tugged her onto her feet and into the centre of the room and curtsied and then, with the beat of the music loud in their ears, they launched into a jitterbug so fast that Betty lost her breath as they spun and hopped in their bare feet on the rug, turning and spinning and jumping. If they'd been wearing skirts instead of shorts the fabric would have twirled up around them.

'We're hep cats!' Betty called out as she swung Lily around under her arm, and they laughed and shimmied and smiled together as if they didn't have a care in the world.

One song ended and another began, a Glenn Miller tune this time, and Violet and Daisy jumped up to join in, squealing in delight, and a moment later Charles had taken Flora's hand and they joined in, too.

'Come on, Nan!' Daisy shouted. 'You can dance too.'

When Mrs Nettlefold put her sewing to one side and pressed herself out of her chair, her granddaughters each took one of her hands and she led them both in twirls and spins.

Betty watched each of them in turn and was so happy to see Lily smiling, the girls' delight, Mrs Nettlefold's pink cheeks, and the warm and loving glance Charles gave Flora, and thought how lucky she was to be in such a place with these wonderful people.

Later that night, Betty and Lily lay in bed, talking. As they'd grown to know each other, Lily had opened up, little by little. Betty was reminded of Gwen, and all she had lost. She recognised the same aching grief in Lily's sad expression. It pained her to know that so many would lose so much.

'Thank you for the dancing,' Lily whispered across the quiet room. 'It was so much fun. Just what I needed, I think.'

'It was fun, wasn't it?'

'David and I used to go dancing at the Palais Royal in Adelaide. It's a beautiful ballroom and I can still see it when I close my eyes. No one was supposed to drink alcohol in there, but someone always managed to sneak in a bottle of gin or something disguised in a brown paper bag.'

'How do I compare with him as a dancer?' Betty asked. 'And please don't remind me that I stepped on your toes. More than once. I know you'd rather be dancing with your husband, Lil, and I wish that for you more than anything, but I thought I might be the next best thing. Especially since Mr Nettlefold only has eyes for Flora and there was no chance that he might ask one of us. He didn't even dance with his mother, did you notice?'

'Yes, I suppose I did.'

'I think he loves her,' Betty whispered, as if the walls might talk. 'Did you see the way he looked at her tonight? It was so romantic.'

'I did,' Lily replied. 'But he looks at her like that all the time, don't you think?'

'She's not married, is she? At her age, you would think she must be.'

'I can't say.'

'Or maybe she's a spinster. Imagine being her age and never being married.'

'One of my aunts is a spinster,' Lily said. 'Her fiancé went off to the last war and died at Gallipoli. She never married after that. I suppose there was no one left to marry when so many had died.'

'We're lucky, aren't we? I have my Michael and you have your David.'

There was a long silence and Betty thought Lily might have drifted off to sleep while she'd been talking. Betty wasn't offended. She had noticed that Lily had been restless, tossing and turning, had heard her tiptoed footsteps in the dark more than once since they'd begun sharing a room. She needed sleep more than anyone Betty had ever met.

But Lily wasn't asleep. Betty heard the sharp intake of breath, the gasp.

'Lily?'

'Oh, Betty. I don't have my David. I didn't know how to tell you. It was easier to pretend that he's … he's been missing in action in Europe since D-day.'

'Oh, Lil.' Betty's eyes welled.

Lily burst into loud sobs. Betty threw back her blanket, crossed the room and swept Lily up into her arms and held her while she cried.

Chapter Thirty-Seven

Flora

'Thank you for this. It's really beautiful here.'

'It's my favourite spot on the river. I can't believe I haven't brought you here before now.' Charles gave Flora an easy smile.

'You've had us too busy working,' Flora said, grinning.

When he'd mentioned earlier in the week that they should head down to the riverbank for a Saturday-evening picnic tea, it had bucked up everyone's spirits. Violet and Daisy had been missing their father, inevitable at this time of year when the picking needed to be done in a hurry, and the mere mention of the word picnic helped them get through the week. It had been searingly hot. Betty was nursing sunburnt arms—she'd insisted on taking off her long-sleeved shirt despite advice not to—and while Lily had never complained, she seemed more worn out than anyone.

A northerly had blown every day, kicking up dust, scorching their throats as they worked. The sun had beaten down relentlessly on the workers of Two Rivers, and Betty and Lily had amused Violet and Daisy by tipping buckets of water over each other at the end of the day. Everyone had worked long hours and had dropped into bed every night with tired limbs and grit in their hair.

This was exactly what they needed.

The cool evening breeze caught Flora's sigh and it floated away across the gently rippling water to the red dirt banks on the other side of the River Murray. From her vantage point on the bank, it didn't seem that far across, nothing that would deter any competent swimmer.

Unfortunately, she was not one. She'd only ever gone up to her knees at St Kilda beach, rolling down her stockings and hitching her dress to her thighs to feel the relief of cool water on her knees. She was content to watch the river lap at the banks, to listen to the little slap of water on earth, and to lift her eyes to the silver-green gums and the blue and cloudless sky above.

In one direction, the river was a straight line as far as the eye could see; on the other, it meandered and then curled around a bend a few hundred feet away. Under the swaying branches, Flora and Charles were on a rug, lying back propped on their elbows, their bodies facing each other at a discreet distance. Charles wore an old pair of swim trunks, judging by the fade in the red fabric, and a cotton shirt half buttoned. The tree provided enough shade that he'd dispensed with his hat, and Flora soaked up the chance to see his face without shadows. He needed a haircut; he was constantly pushing his hair back from his forehead. Since it was the weekend, he hadn't shaved and the laugh lines around the corners of his eyes were working overtime that afternoon. There was something undeniably appealing about a happy, handsome man.

Flora wore her favourite floral cotton dress, unbelted. It was practical and cool in the heat and somehow the frivolity of it made her feel like a woman whose best years might not have passed her by just yet. It didn't seem to matter to Charles what she wore, though. He regarded her the same way, no matter if she was wearing her cut-off overalls and her elastic-sided boots, covered head to toe in red dust, or if she was freshly showered with damp hair. How could he cause such a thrill to reverberate in her very bones with a glance, with a teasing look, with his gaze merely settled on her lips? It was curious and magical and still so overwhelmingly unexpected that Flora had to pinch herself at the circumstances that had brought them together.

'You going to join me for a swim?' Charles asked her. 'It'll cool you off.'

She shook her head. 'I'm perfectly cool here under the tree.'

'You are?' he asked with a teasing tone.

'Definitely.'

He leaning a little closer. 'Then why are your cheeks so red?'

Loud squeals from the edge of the water caught their attention. Betty and Lily were up to their knees in the river, flicking Violet and Daisy, who were dancing on the banks in the arcing spray. The late-afternoon sun caught the droplets and they glistened in the air like an array of stars. There was so much laughter that Flora couldn't quite make out who it belonged to and the entire symphony of it was joyous.

'Lily's needed this,' Flora said quietly to Charles. 'The poor girl.'

He looked over to his daughters once again, as he'd done instinctively every minute to ensure they were safe on the bank. Flora knew by the grim expression tugging his lips into a frown that he was imagining how he might comfort Violet or Daisy if they were ever in the same position as Lily.

'Why do you think Lily didn't tell us about her husband being missing in action?' he asked, puzzled.

Flora shivered at the thought of it, of being told and of having to cope with the dread of not knowing. 'I don't know for sure. Perhaps it might not feel so real if you keep it a secret. All I can say is that I'm so grateful Betty told me about it yesterday. She swore me to secrecy and I promised her I wouldn't say a word.'

'And of course I won't either, but it's a dreadful burden to bear on your own, isn't it?'

Flora observed Charles, with his watchful eyes on the river, his squealing daughters and two young women who were so far away from home. She had been curious for so long about his wife. His loss. His widowhood. Perhaps it might shine a light on why he had fallen in love with her. Flora needed to know. Did she still need convincing that it was indeed love that had drawn him to her, not loneliness?

'Did you have to bear such loss on your own?' she finally asked.

He glanced at Flora, his mouth a line, his eyes narrowed. 'You're talking about Harriet.'

She waited a moment, glanced over to the girls. 'Yes. I'd like to know about Violet and Daisy's mother. About you and Harriet and your marriage. I know that might sound strange to you, but I want to know about her. I look at the girls and wonder how much of her is in them. Daisy must be like her, in her easy manner and her vivacity. But Violet is like you, I think, and not just because she has your black hair and blue eyes.'

'No?'

'She frowns like you do. She's quiet. She's smart and she thinks a lot. She doesn't need the company of others in that secret little world of hers.'

'Is that what I'm like?'

'Oh, most definitely. And you're proving my point right now. How is it that I'm doing all the talking when I was the one who asked you the question about your wife?'

Charles grew silent. Violet and Daisy splashed in the shallows of the river. Betty and Lily were up to their necks, swimming away from the edge.

'You want me to talk about Harriet,' he said.

'Yes,' Flora replied. Did he understand why she was so curious?

'What do you want to know, Flora?'

She was careful, her words considered. 'How did you cope, Charles? You said before how dreadful a burden it is to bear on your own, but you bore it. Who comforted you when you lost her?'

Charles's gaze met hers. His voice was low and she had to concentrate to hear it. 'My mother helped with the girls, has done ever since … you know that.'

'Of course. And she's wonderful with them. But what of Harriet's parents? They're not a part of the girls' lives?' Mrs Nettlefold had told Flora about the brutally cold manner in which his parents-in-law had blamed Charles for his wife's death, about how they had crossed the street to avoid him and any reminder of the grief they believed he had wrought on their family.

'Harriet was their only daughter. Perhaps that's why. I don't know. Some people carry their grief around like a prize, as if they were the only winners in that god-awful competition. It marks them, defines who they are. To see the girls would mean them having to admit that life goes on.'

'How did you keep going after she died?'

'Day by day. What choice did I have? And then the months and years pass, and it gets a little easier.' He sat up, pulled his knees to his chest and rested his elbows on them, his eyes on the river. 'I'll always love her, Flora, if that's what you're asking me.'

'I would expect nothing less of you. She was your wife. She's the girls' mother. I suppose I want you to know that. She must have been a wonderful woman to win your heart because you are the best of men, Charles.'

He angled his head to her, his blue eyes bright. 'Do you know how lucky I feel to be in love again? You're my miracle, Flora.'

They wouldn't hold hands in front of the girls, they'd decided that. But Flora's fingers itched to touch him.

'Do you mind if I ask ... why are there no photographs of Harriet in the house?'

Charles sounded perplexed. 'There are.'

'I haven't seen them.'

'Our wedding portrait hangs on the wall in our ... my bedroom. There's another of Harriet in a wooden frame on my chest of drawers.'

'Not in the sitting room where the girls can see them?'

Charles was quiet. 'They don't remember her at all. I don't want them to be confused. Or sad about not having a mother.'

'I've never heard them talk about her.'

'They used to ask when they were younger, Violet especially. They know she loved them and that she died. They have me. They have their grandmother. And I hope, Flora, that soon they will have you too.'

'Soon, you know that.'

Flora lay back and gazed up at the grey-green leaves of the gum trees, watched them sway like two drunken lovers.

'My brother, Frank, wrote to me when I first came to Two Rivers back in '43. He said that Dad and Jack should learn to look after themselves and that I should strike out for myself and find someone who is worthy of me.' She remembered at the time how she'd felt about this piece of unsolicited advice from her brother, that the notion of finding someone for herself seemed like a plan for someone else's life, not hers.

'I hope you think I'm worthy of you,' he said, his voice husky with emotion.

'More than I deserve,' she replied as she met his gaze, blinking back happy tears.

'Daddy, Daddy!' The girls ran up the bank, laughing, red dirt flicking around their feet. 'Please come and swim,' Daisy shouted.

'Betty and Lily are in the water and we want to go in, too,' Violet chimed in. 'Can we?'

Charles flicked Flora a wide smile as he sprang to his feet. She watched him move, the way his strong shoulders flexed and his long lean legs unfurled. He slowly unbuttoned his shirt and tossed it at her. She had kissed that skin. In that moment, she could taste it again.

'Watch out for the crocodiles!' Charles shouted and the girls shrieked as he chased them to the river. Betty and Lily were out of the water so fast Flora imagined they might have sprouted wings and flown to her side.

'Did Mr Nettlefold say *crocodiles*?' Lily gasped, water dripping from her blonde hair onto her pale shoulders.

'He's teasing,' Betty laughed. 'There are no crocodiles in the Murray.' She turned to Flora. 'Are there?'

On Sunday morning, it was quiet at the Nettlefolds'. It was a mild, late-January morning. Lily and Betty slept. Violet and Daisy had risen early, despite the excitement of swimming having sent them straight to bed, drowsy and exhausted, as soon as they'd returned home the night before. They were playing skip rope outside under the peppercorn tree, one end tied to the trunk, Violet looping the rope up and over, Daisy trying not to catch her feet. Inside, Flora sat with Charles and his mother at the kitchen table. A pot of tea brewed and their bellies were full of boiled eggs and toast.

Flora had spent so many happy meals around this plain wooden table. She knew that underneath the crisp white tablecloth, set with plates and china and a crystal bowl of rationed sugar, its top was scratched and stained, the legacy of cooking and chopping and drawing and children's games. The table told the story of this family, of Mrs Nettlefold and her husband, of their only son and his dead wife, of two little girls who might look back on these years with fond memories instead of stories about what had been lost in the war. How lucky they were to be so young now. Lily and Betty were perhaps ten years older than Charles's children, and often that realisation struck Flora in the heart. They were too young to bear the burdens of a husband and a sweetheart away fighting, to have to face the possibility of such a loss.

Flora sipped her tea and let herself imagine, not for the first time, what a life in this family would be like. To wake up every morning and sit at this table. To be more than a visitor in the house. To share Charles's bed. Her cheeks heated and she looked down into her cup, watched the tiny leaves that had escaped through the strainer swirl and settle. Was it wrong to want it so much?

Charles folded the newspaper and passed it to Flora. 'You might want to have a look.' he said. 'We're getting there.'

Flora unfolded the page and read it. There was progress in Burma. Where was Burma, she wondered? More headlines: a truce in Greece; the Germans collapsing in France; the Russians moving through Hungary; and the Yanks only ninety miles from Manila. Could this be the good news everyone was wishing for? An image caught her attention. Right there on the page, a photograph of Australian artillerymen, bare-chested, using ropes and a jeep to haul a gun into position at Little George Ridge in Bougainville. She looked closely, her heart suddenly thudding. Was this where Frank was? Little George Ridge? She peered close, but the official photograph disguised any trace of their identity, only showing the backs of the soldiers' heads, their bare backs and baggy trousers. They were all anonymous.

She turned the page over. Another screaming headline. 'Resettlement of millions, Gigantic Problem for Post-War Years.'

'Can this be true, Charles?' Flora asked, disbelieving it even thought she'd read the words herself.

'What is it, Flora?'

'This article here. It's saying that fifty million people in Europe have either been called to arms or evacuated from their bombed towns. Or,' she read on, 'they're being forced to work in war factories for the Reich. Fifty million people? That's unfathomable.'

'Hard to think otherwise. After all these years, so much of Europe bombed by one side or the other.'

She blinked, thought of Frank. Had he killed people? Was there much choice when someone was shooting at you too?

Her stomach roiled and gripped. She kept her eyes on the page so Charles and his mother wouldn't see her tears. Another sentence caught her eyes and she stared at it, soaked in its meaning, held it close.

When the war is over and the men have settled down to a normal life …

It wasn't just men who would settle down to a normal life.

Chapter Thirty-Eight

Betty

'Letters?' Betty slapped her hands to her cheeks in sheer excitement. 'Are there any for me?'

'These are yours, Betty,' Flora said, sorting through the lot Charles had just deposited on the kitchen table.

'Is there anything for Lily?' Betty stopped to think about her friend. Some letters would cheer her up, wouldn't they?

Flora sorted through the pile. 'There's one here for me, from my brother Jack.' She put it aside. 'And two here for Lily.'

Betty bit her lip. 'They're not from abroad, or telegrams?'

Flora shook her head. 'These are both from Adelaide.'

'Oh, well. I'm sure when she comes in, she'll be just as excited as I am. A letter is a letter, after all.'

'That's true. And Betty,' Charles said, then paused. 'If a telegram ever did arrive, I would tell you.'

'Thank you, Mr Nettlefold. Thank you, Flora. Is it all right if I have a morning-tea break and go and read these now?'

'Of course,' Charles replied with a nod. 'Come out when you're done.'

It had been months since she'd heard from Michael and Betty could barely contain the anticipation she felt at seeing his handwriting on the envelope. She slammed the back door on her way out and broke into a run until she reached the peppercorn tree and the bench positioned there. She sat, stopped to take a deep breath, and tugged at the string bundling her letters together. She quickly flicked through the envelopes. One from her parents, one from Mrs Doherty, one from an old school friend who she hadn't heard of in positively ages, and three letters from Michael. The others could wait and, with a tremendous excitement thudding in her chest, she shuffled Michael's letters so she would read the oldest one first. It was dated November 1944. She tore open the envelope and unfolded the pages.

Dearest Betty,

Before you worry, I'm very well and all is good here. I'm firing on all six and happy as larry. There's plenty of food and I'm learning to love anything that comes in a tin. I've received all your letters, for which I am very grateful. How many of mine have you received? I don't know what happens to them once they leave us here in _____ so all I can do is keep writing. I'm sharing a tent with some great lads from Sydney, and one is from Balmain, can you believe that? It rains a lot and it's impossible to keep our socks dry, but other than that, I can't complain.

I hope you're not working too hard in the Land Army, although when I told the lads that you had been working in the factory that dehydrates the spuds, they gave you three cheers.

I've been telling them how special you are and what a lucky so-and-so I am that you are waiting for me. Sometimes I think it's the only thing keeping me going, to know that I'll be coming home to you. One of the lads here, Dudley, is already married with two little ones, a boy and a girl. He's been abroad two years now, not quite as long as me, and I know he gets the blues about how much they will have changed by the time he gets home. Have you changed? I hope that if you have, it's only for the better.

Betty Boop, you're in my dreams, did I tell you that before? I think about when we said goodbye out the front of your house and how much I liked kissing you. Your lips were sweet and one day you'll let me kiss you again, I hope. I know I told you not to look back, but I sneaked a look at you that day, as you were walking back up your front path. You were smiling, and it was good to see.

Well, I'll sign off now. Please write soon.

Your loving Michael

Betty looked up the blue sky, pressing the letter to her heart. 'I miss you too, Michael. I think of you every night and I think of that kiss. Where are you?' she whispered.

The second letter was dated the first of January.

Dear Betty,

I suppose I should start by saying happy New Year, but we're not celebrating here today. I have sad news and I don't know where to start so I'll come right out with it. My mate, Dudley, was killed last night. A sniper got him. He was on patrol and I was right next to him when he fell. It's hit us for six is all I can say.

I don't know how much you hear back home about what's going on here, but I wanted to let you know that I'm all right. I haven't had a letter from you for a while, but I know you must be writing to me. You made a promise and I know in my heart you would never let me down.

My dearest Betty, I've been thinking about it a lot and I know this might not be the best way to do it, but when I get home, I'm going to ask you to marry me. People might say we're too young, but I don't feel like a young man anymore. I know in my heart that if you say yes, that thought will keep me safe.

Will you say yes?

Your loving Michael

In that moment, Betty's whole life unfurled in front of her. Her happy reunion with Michael, him so handsome in his uniform, her with red lipstick and a new dress, perhaps a floral cotton with pretty muslin frills around the neck, the kind she'd seen in magazines. With the money he'd earned since he'd been away in the war, they would put a down payment on a home with a yard big enough for a vegetable garden, and she would take all her new-found Land Army skills and plant enough to feed them both and the whole street. And at night, when she rolled over in bed, it would be Michael's face she would see and she would smile and reach for him.

'When the war is over I'm going to marry Michael Doherty,' she whispered to herself, giggling as she wiped tears from her eyes and laughed and sobbed all at once. She held out her left hand and cocked her head to one side. One day she would have pretty hands again, free from callouses created by gripping hoes and secateurs, and the dirt that seemed to find its way into every tiny line on her hands and remain there like a tattoo, no matter how hard she scrubbed. Her ring finger was bare now but it wouldn't be for much longer. She shivered with excitement at the thought.

And just as she was about to leap to her feet to find Lily and Flora and tell them her wonderful news, she stilled. She would write back to Michael answering his question, and she would send letters to her parents and Mrs Doherty announcing the happy news, but here at Two Rivers, she would keep his proposal a secret for now. It would be wrong to shout it to the heavens when her joy would make others feel only sorrow. So she held the secret close in her heart and went back to the house to put her letters in her suitcase, buried deep under her clothes.

Chapter Thirty-Nine

The Dodge pulled into the yard and stopped with a crunching lurch. Flora snipped the bunch of grapes from the vine in front of her and placed it in one of the buckets at her feet. They were full now, and she stood, gripped their handles and lifted them. She blew a strand of hair from her forehead. She really did need a haircut but wasn't sure when she might find the time or energy. She'd snipped her fringe before when it had become long and unmanageable and made a mental note to do that again that night after she'd showered and washed her hair. She began walking towards the drying shed, trying not to let the buckets strike her calves, and made her way towards Charles. He was walking fast towards her with purposeful strides. The sun was so bright, she had to squint to make out what he was holding in his hand.

Something clenched in her chest. Thudded there, faster than her heartbeat.

The post. The combination of his urgent steps and the letters in his hand sent a shiver running up her back and it clenched her throat and shards of her breath caught there and hurt. She stilled, lowered the buckets slowly just before she lost all strength in her fingers, her hands, her arms, her legs.

'Flora.' The brim of his hat was pulled low and all she could see as he approached was his mouth pulled tight, his jaw clenched.

She reached for his hand, gripped her fingers around his fist and pulled it towards her. 'Is it for me?' The tension radiated from him and she almost needed to step back from it. 'Tell me, Charles.' Her voice choked in her throat. 'Hurry up and tell me if it is.'

It seemed to take him forever to answer. 'No,' he rasped, but any sense of relief she felt flickered and died in an instant. 'It's for Lily.'

Lily knew.

As soon as she saw Flora's red eyes and quivering mouth, as soon as Charles took off his hat and held it against his chest. She knew. Her secateurs dropped from her hand into the dirt with a soft thud. A bunch of grapes slipped from her grasp and dropped onto the red earth.

Charles handed her the small grey envelope and she took it, looked at her name, handwritten on it. *Mrs David Hogarth.* Through the window, she could see the telegram was pink. The words *Urgent Telegram* told her all she needed to know.

She blinked away the tears but more came.

Thudding footsteps in the dirt. Betty by her side. A choking gasp. 'Oh, no, Lily.'

Lily turned and walked away, slowly, her feet seeming to sink deep into the dirt, or had they become suddenly heavy? She walked until she couldn't breathe and then stopped to look up at the sky.

Was it David? Was it from her parents in Adelaide telling her that Susan was dead? Had either of them drawn their last breath somewhere far from home?

She'd come here to be close to David, to look at the same sky he'd flown in during his training, to breathe the same air he might have. She stared at the small grey thing in her hands. And finally, she found the courage to open it, slipping her little finger under the fold, ripping it slowly. The pink telegram inside was thin and it was stamped Mildura and the words *Received Telegram* ran across the top in blue ink. And then, typed underneath, Lily's name.

IT IS WITH DEEP REGRET THAT I HAVE TO INFORM YOU THAT FLYING OFFICER DAVID HOGARTH, PREVIOUSLY LISTED MISSING, WAS KILLED IN ACTION ON TENTH JUNE 1944 AND DESIRE TO CONVEY TO YOU THE PROFOUND SYMPATHY OF THE MINISTER FOR DEFENCE AND OF THE MILITARY BOARD.

Betty quietly closed the door of the bedroom she shared with Lily and went to the sitting room. As she stepped inside, Charles shot to his feet, closely followed by Flora and Mrs Nettlefold.

Each of them wore grief on their faces in different ways. Charles was pale, his fists clenched. Flora's eyes were red-rimmed and she sniffed into a handkerchief. Mrs Nettlefold wobbled on her feet.

'She's asleep,' Betty said, barely able to form the words on her lips before the sobs broke, welling and choking her, and then Flora's arms were around her and she held on tight, burrowing into the comfort of her friend's embrace.

Lily packed her suitcase the next morning. She folded her overalls and tucked them inside, along with her gumboots, her elastic-sided boots, her dress shoes, an overall dress, two khaki shirts, one pair of gloves, a tie, two pairs of stockings, her summer uniform, bathing costume, shorts and two floral cotton shirts.

She also packed the bright blue Mildura sky, the sound of a plane flying overhead, the smell of the red earth, the taste of warm sultana grapes on her tongue, the squeals of two little girls, the love and kindness she'd found at Two Rivers and her friendship with Betty and Flora. She placed her hat on her head, her metal AWLA badge on the brim freshly polished, and closed her suitcase. Mr Nettlefold had bought her a train ticket and she was going home to Adelaide.

Her time in the Land Army was over.

She would be taking more than her memories home in her suitcase. She would be carrying an agony that had settled inside her like a stone, as painful as any physical scar, as constant as the northern star.

David had been dead for more than six months. He'd died two days after D-day. How could she have not known it? How was it that she had continued living when he was dead? She'd never met his family and now they were linked by this tragedy. She would have to visit them, tell them how much she loved their son, how much she would always love and miss him. But they'd had him for so much longer than she had. Six months as a smitten friend. Three times as his lover. A lifetime now as his widow and she was only twenty years old. The war had torn apart more families than hers but why did none of that matter in this moment, when her grief was so raw and her future now unimaginable? Why would time not stop? If it could, she wouldn't have to experience another day of this torment. But Lily knew she had as much power over the sun and the moon as she did over the men with guns and bombs who had killed her husband.

The door to the bedroom opened and Betty came in, dressed in her neatly pressed Land Army uniform. 'You ready to go? Mrs Nettlefold's waiting outside. She's determined to drive you to the station.'

'There's really no need …'

'She's fixed on it. And Flora and I are coming too, of course. To say goodbye properly.'

'Really?'

Betty picked up Lily's suitcase. 'You deserve a Land Army send-off, Lily.'

In the kitchen, Violet and Daisy looked solemn and they gave Lily a posy of flowers picked from the front garden. Mr Nettlefold cleared his throat and passed her a brown paper bag.

'Some sandwiches and fruit cake for the journey.'

'Thank you,' Lily said quietly. 'That's very kind.'

'Please accept once again our sincerest condolences, Lily. Our hearts go with you.'

As she stepped out into the back yard, in the small stretch between the house and the vines, Lily took one last look around at the place that would be her final stop in her Land Army journey. She was glad it had been this one, a small property in a home filled with love and a family who understood loss. She had relished the peace and the haven this place had provided her. She had come to Mildura to find a piece of David but he wasn't in the sky or in the air. She would have to find him in her dreams and keep him in her heart, no matter where she was.

The car horn sounded. Mrs Nettlefold sat behind the wheel.

'Don't think she's being impatient,' Betty said quietly, leaning in close, her warm hand on Lily's arm. 'She knows you need to be with your family now and she's worried you'll miss the train.'

The back door slammed behind them and Lily looked back. Mr Nettlefold stood with Violet on one side and Daisy on the other, his arms around them, their little bodies close. She gave them a final wave before walking towards the car.

Flora was in her Land Army uniform too and as Lily approached, she opened the front passenger door seat and stepped back.

'All yours, Lily.'

Betty and Flora didn't let Lily do a thing. At the station, Betty checked her luggage and Flora collected her ticket and bought her a bottle of lemonade. While they waited under the hot shade of the verandah, Mrs Nettlefold moved close.

'Lily, dear?'

'Yes, Mrs Nettlefold?'

'I'm a widow, have been for a long time. In my day, it meant your life was over. Some people wear black the rest of their lives, when their husbands die, as if they have died too. Did you know that?'

Lily listened.

'That wasn't for me. I had a block to work and a boy to raise. And then I saw my own son become a widower, far too young. Life is cruel sometimes. Unfair. You're young. People will judge you, try to tell you what you should be thinking and doing and feeling. Don't let them.' She squeezed Lily's hand, her fingers strong, her grip tight. 'Don't forget to keep living.'

Lily stilled, repeating the words in her head, hoping they would stick and sprout and give her strength when she needed it. 'You've shown me great kindness and sympathy. I'll never forget it.'

'Here's your ticket.' Betty passed it to Lily.

'And your lemonade,' Flora said. 'All set?'

Billowing white smoke wafted over the platform and the train's horn sounded. Lily felt tears welling and she wiped them away with the back of her hand. Mrs Nettlefold, Flora and Betty stood in a row, wearing sad smiles and tears. Lily quickly hugged them all in turn, before shuffling through the crowd of people to step up onto the train. When she found her seat by the window, she looked out. The women were still there, waving furiously. Betty blew her a kiss which made Lily laugh. Flora saluted her and Lily's heart swelled.

Her last glance was for the wise Mrs Nettlefold.

Don't forget to keep living.

Chapter Forty

Flora

Flora was spraying in the drying shed when the telegram arrived. She was up on the ladder, as high as she could climb without toppling over into the dirt, spraying the fruit with oil emulsion. The day was pleasant and warm. A cool change had swept through the evening before and Mrs Nettlefold had thrown open all the windows in the house to cool it down while the respite lasted. It had felt like a novelty to pull on a blanket at night time instead of kicking off the sheets.

Flora's stomach grumbled. She wondered what Mrs Nettlefold had whipped up for morning tea and then laughed at how jealous Jack had sounded in his latest letter that she feasted on scones with cream and honey biscuits and that there was always fresh milk and real butter and cream out there on the block.

'Flora!'

She looked back to the house, squinting into the sun. Mrs Nettlefold was rushing towards the drying shed, her apron flapping and her arms pumping, the panic in the old woman's voice becoming more distinct as she drew nearer.

Flora felt ice in her veins.

Mrs Nettlefold gripped the ladder, steadying herself against it or from concern that Flora might tumble down. 'Flora. You must come to the house.'

'What is it? Tell me.'

Tears welled in the older woman's eyes. 'A telegram.'

The small grey envelope trembled in Flora's hands. The bold word in blue, *Telegram*, on the top right left no doubt about its purpose. She stared at it, at her name, and the loops and strokes of the postmaster's cursive.

Miss Flora Atkins
c/o Two Rivers
Mildura

A wave of nausea rolled over her.

'A cup of tea,' Mrs Nettlefold murmured. 'We'll need a cup of tea.' She fussed with the kettle on the stove and Flora heard the china clatter of teacups on saucers but her attention was entirely focussed on the small grey envelope in her hands.

The house was still. Where was Charles? He and Betty were working at the other end of the block and mustn't have heard the shouts.

Flora stared at her name. There was news inside of Frank. She closed her eyes for a moment. Whatever news was about to be revealed was now a fact she could do nothing to change. The straightforward act of reading it could not alter a thing about it.

'Why don't you sit, Flora?' Mrs Nettlefold laid a hand on her arm. Flora couldn't feel the gesture of comfort. She was numb.

'Flora?'

'No, I can't. I need to go …' Without even thinking about it, her feet carried her to the back door and then she heard it slam behind her, ten feet and a million miles away

She ran to the bench under the peppercorn tree and sat, trying to focus and breathe. She slid an index finger along the flap and slowly ripped the envelope open. Inside, there was a folded pale yellow sheet of paper and she slowly eased it out.

Yellow, not pink. The pounding in her chest became a dull thud.

'Flora!'

Charles was running towards her at such speed that his hat flew off into the air and every boot step on the red, dry ground created a cloud of dust. He came to a quick stop, his breaths loud and fast, his chest heaving inside his shirt. 'Wait,' he managed. 'Don't open it yet.' He lowered his chin, propped his hands on his hips and tried to catch his breath.

Flora looked up at him through her tears. 'It's Frank. It has to be.'

How could thin sheets of paper be so dangerous?

He came to her side, slipped an arm around her shoulder and pulled her in close. 'You're not alone, Flora. Whatever news it brings, I'm here to share it with you. Your sorrow is mine, too.'

A magpie in the branches above warbled. Ahead of them, the vines were silent, their leaves waving in the hot northerly.

Everything is about to change, Flora thought. The war had torn apart people's families—Lily's just the week before—so why should she be immune?

Flora stiffened her spine and unfolded the telegram. It shook in her hands and she had trouble making out the words.

'Do you want me to read it first?' Charles asked tenderly.

Flora shook her head. 'No. I'll do it.' She sucked in a lungful of air, steadied herself.

The telegram was stamped with the place and date: Mildura, 29 January 1945. There were two pages filled with navy ink, with a handwritten message.

L/CPL ATKINS WOUNDED IN ACTION. I REGRET TO INFORM YOU THAT L/CPL FRANK ATKINS 2/11TH FIELD REGIMENT HAS BEEN WOUNDED IN ACTION 2ND JANUARY. THE MINISTER FOR THE ARMY EXTENDS HIS SINCERE SYMPATHY.

Flora dropped the pages into her lap. Charles reached for them, studying them in silence. Finally, he swore softly and let out a deep breath.

Flora flopped forward, dizzy, and dropped her head between her knees. Charles rubbed circles in her back as she gulped for air.

'He's alive, Flora. Did you see that? He's been wounded in action. He's alive.'

Flora covered her face with her hands and wept. Charles waited, his hand on her back. He had promised she wouldn't have to bear this alone.

She gasped for breath. 'It doesn't even say how badly injured he is. How can I know from that?'

'You can't. Here's what we're going to do. We're going to the post office in Mildura so you can send a telegram to Frank, letting him know you've heard the news, that you're wishing him a speedy recovery. He'll want to know that you know. He'll want to know that you're not worrying.'

'Yes,' she said, dazed.

'And they we'll send one to Jack.'

'Jack,' she gasped. 'Of course.'

'And then we'll wait for more news. We'll find out if he's coming home or if he's in hospital and we'll send him every good wish for a speedy recovery. And while that's happening, you're not going anywhere.'

When Flora slowly sat up and opened her eyes, there was two of everything: two houses, two Marjories, two Charleses. 'Can we just sit here a moment? I feel dizzy. I think I might be sick.'

'Yes.'

'He's alive,' she said with a loud exhale, her thoughts jumbled and her head in a spin. 'Is it wrong to be relieved, Charles? That he's injured instead of dead, I mean? What if it's enough to see him home for good? And what if that means it's someone else's brother or husband or fiancé or sweetheart who's still there, in danger?'

'You mustn't feel guilty about being glad he's alive, Flora.'

Flora wiped the tears from her cheeks. 'I'll have to look after him. You know what that means for us, don't you?'

She pressed the palm of one hand to his cheek. His skin was warm, the bristles of his beard prickly, his jaw strong. He sighed, closed his eyes and leant in to her touch.

'Frank is your family, Flora. And that means he's mine too. He comes first.' Charles got to his feet and held out a hand to her. 'Let's go send that telegram.'

'Yes,' Flora said, holding on tight to him.

'And we should tell my mother the news. She's worried sick for you.'

It was a week before more news arrived, and when it came it was in the form of a field-service post card.

Charles and Mrs Nettlefold were by her side when she flipped it over.

Flora peered at the scribblings, trying to decipher them.

'*I am quite well*,' she read. '*I have been admitted into hospital*—he's crossed out the word *sick* but left *wounded* there.'

Charles studied the words. 'He's wounded and hopes to be discharged soon. *I have received your letter dated January 29th. Letter follows at first opportunity.*'

'And he's signed it!' Flora exclaimed and threw her arms around Charles. She found herself laughing, almost hysterical, so delighted and relieved.

At that moment, Betty joined them. She whipped off her hat and stammered, 'Frank? He's all right?'

'Yes,' Flora said and hugged Betty too. 'He's signed the card! In his own hand. I'd know it anywhere. He must be safe and well, and not too seriously hurt.'

'Oh, Flora, that's wonderful news.'

That night Mrs Nettlefold made a special dinner of ham croquettes with salad and devilled eggs. They were

Flora's favourite and she loved that Mrs Nettlefold knew it. She ate up every morsel as if it were caviar and salmon from a feast fit for a king. Her world had been tilted on its axis for years now and finally, perhaps, it was settling again. Even though she knew he was injured, Frank was coming home. He had survived the war. She didn't have to skim over the obituaries in the newspaper any more, wondering if she might have to craft one for Frank one day. That was all she and her dear departed father had wished for when he'd enlisted so many years ago, that he would come home. The only question now was when that might be.

'Here's to absent friends.' Charles lifted his glass of sherry and Flora, Betty and Mrs Nettlefold did the same. Violet and Daisy lifted their glasses of milk.

'And to those coming home just as soon as can be,' Betty said with a wide smile.

'To the end of the war,' Mrs Nettlefold managed in a croaky voice, the emotion of the sentiment too much for her.

'To peace,' Charles added, and the table was quiet as they each said a silent prayer.

That night, Charles came to Flora's room and stayed until the sun came up. She craved his touch now, felt incomplete without it, and she committed every inch of his body to memory as he lay beside her, an arm under her neck, a leg draped across her. She stroked his cheek, brushed her palm against the stubble on his chin, tasted him on her lips as he absentmindedly ran his hand through her hair, twisting the short strands in his fingers.

'One more week,' Charles murmured, pressing his lips to the top of her head. 'I can't believe you'll be gone and this room will be empty again.'

'The season's over. You've delivered all the fruit to the co-op. The girls are back at school. You know, being out here reminds me, more than anywhere else, that the seasons change and the sun rises and sets in the sky, no matter what's going on in the hearts of those who stare up at it. Life goes on, doesn't it?'

'Mine won't without you here.'

'It will,' Flora replied. 'You know your own strength, as do I.'

He signed. 'I would do the same for my daughters. It's the blessing and the burden of being a parent. He's your brother. He's your family.'

How had she been so fortunate to have found this man? 'I love you, Charles Nettlefold.'

'And I love you, Flora Atkins.' He kissed her and she held on tight to him, her face burrowed into his neck.

'When I come back, it won't be to this room, will it?' Flora asked.

'I damn well hope not. This bed is too small.'

They listened to the sounds of the early morning. The house creaking, the birds beginning their chorus. Then there were footsteps and the back door slammed. Flora tensed. Mrs Nettlefold was heading out to collect the eggs and milk Marjorie.

Charles chuckled. 'She knows.'

'About this?' Flora felt a flush of mortification creep up her neck and face. She remembered back two years earlier, in the shoe shop in Mildura, when she'd overheard two old busybodies suggesting that all the Land Army girls were interested in was a job in the country as a shortcut to finding a husband.

As if this journey had been a shortcut.

'I hope she doesn't think less of me because of it. I couldn't bear that, Charles.'

'Less of you?' Charles said, tracing a line from her shoulder to her elbow, to her wrist, to her fingertips. 'She keeps asking me why I haven't done more to make you stay. She's made it quite plain to me that she wants to be your mother-in-law one day.'

'Wait ...'

'Where else did you think this was leading, Flora?' Charles shifted so he could look directly at her. 'I want you to marry me.'

'You do?'

'Yes. You have to know it.'

Did she? 'When were you going to ask me?'

His gaze softened, and he dropped his forehead to hers. 'When the war is over.'

'Oh, Charles. When the war is over, I'll say yes.'

Heidelberg Rehabilitation Hospital
May 2nd, 1945
Dearest Charles,

I write with the happiest of news: Frank is finally home. It took much longer than we expected—and longer than I outlined in my last letter to you—but he is in Melbourne, at the hospital listed above. I write this letter by his bedside while he sleeps. He is well and recovering, but it's been a long journey.

It's only now that I've been able to get to the bottom of the extent of his injuries. He was shot on patrol in New Guinea. The bullet went through his shoulder and came out the other side. He was evacuated to Townsville, where they patched him up, but he had some setbacks with infection, so it's only just now he's been able to come home to Melbourne.

I had been pacing the floor for months at home while we were waiting for him, sending Jack and Doreen a little stir crazy. Honestly, they should have had a honeymoon, even if it was a couple of nights in the Dandenongs. As it is, they've had to begin their married life with me in the house. I'm used to fussing over Jack, as you can imagine, but having one extra person in the house, and his wife no less, somewhat changes things. As it is, I'm away every day here at the hospital with Frank. He sends cheers to you, by the way. He's heard a lot about you and the girls and my time spent in Two Rivers and has made me promise to take him there one day. It was a promise easily made.

He'll be here for a few months more at least. He has become dependent on the morphine used to ease the pain of his injuries and he also has malaria. The poor thing can't take a trick. I find myself with plenty to do here, helping out with the other men in his ward, writing letters for them when they can't and providing company when they are missing loved ones, and simply being a womanly presence to temper their frustrations and anger at their circumstances.

Charles, this isn't the only news I have to share with you. I hope you'll forgive me for not mentioning this until now. I'm expecting. I wasn't sure at first if I was too old for it to continue, but it seems I'm well enough to be nourishing this new life inside me, which is the most wonderful gift you will ever give me, after your love. I am perfectly well and healthy, and taking care to rest when I need to. I am in the care of a good doctor so you needn't worry about anything.

We made our promise to each other and I will keep it. When the war is over, I will marry you.

With my fondest regards,

Flora

Chapter Forty-One

Flora must have dozed off because she woke to the sound of insistent knocking on the front door of the house in Camberwell. She roused, looked down at her swollen ankles propped up on pillows at the other end of the settee and shifted her weight from one hip to another.

'Don't get up,' Doreen told her. 'Jack's getting the door. Probably one of those encyclopaedia salesmen or something. Who else calls at this time of night?'

Flora lay back on the pillow Jack had propped under her head an hour before. After supper they'd settled in the sitting room to listen to the radio. Jack liked *Dad and Dave* and it was about to start. Flora had had a tiring day. The trips to Heidelberg seemed to be getting longer and longer, the tram and bus more crowded and uncomfortable the bigger her belly grew.

There was a mumble of voices and heavy footsteps in the hallway, long strides she would know anywhere. 'Charles?' she murmured.

It was him. He wore his best suit, a heavy coat over it, and carried his hat in his hand. She knew him well enough to recognise the expression on his face was a mix of confusion and love. That was exactly how she'd felt since she'd discovered she was pregnant.

It only took three steps for him to cross the room, kneel at her side, clasp her hands in his and kiss her until she was breathless.

'Flora,' he managed, his voice gruff.

'What are you doing here?'

If he'd heard her, he didn't answer. He released her hands and smoothed his own over her gently swelling belly, the span of his fingers almost covering her bump. When he kissed it through the fabric of her dress, she entangled her fingers in his hair.

'I'll put the kettle on, shall I?' Doreen scuttled from the room and closed the door behind her.

'That's Doreen,' Flora said.

'Who?' Charles shook his head a little, confused.

'My sister-in-law. And you met Jack. He answered the door.'

He let out a huge sigh and squinted his eyes in disbelief. 'Why didn't you tell me?' His eyes gleamed with unshed tears and in that moment she loved him more than she'd ever thought possible.

It was a fair question and one Flora had gone over and over in her head all these months. Before she was sure, she had assumed the stress of Frank being home and so unwell had interfered with her cycle. But when it became clear that it might be something else, when she was sick in the mornings and when her stomach tightened and enlarged, she had visited the doctor to be sure. When the test had returned a week later, positive, she had taken heed of his warning.

'You're an older woman, Miss Atkins.' He'd hesitated over *Miss*. 'There is every chance you won't carry to full term. It's nature's way. There are also options available to you if you don't want to continue the pregnancy. I note you're not married. But please, let me recommend someone medically trained and safe.'

She wanted nothing more than to continue the pregnancy and, it seemed, nature was equally as determined. That's when she'd slipped on her father's wedding ring. It had become both a way of keeping him close to his grandchild and deterring the prying eyes of strangers. Flora was well aware of what people said about unwed mothers and didn't want to hear any suggestions as to what she should do when the baby was born.

'The doctor warned me and I didn't want to worry you if something did go wrong. You've lost so much already, Charles.'

He stared at her. 'You're here all on your own.'

'I'm not. Truly. I have Jack and Doreen. They're doing a wonderful job of looking after me. And I have Frank.'

Charles ran a hand through his hair. She knew he was longing for his hat so he could jam it back on his head like an exclamation point on the gesture. 'What have people said to you? You're unmarried and expecting. I know what people can be like. I won't have you put through that.'

Flora smiled, held up her left hand and wriggled her fingers.

He took her left hand in his, rubbed a thumb over the wedding band on her ring finger.

'It's my father's,' she explained. 'All that Land Army work has given me big strong hands and my mother's simply didn't fit.'

She glanced across the room to the wedding photograph sitting on the mantelpiece above the fireplace. Charles followed her gaze, and moved to sit beside her. She made space beside her on the settee.

'That's your father?'

'John Henry Atkins. Jack is named after him. But he's been Jack since he was in short pants.'

'Jack takes after him. And you look like your mother. So much.' Charles smiled down at Flora, rubbed his hand over her belly. 'I wonder if it'll be a boy or a girl.'

'I honestly don't mind,' Flora said.

Charles lifted her hand, kissed her ring. 'I would have liked to have met him, your father.'

'You would have liked him. You'll have the next best thing in two brothers-in-law who are like him too.'

'Can I meet Frank while I'm here?'

'You're staying?'

'For tonight. I'm back on the train tomorrow to Mildura. Flora … if you honestly thought I'd receive your letter and not jump on the next train.' He sighed and shook his head. 'If I could have flown here, I would have.'

'Pull me up,' she asked him and he tugged her to a sitting position. Side by side, she rested her head on his shoulder and wrapped her hand around a bicep. 'I know you would have. How are the girls?'

'They are over the moon about having a baby brother or sister. It's all they can talk about.'

'You told them?' She laughed.

'They were there when I opened your letter. How could I keep that a secret? I was thrilled for us and angry you hadn't told me sooner and scared for you all at once. And my mother is ecstatic, as you can imagine. She's begun knitting already.'

'I'll come back to Two Rivers as soon as I can. Tell them I miss them dreadfully.'

'Have you missed me?' he asked.

She kissed his cheek, softness on his rough skin, and whispered, 'Let me show you how much.'

Chapter Forty-Two

Wednesday 15 August 1945

Lily Hogarth was with her parents in the sitting room of her family's house in Buxton Street, North Adelaide, listening to the ABC, all of them concentrating so hard on the broadcast they hardly breathed for fear they might miss a word.

'Hello Citizens—'

'It's Prime Minister Chifley,' Mr Thomas startled.

'Sshh,' Mrs Thomas demanded, her hand splayed on her chest as if to stop her heart from exploding out of it.

'The war is over. The Japanese Government has accepted the terms of surrender imposed by the Allied nations and hostilities will now cease. At this moment, let us offer thanks to God. Let us remember those whose lives were given that we may enjoy this glorious moment and look forward to the peace which they have won for us. Let us remember those whose thoughts turn towards gallant loved ones who will not be coming home.'

Lily's mother burst into tears and her father went to her, enveloping her in an embrace so uncharacteristic that Lily couldn't help but stare. They were happy tears, she knew. Their daughter had survived the war. Susan was in London, safe, tending to troops injured on the Continent. They were allowed to feel happiness on a day such as today.

Church bells chimed from the radiogram, ringing with joy and sadness. When the news bulletin began, Lily stood and knelt in front of the wireless, her stockinged legs pressing into the Persian rug, her ear hard against the oak cabinet from which news of the victory over Japan was blaring.

'It's nine o'clock Wednesday morning August the 15th, 1945, and it's peace. The pent-up emotions of almost six years of strain burst in a giant chorus of overwhelming happiness.'

And then General Douglas MacArthur's gruff American voice boomed. 'My fellow countrymen. Today the guns are silent. A great tragedy has ended, a great victory has been won.'

'Did you hear that?' Mr Thomas exclaimed. 'The bombs worked. Hiroshima. Nagasaki. Pity that Roosevelt didn't live to see this day.' His voice caught in his throat. 'Or Curtin. Hard decisions can wear down even the strongest of men.'

It was over.

Lily had been fourteen years old when the war had begun, untroubled by the slings and arrows of life, with nothing but a happy and privileged future predicted for her in her comfortable world. Now she had learnt that she could take nothing for granted any more. And as much as MacArthur might believe that a great tragedy had ended, Lily knew that her personal one would endure. It would never be over.

She'd had months over the long winter to think about who she was now and what would come next for her after the war had ended. She would never go back to that comfortable life she'd had before the war. Years of work in the Land Army, all that she'd seen and done, all that she'd learnt and endured, had liberated her. She'd had a wage of her own, the freedom to choose where she was going to work and what jobs she did. She'd found the joy of real female friendship, and learnt how important it was to have such friends to help her cope with the worst the war had wrought.

David would never return, his life sacrificed like so many others for king and country, but to pretend he hadn't existed would be not only a betrayal of her husband but of the person she had become.

Don't forget to keep living. She long remembered Mrs Nettlefold's advice, had memorised it on the long train journey home back to Adelaide in January.

She'd made a decision about her future. She'd been at home for six months as a widow, her life on hold, in a limbo she hadn't chosen, and it had taken all that time for her to find her courage. Susan had written often during that time, asking how her younger sister was, reassuring her that she would recover and, in her last letter, which had only arrived a week earlier, Susan had made Lily an offer she had decided she couldn't refuse.

Come to London, Susan had offered. She was now based in Eastbourne, in Sussex, treating repatriated prisoners of war who'd been freed from camps all over Europe as the

Allies had advanced. *They're all Australian boys,* Susan had written. *Won't you take the next boat over and come and work with me? We need all the help we can get and the Anzacs would love to see a friendly face from home. Once they're well enough, they're sent back to Australia, but some of them are in pretty poor shape so it'll take some time. It's all hands on deck and if you don't mind doing whatever we ask of you, I'd have you tomorrow. Think about it, Lily.*

She had thought about it. Her world could be bigger than Buxton Street. Bigger than Adelaide. Bigger than Australia.

She was going to London.

Betty Brower stood in the middle of Martin Place with thousands of other Sydneysiders who'd all rushed into the streets that morning when they'd heard the news.

She had been home on leave from the Land Army when the bombs dropped on Hiroshima and Nagasaki, and eating breakfast when she'd heard Prime Minister Chifley's announcement on the radio that Japan had surrendered. Like every other person in Sydney, she rushed into the streets, following the crowd onto buses to head into the city.

Chifley had declared two public holidays so anyone who had been heading into their offices or factories or shops simply turned back and joined the masses gathering in the streets. People were packed tight as sardines in Martin Place, from above Castlereagh Street across Pitt Street and past the Cenotaph.

Betty found herself laughing and crying in equal measure, sometimes in the same minute. Someone handed her a paper hat made out of that morning's newspaper and she slipped it on her head. People waved streamers and Union Jack flags and someone had a Stars and Stripes, too, and there were victory shouts in one ear and singing in the other. Anyone with a whistle kept for air-raid warnings found it and blew until their lungs must have been on the verge of collapse. Hats flew in the air and landed who knew where. A man next to Lily exclaimed, 'My glasses!' and dropped to his knees to search for his precious spectacles underfoot.

Betty could hardly hear herself think in the crush and the loud thudding in her ears. The last time she'd been in a crowd like this she'd been evacuated from Woolworths in an air-raid drill. Now, it was to celebrate victory.

She pushed her way through the crush towards the Cenotaph. A young woman in front of her had drawn VP Day on her forehead and cheeks. Everyone was smiling and laughing and so, so happy. A clapping crowd surrounded a man doing a highland fling. A group of young people danced with British and American soldiers, standing in a circle doing the hokey-pokey. A tram was trying to make its way through Pitt Street, crowded with people inside coming to join the celebrations and others jumping on and cheering.

'Look at that!' There was a shout and Betty looked around to see a sea of fingers pointing up to the side of a building in Martin Place.

'What is it?' an old man called, his voice croaky from singing.

'It's Hitler!'

The crowd erupted. Two men had looped a rope around the neck of a shopfront mannequin and were dangling it out a window, lowering it to the crowd. A swastika had been daubed on its torso and they'd drawn a toothbrush mous-tache above its mouth.

Girls began to yell and old men shouted and when the mannequin was lowered, the rope became slack and col-lapsed to the ground. Betty pushed through the crowd to see it. A man swung a leg back and kicked the Hitler in the groin, once, twice, three times, and there was wild cheering and a young office boy bent over and smashed his fist into the mannequin's head.

Betty kept walking, being jostled good-naturedly. She wondered if she would see anyone she knew, so they could share the joy of victory and peace, but she was surrounded by strangers. When a young American soldier appeared in front of her, she reached up, took his face in her hands and gave him a smacking kiss right on the lips.

'Why, thanks, miss,' he said, beaming, and disappeared into the throng.

The sound of the crowd was so loud that Betty didn't hear it at first, but when faces turned skywards she looked up. A Mosquito flew overhead, directly over the GPO, and people gasped and cheered, and it turned steeply and flew back around. Car horns sounded, people sang, and army lorries crowded with people were almost at a standstill as they negotiated the throng.

It took her longer than she expected but she finally made it to the Cenotaph. In the cacophony of noise all around her, it was somehow quiet there. Flowers had already been laid on the plinth, and others stood, their hats pressed to their chests, in silent prayer. So many had paid the highest price and they would never be forgotten. She elbowed her way through and swept her hands over the words engraved in gold on the stone block, *Lest We Forget*, and she thought of her friend Gwen's fiancé, Reggie. Michael's brother, Patrick. Lily's husband, David. All the boys she'd gone to school with and all the husbands and fiancés and sweethearts of every Land Army girl she'd worked with during the past two years.

And her dearest Michael, who was alive, who had survived. He would be coming home to her. She couldn't wait to kiss him, to hold him, to tell him how proud she was of him, and to tell him all the things that she hadn't been able to put in her letters. How scared she'd been when she'd enlisted in the Land Army. How had she lasted two-and-a-half years? The girl who'd cried for two weeks straight at her first posting? That's the other thing she would make sure she told Michael. About how brave she'd become. How pleased and proud she was that she'd served her country in the best way she could. About her dreams for a future life for them bigger than being a shopgirl or a grocery boy.

About a life they might have together if they were fearless enough to search for it.

She crossed herself, said a prayer for him, and headed home to see Mrs Doherty.

'I have the paper. Do you want to see it?' Flora pulled up her chair beside Frank's bed at the Heidelberg Repatriation Hospital in Melbourne. He looked better today. Less yellow. She wasn't sure why she was speaking quietly to him, as there was little privacy in the ward of seven patients and, anyway, every single one of them was cheering and whooping with laughter, trying to be heard above the wireless blaring and the car horns beeping outside from the street. There were running footsteps in the hallway beyond the ward doors, and whistles, and a group of people singing 'There'll Always Be an England'.

'C'mon, Flora. Read it to us,' called Benny from the next bed.

'Can anyone have a private conversation around here?' Flora replied with a grin.

'Nothing's private around here, hey lads?' John from Geelong laughed.

'And you should know that by now, seeing as you've been here every day since Frank arrived. I reckon they should give you one of them nurses' uniforms, make you an honorary one.'

The boys cheered and Flora's cheeks flushed. She looked around at the men she'd grown to know during the past six months. Benny. Tom. John from Traralgon. John from Geelong. Harry and Bryan. They'd kept each other's spirits up during their long recoveries from their war injuries and their illnesses. They'd come from prisoner-of-war repatriation camps in England, from Townsville as their war injuries had improved, and from the battlefields of New Guinea. They were the lucky ones and they knew it. After the deprivations they'd known, the luxury of regular food, clean sheets and attentive care was not lost on them. And the proximity of the Old England, Henry Barkly and Ryan Hotels made their recovery all the sweeter. They didn't even bother to change out of their pyjamas or dressing gowns before heading down for an ale.

'It's every bloke's god-given right to have a beer,' Bryan had announced one afternoon and there was unsurprisingly no disagreement.

'Where's Harry?' Flora asked, noting his empty bed.

'He's got an appointment with Dr Ryan,' John from Traralgon laughed.

'You mean he's at the Ryan Hotel?'

'Who can blame him on today of all days?' Bryan laughed. 'If this isn't the day to have a bloody beer or two, what is?' Flora believed herself to be accustomed to the way men spoke with each other, having grown up in a household full of them, but these boys were something else. She'd grown to love each and every one of them these past months. She'd seen them through tears and heartbreaks and agonising pain. Held their hands when they'd discovered they'd been abandoned by wives or sweethearts who either couldn't face their injuries or had found the waiting too long and hard. All they wanted to do was go back to their ordinary lives. They wanted normality, quiet, a distance from the horrors.

Flora and Frank shared a smile at the antics. He was coming back to her, her little brother. His symptoms had eased and his humour was returning. She couldn't wait to see him cheeky again, teasing, out on the town in a black suit and his hair slicked back with pomade like Frank Sinatra, flirting with anyone who walked past.

Flora stood, holding a newspaper in her outstretched hands.

'Sit down, Flora,' Frank urged from his position in bed, propping himself up against overstuffed pillows. 'Don't exert yourself. Take a load off, love.'

'I'm all right. I'm marvellous, in fact.'

'Listen to your brother,' Benny called. 'A woman in your condition needs all the rest you can get. I don't know how you've done it, being here every day for Frank. He doesn't deserve you, Flora.'

'No, he doesn't,' said John from Traralgon, who hobbled towards Frank's bed, a wooden crutch propped under each arm. Flora was no longer shocked when she saw his right pyjama leg pinned up at the knee.

'Surely that baby is coming any day now. Look at the size of you.'

Flora turned to glare good-naturedly at Bryan. 'Not for two months, at least, so stop your blathering and listen, will you?'

Her baby. Her miracle. She looked down at her rounded belly, her smocked dress exaggerating the bulge beneath it. She cleared her throat and the men finally quietened.

'This is the Victory edition of *The Herald*,' Flora started and the boys broke into a rousing chorus of 'Rule Brittania'.

'*Peace. World hails Jap surrender. Hirohito to order cease fire.* Oh, look. People were dancing this morning in Collins Street.' She flipped the front page around so the boys could see. Except for Bryan, of course.

Flora continued. '*A party of specially selected Australian servicemen left Australia at dawn today for Manila to get to work on tracing and rehabilitating Australian prisoners of war held by the Japanese since the fall of Singapore three and a half years ago.*'

John from Traralgon piped up. 'That's the 8th Division. My cousin Hedley.'

'My brother, Terry,' said Benny. 'They'll be right. They'll all be home soon, you'll see.'

'*Australia has been at war for five years, eleven months and eleven days,*' Flora read.

'And it's bloody well over,' Frank said from beside her, and when he reached for her hand, she folded the paper and sat with him.

'Dad would be so proud of you today,' Flora said, her voice choking. 'For what you did for the country, for our family.'

'And you,' Frank smiled. 'Two years in the Land Army is nothing to sneeze at, Flor. You did your bit.'

Her thoughts turned to Lily, at home in Adelaide with her family. How awful today must be for her. And Betty— what a day of rejoicing up there in Sydney. How wonderful for her to know that Michael would be coming home soon and that they could begin their young lives together.

And she would be going home, too. Not to Camberwell, but to Two Rivers.

She would be going home to the place of her heart, to her baby's father, to its two siblings, to its grandmother. To her new family. Charles had been patient and understanding, cautious and concerned during her confinement. She understood what he'd gone through and she knew he struggled with being so far away from her should anything go wrong, but he bore it. He knew and understood her too well to think she would do anything except be at Frank's bedside each day as he recovered. They both had responsibilities and obligations, had had their hearts torn in two by being apart. But they'd survived it.

'Frank! Flora!' It was Jack at the door to the ward, buoyant, beaming. He ran to them, his shoes clicking loud on the linoleum, and threw his arms around Flora. Little shreds of paper rained down on her from the brim of his hat. He whipped it off and shook Frank's hand heartily. 'I came as soon as I could. The trams are all caught up in the crowds. The streets are chock-a-block. You wouldn't believe it. I almost got run over by a horse and cart on Collins Street. People are coming from everywhere.' He sat on his brother's bed, patted Frank's thigh. 'How you doing, old boy? You look better.' Jack turned to Flora. 'Doesn't he look better?'

'He does,' Flora replied. 'He'll be ready to leave next week, the doctor says.'

'That's bloody marvellous, Frank.'

'You're telling me,' Frank replied with a weak grin. 'I can't wait to get out of here. To get my life going again. To see what peace will bring me. Will bring us all.'

Flora exchanged glances with her brothers. They listened to the celebrations in the room, the blaring radio, the shouted conversations.

'Here's to dear old Dad,' Jack said finally. 'If only I had a beer to give him a toast.'

Frank moved in his bed, sat up a little. 'To absent friends. May they rest in peace.'

Chapter Forty-Three

Flora

The train pulled into Mildura station, its smoke billowing around the platform like winter fog. Flora buttoned her coat against the late-August cold, although it didn't do up all the way now. It felt so strange to be wearing civilian clothes after all the times she'd made this same journey in her khaki Land Army uniform. But the war was over and she, like the war, was officially retired. Thirty-three years old and retired. The thought amused her. Her gloved hands gripped the handles of her handbag and she turned to Frank.

'You ready?'

He winked. 'I've fought the Japs, Flor. I reckon meeting your future mother-in-law will be a breeze. And I can't wait to see your bloke again. Maybe this time I'll buy him a beer.'

Her bloke. Her Charles. He'd come down to Melbourne as often as he'd been able to during the past couple of months to see Flora and he'd even accompanied her to the repatriation hospital in Heidelberg so he could get to know Frank. They'd become mates, just as she knew they would.

Flora held out a hand to Frank. His grip was tighter and stronger than it had been since he'd come home. The doctors had warned that he would have recurring bouts of malaria, with chills, fever and weakness, for some time before he was fully recovered. She and Charles had asked Frank if he would like to recuperate at Two Rivers and his answer had been a swift yes.

When she stepped off the carriage onto the platform, she heard them immediately.

'Flora! Flora!' A moment later, Violet and Daisy had thrown their arms around her.

'Hello, you two.'

'I didn't recognise you in your real clothes,' Violet said, her voice muffled into the woollen fold of Flora's coat. 'But Daddy saw you first.'

'How are you, Daisy?'

Daisy was crying and Flora wrapped an arm around her. 'Don't cry, sweetheart. This is a happy day.'

'You've brought the baby home,' Daisy shouted.

Flora's eyes welled. 'Yes, I have.' She patted her belly. 'When we get home I'll let you put your hands here and you might feel it kick.'

The girls stared at each other, wide-eyed.

'Violet,' Flora said, and she felt a surge of love for Charles's oldest daughter. 'It's so wonderful to see you again.'

'Welcome back, Flora,' Violet beamed.

'Violet, Daisy. This is my brother, Mr Atkins.'

'Hello there,' Frank said cheerily. 'I've heard all about you two.' He tipped his hat to them. 'I'm very pleased to meet you, Miss Nettlefold.' He looked from Violet to Daisy. 'Miss Nettlefold.'

Violet held out a hand and Flora marvelled at how grown-up she already seemed. Would she need a mother? For that's what she would be to them now, wouldn't she? She watched Violet and Frank shake hands earnestly, and then Daisy copied her sister. Yes, no matter how old they were, they would always need a mother. Flora knew in her heart that every woman did. She herself had felt the loss of hers more keenly during her pregnancy than she ever had before. As a young woman and an expectant mother, she'd had no one to confide in, no motherly influence, no comforting words from someone who knew her better than anyone. That's what she could be to these two girls. And that's what she hoped Charles's mother might be to her.

'Flora.' Charles was at her side, his hand on her elbow, and she turned.

She exhaled. 'Charles.'

He took off his hat, dipped his head and pressed his lips to her cheek. She breathed him in.

Their journey to each other was over. She'd reached her destination at last. Her future lay ahead of her here in northern Victoria, in the azure sky, in the red dirt of Two Rivers, and in the hearts of those she loved the most. She would be a wife to Charles. A mother to Violet and Daisy. A daughter-in-law to Mrs Nettlefold. A sister to Frank and Jack and a sister-in-law to Doreen. An aunt to their children. And, most importantly, a mother to her unborn child. A hand drifted to the swell under her coat and she covered it with her own.

'Everything all right?' Charles whispered.

She nodded. 'Yes.'

Two-and-a-half-years earlier, her world had been small and sheltered and lonely. Now her horizons were as big as the sky.

'Good to see you, Frank.' Charles held out a hand and they shook firmly. 'You're looking well.'

'Tired but well.'

'That's terrific news. You're going to like it at Two Rivers. There might even be some work for you when you're well enough.'

'Good to know,' Frank said. He sent a scrutinising look Charles's way. 'You going to make an honest woman of my sister, then?' Frank winked at Flora and glanced at her stomach. 'You haven't got long.'

Charles grinned. 'That's the idea. You of a mind to give her away?'

Flora was flooded with joy at the thought.

'Too bloody right I'll give her away. I've been telling her for years that she needs to strike out and find a life for herself. Lucky for you she listened to me, hey?' Frank chuckled, which made Flora laugh. She'd missed his humour, his cheek, but she didn't have to miss it any more. The ties that bind are strong, she knew. There was lots to catch up on and they had all the time in the world now.

Her war was over. Troops were coming home in their thousands. Families were being reunited. Fathers were being introduced to children they'd never met or cautiously reintroduced to children who'd forgotten them. Mothers hugged sons and fathers hugged daughters. Young women were getting on boats to sail across the seas to husbands they'd known only briefly. Men came home to abandonment and grief of their own. Women wept that those they loved would never return.

The war had touched everyone, changed everything.

Charles took Flora's hand in his and she looked up to meet his gaze. 'My mother has an afternoon tea waiting for us at Two Rivers. What say we make a move?'

The girls showed Frank to the Dodge parked in the paddock across the tracks, and Flora followed Charles to the last carriage to fetch the luggage. She had a tea chest coming soon with the rest of her clothes, her books and the items she'd collected when she was younger for her hope chest: dishes, linen, a cutlery setting, cookbooks.

Hope.

It had been sorely tested before Frank had come home.

But it had returned, filling her up, swelling her heart. Her family and Charles's would grow together from this day on.

He turned to her suddenly, took off his hat again and moved in close. His eyes met hers. 'Welcome home, Flora.'

She got up on tiptoes and pressed her lips to his.

At last, recognition

Around 6,000 women served in the Australian Women's Land Army between 1942 and the end of the war. These women left the cities and moved into the country, to farms and orchards, to do the work once done by men. Many stayed on for the duration of the war. It was disbanded on 31 December, 1945, and women returned to their old lives.

After the war, their work and sacrifices were largely ignored and forgotten but they continued to campaign long and hard to have their work recognised. They marched on Anzac Day for the first time in 1991, and in 1994 became eligible for the Civilian Service Medal 1939–1945.

On 20 August, 2012, at a reception at Parliament House, Canberra, the then Prime Minister Julia Gillard presented each surviving member with a certificate and a commemorative brooch to wear. Her comments on the day outlined just how much they had contributed to the war effort.

Women of the Australian Women's Land Army, I've been told to refer to you as the Land Army Girls. So from the Head Girl, I'm very pleased to be with you today for this very, very special occasion.

You're here in Canberra to be recognised in the capital of the nation you served so well. And that long journey here might have been filled by memories, as you journeyed, of all those years ago, when you journeyed from your homes and families to the farms and fields where you were needed the most.

You went to take up the work of the men who had left for the front. Some of them were your fathers, brothers, or even sons. In doing so, you brought victory closer, just as if you had picked up a rifle yourself. Now I know a thing or two about working in a traditionally male domain. But the life I've been privileged to lead is only possible because women of courage like you were there first; in the tough years, the desperate years, when the nation faced its ultimate test.

You helped Australia pass that test. And today—here in the nation's heart—we thank you.

I know it's been a long time coming, these words of thanks. I know you will wear those brooches with a great deal of pride. And I really hope, I genuinely hope they prompt younger Australians to ask you what they mean, because you'll be able to tell them. You'll be able to say 'I answered the nation's call. I stood up to be counted when Australia needed help the most.' And a new generation will learn of the remarkable things you did and the remarkable women you are.

On behalf of all Australians, I thank you for your generosity and your service. The Australian Women's Land Army has achieved a lasting place of honour in the history of our nation. May it be celebrated—truly celebrated—for many years to come.

Acknowledgements

Undertaking the research for this book was a fascinating and enlightening experience.

Firstly, I would like to acknowledge all the members of the Australian Women's Land Army who served their country when duty called. In the 1990s, many of them agreed to be interviewed as a way of preserving their precious stories, and the Australian War Memorial's Keith Murdoch Sound Archive of Australia in the war of 1939–45, Australian Women's Land Army, Transcripts of Oral History Recordings, was an invaluable resource.

I would particularly like to mention the following:

Peggy George nee Hull (Interviewer Judy Wing)
Nancy Thomas nee Willicombe (Interviewer Judy Wing)
Gwen Seddon (Interviewer Judy Wing)
Daphne Phillips (interviewer Judy Wing)
Jean Patterson (Interviewer Ruth Thompson)
Betty Brown (interviewer Ruth Thompson)

Sincere thanks to Dianne Mobbs for generously sharing some of her family history with me. Her father, whom we lovingly called Uncle Reg, served with the 2/27th, and his letters, postcards and other memorabilia have found their way into this book.

Carys: Diary of a Young Girl, Adelaide 1940-42, edited by Ann Barson, ETT Imprint, Sydney, Exile Bay, 2017, is a moving and insightful look into wartime Adelaide and the lives of young people at the time.

I would like to most sincerely thank Dr Susan J. Neuhaus CSC, former Colonel RAAMC, for giving me a copy of her book *Not For Glory: A century of service by medical women to the Australian Army and its Allies*, Susan J. Neuhaus and Sharon Mascall-Dare, Boolarong Press, Brisbane, 2014. The character Susan was inspired by these unsung women and, indeed, by the real Susan herself.

On The Home Front: Melbourne in Wartime: 1939–45, Kate Darian-Smith, Melbourne University Press, 2009, was a treasured resource that I returned to time and time again for its vivid and detailed portrayal of women in wartime Melbourne.

Anyone who writes historical fiction knows and loves the online resource Trove beyond all measure. It is a collaboration between the National Library, Australia's State and Territory libraries and hundreds of cultural and research institutions around Australia, that work together to create a legacy of Australia's knowledge for now and into the future. I warn you, it is a rabbit hole from which you may never emerge.

Turn over for a peek

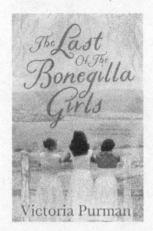

by

Victoria Purman

OUT NOW

Chapter One

9 April, 1954

Sixteen-year-old Elizabeta Schmidt blinked open her sleepy eyes. *The camp.* The words were being murmured from one family to another on the rust-red train. Like a Chinese whisper, they had spread from carriage to carriage, seat after seat, over hats and scarved heads and little children's curls, in hushed and tired voices, like a wave. Their journey was almost over.

Six weeks earlier the Schmidt family had left their home in Hessental to take the train to Bremerhaven on Germany's North Sea coast, and begun their journey on the *Fairsea* around Europe to Malta, then Port Said in Egypt, and to Melbourne via Perth. After a rough voyage over the Great Australian Bight, during which Elizabeta's mother had been sick every day, they'd berthed at Port Melbourne and then crossed a wharf and climbed aboard the train with many carriages. It was almost midnight now, and Elizabeta was tired and anxious, having had only snatches of sleep on the journey. What would they find when the train finally stopped? The leather seats were a small comfort. She and her family had been forced onto all kinds of trains before with nothing so luxurious; they had had no windows and only wooden planks to sit on. Elizabeta didn't mind this Australian train at all.

She pulled her brand-new winter coat tighter around her and lifted the collar to cover her ears. The sobbing from behind her had begun an hour before and the woman hadn't stopped. Elizabeta didn't recognise the words, but thought it might be Russian perhaps, or Ukrainian. Elizabeta had been surrounded by languages her whole life. She still remembered a few words in Hungarian, was fluent in German, and had picked up some English in the classes provided on the *Fairsea* on the voyage over and from lessons from her father. She recognised the harshness of Polish with all its *zeds* and *jheds*; the passionate roar of Italian and the musicality of Greek, in which everything seemed to end in *ki*. People had picked up languages like scraps of food, anything to help survive the war.

The train slowed and lurched and then pulled up with a brake squeal like fingernails on a blackboard, and the woman behind Elizabeta began howling in earnest now.

Someone whispered in German. No matter where they came from, everyone understood some German. '*Sie war in den Lagern. Sie mag es nicht, Züge. Sie verstehen.*'

She was in the camps. She doesn't like trains. You understand.

There were murmurs and nods of agreement all around.

The rattle of the train stilled and Elizabeta stared out the window into the black nothingness. There wasn't a star in the sky. Dim lights brightened an uncovered platform on its own in the empty dark, but there were no buildings to be seen. There was a strange whistling in the dark, a rustle of leaves, perhaps, in the distance. The sobbing woman howled again, which set off a couple of tired children who began to squawk. Slowly, everyone around her stood, collected their belongings and bags, reached for the hands of children, and moved down the carriage towards the open doors. Elizabeta stayed close to her parents, Jozef and Berta, and when her mother asked her to make sure she held her little sister's hand, Elizabeta clasped Luisa's fingers in hers. Her nine-year-old sister looked up at her, her hair coming loose from her thin plaits.

'*Wir sind hier, Luisa*,' Elizabeta said.

Luisa nodded, her eyes wide and frightened. They shuffled to the end of the carriage and stepped off the train onto the platform. Dirt crunched underfoot. Moths danced and crashed into the lights hanging overhead. This wasn't even a station, Elizabeta realised. It was more like a siding in the middle of a field.

The unexpected chill hit Elizabeta and iced her throat. Her father had told her, promised her, that Australia would be sunny and warm all the time. 'It's always summer somewhere in Australia,' he'd said. This was not what she'd been promised. Luisa gripped her hand tighter and snuggled in close, her little body pressed up against Elizabeta's. Ahead of them, their parents were waiting. Their father, wiry and tense, his short hair covered by a peaked cap, was stern and watchful. Their mother, a bag of bones under her thick coat, was sad-eyed and alert. They looked back to their daughters and beckoned them with an urgent wave. Elizabeta quickened her step and tugged Luisa with her, past a man in a uniform handing out something official to each person.

'Elizabeta, Luisa. *Komm.*' Her mother slipped a cord with a name tag attached around Elizabeta's neck, over her layers of clothes and winter coat. Elizabeta felt the string, rough under her fingertips. She wished it were pearls instead. She'd coveted her mother's pearls, the tiny pale orbs on a delicate strand that sat right on her collarbone, so special they had only come out for church on Sundays. But they were back in Germany with a woman from the village, sold off with the new bedroom furniture and the dinner set and the few books and trinkets they'd had. They needed money for their new life in Australia, not pearls, Elizabeta's father had said when he'd sold them.

Berta slipped a name tag around Luisa's head. She looked down at her daughter. Luisa's bottom lip wobbled and her lips were pulled together to cover her chattering teeth.

'*Ihr zeit bald ins bett,*' Berta said, pinching her cheek as if to warm her. '*Schön warm.*' You'll be in bed soon. Nice and warm.

Elizabeta was too old for that loving touch from her mother. She looked up to the black sky. There wasn't even a moon. All she could see was a bench and the word *Bonegilla*, white letters on a black sign that seemed to float in midair. She desperately wanted to be in bed too, nice and warm. She gripped Luisa's hand, and together her family followed the crowd as people shuffled along in their winter coats, their hats, their new suits, their European shoes, along the siding and down a ramp to a dirt road, where a row of chugging pale blue buses stood in formation to take them all to their temporary home in Australia.

Had she slept on the bus? She wasn't sure when the bus pulled up at the camp a few minutes later. The passengers were guided off the buses and shepherded in the dark towards a large and squat reception hall. Inside Elizabeta squinted. The lights were bright after the pitch darkness of the night. Shoes clicked on the wooden floorboards and people found seats in the rows of camp chairs facing the front of the hall. Luisa climbed into her father's lap and laid her head on his shoulder. Next to him, Elizabeta shivered. Her breath was making clouds even though they were inside. She looked around at the sea of faces. She recognised people from the *Fairsea*. There were mothers and fathers who had befriended her parents. Young children she'd last seen playing table tennis on the boat, happily chasing after the flying white ball. Young women her own age who she'd exchanged shy smiles with in one of the boat's dining rooms. She remembered laughing with them as their wayward plates and cups seemed to have become possessed, sliding from side to side across the dining table when the ship listed in rough weather across the Great Australian Bight. She recognised in their expressions what was in her heart: hope, but fear too. Like her, they'd left everything and everyone they'd known and taken a leap of faith, a journey into the unknown. She wondered if this new place felt like limbo to the other girls too.

Suddenly the crowd hushed. People craned their necks and looked forwards. Elizabeta lifted herself out of the canvas chair to see above the heads in front. A man in a grey suit and a dark blue tie stood at the front of the hall on a stage with a microphone on a stand. In his hand he held some sheets of paper and he was saying something in English. Elizabeta tried very hard to concentrate on his words, but she was tired and disoriented and everything echoed in the cold hall. She tugged on her father's coat. He knew some English, absorbed while working at an American army base in Germany in the years after the war. He'd been teaching Elizabeta ever since they'd got their papers to come to Australia

'*Was sagt er, Vati?*' What's he saying, Dad?

Her father listened and then whispered to Elizabeta in German, 'He says welcome. He's talking about what we're allowed to do and not do. Where the showers and toilets are. There is hot water. There is food in the mess if we are hungry.'

Elizabeta felt too tired to eat. Luisa was asleep in her father's arms and Elizabeta listened as he continued to translate. 'And now he's saying that we are all new Australians now and that we must learn English as soon as we can. Bonegilla is about the future, not the past.'

'New Australians,' Elizabeta whispered slowly. Bonegilla. *Bon – a – gilla*. Elizabeta said the name over and over in her head. It sounded Italian but they were somewhere in the middle of Australia. How could that be?

There was applause and everyone stood. Jozef held onto Luisa, and Berta moved closer to stroke her youngest daughter's hair.

'Ve is new Australians,' Jozef announced in English, and Berta shooshed her husband with an exhausted smile.

She had been seasick almost the entire voyage from Bremerhaven. It had been Elizabeta's job to mind Luisa while their mother stayed in her cabin, her stomach roiling, unable to keep any food down. She was bone thin and her skin was grey. Maybe now they were here in Australia her mother's spirits would lift. She might find solid ground on which to plant her feet, on which to feel safe and to be well enough to love her children again. It was the pearls, Elizabeta knew. If only her mother had been able to keep her pearls, she wouldn't be so sad.

There was more shuffling, but now it was across the camp into the cold and mysterious night, as they followed directions to the accommodation block to which they'd been assigned, ticked off on a list on a clipboard. Elizabeta saw a red door. Her father stepped up the small stairs and pushed it open. He smoothed his calloused hand down the wall inside and flicked on the overhead light. Berta gasped and for a moment stood staring. From behind, Elizabeta looked past her. It was small.

'*Komm herein,*' Jozef urged and Berta took the three steps and was inside, Elizabeta and Luisa close behind her, clutching a fold in her coat.

It was called a hut but it wasn't separate. It was one of a number of compartments in a long dormitory. Elizabeta counted three doors and three windows in this building alone.

'*Mein Gott,*' Berta murmured.

There wasn't much inside the tiny space. Four narrow beds with metal legs on a linoleum floor. Each had a grey-and-white striped mattress on it, barely thicker than a folded blanket. On each bed were five blankets, neatly folded white sheets, a pillow and towels. Next to the towels were four silver trays with melamine dinnerware stacked in a pile. There was two of everything on each tray: cups and saucers, plates, soup bowls, knives, forks and spoons. There was a small wooden table in the room, upon which was a pale yellow packet of something that looked like medicine, two canvas folding chairs, a jug, a basin, a brush, a broom, a bucket, a shovel and a rake. Elizabeta looked up to the bright bulb hanging in the centre of the ceiling and blinked. There were two huge moths dancing in the light. They were so big she thought they were birds come to sleep in their room.

It was no warmer inside the hut than out. Elizabeta's breath clouded. Jozef examined the tools while Berta quickly made up the beds and the girls slipped between the sheets, still wearing all their clothes. She covered them with all five of their thin grey blankets.

'*Gute Nacht, Elizabeta*,' Jozef whispered as he leaned down and kissed his daughter's cheek.

'*Du auch, Vati*.' She watched the moths flit as her parents made up their beds before finally turning out the lights.

Elizabeta lay in the dark and the cold, too nervous to sleep. As her father gently snored, her mother breathed quietly and Luisa kicked her legs about in her sleep, her mind raced. It was cold, the sheets and blankets scratched against her legs and she fought against the tangle of her coat and her clothes underneath. What would she find tomorrow? What would this Bonegilla be like in the light of day?

Back in Germany, when her parents had been approved for migration and received their immigration papers from the Australian government, Elizabeta had told her teacher that her family was leaving for Australia. He'd walked to the bookcase and pulled down an atlas, flipping pages under his chalky fingers.

'It's the other side of the world,' he'd told the class.

She would miss her friends, she knew, but for a long time, Elizabeta had wanted to be far, far away from Germany, and the other side of the world seemed like just the right place to be, far away from everything.

Most of all, she wanted a safe place and a fresh start, far from their memories and their history, a place where they might one day, finally, belong. It didn't seem like much to ask. As she grew warmer under the blankets, the soft breathing of her family was a lullaby as she fell into her first sleep on Australian soil.

Chapter Two

A thump, thump, thump on the roof woke Luisa first.

'*Mutti. Vati,*' she cried out, half asleep. '*Was ist das?*'

Elizabeta had heard those noises too. She lifted her head from the hard pillow and looked around the bare hut. It was still cold and her breath made smoke in the air above her face. A pale light leached in through the mist their condensed breath had made on the hut's single window. She was still wearing all her clothes from the day before but one sock was missing. Her toes rubbed against the scratchy sheets.

'Shoosh, Luisa,' she whispered. A few steps away, their parents were two unmoving shapes under their blankets.

'I'm scared,' Luisa sniffled.

'It's only a bird,' Elizabeta whispered sleepily. She yawned and pulled the blankets up to her chin. 'It's a mother bird looking for food for her babies.' She was still so tired. She didn't want to move from the warm cocoon her body had made, despite the cold in the room. Her eyes drifted closed.

There were two light footsteps on the wooden floor. Elizabeta pulled back her blankets and Luisa slipped in next to her big sister.

'There are birds here in Australia?' she whispered.

'Oh yes,' Elizabeta said quietly. 'And kangaroos. They bounce down the streets here, yes? They hop on their two big feet and they have a very strong tail. You can climb on their back for a ride, like you can on a camel or an elephant.'

'Kangaroo,' Luisa said out loud and began to giggle.

'And my teacher told me we will see natives wearing grass skirts, too. And that there will be beaches and swimming and big, blue skies full of sunshine.'

Elizabeta slipped an arm around her sister and they lay quietly, listening for more of the mysterious sounds, waiting for their parents to wake up. Luisa's breath was hot on her neck and Elizabeta pulled her close.

There should have been another sister in between them, bridging the seven-year gap in their ages, but Angela hadn't survived two months. Elizabeta didn't know how she'd died. One day she was there and the next day she was gone, and then they were in church and she was buried in the cemetery alongside it. She still didn't know how to ask to her mother what had happened. There had been so much suffering in those years that she wondered whether they had simply run out of ways to talk about loss, about war and displacement and a dead baby. There had been a decade of grief circling around their lives like a crow.

Almost three years after the baby died, when the war was over, after they'd been deported from Hungary and were living in Germany, Luisa was born. She had immediately made everyone so happy. Elizabeta had loved her from the moment she'd first held her. Her arrival had created a fresh start for the family. Jozef had work, and so did Berta, and there was food on the table and enough money left for little things. A string of pearls for Berta for her birthday. A new pipe for Jozef and a leather pouch for his tobacco. New shoes for Elizabeta and a new blanket for Luisa. A brand-new set of aluminium pots and pans for Berta's kitchen.

They had lived a simple and quiet life until the day, a year ago, when Jozef had arrived home brandishing a pamphlet, *Gluck in der neuen Heimat*. Happiness in your new homeland. They had been looking for happiness in a new homeland and hadn't found it yet. Germany had never felt like home to them. That night, her parents had had serious discussions around the kitchen table. Elizabeta found the pamphlet on the kitchen table the next morning and had pored over it, reading all about the Australian way of life. Her parents had continued talking into the night on many nights that next week. Finally they decided to apply to migrate to Australia. Elizabeta hadn't wanted to go. She liked going to school and she liked her friends. There was even a boy in her class, Aleksander, who smiled at her and walked her home two times a week. Her life was just beginning and her parents had decided to wrench her from it, and she had cried when they'd left their village and got on the train and cried when they'd walked onto the *Fairsea* at Bremerhaven, all their worldly belongings in four suitcases and a trunk. They'd left behind most everything—but the brand-new pots and pans came with them across the other side of the world.

Once they were on the boat, Elizabeta made the decision to stop crying about having to leave. It had only made her parents upset, particularly her mother. Elizabeta was old enough by then to understand and remember what they had been through already. Her father said they were going to Australia for a better life, and she had decided to believe him. After all that had happened, perhaps it would be best to leave everything behind and not look back. It would be nice to finally belong somewhere, to know there was somewhere in the world that wanted her family.

Elizabeta had never felt the tug of loyalty to any country. She'd never truly imagined she belonged anywhere. In Hungary, where she and her parents had been born, they were treated like Germans, with suspicion. When her family had been deported to Germany, real Germans looked down on them as refugees. But they had German names and spoke German, didn't they? She was still as confused as ever by it. When she'd asked her father about it once, he'd told her that when the war was over, important politicians carved up countries and decided what to do with German-speaking people like them from countries that didn't want them any more.

'They think we are Nazis because we speak German,' he'd said. 'That's why we were put on those cattle trains in Budapest by the soldiers. That's why we are in Germany.'

But all that was past now. Today was to be her first Australian morning.

She wondered, as she curled up on a thin mattress on a camp bed in a small room in an ex-army hut, swathed in blankets and warmed by her sister's breath, what Australia would feel like when she opened the door and saw the big blue sky full of sunshine for the first time.

By the time the Schmidts left their hut for the walk to the mess hall, Elizabeta felt as if she hadn't eaten in a week. There had been sandwiches on the train the day before, on the journey from Port Melbourne, but she'd shivered them away all night in the cold hut. She was impatient for her family to gather up their trays and plates and bowls and spoons and cups and walk across Bonegilla for breakfast.

Their shoes crunched on the frosty grass as they walked. The sky was a pale blue and as she followed her parents and kept an eye on Luisa, it struck Elizabeta that for the first time in six weeks the air wasn't filled with the smell of salt and the sound of waves. She took in a deep breath. Bonegilla smelled like something new, like fresh air and open fields, and the spindly trees dotted here and there, with almost-white trunks and leaves long and thin and grey-green, had a scent like peppermint. And there were birds, black-and-white birds, in the branches of the tree, singing, as if they were calling out hello to everyone below.

There was a low hum from the conversations happening all around them as people walked to breakfast. They had to stop and wait as a truck rumbled past on the road, black smoke spewing from its exhaust. There was a picture of a ram with curling horns sticking out of its woolly coat and letters and words painted on the side in English. Elizabeta tried to spell them out, but her reading was still too slow and it went by too fast.

The camp was big. In the dark of the night before, there had been dim street lights and a chill wind blowing in from somewhere cold. This morning, she couldn't seem to see the end of it, no matter where she looked. The camp was filled with accommodation huts like theirs, neat row after row of pale green corrugated iron buildings with the same red doors. In the distance, there was a collection of bigger buildings and one in particular seemed to be the centre of people's comings and goings. The mess.

And there weren't only buildings but people, coming out of every building and walking along every road and in every direction. The camp had come to life while she was waking up. Two women walked by, laughing, their hair wrapped in coloured scarves knotted at the back of their necks, with fabric bags over their shoulders, stuffed to the brim with clothes, the sleeves spilling out as if there were arms inside trying to crawl out. A group of young men jogged past, dark-haired and wiry, wearing T-shirts and canvas shoes, bouncing a ball, speaking Greek. Three young women walked by arm in arm, smiling.

Elizabeta took it all in, dawdling behind her parents. When they called out her name, she scurried after them and when they reached the front door of the mess hall, they waited politely at the end of the queue.

talk about it

Let's talk about books.

Join the conversation:

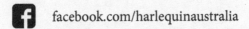 facebook.com/harlequinaustralia

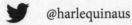 @harlequinaus

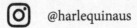 @harlequinaus

harpercollins.com.au/hq

If you love reading and want to know about our
authors and titles, then let's talk about it.